THE PROPHET OF PATMOS

ABBREVIATIONS USED:

| Enc Brit | Encyclopaedia Britannica |
| His Eccl | Historia Ecclesiastica |

St. John, the author of Revelation. Icon in the vestibule of the kapholikon of the Patmos Monastery of St. John the Theologian. Its original appearance dates back to the XII century.

ADELBERT SCHOLTZ

THE PROPHET OF PATMOS

A HISTORICAL NOVEL ABOUT SAINT JOHN THE THEOLOGIAN

RESOURCE *Publications* · Eugene, Oregon

THE PROPHET OF PATMOS
A Historical Novel about Saint John the Theologian

Resource Publications
An Imprint of Wipf and Stock Publishers
199 W. 8th Ave., Suite 3
Eugene, OR 97401

www.wipfandstock.com

PAPERBACK ISBN: 979-8-3852-4404-1
HARDCOVER ISBN: 979-8-3852-4405-8
EBOOK ISBN: 979-8-3852-4406-5

READ THIS FIRST

This novel is partly based on a historical document, the biblical book of Revelation, as well as information contained in extra-biblical sources. It is, though, a work of fiction. Much of the words and actions ascribed to the characters in this novel, as well as the family ties of John, the author of Revelation, sprouted from the imagination of the present author.

The story presented here is based on the present author's commentary on the book of Revelation: *The Prophecies of Revelation – a Reconstruction of the Visions of John of Patmos* (Mauritius: Lambert Academic, 2017). In that book, it was demonstrated with the necessary computerized reconstructions of the night sky over Patmos during AD 96, that John actually described the starry heaven with its constellations and planets and that these sights suggested certain aspects of the battle between the forces of good and evil, in which Jesus Christ, the Lamb of God, proved to be the victor.

John often mentioned earthquakes, a volcanic outburst, and a locust plague, which he also linked to his convictions and message.

The present book is an endeavor to creep, as it were, into the mind of John and to guess what he must have experienced as an exile on the Greek island of Patmos.

Although this novel can be classified as historical fiction, all efforts were undertaken to make it as credible and lifelike as possible. All the characters, apart from those mentioned in the New Testament and other historical records, are the products of the author's fantasy.

The reader will notice that every episode has a date – some of them real and others imaginary. These dates are according to the Gregorian system, which was an improvement on the older Julian system, introduced by Julius Caesar and which was in use at the time of John of Patmos. At that stage, the difference between the two systems would have been negligible and it may be assumed that John also lived according to the dates given for his various visions.

However, the conventional-style year dating used in many parts of the world was only created by the monk Dionysius Exiguus during the sixth century AD. This convention is based on Exiguus' determination of the year in which Jesus of Nazareth was thought to have been born. The prefix "AD" before a date is the abbreviation for "Anno Domini", which is Latin for "in the year of the Lord."

Although we have inherited the Roman names for the months of the year, the ancient Romans used their own system for numbering the years. Since the numbers of the years according to this system won't make any sense for readers of our time, the Gregorian system is rather used, as in all history books dealing with antiquity.

The English names for the days of the week are also used.

The names of the biblical characters in this story are those used in English translations of the Bible, as well as translations of other historical sources. The names as pronounced in those days will be explained in footnotes in relevant cases.

The footnotes will also contain explanations of unfamiliar concepts. Several text boxes are added to provide some background information to certain events and topics.

The sources of certain bits of information will be given in footnotes and a bibliography is to be found as an appendix.

The quotations from the book of Revelation will display the chapters and verses as we find them in modern Bibles. It has, though, to be remembered that the convention of dividing biblical books into chapters and verses only dates from the thirteenth century.

PREFACE

The preparation for this book started around 1973. At that time, I was doing research for my first doctorate in the history of Christianity and my thesis dealt with the life and work of the Rev SJ du Toit, a prominent figure in the Nederduitse Gereformeerde Kerk (Dutch Reformed Church) in South Africa during the last quarter of the nineteenth century. He was a prolific writer and he made much of the so-called "unfulfilled prophecies" of the Bible. He even wrote a commentary on the book of Revelation. He was an enthusiastic supporter of the theological system known as "chiliasm" or "postmillennialism" and he interpreted especially Revelation 20 in a very literal sense. He expected a wonderful condition, lasting exactly one thousand years, sometime in the future, during which Christ and the faithful would rule the world.

My studies convinced me that chiliasm had it wrong. I preached many sermons from the book of Revelation during my ministry in the church and that forced me to analyze the text of this biblical book carefully.

One of my hobbies is astronomy. I built my own reflector telescope with an aperture of 32 cm and I spent many a night in awe of the beauty of the night sky. I often read literature about the stars and I got interested in how the ancients experienced the starry skies. That led me to the discovery that John, the author of Revelation, was actually describing the starry heavens with his visions. He clearly and often mentioned some constellations, as well as the sun, the moon, and the stars in general. It became clear that he regarded the stars as angels and messengers from God and he read a message from God in the stars – of which he left us a fascinating record.

Almost all commentaries on Revelation assume that John was in a trance or state of ecstasy while living in exile on the island of Patmos off the coast of Asia Minor and that Christ and some angels spoke directly to him while he was experiencing extrasensory and supernatural visions and that Christ even dictated the letters to the seven churches of Asia Minor to him. In this novel, I will endeavor to demonstrate –

- That John, in fact, observed the starry skies and certain other natural phenomena such as thunderstorms, a locust plague, earthquakes, and a volcanic outburst during AD 96;
- That John interpreted his observations of the skies and other natural phenomena against the background of the primitive worldview of his time;
- That it is possible to reconstruct the positions of the stars and planets in the sky as he saw them on certain dates; and
- That these constellations, stars, and other natural phenomena suggested certain spiritual messages to him, which he interpreted while being inspired and guided by the Holy Spirit.

No other commentator on Revelation of which I know of has endeavored to recreate the starry skies above Patmos during the nineties of the first century. I did exactly that with the help of a computer program and I discovered what John really saw while having his visions. We are much better able to understand his message if we can recreate his visions and not simply interpret the literal words that he used to describe his visions.

This historical novel is meant for all Bible students, people who wish to understand the most enigmatic book in the Holy Scriptures better. This includes the informed lay person, but also the learned theologian. Although Greek and Hebrew words are often used in the text boxes and the footnotes for the edification of those who can read the original biblical languages, no real knowledge of these languages is necessary to enjoy and understand this book.

Adelbert Scholtz, Somerset West, South Africa, February 2025

PROLOGUE

Monday, 12 April AD 43

My father, who is a learned priest, left home before dawn to perform his duties at the temple on this very important day, Passover.[1] This is the most important feast of the year and Jews from all over Judea and Galilee, and even further away, flocked to the city of Jerusalem to take part in this event.

Our home is crowded. We provide lodging for a family of six, consisting of my father's cousin Ariel, his wife Miriam, and their four daughters Hannah, Sarah, Deborah, and Amirah. I and my two younger brothers, Saul and Samuel, also need a spot to sleep. The guests arrived three days ago and they are supposed to leave only after a whole week, after the end of the festivities.

Because I grew up without sisters, I find it somewhat strange to live in close proximity to four girls. However, Hannah, who is also twelve years old, as I am, struck up a friendship with me and we explored the alleys and streets of our part of the city, the south western corner, next to the Gate of the Essenes or Nazoreans.[2]

My father reminded us: "We Nazoreans are very hospitable people. Whenever people from our brotherhood or sect ask for lodging with us, we share all our belongings with them. Even if we are poor."

Last night, my father explained to all in the house what the meaning of this feast is: "There was a time when the children of Israel were slaves. They lived in the country of Egypt and had to

---

[1] Hebrew: *Hag happesach* (חַג הַפֶּסַח) – usually translated as "Pascha".

[2] The Essenes, a Jewish sect at the time of the New Testament, isn't mentioned in the Bible. They do appear under the name of "Nazoreans" – not to be confused with "Nazareans" (Matt 2: 23; 26: 71; Luke 18:37, John 18:5, 7; 19: 19; Acts 2: 22; 3: 6; 4: 10; 6: 14, 22: 8; and 26: 9) See: Epiphanios, *Panarion,* 29(7:7), 30(1 & 2:7); Dann, "The Essenes"; Kinzig, "The Nazoreans", 464.

work very hard for the Egyptian king, by building cities with mud bricks and stone blocks and doing other hard and dirty work.

"But God sent ten plagues to convince this king that it is wrong to keep our people as slaves. God also provided a leader with the name of Moses. The night before our forefathers managed to escape from Egypt, they only ate unleavened bread because there wasn't time to bake ordinary bread – and that's what we will also be doing. All you children must take part in what we as a family are going to do.

"However, I must go to the temple tomorrow early to help with the sacrifices. There will be so many people that it will be better if you kids stay at home. We don't want you to be trampled underfoot by the thousands of people in the courtyards of the temple. John, you and Hannah must look after the little ones until your mothers come home later during the day."

4

Saturday, 5 September AD 43

All our extended family members are sitting in our synagogue on this Sabbath – my widowed grandmother, my parents, uncles, aunts, cousins, and nieces. I am especially glad to see my cousin Hannah again.

And today, all the attention is focused upon me because it is my bar mitzvah. This is my transition from boyhood to manhood because I turned thirteen earlier this week.

Since my father is a learned priest and a rabbi, he taught me to read and write. And, therefore, I must read a part of the Torah[3] today. I chose the following passage:

> "Ye shall make you no idols nor graven image, neither rear you up a standing image, neither shall ye set up any image of stone in your land, to bow down unto it: for I am the LORD your God. Ye shall keep my sabbaths, and reverence my sanctuary: I am the LORD. If ye walk in my statutes, and keep my commandments, and do them; then I will give you rain in due season, and the land shall yield her increase, and the trees of the field shall yield their fruit. And your threshing shall reach unto the vintage, and the vintage shall reach unto the sowing time: and ye shall eat your bread to the full, and dwell in your land safely."[4]

I chose this particular passage since it was instilled in me by my father that the Romans, who took over our country and treat us like dirt and with disdain, just as the Egyptian king did to our forefathers, worship all sorts of idols. We all hate the Romans, especially

---

[3] The Torah, the Jewish Law Book, is comprised of the first five books of the Bible, traditionally attributed to Moses as author.

[4] Lev 26: 1–5.

because they despise our religion. They think they are superior by worshipping many gods, while we worship only a single God, the only true God who created everything.

Afterwards, our whole family retire to our house where some of the neighbors join us for a meal.

My father takes the word before the food is served: "John[5], my son, I want to remind you, yet again, that you are named after a famous person, John the Baptist, a great prophet. You were born, thirteen years ago, a day after that cruel King Herod Antipas of Galilee had his head chopped off. He did this to please his step-daughter and her mother because they hated this prophet.

"John's bloody head was presented to his stepdaughter as a gift on a golden platter. We don't know what she did with this chopped-off head, but her mother was pleased to be rid of John because he criticized her marriage with the king after she was divorced from her first husband, the half-brother of this king. I was told that she spat on this head to show her hatred and disrespect for John. I also heard that John's head was later chucked onto a garbage heap where his disciples found it."

We all shudder by the thought of such a grizzly and ghastly scene.

My father continues: "This John was a distant cousin of mine and it is my prayer that you will follow in his footsteps. Now that you are thirteen years of age, you are old enough to take control of your own life. You may choose to do the right thing, or to do the wrong thing. You may choose to do good, or to behave badly. That's up to you now. But you were always a boy who didn't put us to shame and I am confident that you will continue along the right path,

---

[5] The name "John" in Hebrew is יְהוֹחָנָן or יוֹחָנָן (*Yehochanan* or *Yochanan*) meaning "Yahweh is gracious". It is mentioned in 2 Chr 17: 17, 2 Chr 23: 1, Neh 12: 22–23 and Jer 42: 8. In Greek it is written as Ἰωάννης (*Ioannes*).

or as our prophet Jesus[6] said, the narrow road that leads to salvation and not the broad road that leads to destruction."[7]

My mother, who sits next to me, presses my hand in encouragement. She adds: "Your father took me once down to the river Jordan where John was baptizing people. I will never forget that day. That was when he also baptized Jesus. The sun suddenly disappeared, the stars became visible and a strange wind blew over us all. John explained that that wind was the breath or spirit of God blowing over all of us, but especially over Jesus who was stepping out of the water at that moment, while he was wet from head to toe. That wind must have chilled him with all his wet clothes."

It is highly probable and possible that Jesus saw events coinciding with his baptism by John the Baptist as God's calling to become the savior and king of Israel (Mark 1: 9–11; Matt 3: 13–17; Luke 3: 21–22). The total solar eclipse of 24 November AD 29 at about 10:40 local time over Galilee[8] most probably happened when Jesus was baptized and that he saw this as a sign that God called him to become *the* Messiah. The report of this event in Mark 1: 9–11, the oldest gospel, must be quoted in full:

---

[6] Jesus' name in Hebrew or Aramaic – the home language of the Jews at that time – was *Yehoshua* (יְהוֹשֻׁעַ), which means: "Yahweh is salvation or deliverance," the same name of Joshua, the successor of Moses as leader of the Israelites

[7] Matt 7: 13–14.

[8] Although the Gospel of Matthew states that John was baptizing at the river Jordan in the "wilderness of Judea" (Matt 3: 1), John must actually have been in Galilee to the north of Judea at that time since Herod Antipas, the ruler of Galilee, had him arrested shortly after Jesus' baptism – and that could only have happened within Herod's area of jurisdiction (Matt 14: 3; Mark 1: 14; Mark 6: 17; Luke 3: 19–20). It also appears from the chronology in the Synoptic Gospels that Jesus concentrated his ministry initially to Galilee and only appeared in Judea at a later date.

"It happened in those days, that Jesus came from Nazareth of Galilee, and was baptized by John in the Jordan. Immediately coming up from the water, he saw the heavens parting, and the Spirit descending on him like a dove. A voice came out of the sky, 'You are my beloved Son, in whom I am well pleased.'"

All three synoptic gospels report that the heavens were opened directly after Jesus' baptism – most probably the stars in the sky that became visible during day-time when the light of the sun was blocked by the intervening moon during the eclipse.

It must be remembered that the ancient Israelites thought that God's heaven was directly beyond the stars and that the stars were, in fact, angels (Neh 9: 6; Job 22: 12–14; Job 38: 4–8; Ps 104: 3; Ps 148: 2–3; Isa 40: 22). In other words: when the stars unexpectedly became visible during day-time it seemed as if the heaven, the abode of God and the angels, was miraculously opened.[9]

During a solar eclipse "a pronounced fall in temperature" is experienced, due to the blocking of the rays of the sun. That causes a wind to blow from the warmer areas outside the path of the moon's shadow to the cooler areas where the heat of the sun is absent.[10]

That must also have been the case with the eclipse of 24 November AD 29 and people would also have noticed the sudden wind – apart from the appearance of the stars in the sky.

The Greek word for "wind", πνεῦμα (pneuma), is also the word used for "spirit", just as the Hebrew word for "wind" is also the word for "spirit" (רוּחַ – ruach). For the Jews, therefore, there was no real difference between a spirit and the wind or breath and,

---

[9] Scholtz, The Prophecies of Revelation, 30–41.
[10] Enc Brit, "Eclipse: sun".

8

therefore, the gospels reported that the (Holy) Spirit "descended" upon Jesus at his baptism (Mark 1: 10; Matt 3: 16; Luke 3: 22) – while it was only an unexpected but ordinary wind that blew.

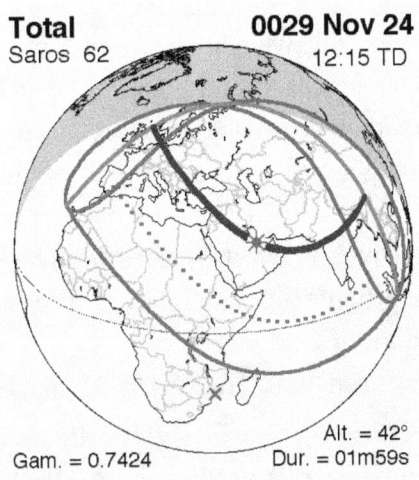

The path of the moon's shadow, where a total solar eclipse was visible, passed through the northern parts of Palestine on 24 November AD 29. The duration of totality was 2 minutes.[11]

A computerized reconstruction of the maximum extent of the almost total solar eclipse at 10: 40 local time on 24 November AD 29, as seen from Caesarea-Philippi, north of the Sea of Galilee, when almost 94% of the sun was blocked by the moon. A total eclipse would have been visible further north on the banks of the Jordan.

Mark – the oldest gospel – merely reported that Jesus saw the Spirit (or the wind) descending on him *like* a dove or a pigeon (the Greek

---

[11] NASA, Eclipse Website.

word may mean both species of birds) – not in the *form* of a dove. Luke 3: 22, though, added that "the Holy Spirit descended in a bodily form" on Jesus.

My father: "As you know, we belong to a group of Jews or Israelites who keep ourselves apart and pure. We call ourselves the Nazoreans[12], but other people refer to us as the Essenes. We are Nazoreans because we are the true branch of the house of Israel. Some of us prefer the name of Ebionites[13] because we abhor riches and luxury and we live in poverty, just as John the Baptist and Jesus did. After all, our prophet Jesus taught us: 'Blessed be ye poor: for yours is the kingdom of God.'[14]

"Jesus also told us: 'The Spirit of the Lord is upon me, because he hath anointed me to preach the gospel to the poor.'[15]

"Unfortunately, many of our priests have defiled themselves by becoming allies of the pagan Romans. They flaunt their prosperity and riches. God cannot condone and tolerate that.

"We have to follow the examples of these two great prophets of our tradition, John the Baptist and Jesus of Nazareth. They were related to each other as cousins and we had high hopes that they could lead our people back to God. Both were, however, executed in a cruel manner by the enemies of our God – that crazy king Herod and that heavy-handed and haughty Roman governor, Pontius Pilate.

"We saw Jesus as our future king, the son of David who would chase the Romans away with the help of God's angels. Some-

---

[12] The name of "Nazorean" is probably derived from the Hebrew word "branch" as used in Isaiah and Daniel, namely נֵצֶר (*netzer*).

[13] The name "Ebionite" is derived from the Hebrew אֶבְיוֹנִים (*Ebyonim*), meaning "the poor".

[14] Luke 6: 20–21.

[15] Luke 4: 18.

thing remarkable happened a year before you were born. When your namesake, John, baptized Jesus in the Jordan up north in Galilee, a miracle happened, as your mother just reminded us. The sun suddenly disappeared, it became dark, and the heavens were opened. All the people who witnessed this, saw it as a sign that Jesus was destined for great things. I know this, because we were there.

"Jesus often called himself the 'Son of God' and thereby indicated that he was God's chosen messiah to become the new king of Israel.[16]

"And now, my son, a very important new phase of your life is to start. In order to prepare you for the priesthood and to become a teacher of the Law, we are taking you to our sect's school in the desert, overlooking the Dead Sea. There you will get to know all the Scriptures intimately, also by making copies of them for use in our synagogues and even at the temple.

"How do you feel about that?"

I like all the attention given to me and I answer with a smile and a clear voice: "Father, I am proud to be your son. You were always a good father and I love you, just as I love my mother. It will be an honor to become a pupil at our school in the desert."

My father: "We will visit you at least once a year to take to you new clothes. You will come back to Jerusalem for all the important feasts and then you will stay with us, of course."

Later, when all the guests have left and it became dark, my father takes me to the roof of our home: "My son, look at that moon, there on the eastern horizon."

Instead of being white, I see a red full moon and I ask in

---

[16] See 2 Sam 7: 14; 1 Chr 17: 13; 1 Chr 22: 10; 1 Chr 28: 6; Ps 2: 6–7, 12; Ps 89: 26–28 and John 1: 49 where the expression "Son of God" was used exclusively for the king of Israel. No other personage in the Old Testament was ever called a "son of God", except for the angels (Job 1: 6 & 38: 7).

11

astonishment: "How did that happen?"[17]

"That's a sign of God."

"What does He want to tell us?"

"I am sure He's blessing your bar mitzvah. When you were three years old, the moon also looked the same. That was on the day that our greatest prophet, Jesus, was crucified by the hated and damned Romans. We saw that as a sign that Jesus would return as he had promised to do."

"And did he come back?"

"Yes. He did come back. After three days in the tomb. He stood up again. His two friends, Nicodemus and Joseph of Arimathea, nursed him with a mixture of herbs and spices to heal his horrible wounds. I had the privilege to see him once when he secretly appeared to his friends and supporters."

"And the moon looked like this when he was crucified?"

"Exactly. His friends took him off the cross and laid him in a new tomb just before it became dark. And then they closed the tomb with a big stone while a red moon was rising in the east."[18]

"And what happened to him after that?"

"Oh, he disappeared after a few weeks when he was strong enough to travel. He was afraid that the Romans would catch him again and make double sure that he really died on that cursed cross. We hoped that he would come back and become our king, but he

---

[17] A total lunar eclipse was visible over Jerusalem on 7 September AD 43.

[18] Jesus was probably crucified on Friday, 3 April AD 33. An eclipsed moon rose in the east shortly after sunset.

went into hiding, somewhere. I suppose that he must still be alive, somewhere."

"How many people know about that?"

"Not many. We wanted to keep his recovery a secret and almost everybody believes that he blew out his last breath while hanging on that cross. But we know better. James, the brother of Jesus, who become the leader of us Ebionites, insists that we must be ready at all times for the return of Jesus. He ought to know because he is Jesus' brother."[19]

I run down the steps next to our home to fetch the rest of our family. After my father has explained to them the meaning of the red moon, he adds: "John, I think you are destined to become a prophet, the same as John the Baptist. God is calling you.

I ask: "Do prophets have dreams of the future?

"Certainly. Did you have any dreams of things that may happen to you in the future?"

"Oh, yes. Only last night I dreamt that I and Hannah are getting married. I have also dreamt that I was writing books. That's perhaps because I am going to our school in the desert where I will do much writing, as you told me."

My father smiles broadly and gives me a hug.

Hannah giggles somewhere in the background.

---

[19] James 5: 7–8.

Saturday, 23 April AD 50

The Passover feast falls on the Sabbath this year. I arrived yesterday from our school in the desert to attend the festivities in Jerusalem, together with some of my fellow students. As a young man of twenty, I am confident that God will bless my future career as a priest and a teacher of the Law. I am still too young to be admitted to the priesthood, but I think that I know the Scriptures well enough by this time to accept that role when the time comes.

My father wishes to talk to me before we depart to the temple and we eat an early breakfast on the roof of our home just when the first glimmers of sunlight appear in the east.

The Passover always takes place when the moon is full and we see the full moon as she is setting in the west.

"Father, look! That moon is getting red again!"

"Indeed, my son. What do you think God wants to tell us this time?"

"I think he approves of what we are doing at the school nowadays."

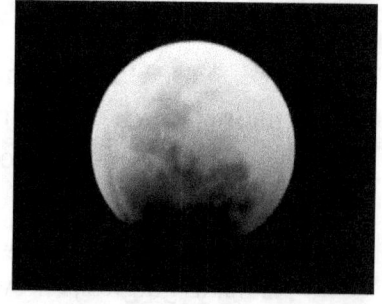

"Tell me more."

"We are collecting the teachings of Jesus, our great prophet. Unfortunately, he never wrote anything. He didn't follow the example of our ancient prophets who wrote several holy books – Isaiah, Jeremiah, Ezekiel, Amos, and the others. I was given the task of talking to people here in Jerusalem who knew him, including his brother, James. Unfortunately, all the apostles of Jesus are gone – some of them are already dead and the others are spreading his message all over the world, even deep inside Africa and in India."

"That sounds like a wonderful project."

"God tells me through that red moon that He approves of our work. I must write down all the sayings of Jesus that I can gather from people who heard his sermons. He was a wonderful story-teller and I must also write down those stories."

"Fantastic. I totally agree that something like this must be done. God will certainly bless your task. I met somebody a month ago who was also gathering stories about Jesus – a man called Saul, but he also has a Latin nickname, Paul. That is because he is a smallish man, but he is very energetic and he also knows the Scriptures very well, because he studied here in Jerusalem under Gamaliel, one of our chief teachers of the Law."

"Where did he come from?"

"Antioch in Syria. He's originally from Asia, from the Roman colony of Tarsus and that makes him a Roman citizen. He grew up in a Greek environment and his Greek is better than his Hebrew and Aramaic, but it was possible to talk to him."

"Why did he come here?"

"That's an interesting story. A few years ago, shortly after he had finished his studies with Gamliel and he joined the party of the Pharisees, he started rounding up the followers of Jesus. He was on his way to Damascus to make life difficult or the Nazoreans living there, but then the good Lord intervened. He had a vision of Jesus. Jesus spoke to him and he fell onto the road, bumping his head severely. His eyes were so swollen that he couldn't see for a few days."

"And then?"

"And then he was baptized. He became a follower of Jesus. He is convinced that Jesus spoke to him, there on that road."

"But Jesus died some time ago already, at the place where he was hiding after he had survived his crucifixion."

"Quite right. And Paul is convinced that Jesus was taken up into heaven and that he spoke to him from there."

"Remarkable."

"Yes, it is remarkable. But he also claims that Jesus told him that it's not necessary for converts from paganism to keep the laws of Moses anymore."

"That's strange, because Jesus always taught that his followers must obey God's commandments diligently as he gave them to Moses."

"Quite right. And then some of us went to Antioch to convince his followers to do as Jesus taught us. Peter was one of those who went.[20] That caused some confusion and Paul was sent by the synagogue there with some helpers to come and argue with us here in Jerusalem."

"Were you part of those talks?"

"Yes. I was, apart from the fact that I'm a priest at the temple, also one of the seven elders at our Nazorene synagogue. We argued for two full days. In the end, our leader, James, whom you know as the brother of Jesus, declared that the pagans who wanted to become followers of Jesus, only had to adhere to the rules we set for all Gentiles who want to become proselytes of our faith."[21]

---

[20] Gal 2: 11.
[21] This meeting is described in Acts 15 and Gal 2: 1–19.

THE STORY OF JOHN OF PATMOS
(IN HIS OWN WORDS)

Sunday, 3 January AD 96

Where I am standing next to the main street of Ephesus, I watch the procession of worshippers as they sing and laugh on their way to the temple of Divus Julius, where a statue of Emperor Domitian is to be unveiled. This temple is devoted to the cult of the Divine Julius Caesar, the founder of the Roman Empire and first *de facto* emperor. He was elevated to divine status after his death by the Roman Senate and temples for his cult were erected all over the empire, also here in Ephesus.

I watch the procession to see whether any Christians are participating. If they do, they will be excommunicated for denying Jesus Christ as their Savior and only Lord. Fortunately, I don't see any of them.

Early this morning, just after dawn, I conducted a religious service for the faithful Christians here in Ephesus, where I am the overseer or bishop. I denounced the pagan cult of Caesar – especially the homage that was due to be paid to the giant statue of Emperor Domitian.

I reminded my flock that God severely punished the Jews for rejecting Jesus Christ as their Savior and Messiah by allowing the Romans to utterly and totally destroy Jerusalem with her temple more than twenty-five years ago. I urged them to stay away from the festivities later today if they didn't want the wrath of God to descend upon our Christian community.

It was also necessary to praise my flock for enduring the hardships of their faith in a pagan city, such as Ephesus. Tradesmen and shopkeepers were only allowed to do business if they could display the official stamp of the Roman Empire that they had adhered to the official imperial cult by worshipping at the temple dedicated to the Divine Julius. They were regarded as traitors if they refused to do so and had to endure austerity and deprivation.

19

Friday, 8 January AD 96

It is cold and I am feeling miserable where I sit down on the cold stone floor of this stinking prison cell in Ephesus. There are three other men with me in this cell. The place smells of shit, piss, and vomit, although there is a hole in the floor that can be used as a latrine.

Early this morning, I was grabbed by a bunch of Roman soldiers. One of them read the charge in Latin, which I, fortunately, can understand: "You are hereby accused of disrespecting and insulting Caesar Domitianus Augustus Germanicus[22] by publicly refusing to pay homage to him at his image and by telling your flock that one Jesus Christ is the only deity worthy of worship, thereby denying the divinity and majesty of Caesar. That amounts to the crime of treason. You are to be tried by the city's magistrate."

    I was merely given the opportunity to grab a tunic before I was marched off to this prison.

---

[22] Caesar Domitianus Augustus Germanicus ruled as Roman emperor between AD 81 and 96.

While I sit with my back against the stone wall of the cell, shivering from the cold and the shock, one of the other prisoners asks: "And who are you, old man?"

I reply: "I'm John. I'm the overseer of the Christian church, here in Ephesus and the western parts of Asia."[23]

The same voice: "Oh, I've heard of you. Your name betrays that you're one of those despised Jews. I detect a Jewish accent when you speak Greek."

"Yes, I am Jewish. But I am also a Christian."

Another voice: "What's the difference? As far as I've heard, Jews and Christians all pray to the same God. There can't be too much of a difference."

"Yes, there are similarities. We read the same Holy Scriptures, except that we also read the letters of the apostle Paul and the memoirs of our Savior, Jesus Christ. And, if I may ask: Who are you gentlemen? Why are you here?"

First voice: "I'm Stephanos. My neighbor picked a fight with me and I had to teach him a lesson by tapping him gently on his skull with my heavy hammer."

Second voice: "And for that you will certainly also lose your miserable head. I'm Philip. And I was caught stealing the purse of an old man at the market. What I didn't know, was that the young man next to him was his son. This chap chased me and caught me."

Me: "And what will happen to you?

Philip: "The magistrate will most probably order that I be whipped and stay a year in this foul-smelling dungeon."

A third voice speaks for the first time: "My name is Joel. I'm also a Jew like you, but I'm not a Christian, although I think that we have met in the past. But I think you and me will both get the death

---

[23] In Antiquity, the name of "Asia" was applied to the part of the world nowadays called "Asia Minor", more or less modern Turkey, especially the western parts.

penalty for insulting Caesar. Did you also refuse to worship a human being as a living god?"

I reply in Aramaic: "Dear countryman. Good to have you with me. Yes, it's possible that we have met in the past. Maybe both of us will become martyrs for our faith. But I simply couldn't bring myself to burn a bit of incense at the statue of Caesar."

We all sink into silence while we contemplate our possible and probable misfortunes and destinies and fates.

Half-an-hour later, I hear somebody calling my name. The sound comes from the small grilled window of our cell and I recognize the voice of my dear friend, Prochorus.[24]

"John! John! I brought you some bread. And your coat. Can you take them?"

"How on earth did you get in?"

"Bribed one of the guards. Here, take this. I must run again."

Stephanos, a big man, picks me up so that I can reach the grated window and grab the precious bread and my coat.

I share my bread with my fellow prisoners and they are very grateful for the gift.

After a while I ask my new friends: "It seems that at least three of us won't leave this place alive. Are you ready to make peace with your Creator?"

Joel: "I know that the God of our fathers will accept me into his heaven."

Stephanos: "My soul will only rot in Hades."

These remarks give me the opportunity to tell my new friends of Jesus Christ, who ascended into the heaven of God to prepare a place for us with God and his angels. All three my new friends accept the good news that we can gain a place in heaven,

---

[24] In Greek: Πρόχορος (*Prochoros*) – meaning "leader of the chorus" (see Acts 6: 5).

even if we are only ordinary folk, not members of the elite. The only condition is that we must believe in Jesus Christ, the eternal Son of God. I baptize all three of my new converts by sprinkling a few drops of our drinking water over their heads.

"Now all of you are the property of Christ," I assure them.

They smile drily and Stephanos weeps. He wipes his tears and running nose with his dirty sleeve.

During the day, I think back on my life up to this point. Even if I may say so myself, I can state that I have had a very interesting and even exciting career with many memorable experiences, although not all of them were pleasant.

Joel asks me: "Please tell us about yourself, old man? How did you become a Christian? How were you appointed overseer of the assembly of the Christians here in Ephesus?"

I willingly oblige. I see this as an opportunity to tell these men more of their new faith. After I have told them about my youth in Jerusalem, I continue:

"At the school of our sect in the desert I proved to be a star pupil. Within four years I could quote from memory every part of the Torah, the books of the prophets and other sacred writings. My favorites were the prophecies of Daniel, Zachariah, and Enoch. It helped to get to know all these Scriptures intimately by making neat copies of them. I'm especially proud of a very neat copy of the book of Isaiah that I copied onto a long parchment roll.

"I was taught more than just the ancient Scriptures. We got lectures on the starry skies. I was taught that there are three heavens. The first one is the heavens filled with clouds and birds. The second heaven is the heaven of the stars and the planets. It was explained that these celestial beings could be grouped into clusters, consisting of certain personages, animals, or objects, called constellations.

The Beth Alpha mosaic with the Zodiac (5ᵗʰ century AD). The personified sun occupies the center and is surrounded by the moon and some planets and stars. The figures in the corners represent the four seasons. The twelve figures within the outer circle contain the Hebrew names and pictures of the signs of the Zodiac.

"Seven of these heavenly objects, called planets, move through all these constellations and we could read from their movements the intentions of God. The planets also supplied the names of the differrent days of the seven-day week."[25]

---

[25] The seven moving bodies in the sky, visible to the naked eye, are the sun, the moon, Mercury, Venus, Mars, Jupiter, and Saturn – to use their Latin/English names. We still use the ancient names of the days of the week and we can recognize Sunday, Mo(o)nday, and Satur(n)day.

> There are numerous indications that the Israelites/Jews of biblical times and later, were familiar with Babylonian astrology and influenced by it.[26] Among the ancient documents of the Essenes, dating from before the destruction of Jerusalem in AD 70 and discovered at Qumran since 1947 near the Dead Sea, astrological texts were found.[27] The best example of a Jewish Zodiac is the mosaic floor of the synagogue of Beth Alpha in Israel from the 5th century AD.

"We cannot accept the ideas of the pagans that these stars and planets are deities because there is only a single God, the Creator of everything. Therefore, these stars and planets had to be God's angels, as well as deceased heroes – but also evil spirits in some cases.

Joel" "And the third heaven?"

"Yes, and the third heaven, beyond the stars and planets, that's the dwelling of God. His throne, from where He can oversee his whole creation, is situated at a point in the far northern sky, the point around which everything on earth and in the heavens revolves.

"We also learnt that the abode of the dead, Sheol – also called Hades by the Greeks – is situated somewhere beneath the surface of the earth. That's where the dead await Judgment Day and where unrepentant sinners are being punished for their evil deeds – although in a deeper part of this abyss. The earth is a flat disc and it is held up by pillars that stand in waters, the source of the waters that bubble up from fountains and springs. There are also sources of water in the heavens, which come down as rain.

"We were all required to study the texts in the Sacred Scriptures where these ideas and insights were revealed.

---

[26] Scholtz, *Revelation*, 27–41.
[27] Jacbus, "The Zodiac Sign Names", 311–12.

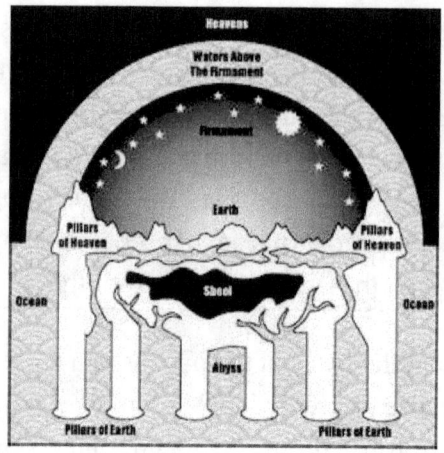

"We students were also taught some of the healing arts, which included the use of herbs, shrubs, and roots to treat different ailments. My father assured me that our great prophet, Jesus, was a very skilled healer.

"In order to be able to get along in the world, we were also taught Greek and Latin. Greek is, after all, the language of learning and philosophy and Latin is the language of the Romans who govern us and under whose laws we must live.

"And, of course, we were also taught some arithmetic. That helped us to understand numbers. We learnt that the Greeks and the Romans used different types of symbols for all the various numbers.

Stephanos interrupts me: "I'm honored to meet such a learned man as you! Was all your time taken up by studying and copying books? What else did you do?"

"Good that you ask. Apart from studying, we also had to do manual work at our school there in the desert – tending the animals and the garden, repairing the buildings, and helping in the kitchen. We had to take a bath regularly and keep our clothes clean, so as to be presentable and pure when praying to God. We always wore white clothes to show that we want to be pure – from the outside, but also from the inside.

"It was also required of me to live as a Nazarite, which meant that I could not shave my hair or my beard and I had to devote my whole life to the service of God. Some of my fellow Nazarites decided to live celibate lives, but I decided that I would like to marry – especially as I enjoyed the company of my cousin Hannah every time when I visited Jerusalem and her family stayed with us. After all, my father who was a priest and who also took the vows as a Nazarite, did get married and fathered three sons.

"When I was twenty and a fully grown man, I got engaged to this distant cousin of mine. She had already grown into an attractive and strong and intelligent woman. Our parents decided that we would make a nice couple, especially since we were good friends. As a future priest, it was required of me to marry somebody from my own tribe and extended family."

Joel asks: "And when did you get married?"

"Only five years later, when I had completed my studies and moved back to Jerusalem to start my service at the temple and at our synagogue. Our firstborn, a son, was born a year later."

Joel again: "And where is your wife now? Is she also living here in Ephesus with you?"

"Unfortunately, no. She died three years after we got married directly after the birth of our second son. She bled to death and I was powerless to help her, even if I was trained in the healing arts. That meant that I had to bring up my two sons on my own, although my mother and my mother-in-law also helped me with them."

Philip: "I've also lost a wife. She was murdered by Roman soldiers after they had raped her. I will never forgive the Romans for what they did."

We fall silent out of respect for the dead.

27

After a while, Joel asks: "Did you become a priest in the end, just as your father?"

"Yes, I became a priest and a teacher of the Law or a rabbi at the age of thirty-one,[28] but I also helped at the temple in the time before that. The night before I was consecrated as a priest, a red moon was seen just after the start of the Sabbath at dusk when the stars came out.[29] I remembered that my father told me that a previous red moon was a sign from God, telling me that I was destined to become a prophet, just as John the Baptist and Jesus of Nazareth.

"As a Nazarite, I decided not to remarry. I couldn't bring myself to take another woman in the place of my beloved Hannah. I regularly did duty at the temple."

Joel: "You mentioned that your parents thought that this Jesus was a great prophet and that they hoped he would restore the kingdom of Israel. My parents also told me something of the sort. But his hopes were dashed when the Roman governor had him crucified because he called himself the king of the Jews. Everybody was sorry when he died. Were you also one of his followers at that time – seeing that you call yourself a Christian now?"

"Yes, indeed. Most of us Essenes were also members of the movement that regarded Jesus as a great prophet. Some of us even decided to record in writing some of our memories of him – especially of his wisdom and sayings and stories.[30]

---

[28] Polycrates, bishop of Ephesus during the second part of the second century AD, wrote in a letter to Victor, bishop of Rome, about the prophet John "who became a priest wearing the mitre, and a witness and a teacher – he rests at Ephesus" (Eusebius, *Hist Eccl,* Liber V/xxiv/2–3).

[29] A total lunar eclipse occurred on Friday, 18 September AD 61. It was visible in Palestine just after nightfall when the Sabbath started.

[30] The source called "Q", which was later incorporated into the Gospels of Matthew and Luke, as well as the narrative sections of the Gospel of John.

"I also got to know James the Just[31], the son of Joseph and the brother of Jesus. He became the leader of this movement after Jesus departed. Unfortunately, he was murdered by a mob a year after I had become a priest. I was so ashamed to be a priest because the mob killed James after Ananus, our high priest, had ordered them to get rid of this tireless and tiresome prophet. James could not keep silent about the abuses of the Sadducees. That was the party of the rich and powerful to which the high priest and his family and friends belonged. They were known as the Sadducees."[32]

Stephanos: "Was this James a very holy man? You also called him a prophet?"

"Oh, certainly. He was known for praying at the temple very often. He abhorred riches and the haughty attitudes of rich people – just as the other members of our sect, the Essenes. We were also called the Ebionites, the 'poor ones'. James even wrote a letter to the members of our movement, the true member of the people of Israel who are living all over the world, not to fall into the temptation of treating rich people better than poor people in their synagogues.[33]

"After he was murdered, James was succeeded by Symeon, another brother of Jesus, as leader of our movement or sect."[34]

Joel: "But your great prophet, Jesus, who thought of himself as king of the Jews, must have been a rich man? What else?"

"No, never. He didn't even own a home of his own, but he and his pupils stayed with family members or friends whenever they travelled through the country.[35] He also taught his followers:

---

[31] James' name in Greek is Ἰάκωβος (*Jakobos*), the Greek form of the Hebrew name of Jacob.

[32] James was murdered in AD 62.

[33] James 2: 1–9.

[34] Eusebius, *Hist Eccl,* Liber III/XI and XXXII.

[35] Luke 9: 3–5; 10: 1–3; 22: 35.

'Don`t gather treasures for yourselves on the earth, where moth and rust consume, and where thieves break through and steal; but gather for yourselves treasures in heaven, where neither moth nor rust consume, and where thieves don`t break through and steal.'"[36]

Joel again: "And how did you come to stay here in Ephesus? I moved here during the war against the Romans after the soldiers had burnt down my house on my farm near Capernaum."

"That was also my lot. During April, ten days before the start of the feast of Passover, I was many stadia north of Jerusalem when the bulk of the Roman army moved towards Jerusalem from Syria under the command of Titus, the son of Caesar Vespasian.

"I watched them from a hill overlooking the plain of Jezreel and I saw the soldiers with their body armor, helmets, shields, spears, and swords, marching at the beat of drums and trumpets.

"There were also archers and slingshot-throwers, as well as horsemen and drivers of chariots and wagons carrying their equipment. It was a most impressive and frightening sight.

"I was later told that there were four full legions, each of them comprised of six thousand men. It took them hours to pass the

---

[36] Matt 6: 19–20.

30

spot where I was watching them, even if they marched over a wide front.

"While I was watching them, a thunder storm broke over our heads. They just kept on marching and blowing their trumpets and waving their banners and standards with depictions of eagles and other idols. Whenever I experience a thunder storm nowadays, it is as if I hear those trumpets again. That sound follows me, wherever I go."

Joel: "Did you flee immediately to Ephesus?"

"No. I took my two sons who were with me and we moved as fast as we could to our old school in the desert. It was clear that the Romans left burnt-down homes, violated, and killed women and children and destroyed orchards and vineyards in their wake. We had to warn the people there of the approaching danger. We could only start after the marching columns have passed us and the road was open again. I convinced them that it was only a matter of time before Jerusalem would fall and the soldiers started to look for Jews in other parts of the country.[37]

"Our Teacher gave the order that we close down the school and only return after the end of hostilities when it was safe again. We – that's me and my two sons who were thirteen and eleven years old at that time – helped to pack our precious library into big jars and to hide all of that in almost inaccessible caves overlooking the Dead Sea.

"The work to hide our library took a long time. We even saw the smoke and flames while Jerusalem was burning after the Romans broke through the last defenses. And then we fled, although a number of men refused to go. They argued that God would protect them. They also wanted to guard our books in the caves."

---

[37] Jerusalem was conquered and razed by the Romans on 30 August AD 70.

Joel: "The lot of them perished. I heard that from people who saw their skeletons strewn all over the place. The Romans torched all the buildings."

"Yes, that's sad. Our Teacher advised us to move to a place where there were other Jews, far away from Judea, in order to avoid certain capture by the Roman soldiers who would make slaves of us – if they didn't kill us. We decided to move to the town of Pella on the other side of the river Jordan in the country of Perea where a Jewish community was living, consisting mainly of people of our sect and who would welcome us. People from Jerusalem joined us there."

Joel: "I also heard that nobody dared to return to your school in the desert after the war. The place was totally ruined, anyway. There was nothing left to return to."

"That's right."

Stephanos, the killer, who was mostly silent, remarks: "You obviously didn't stay there in Pella forever. How else did you land up in this rat hole?" He points with his finger in all directions.

"Of course, you're correct. I didn't stay in Pella. After a few months there, during which both my sons had their bar mitsvah, I became restless. I wanted to be a teacher of the Law, but there were almost no books available at that spot. Our Teacher advised me to move to a city with a big school, which I could join. His first choice was Alexandria in Egypt with the largest library in the world. There is a famous Jewish school, founded by the late learned scholar, Philo the Jew. He also recommended Ephesus, the largest and most important city in Greece with a famous library. There was, in addition, a sizable Jewish community with their own schools and synagogues.

"The Teacher added: 'Brother John, I've observed that you sometimes go into a state of deep thought – even when you were a student with us. It is almost as if you are no longer with us, but in another world. You are just absent, gone, lost in thought. I believe that is when God's Spirit is taking hold of you. With this prophetic gift of yours it is important that you depart to an important city like Alexandria or Ephesus where your talents and gifts and skills can develop further.'"

Stephanos: "And then you chose Ephesus?"

"Yes, but almost by accident. I took my two sons, who needed a good education – although not one of them would be able to become a priest because the temple in Jerusalem went up in flames – and we walked to the port of Tyre. This is an old Phoenician city where we were bound to find a ship to take us somewhere.

"Since we had no money, we had to find a ship's captain who

was willing to take us on as crew members. The three of us were prepared to pull the oars of the ship when the wind for the sail failed, along with some other oarsmen, and we set sail for Piraeus, the harbor quarter of Athens, the destination of this captain. That meant that we could travel to a destination not too far away from Ephesus."

Joel: "And did you find any Jews there who helped you?"

"By the grace of our good Lord in heaven, we found a Jewish couple with the names of Priscilla and Aquila in the harbor of Piraeus. They were originally from Pontus, the Roman province on the south coast of the Black Sea, but also the first Christians I had ever met. When I enquired around where I could find a Jewish synagogue, I was directed to this couple who just returned from Rome. They introduced me to their friend Timothy, a fellow-Christian, who grew up with a Jewish mother and a Greek father. He was bishop of Ephesus at that time. He visited his counterpart in Rome, where he and his old friends, Priscilla and Aquila, found each other again after many years.

Joel: "Did these people take you to Ephesus?"

"Yes, they did, in due course. And they also explained to me that they all became friends and colleagues of a missionary or apostle, named Paul, many years ago. I heard of Paul from James in Jerusalem, who told me that he and Paul differed on how one must live as a follower of our prophet, Jesus of Nazareth. My late father also told me of a meeting he had with this Paul."

Joel: "And how did James and Paul differ?"

"James, the apostles, and all his followers in Jerusalem and Judea, including my father, were convinced that all converts to the sect of the Ebionites or Nazoreans, the followers of Jesus, had to be circumcised and had to follow all the laws of Moses – just as all the other faithful Jews.

"Paul, on the other hand, thought that the Law of Moses

34

didn't apply anymore because Jesus, the divine Son of God, made that unnecessary.[38] When he suffered on the cross, he took upon him the punishment, which all sinners deserve, namely eternal damnation. Of course, that didn't mean that Christians could lead immoral or criminal lives, but they were no longer obliged to submit to circumcision and other purity and ceremonial laws."

Joel: "Was that the only difference?"

"No, not by far. Paul maintained that Jesus was really a divine being who adopted a human body. He is actually the eternal Son of God and the equal of his Father, although nobody realized it during the time when he was wandering the earth. They were bound together by the Spirit of God, another divine personage, who impregnated Mary, the mother of Jesus while she was still a virgin.

"We Ebionites or Nazoreans always regarded Jesus as a mere mortal, an ordinary, yet very gifted, descendent of king David whose parents were Joseph and Mary and who was born in the normal way. When he called himself the 'son of God', he only meant to explain that he was to be the next king of Israel – just as the Israelite kings from the House of David were also called sons of God in our Scriptures."

Philip: "That's what the ancient Egyptian Pharaohs did and what Caesar in Rome also claims. They all said that they were descended from some or other god, like Osiris or Zeus or Jupiter, or some other god."

Joel: "And then these Jews convinced you of Paul's ideas?"

"Yes, they did. What convinced me that they were on the right track was the fact that the sun disappeared inexplicably on a Wednesday morning, the day after I had met them. I saw that as a message from God that I ought to join these three Christians.

---

[38] See Acts 15 and Gal 1–2.

"What also convinced me as a prophet was that God wanted the traditional religion of Israel to be supplanted by the Christian faith. After all, He allowed the Romans to utterly and totally and completely destroy Jerusalem with her temple. After that, it became impossible to worship at the temple and to bring the sacrifices prescribed by the Torah. He allowed thousands upon thousands of Jews, including all the corrupt priests, to be killed during the war. God punished them for killing James and not accepting Jesus as God's ultimate Messiah."

A total solar eclipse was visible at Athens on 20 March AD 71. The Gospel of Mark seems to have referred to this eclipse in Mark 13: 24 – "But in those days, after that oppression [the destruction of Jerusalem and the temple in August AD 70], the sun will be darkened, the moon will not give her light..."

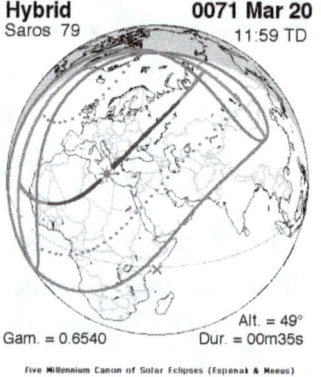

The path of the moon's shadow on the surface of the earth on 20 March AD 71, as computed by NASA. A computerized reconstruction of the solar eclipse visible at Athens on 20 March AD 71, more or less at 11:20 local time.

People in Athens experienced the eclipse around midday. This configuration would have held a message for Christians at that time because the eclipsed sun lay within Pisces, the Fishes, and next to Aries, the Ram. The Fish was an ancient symbol for Jesus Christ and the Jews traditionally regarded Aries as a lamb – which is also a symbol of Jesus Christ. Christians would have interpreted this eclipse as a sign that Jesus was indeed the "sun of righteousness" (Mal 4: 2) and "the Lamb of God" (John 1: 36). Aquarius, the Water Carrier, could have been interpreted as a symbol for John the Baptist who baptized Jesus, when he was confirmed as the Son of God when another eclipse occurred.

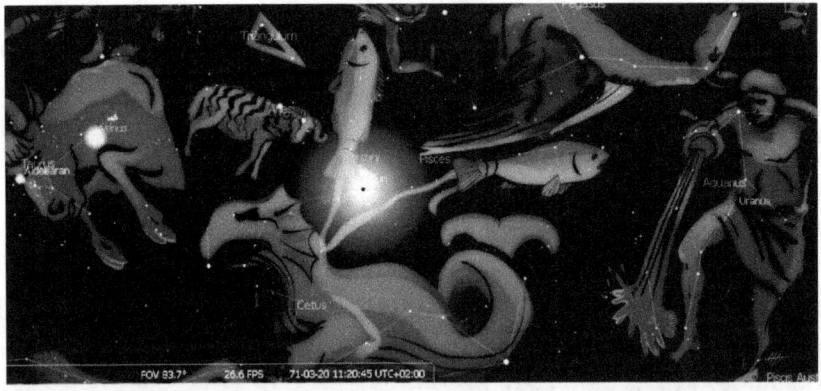

A computerized reconstruction of the heavens with the constellations of stars that became visible during the solar eclipse of 20 March AD 71 in Athens at 11:20

Philip asks: "You claim to have a prophetic gift. So, this mysterious event of the disappearing sun must surely have made a deep impression upon you?"

"Oh, yes, it did. I remember that clearly. My father told me that the sun also disappeared on the day when Jesus was baptized by my namesake, John the Baptist. That was when he was called to become the Messiah and king of Israel. I saw the disappearance of the sun at Athens also as a calling from God – and my three new friends shared my conviction.

"What was remarkable, is the fact that the invisible sun was in the constellation of the Fishes at that moment. Timothy explained to me that the Christians in Rome used the fish as a symbol for Christ. The word for 'fish' in Greek, as you well know, is ΙΧΘΥΣ.

37

That is also the abbreviation for 'Jesus Christ, God's Son, Savior.'"[39]

Philip: "And why did this Paul's conclusions differ from those of James and the Jewish followers of this Jesus?"

"My new friends explained that Paul also had a prophetic gift. He often had visions and revelations. Jesus spoke directly to him and assured him that he survived his death on the cross and was taken up into heaven with a spiritual or heavenly body so that he could fit in between the stars, the angelic spirits. Although the people in Galilee, Judea, and Jerusalem regarded him as merely an ordinary man, Paul concluded that he was actually the divine Son of God, the equal of his Father, whom he joined in heaven."

Philip asks again, "And how did you reach this place?" while pointing with his index finger to the floor of the cell: "Was it with the help of your new friends?"

"Yes. That was easlly done. A few days after my encounter with Priscilla, Aquila, and Timothy, we found a ship that took us to the harbor of Ephesus. On the way, we stopped over at a few islands, including Naxos and Patmos. My new friends paid for me and my sons' passage because they wanted to appoint me as a teacher in Ephesus. They only required of me to study all the letters of the late apostle Paul, which he wrote to various churches in Greece and Rome, as well as his two personal letters to Timothy. Copies of all these letters were being kept at all the Christian congregations, together with a short description of the life and death of Jesus, written by his disciple John. After reading all these new Scriptures, I regarded Paul's visions and revelations as trustworthy and inspired by God's Spirit. I became a committed Christian teacher."

Philip, the pick-pocket: "Were there also some other teachers at your school?"

---

[39] ΙΧΘΥΣ (*ICHTHYS*), the Greek for "fish" is also the abbreviation for "Ἰησοῦς Χρῑστός Θεοῦ Υἱός Σωτήρ (*Iēsoûs Chrīstós, Theoû Huiós, Sōtḗr*).

The restored house in Ephesus in which the Virgin Mary purportedly lived. It is now in use as a chapel.

"Yes, there were a few. The most important and famous of them all was this former disciple and apostle of Jesus, namely John, who took Jesus' mother, Mary, under his care. They settled in Ephesus where she was later buried. After his death, some of the other teachers at the school completed John's description of Jesus' life by adding some of the teachings of John and Jesus to the skeleton of the original book. I don't quite agree with all these additions, because they, in effect, turned John and Jesus into Greek philosophers – instead of Jewish prophets."

Joel: "Wasn't there some sort of a scandal connected with this other John?"

I laugh: "Ah, yes! There was. Some pagans wanted to make a fool of this John and they concocted an evil plan. We rented the school of Tyrannus, where Paul also taught when he was in Ephesus.[40] We used it during the afternoons when most people were resting during the hottest time of the day and the school was empty. One day, a wild woman suddenly stormed into the school. She

---

[40] Acts 19: 9.

wasn't dressed properly with wild hair and her breasts hanging out. She yelled at the apostle John: 'You crook! You scoundrel! You owe me money! You slept with me, without paying! You devil, I will make you pay what you owe me!'"

Stephanos, the hammer man, is leaning forward to listen better: "How did this John react? If something like that would have happened to me, I would have grabbed this witch by her hair and thrown her out."

"He didn't do anything. A few young men grabbed this wriggling and wicked woman and removed her, not very gently. While they were struggling and wrestling and fighting with her, I stood up and declared with a loud voice that I know John as an honorable and honest man who would never do such a thing as hiring the services of a whoring and wayward woman. The rest of the congregation applauded my words."

Stephanos: "Ha-ha, so this plan of those pagans fell flat. So, you got to know some people who knew Jesus personally, as well as friends of Paul, the apostle?"

"Indeed, indeed. In Athens, I also got to know John Mark, another of Paul's helpers. He told me that he was planning to write a book on Jesus and was collecting memories about Jesus from as many Christians as he could find, including the stories he heard from Paul and also from Peter, one of Jesus' apostles in Rome. I told him that the Ebionites already had compiled a book containing some of Jesus' sayings and teachings, but that I didn't have a copy. He was unaware of this and he hoped to gather as much material as possible, although most of the people who knew Jesus personally were already dead.

"When we discussed the disappearance of the sun soon after my arrival, he told me that he was convinced that Jesus must have predicted that such a sign would occur soon after the destruction of

40

Jerusalem."

Joel, the Jew: "Were you ever accepted as a proper prophet in Ephesus?"

Ruins of the Library of Celsus in Ephesus. The possibility exists that the school of Tyrannus was connected to this library.

"Certainly. The fact that God had given me so many signs by creating a red moon and making the sun disappear, He made sure that I got the message that I had to be a prophet, also in Ephesus. My career as a prophet started soon after I became a priest in Jerusalem. When the high priest ordered the murder of James a year later, I warned my fellow priests and the members of our sect that God would punish Jerusalem harshly for this crime. That did happen when the Roman soldiers demolished everything in the city and took thousands of people as slaves.

"The other teachers in Ephesus also accepted me as a prophet. It was later a privilege that my two sons were also my students. Timothy was the leader of the church, here in Ephesus. His title was bishop. But when he grew old and frail, it was decided that

I take over the leadership and oversee the churches in these western parts of Asia. And this is where I am today."

Mosaic of Roman legionaries

Philip: "What happened to your three friends from Athens?"

"Aquila and Priscilla travelled on to Pontus where they grew up. Timothy – as I told you – was bishop of Ephesus. He died recently when he tried to preach the gospel to a crowd of people who were worshipping the mother-goddess, Artemis. Some of the worshippers threw the old man down and he was trampled to death by the angry and aggressive mob. It was really sad and we all felt sorry, somber, and even sick at heart."

Sunday, 10 January AD 96

Today is the Lord's Day, the day of the week on which we commemorate the resurrection of Jesus when he first appeared to his followers after having been crucified. We skipped the Jewish Sabbath yesterday.[41]

I recite a part of a book by a prophet, which I can do in Hebrew and Greek. After a short explanation of how this prophecy applied to the life and work of Jesus, I do a prayer. The four of us kneel while I pray. Thereafter, I and Joel sing two Hebrew Psalms and I teach my new converts some Christian hymns. Some of the prisoners in other cells join in and I gather that there must be more Christians in this prison.

Shortly after the guard have pushed some breakfast through the bars of the gate to our cell, two soldiers appear to fetch Stephanos, the hammer man. While they try to shackle his legs, he bangs their heads together with great force. Hy grabs the sword of one of them and storms out. He disappears along the winding passage. A few seconds later, we hear a horrific scream as somebody is pierced by a sword or another weapon. We don't know whether Stephanos or somebody else was the victim.

I advise my two companions not to try to escape through the open gate of our cell, because we are unarmed and we will surely be slain if we ventured out. The two unconscious guards recover after I have poured some water onto their faces and they lock the gate of our cell as they depart.

One of them says: "Thanks for reviving us. It will certainly help you in court that you didn't take advantage of us."

---

[41] It is clear from Matt 28: 1; Mark 16: 9; John 20: 1, 26; Acts 2: 1; Acts 20:7 and 1 Cor 16: 2 that the first Christians regarded Sunday as the "Lord's Day" in commemoration of Jesus' reappearance from the tomb.

Philip: "Ha-ha! I almost castrated both of you with your own swords, but this old man stopped me."

It proves to be a wise decision not to have made use of the opportunity when the two guards were unconscious. After about half-an-hour, four guards appear. They chain Joel first and do the same to me. We are led out through the passages of the prison.

One of the guards mumbles: "Are you ready to meet the magistrate? His name is Macinus Olivetius. He has the rank of a praetor. So, you had better behave yourself when in his presence. Understood?"

We both nod our heads, too shaken to say anything.

As we are marched along the corridor, we encounter the corpse of a dead soldier – obviously the man killed by the fleeing Stephanos. Just before we reach the outer gate, we see the mutilated body of our late friend. His dash to freedom only led to his untimely demise. He must have been cornered by a whole squad of guards.

There is blood all over the place and Joel remarks that Stephanos must have wounded some of the guards who stopped him. I say a silent prayer of thanks that I was able to lead this man to

Jesus Christ two days ago and to baptize him.

We appear before Macinus Olivetius in the Praetorium or court house. The charge is read and we are requested to plead.

Joel pleads guilty, but also argues that the Jews have been granted special permission by the Roman Senate to practice their religion without interference from the Roman authorities. In addition, he has receipts at home to prove that he had paid his taxes, including the *Fiscus Judaicus,*[42] which exempted him from worshipping at a Roman temple dedicated to the cult of Caesar.

Macinus: "But it's impossible to continue with your religion because your temple has been razed many years ago. Why not embrace the official religion of the *Imperium Romanum*, together with your traditional religion? Many people do that."

Joel: "Although our temple is gone, we can still continue with our religion in our synagogues. We don't harass anybody and we are law-abiding citizens in all other respects. Our Law forbid us to worship idols, though."

Macinus: "Yes, you seem to have made a valid point. As a Jew, although your race is regarded as a despicable lot because you lost the war after starting a futile and foolish rebellion, I cannot find you guilty of sacrilege or insulting Caesar or anything else. You are free to go, although you must still pay the *Fiscus Iudaicus*."

I secretly wonder whether Joel has denounced his newly found Christian faith, but then I decided that he could legally rely on his Jewish ancestry – which he just did.

As Joel walks out, he grabs my shoulder and whispers: "I will pray for you, my brother in Christ."

I get tears in my eyes.

---

[42] Jews (and Christians) were obliged to pay a special tax, the *Fiscus Iudaicus*, for the upkeep of the temple of Jupiter in Rome, equal to the temple tax the Jews were required to pay before the destruction of the Jerusalem temple.

A golden coin minted by Emperor Vespasian after the destruction of Jerusalem in AD 70. The reverse side shows Judea as a captive woman, guarded by a soldier with a helmet and a shield. IVDEA CAPTA coins were minted for 25 years by Vespasian and his sons and successors, Titus and Domitian, in order to warn any nation that it would be futile to rebel against Roman rule.[43]

And then it's my turn to be tried. The magistrate remarks that it is well-known that I'm the leader of the Christians in these parts. He asks: "Why did you refuse to pay homage to Caesar as a living god?"

This question has been asked many times in the past by pagans, which gave me the opportunity to give my testimony why I became a Christian. This testimony resulted in a few cases where the pagans were so impressed by the beautiful Christian faith that they decided to convert to Christianity. I decide to try the same with this magistrate and I declare with great conviction that I cannot give up my faith and that my highest loyalty is with Jesus Christ who was willing to suffer crucifixion for my redemption.

Macinus, who listened carefully, responds: "Old man, you have broken the law. No doubt about it. You insulted Caesar with your sermon a few days ago and that is a capital crime. But it is also clear to me that you are an honorable man. Otherwise, the Christians would not have chosen you to be their leader. How old are you, by

---

[43] Ngo, "Judaea Capta Coin".

the way?"

"Sixty-six, milord."

"Yes, I can see your grey hair and I respect that. There are some attenuating circumstances, including your age and the fact that you didn't try to run away when your cell's door was hanging open. I will show you some mercy. I sentence you to banishment and exile on the island of Patmos, which falls under my jurisdiction as magistrate of Ephesus.

"Guards, shackle the legs of this man and take him on a military galley to Skala, the main town on Patmos. Leave him there to do as he pleases.

"Old man, I warn you. If you ever try to escape from Patmos, you will be hounded and hunted and harassed and arrested and then thrown back into prison for the rest of your life. Understood?"

I use my best Latin to thank the man for being merciful and sparing my life. I add: "May God have mercy upon your precious soul!"

Silently, I tell myself: "This man, of course, hopes that I will die on Patmos. How on earth will I be able to survive there without money, friends, or enough clothing? But, on the other hand, I'm sure that God will protect me, somehow. I am in his hands. And, who knows, perhaps I have convinced this man to become a Christian with my testimony! I noticed that he became nervous when I spoke of the never-ending horrors of Hades with its flames and fires and fumes and never-ending tortures and torments."

Sunday, 17 January AD 96

It took me five days to reach Skala, the main town on Patmos. I arrived without any luggage, except for my cloak that Prochorus had smuggled into my prison cell. I hoped to find lodgings with Christians or Jews on this island because I am totally destitute.

Roman shackles

After enquiring all over the place, it seemed that only pagans are living on this island. Nobody knew of any Christians or Jews. Because nobody would take in a shackled prisoner, I didn't sleep that first night because I just kept on walking to stay warm. It wasn't impossible to walk with the shackles, but it proved to be difficult.

A soft cold winter rain fell at times and it made me feel more and more miserable and melancholic, pathetic, and pitiable. There was half-a-moon in the sky and this heavenly body's light seeped through the clouds so that I could see where I was going.

It later transpired that I shuffled in a southerly direction.

Shortly after dawn, I encountered a shepherd leading his flock of sheep from a cave in the hillside. I asked him: "Do you mind if I seek shelter in your cave against the rain and the cold?"

He smiled: "Old man, you are welcome. I see that you are a prisoner of the Romans with those shackles on your ankles. I hate the Romans and anybody who is treated badly by the Romans is automatically my friend. Let's go back into the cave and I will share my breakfast with you."

I grabbed the hands of this generous man out of gratitude for

48

his kindness. He introduced himself as Andrew[44]. During breakfast I told him my story.

"You are welcome to make yourself at home in this cave. I don't have space for you in my hut where I live with my wife and five kids. My sheep sleep in here at night, especially during winter, but I will clear a spot for you where you can lie down. I will give you a few sheep skins to lie on and to cover yourself at night. Perhaps I have some old clothes that I can fetch from my hut down there so that you can get rid of your wet clothes."

And so, I found a spot to stay on this smallish island. It wasn't ideal and at night the sheep sometimes kept me awake, but it was, nevertheless, dry and safe and sheltered from the icy wind.

And today Andrew arrives with his friend, George[45], who is a blacksmith. He has a heavy hammer and a big iron chisel in his hands. He makes me lie down on the stone floor of the cave and smashes the shackles to free my legs. Out of gratitude, I preach the Gospel of God's grace and forgiveness to them, with the promise of life eternal after death. Both listen with attention and concentration.

George smiles: "Old man – or may I call you John? – what you tell us, makes lots of sense. The people on this island worship at the temples dedicated to Artemis, Apollo, and Aphrodite on the northern part of this island. I actually prefer Zeus, the father of the gods, but there is no temple for him on this island. But your God, who is the father of Jesus Christ and all believers, seems to me to be a better bet than Zeus. I like that bit about avoiding or escaping Hades after death and joining all the angels in the sky."

---

[44] The name "Andrew (Greek: Ἀνδρέας – *Andreas*) means "manly".

[45] The name "George" (Greek: Γεώργιος – *Georgios*) means "farmer" or "tiller of the soil".

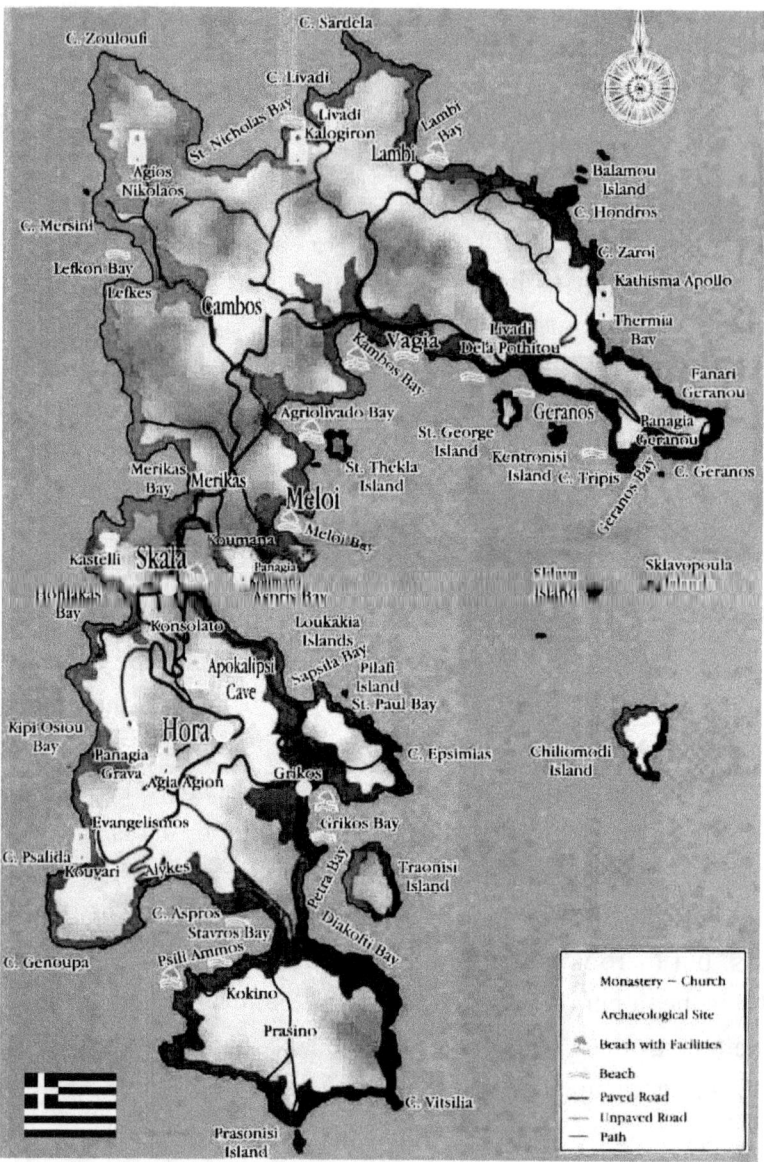

Patmos: The Holy Apokalipsi Cave (Ιερό Σπήλαιο της Αποκαλύψεως – *Hiero Spilaio tis Apokalypsteos*), in which the prophet John lived according to tradition, is in the southern half of the island. It is likely that John visited the beaches at Groikos (Γροικος) Bay or Sapsila (Σαψιλα) Bay (Rev 1: 8 and Rev 13: 1). He must also have visited the main town Skala (Σκάλα) often.

50

The cave in the southern part of Patmos in which John is said to have lived as an exile and where he wrote the account of his visions. This site, which is now part of the Monastery of the Apocalypse, together with the Monastery of St John the Theologian, were declared world heritage sites in 1999 and are popular tourist destinations. The cave is in use as a chapel.[46]

Aerial photo of Patmos taken from the south, showing its irregular coastline with various beaches. It is about 12 km long. There are some smaller islands associated with Patmos (Rev 1: 9).

---

[46] Unesco, *The World's Heritage,* 603.

Andrew agrees with his friend. I take the two to a nearby pool where the sheep usually drink and I baptize both as Christians. I explain to them that today is Sunday, the Lord's Day, the day on which we gather as Christians and praise the Lord. I teach my two new friends some hymns. I hope that this will be the start of a Christian congregation on this little island.

Sunday, 31 January AD 96

During the last few days, I felt very lonely, despite the occasional company of Andrew and George. I miss my Hannah, as well as my two sons who became missionaries in Persia.

There is, though, great joy and gratitude and relief in my heart because my dear friend, Prochorus, arrived yesterday.

I asked him: "How did you find me here, at this spot?"

"Simple. Easy. I kept my God-given eyes and ears open and used my God-given mind."

"Yes? How?"

"I was in the court house on the day you were sentenced. I kept myself hidden because I didn't want to make things more difficult for you by talking to you or by helping you. The guards might have kicked and hit and mistreated both of us if I did that. But I heard that you were to be exiled to Patmos. I watched the harbor of Ephesus to see when you were to be transported to Patmos."

Me: "The good Lord will surely bless you, my kind friend."

Prochorus: "In the meantime, the assembly over there in Ephesus started praying for your safety. Some money was collected and I was tasked with bringing it to you so that we can buy food. I've also brought some of your possessions so that you can live more comfortably. I also brought your stack of papyrus sheets, a few reed pens and ink, in case you wanted to write some letters."

"God is merciful and wonderful and thoughtful."

"Amen, halleluyah, amen. When I arrived here on Patmos a few days ago, I enquired all over the place to find you. Some people saw you after your arrival, but nobody knew where you were staying, until I happened to find a blacksmith named George. He directed me to this cave."

During the late afternoon, when the day's work has been

completed, I celebrate the Lord's Day with my little flock consisting of Prochorus and the families of Andrew and George – my only converts on Patmos, as yet. After Andrew and George and their families have left, we have our supper.

Prochorus announces: "I was lucky. I found some happy weeds[47] this morning and I added some to the broth we are having tonight."

My training at our desert school included the healing arts and we were informed about the properties of this weed. I was anointed with its oil while serving in the temple.[48] It has the effect of lifting the spirits in downhearted people and I conclude that I will certainly welcome the effects of this plant's leaves on myself.

After supper, I go and sit outside the cave, while feeling the effects of the happy weed. I tell Prochorus that I need some solitude and silence because Andrew's sheep keep on making noises. He promises to get our primitive beds ready and stoke our fire. He fortunately brought some rugs from Ephesus along and with those we feel as if we are living in luxury – even with lots of restless and noisy and stinking sheep with us in the cave.

I start watching the night sky. During my life as a priest in Jerusalem and my stay in Ephesus as a teacher, I had little time to watch the stars, as I was used to do when I was a student at our school in the desert. Tonight, though, the sky is clear and I look in wonder and awe at all the dots of light in the sky and the clusters and constellations they form. No planets are visible.

---

[47] The name the ancients gave to *Cannabis Sativa*, also known as Marijuana. It was used as a pain killer and in religious ceremonies due to the ecstatic frame of mind or euphoria it caused. Archaeologists have found traces of the plant in ancient sites in Israel (Fox: "Archaeologists Identify Traces of Burnt Cannabis").
[48] Ex 30:22–25.

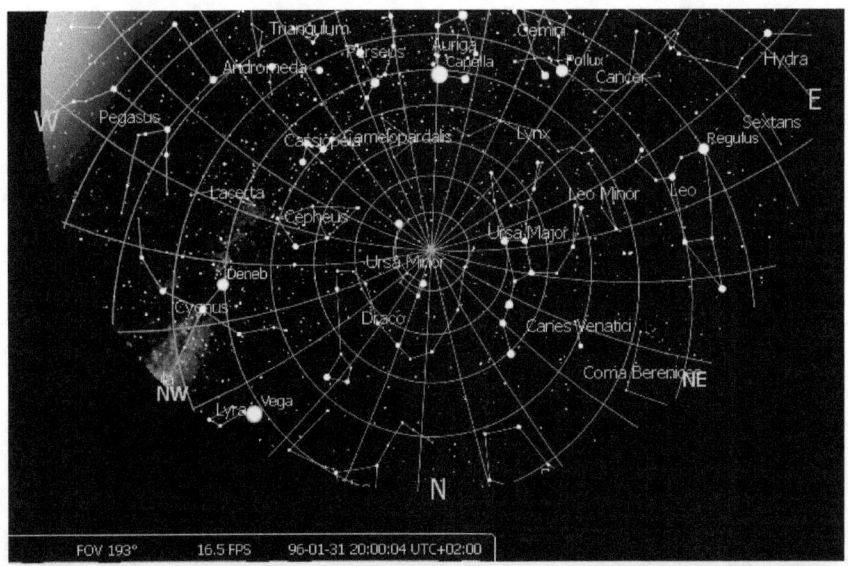

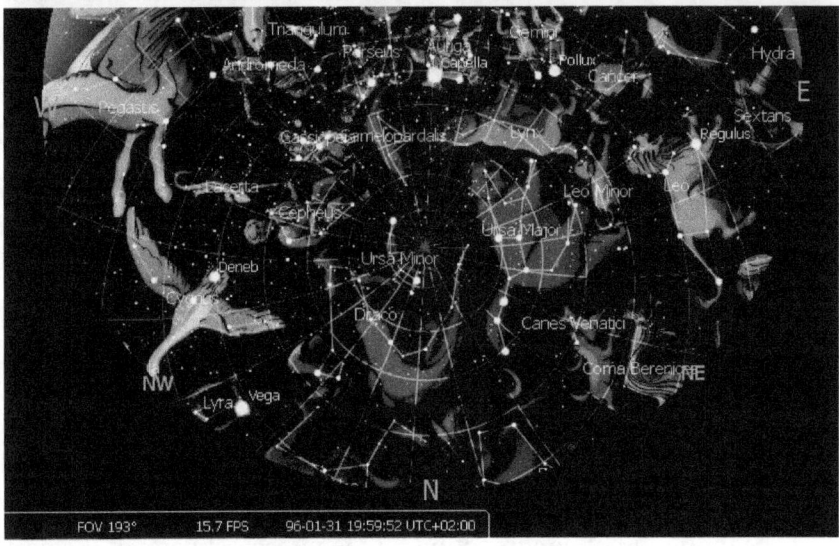

Computerized recreations of the night sky over Patmos, looking north, on Sunday, 31 January AD 96, at around 20:00 local time. The second illustration contains drawings depicting the personages, animals and objects that are connected with the different celestial constellations. The illustrations also contain grid lines emanating from the celestial north pole.

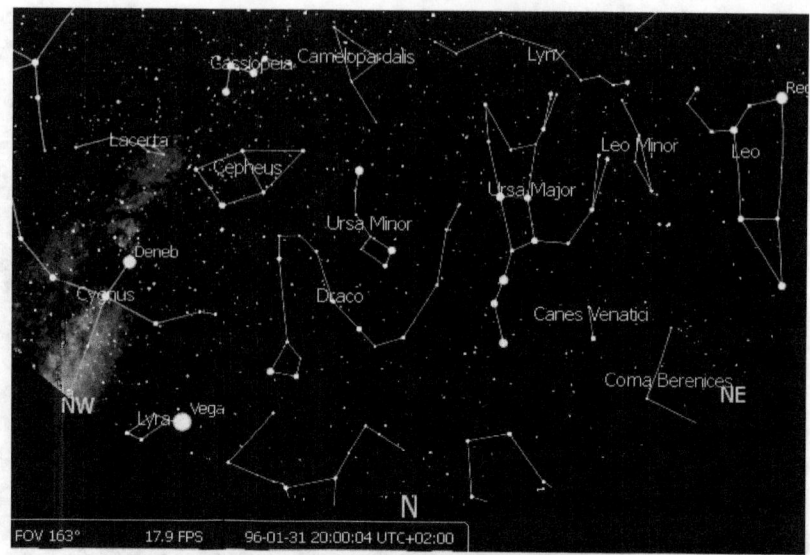

A close-up view of the circumpolar stars and constellations, as seen from Patmos on 31 January AD 96 and looking north. The celestial North Pole is just above the "o" in the name "Ursa Minor".

As I explained to my friends in prison in Ephesus, according to the Scriptures, these constellations and stars are real spiritual beings – angels and even demons.[49] Of course, God Himself is not visible because he is hidden from human eyes. It is, though, possible to locate the spot in the northern sky where his invisible throne must be situated.

I remember what the Scriptures said of the king of Babylon:

"You said in your heart, I will ascend into heaven, I will exalt my throne above the stars of God; and I will sit on the mountain of congregation, in the uttermost parts of the north ..."[50]

---

[49] 1 Kgs 22: 19; Job 38: 4–8; Ps 148: 2–3; Ps 103: 20–21; Neh 9: 6; Dan 1: 2–3.
[50] Isa 14: 13.

There are some other places in the Scriptures where something similar is taught and I recite those to my companion.[51]

More or less, at the spot where the throne of the Almighty Creator of heaven and earth is situated, I notice the chariot of the prophet Elijah with which he ascended into heaven.[52] There are seven prominent stars in this constellation.

While I look more intently, I notice that these stars form the outlines of a throne. Directly below Elijah's Chariot, I notice the Quiver[53], the container or basket in which an archer keeps his arrows.

Seven of its brightest stars form an arc below the throne of God and I can't help but to be reminded of the Menorah, the lamp with seven arms that used to stand in the Jerusalem temple and that was looted by the Romans when Jerusalem with her temple was destroyed during the war.

---

[51] I Kgs 22: 19; Job 37: 22; Isa 2: 2; Is 11: 9; Isa 65: 25; Enoch 14: 18.

[52] The Jewish name for the constellation of Ursa Minor, the Little Bear (see: Allen, *Star Names,* 451).

[53] The Jewish name for the constellation of Draco, the Dragon, was "the Quiver" (see: Allen, *Star Names,* 203).

I try to imagine how Jesus Christ in his glory, next to his Father on the heavenly throne, must look if human eyes could have seen him. I conclude that he must have been clothed as a king or a Roman judge, the Judge on Judgment Day. He will be flanked by his archangels.

Christ on his throne and dressed as a Roman judge, with four archangels – mosaic in the basilica of San Apollinare Nuovo, Ravenna, Italy (6th century).

In my mind, I picture Christ holding the seven stars of Elijah's Chariot in his right hand, while being illuminated by the seven lamps in front of him. He must be the "Son of Man"[54] as mentioned in the prophecies of Daniel and as he referred to Himself on occasion, according to the memoirs we have of his life and words. He must be

---

[54] An expression from Dan 7: 13; 10: 1 & 5–6.

a figure with white hair, a shining face, a long robe and a golden sash or belt to portray his eternity and majesty. With his feat he tramples upon his enemies.

The thought occurs to me that Christ, who led me to this forlorn, far-away, and forsaken island, and gave me the opportunity to gaze at his throne, must have a message for me. What would that message be?

Suddenly, I can hear a loud voice speaking to me, which makes me feel dizzy. The voice orders me to write down everything that I see and send the message to the seven Christian assemblies in Asia, namely Ephesus, Smyrna, Pergamum, Thyatira, Sardis, Philadelphia, and Laodicea – the churches of which I am the overseer.

I hear the waves of the sea crashing against the coast of the island and those sounds accompany the Voice, which announces that the seven stars in Jesus' right hand represent the seven guardian angels of these assemblies, while the seven lamp stands of the Quiver constitute these seven assemblies.

Next to the seven lamp stands, I see the outlines of a sword in the stars, directly to the left of the seven lamp stands. That sword must represent Christ's message and words, since it emanates from his mouth. With that sword, He will condemn pagans and unrepentant Jews to Hades, while he will order the faithful to be worthy of heavenly bliss. Some of the older members of my church in Ephesus told me that they remembered that Paul explained to them that the Word of God can be regarded as the sword of the Spirit, a weapon to fight Satan and all evil forces.[55]

This sight of God's heavenly throne and all the angels gives me the conviction and assurance that Jesus Christ is in command

---

[55] Eph 6: 17.

and seated on his throne, despite the might of the Roman Empire with her military legions.

A cold wind has picked up and it blows over me where I sit in this exposed spot outside the cave. This wind must be the breath of God, his Spirit, that took hold of me and made me see all the sights in the heavens. I regard it as a great privilege that God is using me as a prophet and that his Spirit is inspiring me.

Monday, 1 February AD 96

After my encounter with the glorified and exalted Jesus Christ last night, during which I was profoundly moved by the Spirit of God while I forgot about my surroundings, I woke up this morning with a smile on my face. I realize that God had sent me with a divine plan to this island. I am to receive messages from Christ, which must be passed on to my fellow-Christians on the mainland. My studies, my work as a priest and teacher of the Law, and my leadership position in Ephesus all led to this point where I was to become God's messenger and prophet. The predictions of my father, the Teacher at our school, and others that I was destined to become a prophet, as well as the signs in the heavens of a red moon and a disappearing sun, were all leading up to this point. And that is the real reason why I am an exile on Patmos!

This realization comes almost as a shock to me. I must ask myself: Am I worthy of this task? Am I fit to be God's messenger?

After the sheep had been led away by Andrew and we had breakfast, prepared by Prochorus, we sing two Psalms in Hebrew and I recite a part of the prophecies of Ezekiel in which he described four heavenly beings with the appearances of a man, a bull, a lion and an eagle, respectively.[56]

I tell my companion: "I want to dictate to you something that you must write down on a sheet of papyrus. Keep it in a safe place because I am sure that there will be more messages that I receive from the Spirit of God and from Christ. They will have to be sent in due course to our Christian brethren on the mainland."

Prochorus fetches the required writing materials and we sit down in the entrance to the cave to have enough daylight. I start to dictate, while Prochorus takes down my words:

---

[56] Ezek 1: 10.

Revelations 1: 9–20
The appearance of Jesus

9. I, John, your brother and partaker with you in oppression and kingdom and perseverance which are in Jesus, was on the isle that is called Patmos because of God`s Word and the testimony of Jesus Christ.

10. I was in the Spirit on the Lord`s day, and I heard behind me a loud voice, as of a trumpet

11. saying, "What you see, write in a book and send to the seven assemblies: to Ephesus, Smyrna, Pergamum, Thyatira, Sardis, Philadelphia, and to Laodicea."

12. I turned to see the voice that spoke with me. Having turned, I saw seven golden lampstands

13. And in the midst of the lampstands was one like a son of man, clothed with a robe reaching down to his feet, and with a golden sash around his chest.

14. His head and his hair were white as white wool, like snow. His eyes were like a flame of fire.

15. His feet were like burnished brass, as if it had been refined in a furnace. His voice was like the voice of many waters.

16. He had seven stars in his right hand. Out of his mouth proceeded a sharp two-edged sword. His face was like the sun shining at its brightest.

17. When I saw him, I fell at his feet like a dead man. He laid his right hand on me, saying, "Don`t be afraid. I am the first and the last,

18. and the Living one. I was dead, and behold, I am alive forevermore. I have the keys of Death and of Hades.

> 19. Write therefore the things which you have seen, and the things which are, and the things which will happen hereafter;
> 20. the mystery of the seven stars which you saw in my right hand, and the seven golden lampstands. The seven stars are the angels of the seven assemblies. The seven lampstands are seven assemblies."

While Prochorus takes the writing materials back into the cave to store them on a shelf, out of reach of the sheep, I happen to feel a Roman coin in the pocket of a cloak that Prochorus has brought – a Sestertius.

The deified son of Emperor Domitian who died at the age of nine, is depicted on this coin. He is sitting on a globe (the earth) with his arms stretched out and surrounded by seven stars, while holding one of them in his left hand – almost like the seven stars in the right hand of the glorified Christ that John had seen.

The inscription surrounding the figure, DIVUS CAESAR IMP[ERATOR] DOMITIANI F[ILIUS], means: "THE DIVINE CAESAR, SON OF EMPEROR DOMITIAN". The boy is depicted as baby Jupiter, head of the Roman pantheon of gods. If Domitian's son was depicted as a god, then his father must also have been regarded as a divine being.[57]

---

[57] Franz, "The King and I".

I take a good look at it and notice that it contains a hidden message, namely that Emperor Domitian regards himself as a living god.

The message on this coin is certainly and precisely and definitely the reason why I am on this island as an exile with a criminal record. It was and is and will be impossible for me to ever venerate Caesar Domitian as a living god. I devoted my whole career in Ephesus to win converts from pagan religions and the Jewish faith to the faith of Jesus Christ.

It is sometimes erroneously claimed that the book of Revelation was written by the Apostle John, who also wrote the Gospel bearing his name and the three short letters attributed to him. This cannot be the case. The different styles of writing between these parts of the New Testament rules the apostle as author of Revelation out. The Apostle John would most probably have been dead by the time Revelation was written after the death of Emperor Domitian in September AD 96 when the author of Revelation was allowed to return to Ephesus. There are various clues about the background of the author of Revelation contained in his book that rules the authorship of the apostle out.

Tuesday and Wednesday, 2–3 February, AD 96

The rather shocking experience I had on Sunday night, when I heard the voice of Jesus Christ and I was overpowered by the breath or wind or Spirit of God, keeps me awake tonight. After supper, prepared by Prochorus and laced with a few leaves of the happy weed, I sit down again on a rock outside the cave and start to observe the heavens – expecting a repetition of the night before yesterday.

There was a violent thunder storm during the afternoon, with lightning flashes and loud explosions as the flames from heaven crashed down onto the earth.

I tell myself: "Those loud explosions must certainly be the voice of God. That gives us an idea how awful it will be on Judgment Day for the pitiable pagans and the deranged devils and demons!"

The lightning and thunder during the afternoon brought back memories of the Jewish war of thirty years ago when I heard the trumpets and drums of the Roman legions while experiencing a thunder storm near Jerusalem. After the worst part of the storm had passed, a beautiful rainbow appeared.

In the meantime, it became dark and the stars became visible, but there are still lightning flashes over the horizon to the north.

I am reminded of the experience of the children of Israel during the time of Moses when they camped out at the foot of the mountain of God in the desert:

> "It happened on the third day, when it was morning, that there were thunders and lightnings, and a thick cloud on the mountain, and the sound of an exceedingly loud trumpet; and all the people who were in the camp trembled. (...) Mount Sinai, the whole of it, smoked, because the Lord descended on it in fire; and its smoke ascended like the smoke of a fur-

65

nace, and the whole mountain quaked greatly."[58]

As I was looking in a northerly direction, to the spot where God's throne must be, it is as if I see a door opened into the heavens and I get a vision of God sitting on his throne. The Scriptures often spoke of the doors and windows of heaven, through which the waters above the heaven came pouring down as rain, just as happened earlier today. I remember that the prophet Enoch spoke at length of the doors and windows of heaven.[59]

God's throne is situated just above the seven stars of the Quiver. During my earlier vision, I was told that these seven stars or lamps represent the seven Christian communities in Asia. I also get the insight that these seven stars may be regarded as the sevenfold Spirit of God, sharing the throne with God the Father and his Son, Jesus Christ. This insight reminds me of one of David's Psalms. "God reigns over the nations. God sits on his holy throne."[60]

It is as if the throne is surrounded by a rainbow, but a rainbow that differs from the one that I saw shortly after this afternoon's thunder storm. It looks like an emerald, a green stone, and consists of the bright band of light, stretching over the whole expanse of the sky, called by the Greeks the "Galaxy"[61] or "Milky Way" and which the Jews call "the River of Fire".[62]

In my mind's eye, I see God's glory and I compare it in my

---

[58] Ex 19: 16 & 18.

[59] Gen 1: 7; Gen 7: 11; 2 Kgs 7: 2; Ps 148: 4; Ezek 1: 1; Mal 3: 10; Enoch LXXII/3; Enoch LXXV/1 & 7.

[60] Ps 47: 8.

[61] Greek: Γαλαξίας (*Galaxias*). According to Greek mythology, the goddess Hera nursed the baby Herakles (Hercules). He bit her breast so hard and painfully that the milk from her breast got splashed over the heavens – with the Milky Way as the result.

[62] Dan 7: 10. The Aramaic expression is נְהַר דִּי־נוּר (*nehar ki nuwr*).

66

mind with a jasper stone and a sardius – both are reddish or multicolored stones that can be polished to a high gloss and can be worn as expensive jewelry. The beautiful stars are reflected on the waters of the bay next to the town of Skala to the north and the scene looks like a sea of glass, like a crystal.

My eyes look around and I remember that Enoch wrote that there are four prominent stars – he called them "leaders" – of which each one has dominion over a quarter of a year, calculated as ninety-one days each.[63] I see three of these stars: Arcturus in the Ploughman, Regulus in the Lion, and Aldebaran in the Bull. The fourth one, Altair in the Eagle, must become visible later during the night as the stars move around the earth and God's throne and I decide to remain sitting here on this rock until I see the Eagle.

Then I recall that I recited yesterday a passage from the prophet Ezekiel in which he also mentioned the Man, the Lion, the Eagle, and the Bull.

It is also apparent that these creatures surround God's throne in all four directions. The number of four can be regarded as a number telling us something about the earth or creation. There are four wind directions and four seasons. The world is made up of four elements: fire, air, water, and earth. These four creatures may also be seen as representatives of God's creation. The lion is the king of the wild animals, the bull is the strongest of the domesticated animals, the eagle can fly higher than any other bird, and Man is the pinnacle of God's creation. We humans are, after all, created in the image of God.

Something else strikes me. These four creatures are also representatives of the nations of the earth. The Lion, of course, represents Judah, whose sign is the Lion.[64] The Eagle is connected

---

[63] Enoch 82: 12–20.

[64] Gen 49: 9.

67

to the Roman Empire. The Roman legions march with standards on which eagles appear. The Bull is a representative of Egypt, the country where the Israelites learnt to worship the Golden Calf. The Bull is also connected to their chief god, Osiris. The Man, the Ploughman, represents all the other nations of mankind.

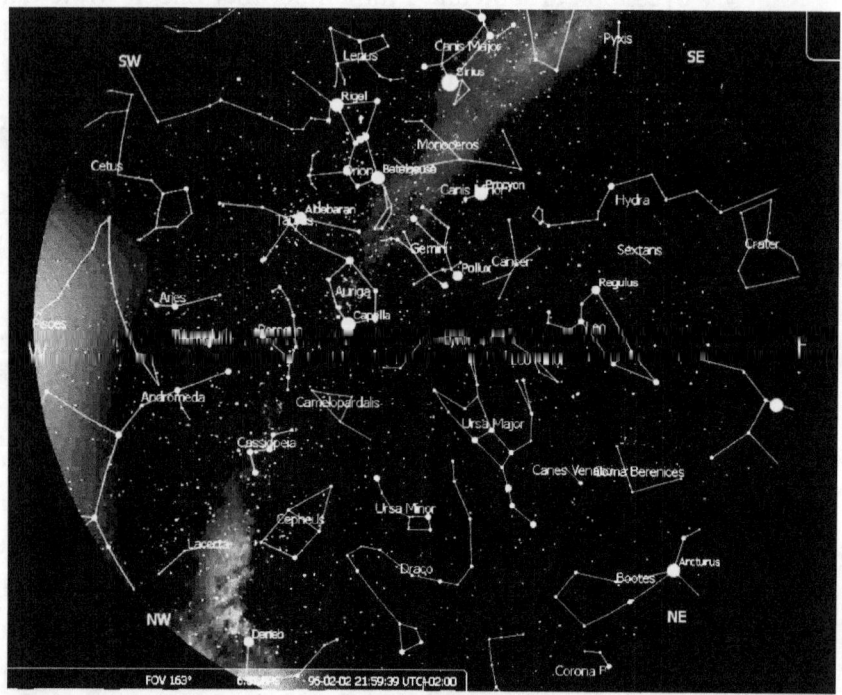

A computerized reconstruction of the night sky over Patmos on 2 February AD 96, at about 22:00 local time, looking north. The bright Milky Way stretches from the north western corner to the south eastern corner. The following living creatures are visible: the Man (Boötes, with its brightest star Arcturus) on the north eastern horizon, the Lion (Leo, with its brightest star Regulus) in the east and the Bull (Taurus, with its brightest star Aldebaran) towards the south west.

A passage from the prophet Isaiah intrudes into my mind:

> "In the year that king Uzziah died I saw the Lord sitting on a throne, high and lifted up; and his train filled the temple.

Above him stood the seraphim: each one had six wings; with two he covered his face, and with two he covered his feet, and with two he did fly." [65]

Because of this, I conclude that these four creatures must each have six wings.

As I watch the hours go by and wait for the Eagle to appear, it dawns upon me that all these creatures must be singing God's praise. I start to sing to myself one of the hymns that we often sang in Ephesus.

Shortly before dawn, I see the Eagle rise in the east. The Ploughman and the Lion are still visible, but the Bull has disappeared behind the horizon.

While I waited for the Eagle to appear, I also watched the constellations on the southern horizon. They appeared and disappeared, one after the other. It also struck me that there must be twenty-four constellations taking turns to appear and to disappear, one for each hour of the day and the night. They also surround God's throne and I decide that they must represent twenty-four elders – twelve from the tribes of Israel and the twelve apostles of Jesus Christ. Their function must also be to sing God's praise.

In Ephesus, I had a conversation with a learned Greek philosopher. He told me that the ancient philosopher, Pythagoras, taught that the planets follow fixed courses in their travels around the earth and they created harmonies and music because the distances between them form harmonious proportions – just as the string on a stringed instrument produce the different musical notes when the strings were shortened or lengthened in accordance with numerical proportions. That convinces me that all these heavenly

---

[65] Is 6: 1–2.

beings, the four living creatures and the twenty-four elders, must sing hymns and Psalms in honor of God all the time.

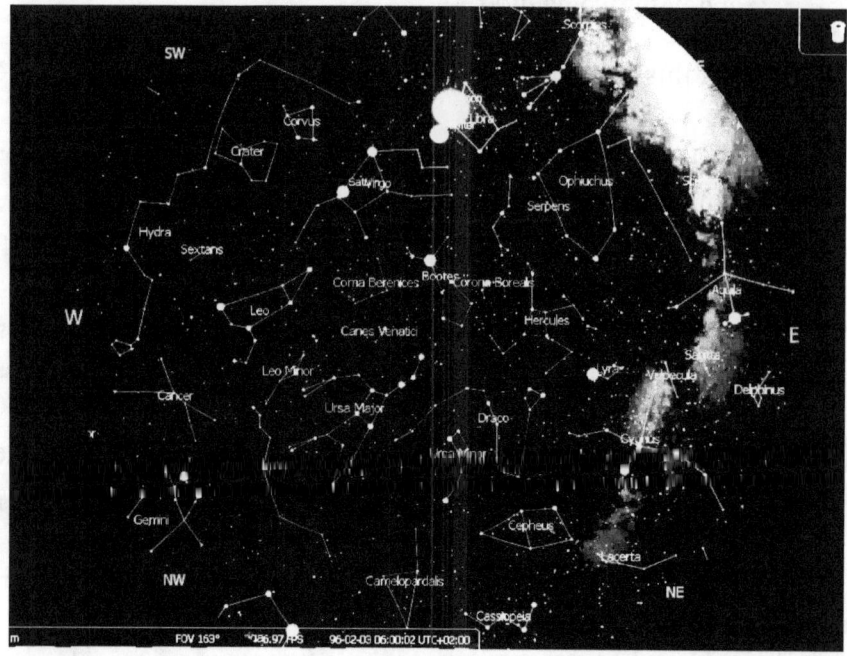

Aquila, the Eagle. with its principal star, Altair, is rising in the east at more or less 06:00 local time. Leo, the Lion, lies to the west and Boötes, the Ploughman, is situated in the middle of the sky. A crescent moon is also visible in Libra.

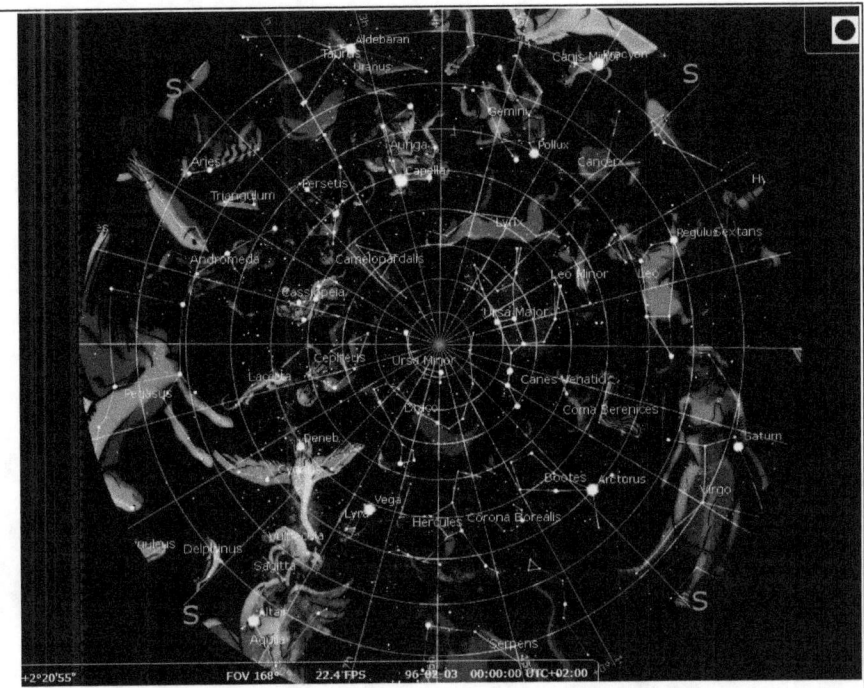

The view of the sky at the terrestrial north pole showing the distribution of the four living creatures around the celestial north pole. Taurus (the Bull) is at the upper left, Leo (the Lion) is at the upper right, Aquila (the Eagle) is at the lower left and Boötes (the Ploughman) is situated at the lower right, next to Virgo. The sky is also divided into 24 segments – one for each hour of the day.

A map of the northern sky (viewed from above) by the medieval German artist, Albrecht Dürer, showing the positions of the four living beings. Taurus (the Bull) is on top (on its back) and Leo (the Lion) is on the left. Boötes (the Ploughman) is visible at the bottom with a big fork in his hand and Aquila (the Eagle) can be seen on the right. The large circle, which is divided into twelve segments, is the path of the sun through the twelve constellations of the Zodiac (Rev 4: 6)

The god of the heavens of the Sumerians, Anu, had his throne at the northern celestial pole and his throne was also surrounded by a lion, a bull, a man, and an eagle. These were the constellations of –

- Leo, the Lion, with Regulus as its most prominent star, which was situated at the summer solstice in those days;
- Taurus, the Bull, whose biggest star is Aldebaran, which marked the spring equinox;

- Aquila, the Eagle, with Altair as its principal star, which ruled the winter solstice; and
- Boötes, the Ploughman or Farmer, with Arcturus as his biggest star, which was somewhat askew and did not quite mark the autumn equinox.[66]

John clearly held the same view as the old Sumerians.

After having observed all four living creatures, I retire to my bed, although it is almost daybreak.

I cannot sleep very long because Andrew appears to lead his sheep out to pastures and water.

Prochorus prepares breakfast and he asks: "Do you want me to write down what you have been watching during the night?"

"Yes, directly after breakfast you must fetch a new sheet of papyrus. I will tell you what to write."

Revelation 4: 1–11
Worship in heaven

1. After these things I looked and saw a door opened in heaven, and the first voice that I heard, like a trumpet speaking with me, was one saying, "Come up here, and I will show you the things which must happen after this."
2. Immediately I was in the Spirit. Behold, there was a throne set in heaven, and one sitting on the throne
3. that looked like a jasper stone and a sardius. There was a rainbow around the throne, like an emerald to look at.
4. Around the throne were twenty-four thrones. On the thrones were twenty-four elders sitting, dressed in white garments,

---

[66] Cornelius, *Geistesgeschichte,* 13, 35–36; Visser, *Openbaring,* 57–58.

with crowns of gold on their heads.

5. Out of the throne proceed lightnings, sounds, and thunders. There were seven lamps of fire burning before the throne, which are the seven Spirits of God.

6. Before the throne was something like a sea of glass, like a crystal. In the midst of the throne, and around the throne were four living creatures full of eyes before and behind.

7. The first creature was like a lion, and the second creature like a calf, and the third creature had a face like a man, and the fourth creature was like a flying eagle.

8. and the four living creatures, having each one of them six wings, are full of eyes around about and within. They have no rest day and night, saying, Holy, holy, holy is the Lord God, the Almighty, who was and who is and who is to come.

9. When the living creatures give glory, honour, and thanks to him who sits on the throne, to him who lives forever and ever,

10. the twenty-four elders fall down before him who sits on the throne, and worship him who lives forever and ever, and will throw their crowns before the throne, saying,

11. "Worthy are you, our Lord and our God, to receive the glory, the honour, and the power, for you created all things, and because of your desire they existed, and were created."

The symbols of the Four Evangelists (Clockwise from top left): a man (Matthew), a lion (Mark), an eagle (John) and an calf (Luke) in the Book of Kells, ca AD 800.

These four living creatures were traditionally seen as symbols of the four evangelists. The lion represented Mark, the calf Luke, the man Matthew, and the eagle John. Irenaeus, the second century theologian was the first to make this association with the evangelists, and this interpretation became tradition, although the text in Revelation does not support this idea.[67]

---

[67] Kovacs & Rowland, *Revelation.* 66.

Sunday, 14 February AD 96

During the previous ten days, I spent some time outside the cave at night, but no message from God came through. There were also a few cloudy nights during which no observations could be made.

I take my place on my rock outside the cave while Prochorus prepares our beds. My attention is drawn again to the spot in the sky where God's throne must be. I see again the seven stars of the Chariot of Elijah and the seven stars of the Quiver. I also observe three of the four living creatures surrounding the throne: The Man, the Lion, and the Bull.

Suddenly, a text from the prophet Isaiah regarding the Messiah pops into my mind:

"He was oppressed, and he was afflicted, yet he opened not his mouth: he is brought as a lamb to the slaughter, and as a sheep before her shearers is dumb, so he opened not his mouth."[68]

A flock of sheep on Patmos. These animals may be descendants of the sheep that John saw every day.

[68] Is 53: 7.

I also remember that my namesake, John the Baptist, reportedly called Jesus "the Lamb of God."[69]

That gives me the confidence to clearly see Jesus Christ next to his Father in the form of a lamb – of which I see a lot every day when Andrew's sheep leave or enter our cave.

Tears come to my eyes while I contemplate the beauty of God's heaven with all the heavenly beings populating the sky. But these tears are also the result of the fact that I feel very lonely, here on this small island with only Prochorus, Andrew, and George with their families as company. They visited me earlier today to hear the Word of God. The other inhabitants shun me.

The realization takes hold of me that the seven stars of the Quiver, which I previously saw as seven lamps stands, as well as the seven assemblies, and the seven Spirits of God, may also be regarded as the seven eyes and horns of the Lamb on the throne. With those, he can see everything in creation.

According to Isaiah, the Messiah in the guise or form of a lamb, was slaughtered. That is exactly what happened to Jesus Christ when his body was broken on the cross.

And yet, he is still alive, because he was resurrected with a spiritual body after his death and taken up into heaven where he sits on his Father's right hand side on the throne.

As I fall into deep thought while the happy weed in our supper takes effect, I hear a voice declaring the seven stars of the Chariot of Elijah to be a book with seven seals. An angel, in the form of the sliver of a crescent moon in the west, asks with a loud voice whether anybody would be able to open that book. I feel sad, because I feel that nobody will be able to open that scroll – nobody in the heavens, nobody on earth, and nobody from the underworld.

---

[69] John 1: 29.

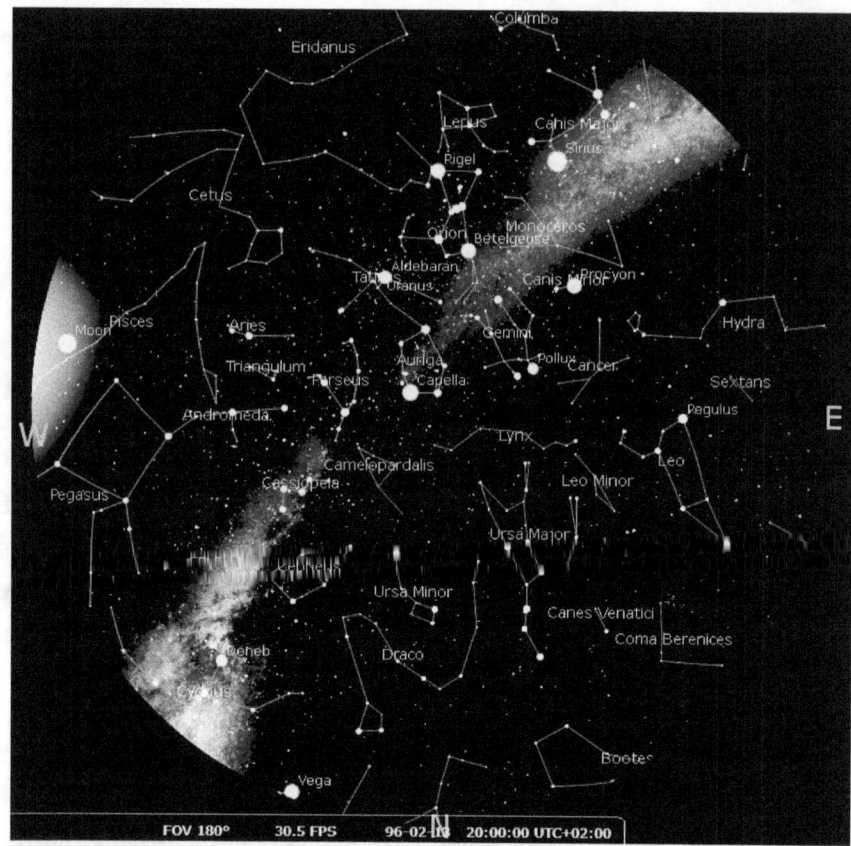

A reconstruction of the starry skies above Patmos on the evening of 14 February AD 96, at about 20:00, looking northwards. Only the outlines of the constellations are shown. The book with the seven seals is Ursa Minor, the Little Bear, with its seven stars and the seven eyes. The seven horns of the Lamb, which are also the seven Spirits of God, are the seven stars on the body and tail of Draco. The angel who called out is the setting crescent moon (1,5% illuminated) in the west.

It is as if one of the twenty-four elders consoles me by declaring that the Lamb will be able to break those seals and reveal the contents of this book. Because this book is held in the hand of God, it can only contain God's plans for this evil and sinful and corrupt world. I am sure that the different parts of this plan will become clear whenever these seals are broken, one after the other.

I am looking forward to what the Lamb will be able to reveal to me – and to the seven assemblies on the mainland to whom I must send my messages. It must be a perfect plan, because the book is sealed by seven seals and seven is, after all, a sacred number.[70]

The Lamb (Rev 5: 6) surrounded by stars and archangels in heaven; some of the constellations of the Zodiac are hidden amongst the foliage next to the angels (mosaic on the ceiling of the Basilica of San Vitale, Ravenna, Italy, 6th century)

I clearly hear the four living beings and the elders singing the praise of the Lamb again. They sang a new song, saying,

> "You are worthy to take the book, and to open its seals: For you were killed, and bought us for God with your blood, out of every tribe, language, people, and nation, and made them kings and priests to our God, and they reign on earth."

The fact that they mention "every tribe, language, people, and nation," amounts to a fourfold mention of the whole of mankind.

---

[70] There were seven days of creation, there are seven planets circling the earth, there are seven days in a week, there are seven basic colors, and there are seven notes in a musical scale.

79

That means that those who were saved by the Lamb may come from any place on earth, whose symbolic number is four. The privileged position of Israel as God's chosen people has been abolished.

And then the thousands upon thousands of angels in heaven – the many dots of light in the sky – start singing God's praise. I start singing with them, because it's a well-known hymn that we often sang in Ephesus. Prochorus hears me and joins me outside.

While singing, I also remember that I have read at our school in the desert that Philo of Alexandria, the Jewish scholar and contemporary of Jesus, also thought that the skies moved according to celestial music.

While we retire to our beds in a corner of the cave, which we have fenced off with some rocks to keep the sheep away from us, I decide that God's plans for this evil and godless and cruel world will certainly be executed because He has the assistance of the Lamb – who is also the Lion of Judah[71] and the descendant of King David and his father, Jesse. The prophet Isaiah also wrote:

"And there shall come forth a rod out of the stem of Jesse, and a branch shall grow out of his roots."[72]

He is, therefore, also of royal blood.

I call upon Prochorus to light a fire and fetch his writing materials. I dictate:

Revelation 5: 1–14
The book and the Lamb

1.	I saw, in the right hand of him who sat on the throne, a book written within and on the back, sealed shut with seven seals.

---

[71] Gen 49: 9.
[72] Isa 11: 1.

2.   I saw a mighty angel proclaiming with a loud voice, "Who is worthy to open the book, and to break its seals?"

3.   No one in heaven, or on the earth, or under the earth, was able to open the book, or to look in it.

4.   And I wept much, because no one was found worthy to open the book, or to look in it.

5.   One of the elders said to me, "Don`t weep. Behold, the Lion who is of the tribe of Judah, the Root of David, has overcome to open the book and its seven seals."

6.   I saw in the midst of the throne and of the four living creatures, and in the midst of the elders, a Lamb standing, as though it had been slain, having seven horns, and seven eyes, which are the seven Spirits of God, sent forth into all the earth.

7.   Then he came, and he took it out of the right hand of him who sat on the throne.

8.   Now when he had taken the book, the four living creatures and the twenty-four elders fell down before the Lamb, each one having a harp, and golden bowls full of incense, which are the prayers of the saints.

9.   They sang a new song, saying, "You are worthy to take the book, and to open its seals: For you were killed, and bought us for God with your blood, out of every tribe, language, people, and nation,

10.   And made them kings and priests to our God, and they reign on earth."

11.   I saw, and I heard a voice of many angels around the throne, the living creatures, and the elders; and the number of them

was ten thousands of ten thousands, and thousands of thousands;

12. saying with a loud voice, "Worthy is the Lamb who has been killed to receive the power, riches, wisdom, might, honour, glory, and blessing!"

13. I heard every created thing which is in heaven, on the earth, under the earth, on the sea, and everything in them, saying, "To him who sits on the throne, and to the Lamb be the blessing, the honour, the glory, and the dominion, forever and ever. Amen."

14. The four living creatures said, "Amen!" The elders fell down and worshipped.

The German-English composer, Georg Friedrich Händel, used the words of Rev 5: 12–14 of the Authorized Version of the Bible for the final chorus of his famous oratorio, the Messiah (1742). The words in the chorus are as follows:

"Worthy is the Lamb that was slain, and hath redeemed us to God by His blood, to receive power, and riches, and wisdom, and strength, and honour, and glory, and blessing. Blessing and honour, glory and power, be unto Him that sitteth upon the throne, and unto the Lamb, for ever and ever. Amen."

With this, he endeavored to emulate the heavenly choirs.

Sunday, 13 March AD 96

My friends, Andrew and George, turn up with their families to worship with me and Prochorus on this Lord's Day. George introduces me to a stranger: "This is Jason. He wants to see you for himself after I have told him about you and your message."

I greet Jason warmly and I ask: "How are you and George connected?"

Jason: "We are neighbors. I am a shopkeeper and I deliver and transport my wares with my horse and cart. See my cart, overt there, with her horse. George helps to keep my horse's hooves in shape and he has fixed my cart more than once."

George: "Jason has travelled a lot. He even visited Rome."

Me: "That sounds great. Tell me about it, please?"

Jason: "Well, Rome is a very, very big city. There are thousands and thousands of people. The place is full of criminals and soldiers and harlots. It's a cruel and evil place and they easily lock you up in prison for even the smallest or silliest of crimes. And then you have to face wild animals inside a new big building that the Emperors Vespasian, Titus, and Domitian had erected a few years ago. The call it the Colosseum."

"What happens there?"

"Horrible things. Evil things. Ugly things. And the despicable Romans love it. No civilized Greek can ever approve of what is happening there. There are all sorts of shows. Armed men, called gladiators, fight and kill each other with swords and axes and spears and other weapons. These gladiators also have to fight wild animals, such as lions, bears, and leopards. Condemned criminals are being devoured by wild animals. And then they have actors who commit all sorts of sexual acts – right in sight of thousands of people! It's despicable. It made me sick!"

Roman mosaic of a gladiator spearing a leopard (Rev 6. 8). The life of an individual did not count for much in those days, even though Rome had an exemplary legal system, but that system worked only for Roman citizens. Criminals, prisoners of war, and rebels were dealt with harshly, usually death by crucifixion as the history during 73–71 BC of Spartacus and his band of rebellious fellow-slaves demonstrates.[73] Thousands upon thousands of Jewish captives were killed by the sword or were crucified after Jerusalem had been taken by the Roman army in August AD 70. In total, more than a million people perished during the war, while ninety thousand youths were sold as slaves.[74]

Me: "That's how I have experienced the Romans. They're civilized barbarians. They're cruel, bloodthirsty, and always on the look-out to see whether there are any other countries that they can conquer and loot and rob. They're a mad, insane, completely crazy lot.

"And they worship a whole bunch of imaginary gods. If these gods were real people, they would have been mindless madmen, feebleminded fools, and immoral idiots. Even their chief

---

[73] Enc Brit, "Spartacus."

[74] Eusebius, *Hist Eccl*, Liber II/XXVI/1-2 & Liber III/V & VII/3).

god, Jupiter, who is the equivalent of Zeus, has cheated on his wife numerous times and sired a whole army of illegitimate children. That's according to the stories they tell their children. Too horrible for words. Fortunately, my people, the children of Israel, are worshipping the only real God, the Lord who created the whole world within six days. I will tell you more about Him, if you like."

Monday, 14 March AD 96

After a bad night, during which I had nightmares in which I fought with wild animals and had to defend myself against a laughing giant of a man with only my bare hands, I leave my bed and go outside to await dawn.

My rest was also interrupted by a violent thunder storm during the night and I can still hear in my memory how the flashes and fires from heaven crashed down onto the earth and illuminated the inside of the cave for an instant. That reminded me of God's promise to punish the godless pagans with fire. The thunder flashes also brought back my recollections of the Roman Army on its way to besiege Jerusalem that I saw thirty years ago. It is almost as if that rolling thunder through the hills sounds like a troop of Roman cavalrymen on the gallop.

Dating from AD 70, this inscribed Roman commemorative stone depicts a horseman wielding a spear and with a sword strapped to his side. John, no doubt, must have seen such horsemen in action (Rev 6: 4).

The stars are bright and shiny and I look again at the spot where the throne of God is, where the Lamb is also sitting. I see again the seven stars of Elijah's Chariot and I remember that I have been told that they also represent seven seals on a scroll. That scroll, I remember, contains God's plans for this evil, immoral, and wicked world – of which I was forcefully reminded yesterday by Jason.

I still feel sleepy and it is as if I am dreaming while I see that the Lamb breaks open the first seal. I am curious to discover what will happen next.

One of the four living beings, the Ploughman, draws my attention to the southern horizon.

Sagittarius (the Archer) and Corona Australis (the Southern Crown).

There I see the Archer[75], the sign of the tribe of Joseph or Manasseh. It consists of a horseman, a soldier, carrying a bow and arrow. There is crown in front of him.

The realization dawns upon me that I am really seeing Christ, the King of kings, and his message of salvation. With his crown or victor's wreath, he is a conqueror and nothing an nobody in this damnable and depraved and disastrous world will stop the progress of his message. This thought makes me feel good.

Since the Archer shows me something of Christ, I decide that

---

[75] Sagittarius is traditionally depicted as a centaur, a being with the upper body of a man and the rump and legs of a horse. John, with his convictions rooted in the Old Testament, would not have seen in Sagittarius this Greek mythological figure but a real horseman or knight on his steed. Hachlili reports that the Jewish depictions of Sagittarius was always that of a man holding a bow and arrow. They "felt that the centaur was a pagan hybrid figure and consequently would not want to use it..." (Hachlili, "The Zodiac in Ancient Jewish Synagogal Art", 224).

he must be sitting on a white horse – a sign of his purity and sinlessness.

I am curious to know what will happen next as the Lamb breaks open the second seal.

Another living being, the Bull, calls me to watch a second horse. I notice the Horse of Nimrod,[76] the great Warrior, on the eastern horizon. One of the fishes of the constellation of the Fishes, directly on the back of the Horse of Nimrod, looks like the outlines of a sword.

The second horse seems to be red, due to the first glimmer of dawn in the east. Red is the color of blood. Its rider holds a sword and it is his task to take away the peace from earth and wage war and spill blood.

This horseman depicts for me the military might and cruelty of the Roman Empire that holds many nations and peoples under its rule by means of its army that is stationed in all parts of the empire and that must defend its borders against attacks from outside and crush insurrections from inside.

The Roman regime is a bloodthirsty regime that is constantly at war somewhere and it thrives on bloodshed – as I was reminded of by Jason yesterday. The most important victim of the godless, pagan, and barbaric empire was surely Jesus of Nazareth who was crucified in Jerusalem by Roman soldiers after having been sentenced to death by a Roman governor.

Many Christians also died a martyr's death during the reigns of Nero and Domitian as emperors. There was wholesale slaughter especially at the end of the Jewish revolt by the Roman army in Jerusalem and Judea.

Dawn arrives and the stars disappear. Andrew comes to fetch his sheep.

---

[76] The Jewish name for Pegasus, the Winged Horse (Allen, *Star Names*, 323).

The sky over Patmos during the early morning hours in March AD 96. Ursa Minor (the Little Bear) with its seven stars (the seven seals) are to be found next to the celestial north pole. Sagittarius (the Archer – the white horse) and Corona Australis (the Southern Crown) are in the south. Pegasus (the winged horse – the red horse), and Equuleus (the Foal – the pale horse), are visible in the east. The red planet Mars (Hades), is to be seen in the south-east inside Capricornus (the Goat). The following living beings are present: Boötes (the Ploughman) and Aquila (the Eagle), while Leo (the Lion), is disappearing behind the horizon in the west.

Prochorus asks: "Anything that I must write for you today?"

"Not yet. Perhaps tomorrow."

I expect to see some more horsemen tonight. There ought to be four of them and I recall the following words from the prophet Zechariah:

> "I saw in the night, and, behold, a man riding on a red horse, and he stood among the myrtle-trees that were in the bottom; and behind him there were horses, red, sorrel, and white."

Something similar is also described elsewhere by Zechariah:

> "Again I lifted up my eyes, and saw, and, behold, there came four chariots out from between two mountains; and the mountains were mountains of brass. In the first chariot were red horses; and in the second chariot black horses; and in the third chariot white horses; and in the fourth chariot grizzled strong horses."[77]

This gives me the confidence that two more horses are due to appear tonight or the night thereafter.

---

[77] Zech 1: 8 and 6: 1–3.

Tuesday and Wednesday, 15–16 March AD 96

When darkness descended, I again sat on my usual rock outside the cave and watched the heavens, expecting to hear from one of the other living beings. But nothing happens. After about an hour, I return to the cave and lie down on my bed after chasing away a lamb lying on my bed.

It must be past midnight when I am woken by some of the restless sheep trampling on my legs and feet. They must have climbed over the barrier of rocks with which we fenced off our beds. I almost have the urge to swear at them in Aramaic or Hebrew or Latin or Greek, but I keep myself in check. If I had known some Phrygian or Persian or Parthian, I would probably have used those languages, although it is doubtful whether the dumb sheep would have understood any of it.

In addition, I don't want to disturb Prochorus' sleep by swearing in Phrygian or Persian or Parthian and insulting the sheep belonging to my friend and benefactor, Andrew.

There is nothing else for me to do, but to get into my robe and to go outside and to watch the heavens again. When I look to the north, where God's throne with the Lamb is situated, I observe the Lamb breaking the third seal on the scroll.

I am not fully awake yet after I have left the cave and it's almost as if in a dream, the Lion, one of the living creatures, catches my eye where he lies in the south-western sky. He tells me to watch the far southern portion of the sky.

On the southern horizon I notice the upper body of the horseman. The Greeks call him the Centaur, a being that must be an abomination in the eyes of God because it is supposed to consist of the upper body of a man with the body and four legs of a horse. At our school in the desert, where I could see this celestial being better,

91

we simply called him the horseman – an ordinary human being seated on the back of a horse.

This horseman holds onto a pair of scales, the constellation of Libra, the Scales, directly to his east.

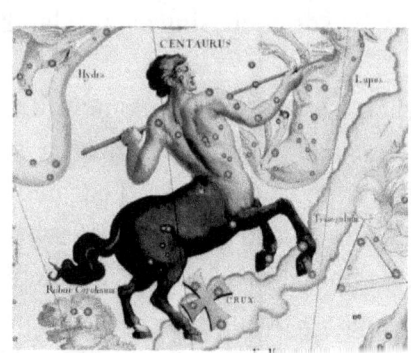

Centaurus, the Centaur (Rev 6: 5), together with the Southern Cross

It strikes me that I can see less of the horseman here on this Greek island than I could see in the Judean desert where the whole constellation rose above the horizon. There are Greek philosophers who think that the earth must be a round globe and that would explain this strange observation, but I can't accept that idea because our Scriptures don't teach anything of the sort.

Because this horse is hidden behind the horizon and only the horseman's upper body is visible, I take it for granted that it must be a black horse – as black as the dark waters of the Aegean Sea to the south, behind which the horse is hidden.

And then I hear a voice warning all mankind to be prepared for a famine. That isn't a strange idea because I and Prochorus, who are poor exiles, often don't have enough to eat. That also reminds me of the famine that raged in Jerusalem during the war and that many poor Christians in Ephesus also often go hungry.

The voice calls out: "A ration of wheat for a denarius, and three rations of barley for a denarius! Don't damage the oil and the wine!" That must be a reference to the habit of Roman armies to destroy the crops, orchards, and vineyards of vanquished people as a form of punishment or vengeance. I witnessed that when I saw the Roman legions marching in the direction of Jerusalem.

During breakfast, my friend enquires: "Must I fetch my pen, ink and a sheet of papyrus?"

"I'm not quite ready for that right now. Perhaps tomorrow."

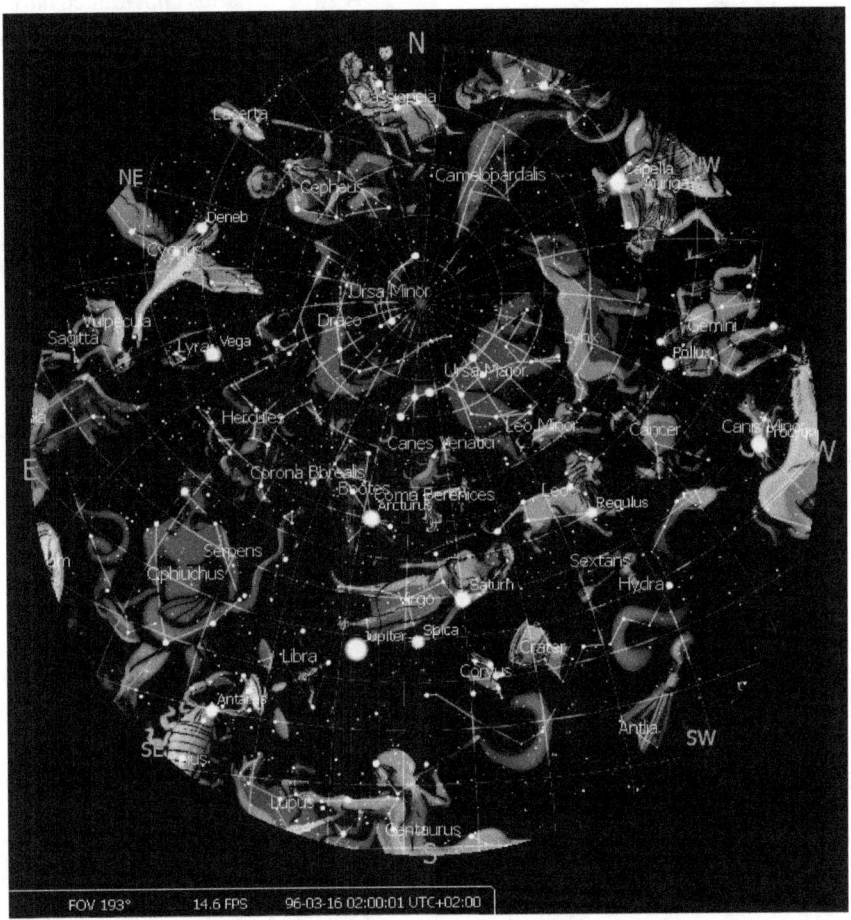

FOV 193°   14.6 FPS   96-03-16 02:00:01 UTC+02:00

The night sky over Patmos during the early morning hours of 16 March AD 96. Centaurus with his spear and Libra, the Scales, lie on the southern horizon. Leo (the Lion), one of the four living beings, is also visible in the middle of the sky.

I feel again in my pocket to find the coin I held there – a denarius – and I look at the image of Emperor Domitian who has crowned himself with a victor's wreath.

A silver denarius coin minted during the reign of Emperor Domitian. At the opening of the third seal, one of these coins – approximately one day's wage of a laborer – was said to be needed to buy a single ration of wheat.[78]

---

[78] Franz. "The King and I".

Thursday, 17 March AD 96

The sheep in the cave start moving around while it is still dark because they expect Andrew at any moment to take them out. That wakes us up.

I get seated on my rock in anticipation of Andrew's arrival and I look forward to another message from God regarding the fourth horse.

I am not disappointed. The Lamb on the throne in the north opens the fourth seal and the Eagle, one of the four living creatures, requests me to watch a faint constellation – the Foal. Only the head of this horse is visible and its body is hidden behind the Horse of Nimrod, next to it.

It is clear that this must be a dark or pale horse. That color reminds me of the color of a decomposing corpse and, therefore, this horse carries the message that this world is characterized by death, distress, and destruction, caused especially by the Roman Empire of which the nearby Eagle is a sign. The rider on this horse must have a name and I decide to call him Death.

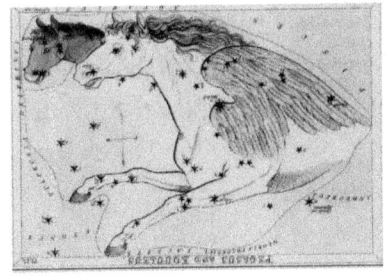

Pegasus, the winged horse (the red horse), and Equuleus, the Foal (the pale horse) from an old celestial atlas.

In my experience, people die mainly from four causes: from sword wounds, from famine, from old age, and attacks by the wild animals of the earth. Four is the symbolic number of the earth with its four wind directions and four elements. These causes of death are especially characteristic of Roman rule: people were killed by the sword during war or gladiatorial games, but also when they were executed as criminals. Famine was often the result of heavy taxation or war. Wild animals were encountered in a circus where gladiators and martyrs had to fight them – as Jason reminded me.

Many Christians in Asia, who refused to participate in the veneration and adoration of the emperor as a living god, had to endure hardship. They were excluded from the trade guilds of their cities and they had to endure many injustices, and that led to poverty in many cases.

It is noticeable that the red planet Mars lies just below the Foal, inside the constellation of the Goat. Mars, or to use his Greek name of Ares, is, of course, the god or war. Roman soldiers venerate him to convince him to aid them during a battle. Mars, on the southern horizon, therefore, reminds me of Hades, the realm of the dead under the surface of the earth.

My memory goes back to the time in August, twenty-six years ago, when the Romans finally broke down the defenses in Jerusalem and torched the city, together with the temple. That night, we could still see the smoke and flames where we were watching in horror from our school in the desert. During the early morning of that fateful day, the red planet Mars, or *Ares*, was inside the constellation of the Crab and ready to pounce upon the Lion, the sign of the tribe of Judah. Three other planets, named after Roman gods, were also besieging the Lion, namely Mercury, Jupiter, and Venus.

Our Teacher at that time declared with tears in his eyes: "My children, that is God telling us something. It is his message that the Roman god of war will crush the Lion of Judah, with the help of those other pagan Gods. It is sad, but it is inevitable."

We all agreed when we saw the flames and the smoke.

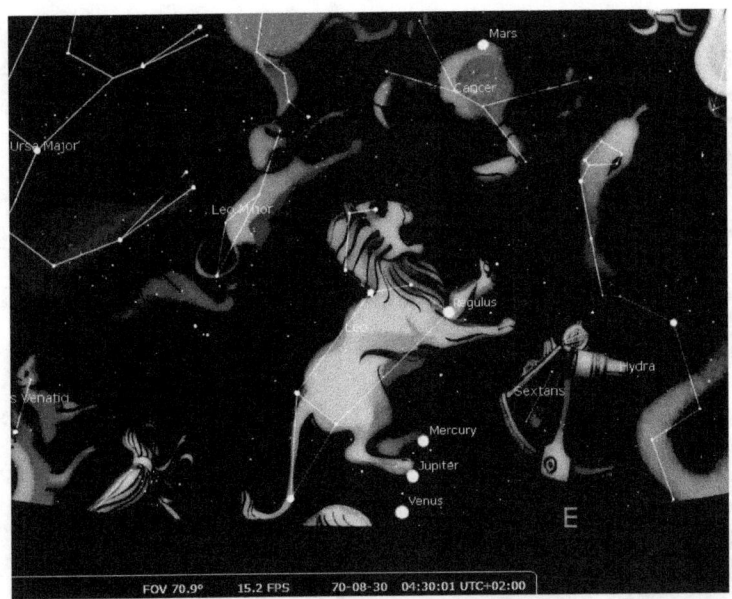

The heavens above Jerusalem, looking east, on 31 August AD 70, when the city fell to the Roman legions. The Lion of Judah is being threatened by the following Roman gods: Mars (inside Cancer), as well as Mercury, Jupiter, and Venus (inside Leo and Virgo). The victors and the vanquished must have seen this configuration as a sign that Jerusalem was doomed on that day.

When I think back of these four horsemen that I could see in the heavens, I decide that they depict four different aspects of the world in which I and my fellow Christians are living. Each horse became visible after one of the seals had been broken. These successive seals on the scroll are the unfolding of God's vision and plans for the world and how this world with its godlessness and blasphemy and pagan superstitions had to be dealt with.

Later, during the day, I and Prochorus wander through a few villages and hamlets of Patmos, trying to buy food and spread the good news about Jesus of Nazareth. Some people have pity on us and invite us in for a few pieces of bread with sheep's milk. Most people listen politely when we explain the gospel, but just smile and tell us that they are quite satisfied with their Greek gods.

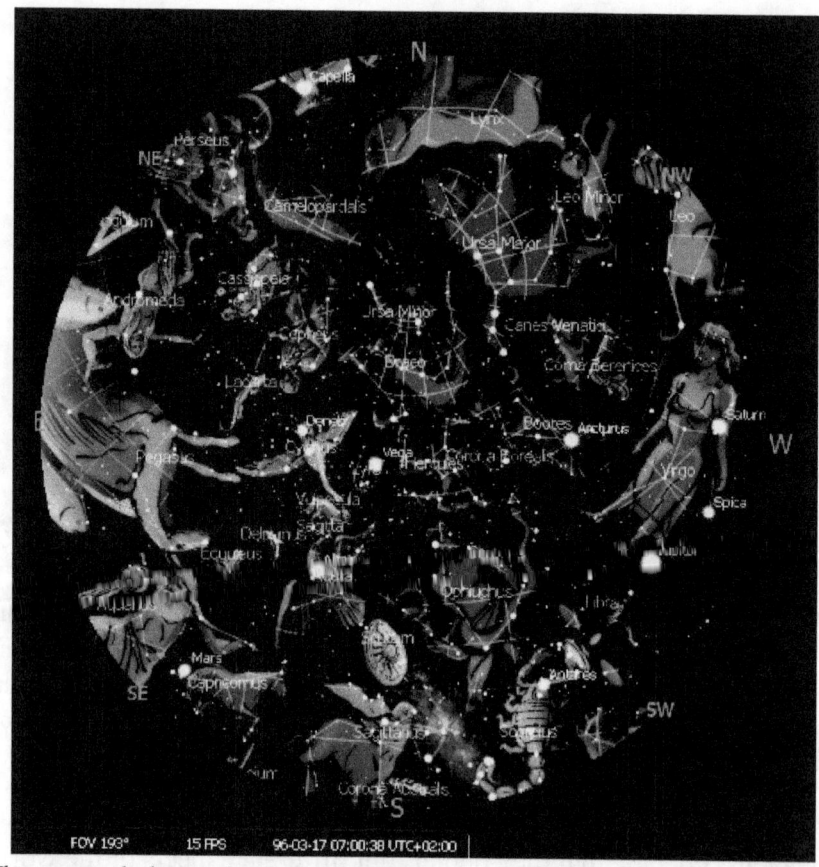

The stars and planets shortly before daybreak on 17 March AD 96, as seen from Patmos. Equuleus, the Foal (the pale horse), is a faint constellation of which only the head is visible, right in front of Pegasus (the red horse). The nearest living creature is Aquila, the Roman Eagle. The planet Mars, the personification of war, is to be found inside the nearby constellation of Capricornus, the Goat.

After supper, I returned to my habitual rock outside the cave to watch the stars again. Nothing happened because I fell asleep on top of that rock and I only wake up a few hours later when it becomes very cold. I return to the cave where our fire is burning very low with only a few embers still glowing. They look like stars and they help me to find my bed in the dark.

Friday, 18 March AD 96

It was still dark when I left my bed this morning because I wanted to see whether the Lamb would open the fifth of the seven seals on that scroll. I am not disappointed.

I glance at the most northern point in the sky again, the point around which everything in the heavens revolves and where God has his invisible throne. I conclude that the constellation of the Quiver, before the throne with its seven stars in an arc, must also be seen as an altar on which offerings and sacrifices for God are being brought.[79]

My eyes are then drawn to the eastern horizon. Just above this, the bright band of the Milky Way stretches across the whole sky. I get the insight that this bright streak of light, a luminous cloud, must represent the countless numbers of victims of the Roman Empire – especially the thousands of Jews who died during the war when Jerusalem was besieged and razed to the ground, as well as all the faithful followers of Jesus Christ, the Lamb, who suffered and were killed on account of their faith.

I heard from survivors of the war that thousands upon thousands of Jewish captives were killed by the sword or were crucified after Jerusalem had been taken by the Roman legions. In total, more than a million people must have perished, while something like ninety thousand youths were sold as slaves

It is almost as if I can hear their cries and sobs while I listen to the waves of the Aegean Sea crashing against the rocky shores and beaches of this island. The wind makes a moaning sound as it blows over the entrance of the cave. They cry to God to avenge them

---

[79] It is clearly stated in Rev 8: 3 that the golden altar is before God's throne. The only constellation that qualifies for that is Draco (or the Quiver in Jewish star lore). The seven lamps were, of course, positioned upon this altar.

and punish those responsible for their painful and cruel deaths.

The suffering of these martyrs is the result of the forces represented by the riders on the red, black, and pale horses who preceded this scene. But there was also the white horse, carrying the Archer, who is destined to overcome all sordid satanic forces.

I am sure that God gives these martyrs in white robes the promise that they will be avenged when their numbers are complete. This thought makes me really sad because it means that the campaigns of the godless pagans against God's children will not end soon – only on Judgment Day, sometime in the unknown future.

Part of a mosaic depicting a procession of 26 saints or martyrs, clothed in white and carrying crowns, in the basilica of San Apollinare Nuovo, Ravenna, Italy (6th century).

The white robes of the martyrs demonstrated that all their sins were wiped away through the blood of the Lamb that flowed when he was crucified by the Romans.

Later, the light of the sun breaks through and clears the heaven of all its stars. Andrew appears to take his sheep away and he brings us some breakfast. I give him the assurance that he will receive a white robe when his soul leaves this earth after his death at some time. He receives my blessing for his kindness.

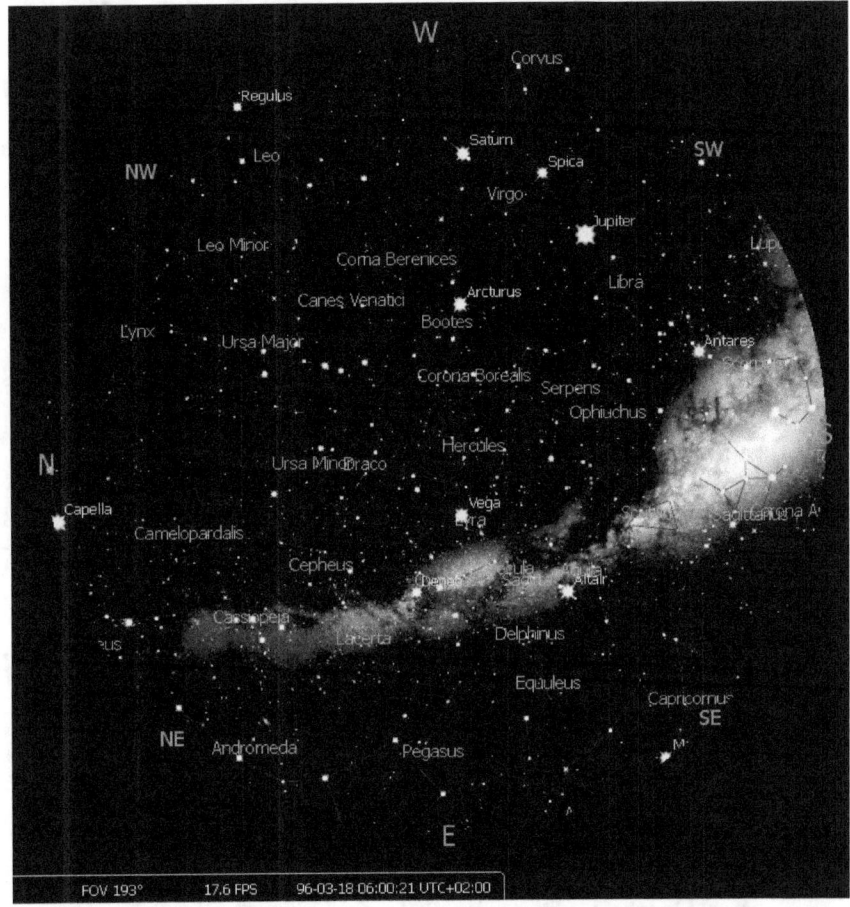

The skies above Patmos during the early morning hours of 18 March AD 96, looking east. The altar that John saw is to be found in the constellation of Draco (called the Quiver by the Jews), which also doubled as seven lamps. The souls of the martyrs clothed in white under the altar are to be found in the clouds of the Milky Way.

After breakfast, I tell Prochorus: "My good friend, I'm ready to dictate to you. Go and fetch your writing instruments."

Revelation 6: 1–11

The first five seals and the four horsemen

1. I saw that the Lamb opened one of the seven seals, and I heard one of the four living creatures saying, as with a voice of thunder, "Come and see!"

2. I saw, and behold, a white horse, and he who sat on it had a bow. A crown was given to him, and he came forth conquering, and to conquer.

3. When he opened the second seal, I heard the second living creature saying, "Come!"

4. Another came forth, a red horse. To him who sat on it was given to take peace from the earth, and that they should kill one another. There was given to him a great sword.

5. When he opened the third seal, I heard the third living creature saying, "Come and see!" I saw, and behold, a black horse. He who sat on it had a balance in his hand.

6. I heard a voice in the midst of the four living creatures saying, "A choenix of wheat for a denarius, and three choenix of barley for a denarius! Don`t damage the oil and the wine!"

7. When he opened the fourth seal, I heard the voice of the fourth living creature saying, "Come and see!"

8. I saw, and behold, a pale horse. He who sat on him, his name was Death. Hades followed with him. Authority over one fourth of the earth, to kill with the sword, with famine, with death, and by the wild animals of the earth was given to them.

9. When he opened the fifth seal, I saw underneath the altar the souls of those who had been killed for the word of God, and for the testimony which they held.

10. They cried with a loud voice, saying, "How long, Master, the holy and true, do you not judge and avenge our blood on those who dwell on the earth?"

11. There was given to each one of them a white robe. It was said to them that they should rest yet for a little time, until their fellow servants and their brothers, who would also be killed even as they were, had been fulfilled.

During the afternoon, I and Prochorus wander through the hills, looking for edible plants, bulbs, and roots, including leaves of the happy weed for our broth tonight.

Suddenly, the earth starts trembling and shaking and rocking beneath us. This is not the first time that I encounter an earthquake, but this one is more violent than anything that I have ever felt. Shortly afterwards, we hear a loud bang, like somebody striking a big drum, but only much louder.

My first thought is: "That must be the sixth seal that the Lamb has opened. Because the sun is shining, I couldn't look in the direction of God's throne."

A few hundred heartbeats later, stones and rocks start raining from the sky.

Prochorus: "Run! We must hide in the cave!"

Me: "Yes! Before one of us gets killed by a falling rock."

We reach the safety of our cave a little later. People from the surrounding areas flock to our cave and they don't even ask permission to hide here. Some of them are from the fishing villages of Groikos and Sapsila on the coast, just below our hill to the east.

One of the villagers cries out: "An evil demon is devouring the sun! Look at it! It's disappearing!"

I take a good look. This differs from the occasion in Athens some years ago when the sun also disappeared. This time, the setting sun is still faintly visible, but a thick cloud of smoke is obscuring it. A small crescent moon in the middle of the sky also gets obscured. The cloud gives it a red color.

Prochorus asks me: "Is this Judgment Day? Is this the end of the world?"

Me: "No. It can't be. God has given me the task of sending his message to the Christian communities in Asia. He wouldn't have given me that task if He had intended to annihilate this world today. No, this can only be a serious warning from God to show all of us that He has the power to eradicate all evil from this world."

I grasp the opportunity to preach to the little crowd that has taken shelter in our cave. All of them listen to me with shock in their eyes and their bodies trembling from fear. I believe that I have moved the hearts of a few of them to accept that they must mend their ways, turn to the living God, and believe in Jesus Christ.

Andrew arrives with his sheep only after sunset. He informs me that he has lost three sheep that have been struck by falling rocks. They will have to be slaughtered for their meat and hides. He also requests me to come and watch outside.

We look at a wonderful spectacle in the south. A huge fire is raging behind the horizon – the biggest fire that any one of us has ever seen. Sparks fly into the air, smoke blows out of the fire, and it seems as if some stars are falling from the sky.

One of the fishermen asks me with a trembling voice: "Old man, is that something your God has sent? Why is He so angry by spitting fire?"

Me: "Yes, and no, dear friend. What you see there can only be an opening to Hades below the earth's surface. Somehow, it blew open and we are observing the fires of hell. The flames of hell are spilling over, somehow. Look, it lies to our south – directly in the opposite direction of God's throne, which lies in the far north. But that is certainly a warning from God."

Prochorus adds: "John, you have taught us in Ephesus about what Jesus had to say in this regard. Can you remember his words?"

A volcanic eruption at night: Stromboli, the small volcanic island north of Sicily. This volcano has been erupting periodically for hundreds of years to produce a lightshow that gives rise to its nickname, the "Lighthouse of the Mediterranean". John of Patmos must have witnessed something similar from afar (Rev 6: 12–17; 8: 8).

I quote the words of Jesus, as recorded in the memoirs we have of him: "Yes. On Judgment Day, the Judge will tell the godless people: 'Depart from me, you cursed, into the eternal fire which is prepared for the devil and his angels.'[80] He also warned us against 'the Gehenna of fire, where their worm doesn't die, and the fire is not quenched.'[81]"

---

[80] Matt 18: 8.

[81] Mark 9: 48.

Prochorus again: "You also taught us that the prophet Isaiah also said something similar, isn't that so?"

Me: "Yes, yes, you're correct. He wrote:

'The sinners in Zion are afraid; trembling has seized the godless ones: Who among us can dwell with the devouring fire? Who among us can dwell with everlasting burning?'[82]

Some of the people who fled to our cave stayed during the night. That reminded me of the prophet Isaiah who wrote:

"Men shall go into the caves of the rocks, and into the holes of the earth, from before the terror of the Lord, and from the glory of his majesty, when he arises to shake mightily the earth."[83]

---

[82] Is 33: 14.
[83] Is 2: 19

106

Saturday, 19 March AD 96

Smoke is still pouring from the opening to Hades in the south. During the night, we felt a few more earth tremors. Although the sun's light struggles to penetrate the smoke, there is enough light for Prochorus to write down my words:

Revelation 6: 12–17
The sixth seal

12.	I saw when he opened the sixth seal, and there was a great earthquake. The sun became black as sackcloth made of hair, and the whole moon became as blood.
13.	The stars of the sky fell to the earth, as a fig tree drops its unripe figs when it is shaken by a great wind.
14.	The sky was removed as a scroll when it is rolled up. Every mountain and island were moved out of their places.
15.	The kings of the earth, the princes, the commanding officers, the rich, the strong, and every slave and freeman, hid themselves in the caves and in the rocks of the mountains.
16.	They told the mountains and the rocks, "Fall on us, and hide us from the face of him who sits on the throne, and from the wrath of the Lamb,
17.	for the great day of his wrath has come; and who is able to stand?"

SEISMIC AND VOLCANIC ACTIVITY IN THE AEGEAN SEA

We may take John on his word that a violent earthquake occurred and that the mountains and islands were moved and shaken. The Aegean Sea and western coastal region of Asia Minor – nowadays

Turkey – is known for seismic activities, namely earthquakes and volcanic outbursts.

Decker and Decker explain: "There is a clear correspond-dence between the geographic distribution of volcanoes and major earthquakes..."[84]

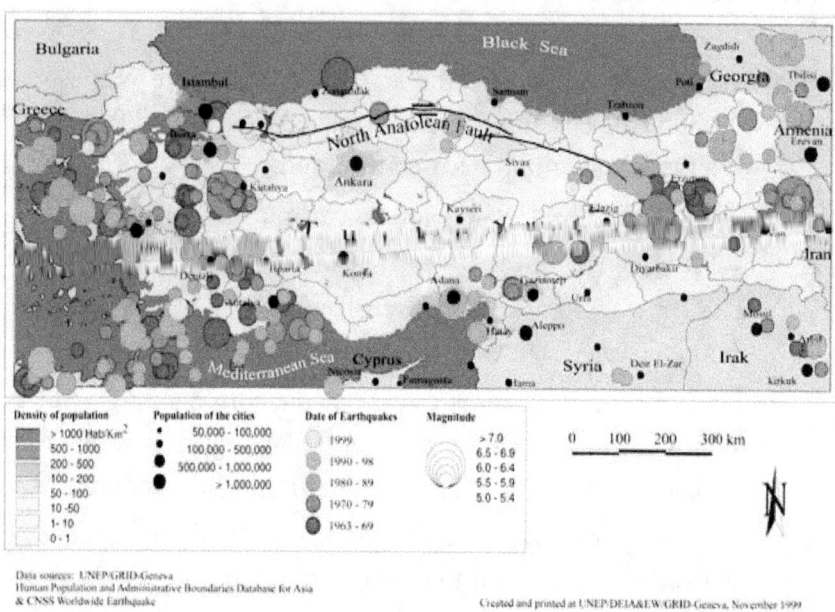

The distribution of the epicenters of earthquakes in Turkey and the Aegean Sea during the last decades of the 20th century.

John of Patmos certainly did experience a violent earthquake that shook the island of Patmos and that he did witness a volcanic event. The steam, dust clouds, ash, toxic gasses, and the smoke of wildfires generated by the volcano must have obscured the sun and the moon, as well as a large part of the sky. The glowing blobs of lava and rocks

---

[84] Decker and Decker, "Volcno".

flying skywards and falling back must have looked like stars crashing onto the earth. There can be no doubt that people witnessing the event must have been struck by panic and tried to hide from the falling debris.

The book of Revelation records at least five earthquakes:

- During the opening of the sixth seal, a "great earthquake" occurred (Rev 6:12);
- During the breaking of the seventh seal (Rev 8:5);
- After the resurrection of the two witnesses, a "great earthquake" happened when 7 000 men were killed (Rev 11:13);
- During the blowing of the seventh trumpet (Rev 11:19); and
- The final one, during the seventh bowl of judgment, described as "a great earthquake, such a mighty and great earthquake as had not occurred since men were on the earth" (Rev 16:18).[85]

Acts 16: 26 reports an earthquake in Philippi in Macedonia where Paul and Silas were being held in prison.

A website dealing with 'Volcanoes in Greece' reports: "Greece has a large volcanic arch, which was created millions of years ago by the sinking of the African lithosphere (Oceania) under the Eurasiatic plate (mainland). This volcanic arch of Greece had an especially intense volcanic activity in the past and created the volcanic landscapes that we come across in many regions and islands around Greece. Most of the volcanoes in Greece and the Greek islands are extinct, however there are some still active. The most important active volcanoes in Greece are situated in Santorini island, Nisyros island, Methana and Milos Island, receiving thousands of visitors every year."[86]

---

[85] Franz, "The King and I".
[86] Kinvig, "Volcanic Threat".

The best candidate for the volcano described by John is certainly on the island of *Nisyros* (Greek: Νίσυρος), about 90 kilometers south-east from Patmos.

An aerial photo of the Greek island of Nisyros with its volcanic crater

The Department of Geology of the Oregon State University reported on Nisyros: "It is suspected that the volcano erupted in 1422. In 1871, an eruption was accompanied by earthquakes, detonations, and red and yellow flames. Ash and lapilli [small stones] were erupted and covered the floor of Ramos, destroying the fruit gardens there. During a three-day-long eruption in 1873, a 20–25 foot (6–7 m) diameter crater formed and ash and blackish mud was ejected. The bottom of Lakki and Ramos was transformed into a lake by hotsaline water that overflowed the crater. The most recent eruption was in 1888. This strong eruption threw out a cylindrical pipe of volcanic material at least 80 feet (25 m) in diameter. Mud, lapilli, and steam were also ejected."[87]

---

[87] Volcano World, "Nisyros".

The volcanic activity on Nisyros was described as follows: "None of the subsequent eruptions of the volcano recorded in historical sources produce molten rock. All of them are hydrothermal explosions due to the existence of superheated steam in the subsoil of the island. Seawater and rainwater descend on the rocks of the island, gather in deep horizons and get heated by magma. The water there is converted to superheated steam and exerts tremendous pressure. When this pressure overcomes the weight and consistency of the above rocks, the steam hurls them through the air causing a hydrothermal explosion. Such were the explosions that were recorded in Nisyros in historical times."[88]

The volcano on Nisyros is a popular tourist destination where low-grade volcanic activity is still going on. A tourist guide states that "occasional bubbles are seen and the sulphureous smell is often overpowering." There are also frequent "subterranean rumbling noises."[89]

No record could be found of an eruption of Nisyros during the first century AD, but such an event cannot be ruled out either, since this volcano has erupted at various times and geological evidence of at least 13 eruptions in the past have been found. Kinvig *et al.* report: "There is no record of any fatalities on the island of Nisyros.... It is important to consider, however that there may have been fatalities that were undocumented." During 2010 there were concerns that the volcano could erupt at any time again.[90]

The fireworks on Nisyros at night would have been clearly visible from Patmos – especially if the observer stood on one of the low hills on Patmos. The glowing lava, dust, ash, gas, steam, stones,

[88] Anaema, "Nisyros".
[89] Sattin & Franquet, *Exploring Greek Islands,* 160.
[90] Kinvig *et al.* "Volcanic Threat", 1101 & 1108.

and other material ejected from the volcano could have showered on places as far as 300 km away.[91] It would have been impossible for John not to have seen the volcano because everybody on Patmos would have been watching and discussing the spectacle.

If the tradition is correct that John lived in a cave on Patmos, then it is very probable that some inhabitants of Patmos fled to the safety of his cave.

Volcanic outbursts often take weeks and even months before they come to an end.[92] It is clear from John's descriptions that volcanic activity continued several weeks and Patmos suffered the effects of this natural disaster for a long time.

It must be remembered that people in the ancient world did not have the faintest idea what caused earthquakes or volcanoes to erupt. Just as they attributed diseases to supernatural causes, such as the influence of evil spirits or magic, they regarded earthquakes and volcanoes as supernatural events, caused by the gods. It is no wonder that John incorporated a seismic event into his visions and regarded the volcano as the entrance to the subterranean netherworld.

The most famous volcanic event from antiquity is certainly the outburst of Vesuvius in October AD 79 when the towns of Pompeii and Herculaneum in Italy were buried under volcanic ash and mud. The most recent eruption occurred in March 1944.[93]

---

[91] Kinvig *et al.* "Volcanic Threat". 1108.

[92] Decker & Decker, "Volcano".

[93] Enc. Brit., "Vesuvius".

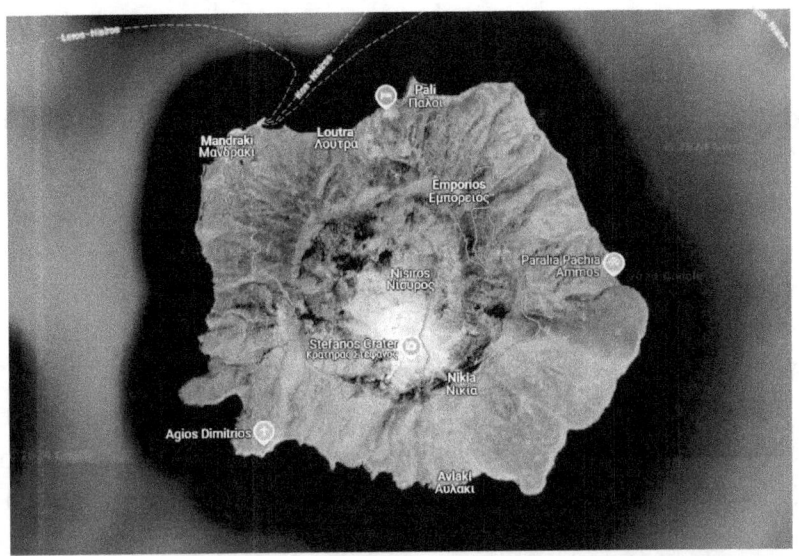

A recent satellite photo of Nisyros, showing the volcanic crater.

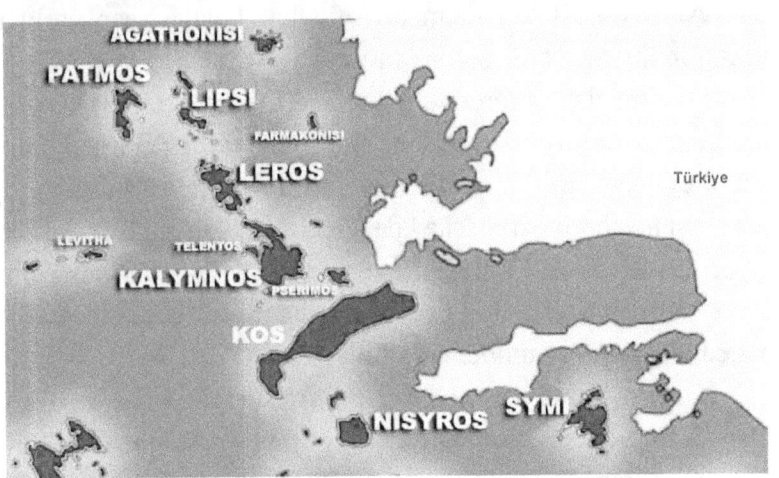

Map of a part of the Dodecanese Sea, showing the relative positions of Patmos
and Nisyros – about 90 km apart from each other (Rev 6: 12–17; 8).

Sunday, 27 March AD 96

More than a week has passed since we witnessed the fire and fury and flames of Hades on the southern horizon. By this time, the worst shock has disappeared and life is slowly returning to normal.

My little congregation assembles this morning early in the cave, just after Andrew has taken his sheep outside. Three new families join our group and after they have confessed their sins and professed their faith in Jesus Christ, they are baptized.

I tell them: "Although the water on your heads will dry very soon, God will always be able to see it. There will be a mark on your foreheads that acts as a seal. That is the mark God has given you to proclaim that you are from now on his property. Nobody and nothing can ever steal you out of the hands of the almighty God."

After this, I tell them all of what I have seen early this morning in the heavens, before dawn.

"On the day before we witnessed the fires of hell from afar, I had the opportunity of observing the souls of the departed martyrs where they were waiting under the altar next to God's throne, right in the most northern part of the heavens. The wide band of the Milky Way or the River of Fire was revealed to me as consisting of the souls of these martyrs. God gave them the promise that they will be avenged when their numbers are full.

"A few hours later, God demonstrated clearly how He will punish all the godless and evil powers of this world when he allowed us to get a glimpse of Hades and demonstrated how this world will be destroyed by fire on Judgment Day.

"We could not see much of the sky due to all the smoke pouring from hell. But that smoke has cleared and the winds have died down so that I could get another glimpse of God's plans for this world last night.

114

"The Milky way was again very bright. I recognized four angels holding back the winds of heaven because there was no wind early this morning. Those four angels were to be found on four corners of the sky. They are the constellation of the Young Woman[94] in the south-east, the Giant[95] in the south-west, the Persian Warrior[96] in the north-west and the Hero or Samson[97] in the north-east.

The Christ monogram surrounded by the four angels at the four corners of the earth (Rev 7: 1), together with the four living creatures – the human being on top, the bull on the right, the lion at the bottom and the eagle on the left (12th century mosaic on the ceiling of the chapel in the Archbishop's Palace, Ravenna, Italy)

"I regard these four angels who keep the storm winds from blowing as a sign of God's grace. He is giving us still some time to repent

---

[94] Virgo (Allen, *Star Names,* 464).
[95] Orion (Allen, *Star Names,* 309).
[96] Perseus (Allen, *Star Names,* 330).
[97] Hercules (Allen, *Star Names,* 242).

from our evil ways before he unleashes the storms on Judgment Day.

"Our Scriptures also mention these four angels at the four corners of the world and who held the four winds of the earth back. The prophet Zechariah wrote: 'These are the four winds of the sky, which go forth from standing before the Lord of all the earth.'[98] The prophet Daniel also mentions 'the four winds of the sky'.[99]

"I am sure you all saw the full moon rising in the east last night. I got the insight that it must be seen as an angel who called in a loud voice to the other four angels that they must not destroy the earth, the sea, and the trees before the full number of God's people are assembled. This angel in the east also carried the seal of God with which the people of God had to be sealed, just as you have been sealed with water when you were baptized.

"In the past, the Jews or the Israelites were the people of God, but since the days of Jesus, that has changed. God has allowed the Romans to destroy Jerusalem and its temple and the Jews were thoroughly humiliated because they refused to accept Jesus as their Messiah and king. The people of God, the new Israel, are all those who believe in Jesus as Christ, as the Messiah, as the Savior.

"A few days ago, I looked at the bright Milky Way and it was revealed to me that that bright band of stars across the sky is the crowd of martyrs who have died for their faith. The new people of God, who replaced the twelve tribes of Israel, are to be found in the twelve signs of the Zodiac. Last night, the following signs were visible: The Young Woman, the Lion, the Crab, the Twins, the Bull, and the Ram. Some of the others appeared later during the night. These constellations must be regarded as symbols of the new Israel, the new people of God, all the believers, all the people who worship the only true God.

---

[98] Zechariah 6: 5
[99] Daniel 7: 2

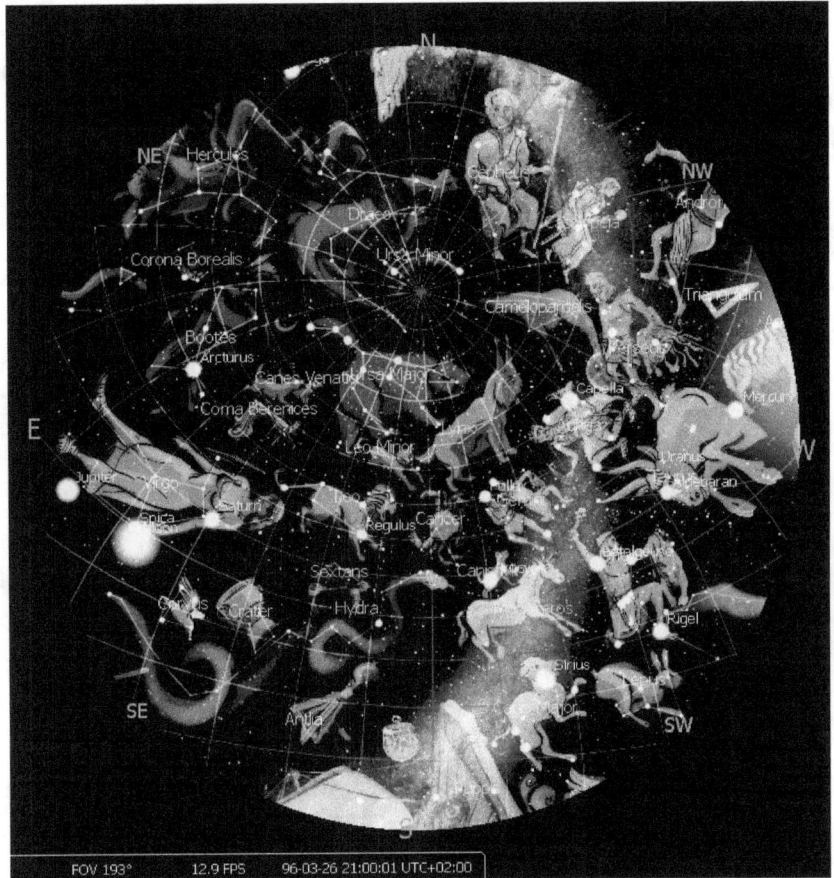

Virgo in the south-east, Orion in the south-west, Perseus in the north-west and Hercules in the north east – the four angels at the four corners of the earth, during the evening of 26 March 96 AD. A bright full moon lies on the eastern horizon, next to Virgo. The following constellations of the Zodiac are visible: Virgo, Leo, Cancer, Gemini, Taurus, and Aries.

"I also concluded that this crowd is infinitely large because untold numbers of people will be added to those who already believe. We can express that multitude with the symbolic number of one hundred and forty-four thousand."

I see the eyes of a few of my listeners blink in disbelief and it is clear that I must clarify my words.

117

I continue: "Let me explain. When I was a student at our school in the desert, we were taught how to interpret numbers. This number of one hundred and forty-four thousand can be broken up into twelve times twelve times one thousand. The number of twelve points to the twelve tribes of Israel – represented by the twelve signs of the Zodiac – but also to the twelve apostles of Jesus who were the founders of his church. The number of thousand is meant to describe a large number, but we can also see it as ten, multiplied by ten, multiplied by ten, or ten multiplied twice with itself. The number of three times ten tells us something about God – God the Father, his Son, Jesus Christ who is also the Lamb that was slaughtered and is still living, as well as the sevenfold or perfect Spirit of God who revealed all the divine messages to me.

"The number of ten reminds us of the ten fingers with which each man, woman, and child do their work. It also points to the fact the God is working. After all, he made the world and He still rules the world from his invisible throne, high up on the most northern point in the sky.

"So, my dear friends, you may all regard yourselves as members of the people of God, the people who are assured of a place in heaven, somewhere in the Zodiac and the Milky Way. You also have received the seal of God. After all, the prophet Ezekiel got this instruction from God:

'Go through the midst of the city, through the midst of Jerusalem, and set a mark on the foreheads of the men that sigh and that cry over all the abominations that are done in the midst of it.'[100]

"Let us worship Him with a few songs that I will teach you."

---

[100] Ezek 9: 4

After all the people have left, I ask Prochorus: "Do you mind, my friend, to take out your writing materials? Please, write as follows:"

Revelation 7: 1–8
The 144 000 people of Israel

1. After this, I saw four angels standing at the four corners of the earth, holding the four winds of the earth, so that no wind would blow on the earth, or on the sea, or on any tree.

2. I saw another angel ascend from the sunrise, having the seal of the living God. He cried with a loud voice to the four angels to whom it was given to harm the earth and the sea,

3. saying, "Don't harm the earth, neither the sea, nor the trees, until we have sealed the bondservants of our God on their foreheads!"

4. I heard the number of those who were sealed, one hundred forty-four thousand, sealed out of every tribe of the children of Israel:

5. Of the tribe of Judah were sealed twelve thousand, of the tribe of Reuben twelve thousand, of the tribe of Gad twelve thousand,

6. of the tribe of Asher twelve thousand, of the tribe of Naphtali twelve thousand, of the tribe of Manasseh twelve thousand, of the tribe of Simeon twelve thousand, of the tribe of Levi twelve thousand, of the tribe of Issachar twelve thousand,

7. of the tribe of Zebulun twelve thousand, of the tribe of Joseph twelve thousand, of the tribe of Benjamin were sealed twelve thousand.

THE TWELVE TRIBES OF ISRAEL AND THE ZODIAC

The people from the twelve tribes of Israel who were sealed are to be found in the Zodiac. John probably connected each sign of the Zodiac with one of the Israelite tribes he listed. Mosaics on the floors of synagogues from the Christian era in Palestine often depicted the Zodiac with Hebrew names and identified the Israelite tribes with the various signs[101] and John could have followed this tradition. The Jews seemed to have used more than one system of connecting the tribes with the zodiacal signs in the past, but the following seems to be the most satisfactory system, while keeping in mind the blessings Jacob gave his twelve sons before his death, as recorded in Gen 49:

- Gad (Aries)
  "Gad, a troop will press on him, but he will press on their heel" – Gen 49: 19
- Ephraim (Taurus)
  "The arms of his hands were made strong, By the hands of the Mighty One of Jacob, (From there is the shepherd, the stone of Israel)" – Gen 49: 24
  "His horns are the horns of the wild-ox: With them he shall push the peoples all of them, [even] the ends of the earth: they are the ten thousands of Ephraim" (Deut 3: 17).
- Simeon (Gemini)
  "Simeon and Levi are brothers; weapons of violence are their swords" – Gen 49: 6
- Levi (Gemini)
  "Simeon and Levi are brothers; weapons of violence are their swords" – Gen 49: 6

---

[101] Hachlili, "The Zodiac", 220.

- Issachar (Taurus)
  "He saw a resting-place, that it was good, the land, that it was pleasant; He bowed his shoulder to bear, and became a servant doing forced labour (Gen 49: 14)."
- Judah (Leo)
  "Judah is a lion's whelp" – Gen 49: 9
- Asher (Cancer)
  "Out of Asher his bread will be fat, he will yield royal dainties" – Gen 49: 20
- Benjamin (Libra)
  "Benjamin is a ravenous wolf. In the morning, he will devour the prey. At evening he will divide the spoil" – Gen 49: 27
- Dan (Scorpius)
  "Dan will be a serpent in the way, an adder in the path" – Gen 49: 17
- Joseph (Sagittarius)
  "The archers have sorely grieved him, shot at him, and persecute him. But his bow abode in strength" – Gen 49: 22–24
- Naphtali (Capricorn)
  "Naphtali is a doe set free, who bears beautiful fawns." – Gen 49: 21
- Reuben (Aquarius)
  "Boiling over as water, you shall not have the pre-eminence" – Gen 49: 4
- Zebulun (Pisces)
  "Zebulun will dwell at the haven of the sea" – Gen 49:13.[102]
- Dinah (Virgo)

---

[102] Allen, *Star Names*: 48, 78, 108, 138, 223, 253, 273, 339, 352, 362, 381 & 464; Clarke, "Jacob's Zodiac".

Whether John had this system in mind, we will never know, but he may well have thought of something along these lines.

There has been much speculation regarding the order in which John named the tribes. Valdez compared John's list of the tribes with all the cases where the patriarchs and tribes were listed in the Old Testament and Apocryphal literature, but found "that John does not follow any logical reasoning when confronted with the internal principles of the other lists, a fact which makes Rev. 7: 4–8 quite unique".[103]

The order in which the tribes are listed does not correlate with the order of the zodiacal signs either.

There does seem, though, as if there is some similarity between John's list and the order of the tribes mentioned in Ezek 48. The main difference is that John included Levi and Joseph as tribes and left out Ephraim, the son of Joseph, and Dan. Dan was left out due to the idolatry of which the men of this tribe were guilty, according to Judges 18.[104] In Gen 49: 17, Dan was also called "a serpent in the way, an adder in the path." In Rev 20: 2 Satan was called "the old serpent" and that may also be the reason why Dan was associated with Satan and therefore deliberately left out from the list in Rev 7.

The pagan sanctuary of Bethel, which was built by king Jeroboam, was situated inside the territory of Ephraim (1 Kin 12: 28–33) and, therefore, Ephraim was also omitted. John held Deut 29: 18–20 in mind when leaving these two tribes out since a curse was placed on every "man, or woman, or family, or tribe, whose heart turns away this day from the Lord our God..."

---

[103] Valdez, "Number 666", 7–13

[104] Jordaan, *Openbaring,* 105.

122

Various groups and sects through the ages claimed that they – and nobody else – were the 144 000 chosen ones who were to be admitted into heaven. The question arises: how are we to choose between these competing groups and sects? Who will decide which one has a better claim? Did John really have a specific sectarian group centuries after his time in mind with his list?

There are also those who restrict these 144 000 to the progeny of Abraham.[105]

It must be pointed out that these groups and sects fail to see that the number of 144 000 sealed saints is a symbolic number. The Bible abounds with promises that all those who believe in Jesus Christ as their Redeemer and have dedicated their lives to God – irrespective of descent, race, or color – may rest assured that they will inherit eternal life in God's heaven.

In other words: the twelve tribes mentioned in Rev 7: 5–8 are composed of the spiritual or symbolic Israel, all the people who have accepted Jesus Christ as their Messiah – not only the members of a certain group or sect or the biological descendants of Abraham.

---

[105] Jong, *Kommt das Zeitalter,* 359–65.

Saturday, 9 April AD 96

This morning early, I awaited daybreak on my favorite rock outside our cave. The fires of Hades in the south have died down and the sky is clean and clear. The beautiful Milky Way struck me again as a cloud of the faithful, the people who believe in Jesus as the Messiah. They are members of humanity in its totality and they come from every nation and all tribes, peoples, and languages. I decide that I must ask Prochorus to write about these four groups – four being the symbolic number of the world with its four wind directions, its four seasons, and its four elements, namely fire, air, water, and earth.

I already saw this countless multitude a few days ago and I ascribed the number of 144 000 to them. But they are, in reality, countless. I also saw them as clothed in white and that must again be the case this morning.

In the past, the heavenly beings were making music and sang songs. This crowd must, surely, also sing the praise of Him who sits on the throne – the Lamb.

I notice that there are also many angels surrounding the throne, together with the twenty-four elders and the four living creatures. A song that we often sang in Ephesus comes to my mind and I sing it to myself while I believe that these heavenly beings are singing along with me.

Cepheus as depicted in Urania's Mirror, c. 1825

One of the elders, the constellation of the King of Aethiopia, called Cepheus by the Greeks, which lies directly next to the heavenly throne, asks me where this multitude in white clothes came from. I'm afraid to give a wrong answer and he explains that they are the victims of persecution and oppression by the pagans. Their clothes are white because they have been cleansed by the blood of the Lamb, of Jesus Christ, who was executed on a cross.

This elder assures me that these saints experience eternal bliss in heaven where they won't lack anything. His promise that they won't suffer from the heat of the sun reminds me of a Psalm: "The sun will not harm you by day, nor the moon by night."[106]

The Lamb must be their shepherd and he leads them to a never-ending source of water. I decide that this spring must be sought in the constellation of Aquarius, the Water Carrier. I visualize him holding a bucket full of water.[107]

This scene shows me something of conditions in heaven after Judgment Day, sometime in the unknown future, when all the chosen of God will be gathered.

Later, during the day, Prochorus asks me: "Anything to write today?" I nod and he sits ready to write while I speak:

Revelation 7: 9–17
The great multitude

> 9. After these things I saw, and behold, a great multitude, which no man could number, out of every nation and of all tribes, peoples, and languages, standing before the throne and before the Lamb, dressed in white robes, with palm branches in their hands.

---

[106] Ps 121: 6.

[107] Aquarius is called דלי (*Deli*) in Hebrew on the Zodiac mosaic on the floor of the 5th century AD synagogue at Beth Alpha in Israel and it means "Bucket".

10. They cried with a loud voice, saying, "Salvation be to our God, who sits on the throne, and to the Lamb."

11. All the angels were standing around the throne, the elders, and the four living creatures; and they fell before the throne on their faces, and worshipped God,

12. saying, "Amen! Blessing, glory, wisdom, thanksgiving, honour, power, and might, be to our God forever and ever! Amen."

13. One of the elders answered, saying to me, "These who are arrayed in white robes, who are they, and where did they come from?"

14. I told him, "My lord, you know." He said to me, "These are those who came out of the great oppression. They washed their robes, and made them white in the Lamb's blood.

15. Therefore, are they before the throne of God, they serve him day and night in his temple. He who sits on the throne will spread his tent over them.

16. They will never be hungry, neither thirsty anymore; neither will the sun beat on them, nor any heat;

17. for the Lamb who is in the midst of the throne will be their shepherd, and will guide them to living springs of waters. God will wipe away every tear from their eyes."

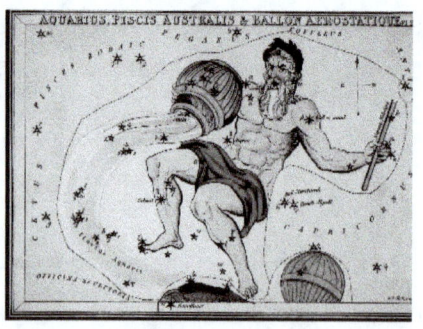

Aquarius, the Water Carrier, printed in 1825 as part of Urania's Mirror

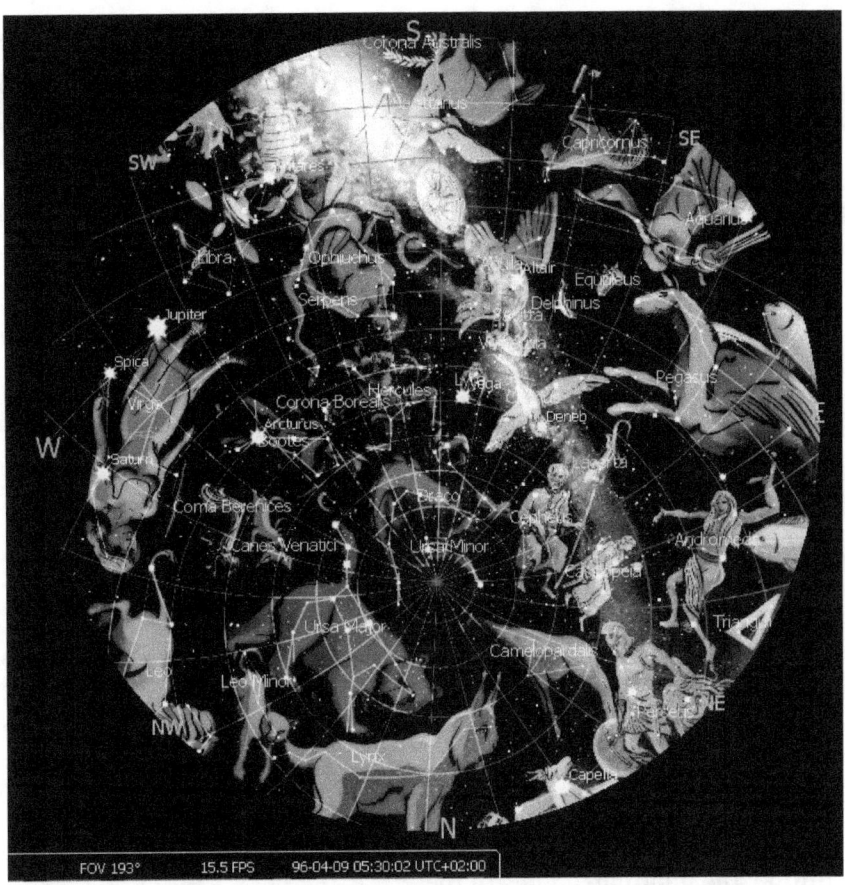

The sky over Patmos during early April AD 96 before daybreak with the Milky Way visible across the sky, looking north. The following three living creatures are also visible: Aquila (the Eagle) in the south, Boötes (the Ploughman) in the west, and Leo (the Lion) is disappearing behind the horizon in the northwest. Aquarius (the Water Carrier) can be seen on the south-eastern horizon.

Tuesday and Wednesday, 26–27 April AD 96

It is a pleasant evening in Spring and I decide to visit my favorite rock outside the cave, once again. Prochorus prepared a delicious supper – a broth with a few morsels of mutton that my friend, Andrew, brought us. The happy weed Prochorus made part of the stew makes me feel content, blessed, and relaxed. I feel ready to receive God's message as a gentle wind blows through the hair on my head. That must be God's breath or his Spirit.

The full moon is rising in the east, just above the clouds of the Milky Way or the River of Fire. Below the moon I observe the bright red star in the Scorpion or Serpent, called Antares by the Greeks.

My eyes wander to the throne of God, high in the northern sky. I see again the seven angels in front of God's throne, the guardian angels of the seven churches in Asia.

The invisible Lamb on the throne opens the last of the seven seals, the seventh star in the Chariot of Elijah. With that, he gives the seven angels each an important task.

The full moon draws again my attention. Something tells me that it is an angel with a golden censer, full of glowing coals. The coals are the red star, Antares, just below the moon. Smoke pours from the censer, the clouds of the Milky Way and of Hades. The thought occurs to me that those clouds represent the prayers of God's people and they are carried right to the throne and the altar of God.

This insight fills me with joy because I know that my flocks in Ephesus and elsewhere are praying for me and that their prayers are not in vain, because those prayers will certainly reach God's throne. That is also what must have happened with all the prayers of the faithful through the ages.

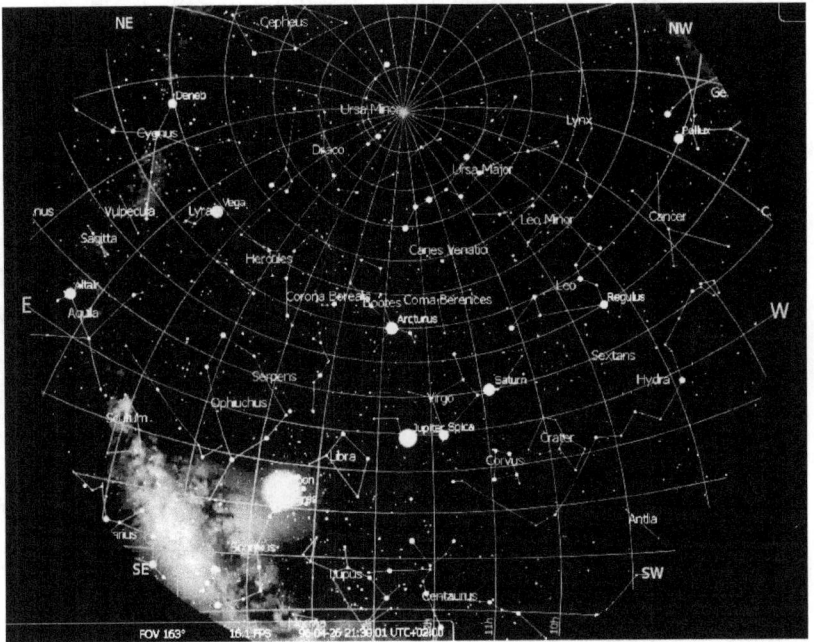

The seven stars in the tail of Draco, next to the throne of God at the northern celestial pole, the altar. It is situated adjacent to Ursa Minor (the Little Bear) – the seven angels who received seven trumpets on 26 April AD 96. The full moon – the angel carrying the censer – is rising in the southeast, directly next to Antares, the bright red star in Scorpius (the Scorpion). The Milky Way lies on the horizon in all directions at that point in time.

It suddenly dawns upon me that it is very silent. The wind has died down and the waves of the sea are inaudible. It is as if the world is holding its breath and waits for something to happen. I sit and watch for a full half-an-hour, waiting for something to happen. I am reminded of the prophet Habakkuk who wrote: "But the Lord is in his holy temple. Let all the earth be silent before him!"[108]

And then the fires of Hades suddenly erupt again in the south. Soon thereafter, a great cloud develops over these fires and a thunderstorm breaks loose. Lightning crashes down upon the earth and I can hear the loud thunder that accompanies the flashes.

Clouds of steam, gas and ash rising from the volcano Chaitén in Chile. All the vapor in the air gave rise to a localized thunder storm (Rev 8: 5 and 10: 4).

It is as if the world is suddenly woken up by this storm because I feel the tremors of yet another earthquake. Some rocks on the hill where I am sitting, get shaken loose and they make cracking sounds as they crash down the hill.

This thunderstorm over the fires of hell awakens memories of the Roman Army on its way to Jerusalem, many years ago. I can again hear the sounds of the military trumpets and drums in my mind. I decide that those seven angels in front of God's throne must

---

[108] Hab 2: 20.

each have received trumpets to announce God's judgment on this evil, horrible, wicked, cruel, corrupt, and godless world.

Mosaic showing the Roman tuba and its size in relation to its player, circa 4th century AD, in the Villa Romana del Casale, Piazza Armerina, Sicily, Italy.

The four events happening at the same time, the thunder, the lightning, the sounds of the rocks, and the earthquake, remind me of the number of the earth, namely four. These four events convince me that the whole earth will experience God's wrath.

I cannot help but to think of Moses who received the instruction to have two trumpets made of silver with which the people of Israel were to be summoned for meetings and gatherings or to be used as an alarm system[109]. The trumpets given to the seven angels are certainly also meant to make important announcements.

---

[109] Num 10: 1–10.

The thunder storm fascinates me to such an extent that I stay seated on my rock, even while big rain drops fall on my head and drench me totally. I want to see whether the rain drops would put that big fire out. It must have been after midnight that I decide to return to the cave, shivering from the cold. Fortunately, the embers of our fire are still glowing and I add some sticks. A few minutes later, the fire burns brightly and I can dry my soaked clothes.

Prochorus wakes up and asks: "What are you doing?"

"Can't you see? I am drying my wet clothes. I sat outside in the rain during the thunder storm after I have watched the stars and the fires of hell and heard their messages."

"I am wide awake now. Do you want me to write anything? The fire is bright enough that I can see what I write."

"Yes, please. I don't have much for you to write, but in the meantime, I can get warm again before I get into my bed and before I forget what I have seen and heard."

Revelation 8: 1–5
The seventh seal

1.	When he opened the seventh seal, there followed a silence in heaven for about half an hour.
2.	I saw the seven angels who stand before God, and seven trumpets were given to them.
3.	Another angel came from the east and stood over the altar, having a golden censer. Much incense was given to him, that he should add it to the prayers of all the saints on the golden altar which was before the throne.
4.	The smoke of the incense, with the prayers of the saints, went up before God out of the angel's hand.

> 5. The angel took the censer, and he filled it with the fire of the altar, and threw it on the earth. There followed thunders, sounds, lightnings, and an earthquake.

After Prochorus has stored his writing instruments, we get into our beds and try to sleep. However, I hear loud bangs outside and that keeps me awake.

After some time, I give up and get dressed again after a very loud bang became audible. It sounds like a blast on a trumpet. Fortunately, my clothes got dry in the meantime and I go outside again. A spectacle is still to be seen in the south where the flames of Hades are again burning high. Stars are again being shot out of that horrible hole – probably devilish and diabolical demons trying to escape.

Andrew and his family join us and he asks: "May we please spend the night inside the cave? There are stones like hail and lumps of burning stuff falling out of the sky. These burning things looks red like red blood clots."

"It's your cave and it's your sheep inside. Make yourself at home. But I think I want to watch this spectacle because I believe God wants to send us a message with this calamity."

As I venture outside, I observe fires in the fields, caused by the burning stuff falling from the sky.

Another loud bang sounds and that sounds like another blast on a trumpet. I decide that that must be the second angel in front of God's throne who has received a trumpet. I look up into the sky that has cleared after the storm and I observe that one of the living beings, the Eagle, is watching all that is going on here on earth. I am sure that the Eagle must be proclaiming God's judgment. To make sure that the world hears it, the Eagle cries out three times – three being the number of the holy Trinity.

The full moon is setting in the west and she is partly obscured by the smoke pouring from the gaping hole of Hades. The moon also looks red as if she is soaked in blood.

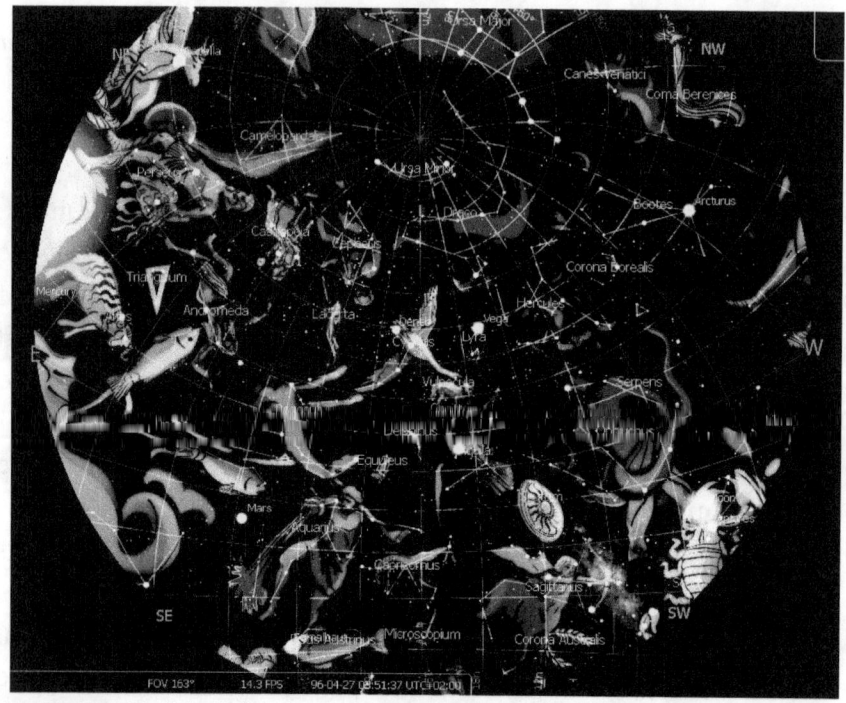

Aquila (the Eagle) visible in the middle of the southern sky during the early morning on 27 April AD 96. The throne of God is situated at the northern celestial pole next to Ursa Minor, with the seven stars on the tail of Draco in front of the throne, representing the seven trumpeters. The full moon (on the border between Libra and Scorpius) is setting in the south-west

Another loud bang follows and a short time later a huge rock, the size of a mountain, crashes into the sea to the east of Patmos. The sea turns red as stones and burning stuff fall into the water. The burning mountain that fell into the water causes a massive wave, which engulfs and rocks many of the fishing boats seeking shelter in the bay at Skala – perhaps a third of them. Some of them are washed up onto the beach and others are smashed against the rocks. The full moon and the approaching dawn make that visible.

Later, the sun appears in the east, but he is obscured by the smoke hanging in the air. I walk down to the beach of Sapsila Bay, east of the cave. Dead fish and other dead sea creatures are being washed ashore by the waves. Somebody warns me not to touch the fish because they have been poisoned by evil spirits.

A third loud bang is heard and I decide that that must the third angel's trumpet that sounded. A few minutes later a burning star falls out of the sky. Somebody screams: "All our drinking water is gone! That monster of a star has splashed onto our reservoir. Blasted! All our water is gone!"

Another voice: "All this red dust has poisoned all our water. Nobody can drink it. It tastes bitter, like Wormwood or Absinth. Hell, it's horrible!"

My memories of the Scriptures kick in. According to Jeremiah, God threatened the people of Jerusalem who did not serve Him:

> "Behold, I will feed them, even this people, with wormwood, and give them water of gall to drink."[110]

The poet of Lamentations cried:

> "Remember my affliction and my misery, the wormwood and the gall."[111]

Andrew leads his sheep out of the cave to graze, but he is dismayed because there is very little for the animals to graze on – much of the

---

[110] Jer 9: 15.
[111] Lam 3: 19.

pastures between the cave and his hut next to the coast have been consumed by fire.

The fires of Hades are still burning behind the horizon and yet another loud blast is heard. That must be the trumpet of the fourth angel. More smoke is spewed into the air, which obscures the sun.

At midday, I become very tired after having spent the whole time on my feet and having had no sleep during the night. I return to the cave and I fall asleep almost immediately. I wake up again when dusk falls and the sheep return to the cave. I remember a clear dream I had. I heard the Eagle that I saw this morning in the sky cry out three times to warn all the people on earth that more calamities and disasters are to come because there are still three more angels who will blow their trumpets.

I take a rest on my favorite rock and I start to think about the meaning of all I have witnessed. I realize that each of the first four trumpets brought about three catastrophes or calamities each and, in each case, a third of a certain category or class of objects or part of creation was affected. The following twelve categories were damaged: the earth, the trees, the grass, the sea, sea creatures, ships, rivers, springs, water supplies, the sun, the moon, and the stars. They can be grouped into four groups: things on dry land, things in the sea, fresh water, and celestial beings.

The numbers of four and twelve are, of course, numbers that mean something. The number of four tells me that the whole of creation was affected. Four is, after all, the number of the world – there are four wind directions and four seasons and the world is composed of four elements: fire, air, water, and earth. Twelve symbolizes completeness and that tells me that the disasters and calamities affected the whole of creation, except for the people. Their turn would certainly come later.

These calamities and woes are surely under the control of almighty God and they must be seen as his warnings to the people of a corrupt and criminal world to turn away from their iniquities and idolatry and insolence and wickedness and accept his power and only worship Him – instead of worshipping all sorts of creatures on earth or in the heavens. People should also recognize that the means for their livelihood – agriculture, fishing, and commerce – are at the mercy of the forces in creation under the guidance of God who created and rules everything.

Andrew's wife has prepared supper in the meantime and we are very grateful for some nourishment. The poor hungry sheep in the cave make a conversation difficult with their bleating. When it turns dark, I go outside again to escape from the suffering sheep. A third of the stars are obscured because of all the smoke rising from the gaping throat of Hades.

It must be clear that God emphasized with each trumpet that only a third of each category of objects was affected. That is God's way of saying that He was not annihilating the wicked world totally or straight-away – He was giving the rest of the world an opportunity to repent and to convince people to recognize Him as the supreme authority in creation. The trumpet blasts were therefore warnings to an evil and godless pagan world.

While Andrew and his frightened family are sitting huddled on some sheep skins, his wife lights a little lamp filled with oil. I call on Prochorus: "Get your pen and some ink and a sheet of papyrus. I must dictate to you another prophecy."

Revelation 8: 6–13
The First Four Trumpets

6. The seven angels who had the seven trumpets prepared themselves to sound.

7. The first sounded, and there followed hail and fire, mingled with blood, and they were thrown on the earth. One third of the earth was burnt up, and one third of the trees were burnt up, and all green grass was burnt up.

8. The second angel sounded, and something like a great mountain burning with fire was thrown into the sea. One third of the sea became blood,

9. and one third of the creatures which were in the sea died, those who had life. One third of the ships were destroyed.

10. The third angel sounded, and a great star fell from the sky, burning like a torch, and it fell on one third of the rivers, and on the springs of the waters.

11 The name of the star is called "Wormwood." One third of the waters became wormwood. Many men died from the waters, because they were made bitter.

12. The fourth angel sounded, and one third of the sun was struck, and one third of the moon, and one third of the stars; so that one third of them would be darkened, and the day wouldn't shine for one third of it, and the night in the same way.

13. I saw, and I heard an eagle, flying in mid heaven, saying with a loud voice, "Woe! Woe! Woe for those who dwell on the earth, because of the other voices of the trumpets of the three angels, who are yet to sound.

Sunday, 1 May AD 96

To my relief, the members of my little flock all turn up for a short service just after dawn. Andrew has already led his sheep from the cave to browse on whatever they can find after the fires and I start to feed my little flock with spiritual nourishment. We sit outside and I sit on my favorite rock while I address those assembled. George has brought two new families along, neighbors of his. They are all terrified by all the events of the past days and they want to hear God's message for them on this Sunday.

Just as we sing our last song, a loud bang is heard from the south. I tell my little flock: "That was the trumpet of the fifth angel. Something bad is about to happen soon."

And, lo! A big star is shot out of the open throat of Hades and falls into the sea where we can see how it causes steam to boil off the water where it fell. It must be very, very hot to produce so much steam.

Andrew's wife asks with the shock showing on her face with her wide-open eyes: "Was that a demon that jumped out of Hades?"

Me: "That's possible. And now he's drowning in the sea. Look at all the steam his gives off in his anger!"

We see how clouds of smoke are still pouring from the furnace, which is Hades, the evil place, the abhorrent abyss beneath the surface of the earth where all the stinking spirits have their hide-out and where the damned dead are being dumped.

Suddenly, a dark cloud materializes out of the smoke and a huge swarm of horrible, horrific, and horrendous creatures descend upon us where we are sitting outside the cave. My first thought is: "Heaven must preserve us against these malicious and malevolent and malignant diabolic creatures!"

Thousands upon thousands of them descend upon us where

139

we are situated on the hillside. We cover our heads with our cloaks, slap with our hands where these vermin hit and bite and scratch us.

George shouts: "These devils are called locusts! They will devour every blade of grass and every leaf from all the trees and shrubs! Andrew, get your sheep to trample these destructive demons with their sharp hooves!"

Andrew jumps up and call his sheep. I, George, and Prochorus help him to chase the sheep all over the spots where these damnable devils have landed. Fortunately, the sheep prevent them from consuming too much of the little bit of grass and leaves on the trees that survived the fire. A stench is given off as their carcasses heap up where they are trampled. The poor sheep also suffer where these obscene, offensive, and outrageous evil spirits worry them.

Andrew yells: "Satan must be behind this. He did it on purpose. He wanted to disrupt the Day of the Lord and make us abandon our worship of the only true God. John, do you think that the good Lord in Heaven will punish him for this?"

"Oh, certainly. I foresee the day when Satan will be chained and bound where he is lurking in Hades. Although…, when Jesus was resurrected from the tomb, he already achieved a significant victory over Satan. This evil spirit's days are numbered! Just wait!"

George: "You mention Satan. My first thought was that it must be Apollyon, the Greek destroyer of the Underworld."

Me: "You must be right. We know that devil in Hebrew as Abaddon, the Destructor. But it's only another name for Satan, the prince of the demons. Something that struck me is that this abyss, this hole into Hades, is in the south. God's throne is in the exact opposite direction, at the far north. It's impossible for them to lie next to each other."

Prochorus: "Remarkable."

Me: "And something else: this Apollyon or Abbadon must

also have been the instigator of the attack of the Roman Army on the holy city, Jerusalem, thirty years ago. The general who conquered Jerusalem became Caesar Titus later when he succeeded his father as emperor. He must be a close associate of this Apollyon or Satan. The same as the present emperor who thinks he's a god or something."

Jason: "Hush, hush. Don't let the authorities hear what you are saying. It could cause you lots of trouble, apart from your exile here. Anyway, have you noticed that huge star that was shot out of that abyss? It must have had the key to that bottomless pit and released these ugly and unsightly and uncouth beasts. John, what do you think?"

Me: "Oh, certainly. Something else: when these vermin came flying along with their clapping wings, it reminded me of the Roman chariots and horsemen that I have heard and seen many years ago when they were attacking Jerusalem."

Prochorus: "These brutes make me think of war machines. They have breast plates, teeth like lions to chew all the plants, glaring eyes to watch their enemies, golden helmets on their heads, and the faces of men. I shudder when I watch them!"

Me: "This is not the first time that Gd has sent such a plague upon the world. I suddenly remember that I have read something of this sort in the book of the prophet Joel where he reminded the drunkards of his people:

'What the swarming locust has left, the great locust has eaten. What the great locust has left, the grasshopper has eaten. What the grasshopper has left, the caterpillar has eaten.'[112]

---

[112] Joel 1: 4.

141

"God also commanded Moses when the children of Israel were held as slaves in Egypt:

> 'Stretch out your hand over the land of Egypt for the locusts, that they may come up on the land of Egypt, and eat every herb of the land, even all that the hail has left.'"[113]

Prochorus: "Remarkable."

Andrew's wife: "How long will we have to suffer all these things? If these little dragons devour all our wheat, there will be no bread for our little ones."

Me: "Heaven alone knows. It might take some time, even something like five months. When that Roman general, Titus, started the siege of Jerusalem during the Jewish War, it took five whole months before Jerusalem fell.[114] Something like that may also happen here. It's possible that God will allow us to suffer for five months, till the end of Summer before the first autumn rains fall and we can harvest our crops."

After our visitors have sung a hymn and left, I ask Prochorus to fetch his writing utensils and take down my words.

Revelation 9: 1–12
The Fifth Trumpet

1.	The fifth angel sounded, and I saw a star from the sky fallen to the earth. The key to the pit of the abyss was given to him.
2.	He opened the pit of the abyss, and smoke went up out of the pit, like the smoke from a great furnace. The sun and the air were darkened because of the smoke from the pit.

---

[113] Ex 10: 12.

[114] The Roman legions started with their assault on Jerusalem during April AD 70. The city fell five months later, at the end of August.

3. Then out of the smoke came forth locusts on the earth, and power was given to them, as the scorpions of the earth have power.

4. They were told that they should not hurt the grass of the earth, neither any green thing, neither any tree, but only those men who don't have God's seal on their foreheads.

5. They were given power not to kill them, but to torment them for five months. Their torment was like the torment of a scorpion, when it strikes a man.

6. In those days men will seek death, and will in no way find it. They will desire to die, and death will flee from them.

7. The shapes of the locusts were like horses prepared for war. On their heads were something like gold crowns, and their faces were like men's faces.

8. They had hair like women's hair, and their teeth were like those of lions.

9. They had breastplates, like breastplates of iron. The sound of their wings was like the sound of chariots, or of many horses rushing to war.

10. They have tails like those of scorpions, and stings. In their tails is their power to harm men for five months.

11. They have over them as king the angel of the abyss. His name in Hebrew is "Abaddon," but in Greek, he has the name "Apollyon."

12. The first woe is past. Behold, there are still two woes coming after this.

After supper, I go outside again to watch the sky and the fireworks in the south. It strikes me that the constellation of the Scorpion lies on the southern horizon, just above the entrance to Hades with its fire and smoke. The realization dawns upon me that the Scorpion can be identified with Apollyon or Abbadon – and with Satan...

The Scorpion, Scorpius, is lying just above the south eastern horizon, as seen from Patmos – directly above the spot where the volcano on Nisyros would have been visible.

A locust plague must have been something that John had never encountered before and, therefore, he described it in superlative terms. However, swarms of locusts are not totally strange to the islands in the Aegean Sea. The island of Rhodes, for instance, experienced such a plague as recently as May 2013.[115]

The locusts come from North Africa and are blown over the Mediterranean Sea by the Sirocco, a hot south-easterly to south-westerly wind during Spring and it can reach hurricane strength.[116]

In 1869, locusts were even blown from West Africa as far as

---

[115] Mason, "Locusts".

[116] Bottenberg et al. "The Mediterranean Climate".

England.[117] The fact that these locusts from Africa seemingly came out of the smoke affirms the deduction that the volcano was to the south or south-east from Patmos.

A locust photographed on the Greek island of Rhodes, May 2013. Its wings look like hair and there are spikes on its hind legs. The front part of its body is protected by a hard shell and its prominent eyes give it an almost human look. Its yellow head looks golden. Its ability to devour lots of plant material gives the impression of ferocious teeth (Rev 9: 7).

---

[117] Enc Brit, "Locust".

Sunday, 8 May AD 96

A whole week has passed since the locusts descended upon our island. Fortunately, other owners of flocks of sheep followed our example and they drove their sheep and other animals with hooves over the locusts and trampled the lot of them.

By this time, it has become known that I worship the God of Jesus Christ, and many inhabitants of this island blame me and my God for the disasters that have befallen us. Many fishing boats were wrecked, dead fish was washed up on the beaches where they rotted, locusts devoured a part of the crops and pastures, deadly earthquakes occurred, many people lost their water supplies, extremely frightening sights were to be seen to the south where the flames of hell suddenly became visible, and burning stuff fell on us and caused fires. The earthquakes, fires, and falling rocks have wrecked quite a lot of homes.

Andrew advised me to lie low. Fortunately, the flames leaking from the abyss in the south died down somewhat and people were no longer so afraid of burning stuff falling from the sky.

And now I sit on my usual rock, early in the morning, before dawn, on this Day of the Lord and I think about what I am going to tell my little flock when they come to worship the God of Abraham, Isaac, and Jacob here with me and Prochorus.

I am not totally awake yet while I watch the heavens, awaiting a message from God.

Suddenly, the abyss, the pit into Hades – or Sheol as it is called in Hebrew – explodes again and another lump of burning stuff is thrown into the sky. That must be a blast from the trumpet of the sixth angel and the second woe that the eagle has announced. This time, human beings are to be targeted directly, as if they haven't suffered enough already. I believe that many people will die on account of the poisonous smoke, dust, and lumps of burning stuff falling onto the earth. That will be the punishment for all their sins and idolatry and crimes.

I look up into the sky. I suddenly realize that the four bright stars that form the square of Nimrod's Horse – or Pegasus, the horse with wings according to the Greeks – represent four avenging angels from the east. They want to cross the Euphrates River to the west, but are held back by the river. The Euphrates is represented by the stream of water from the bucket or bowl of the Water Carrier. When they are released, they have the task of killing a third of mankind and that is what is happening right now when people are dying from the effects of the events of the recent past.

The four stars in the square of Pegasus (the Winged Horse) and the constellation of Aquarius (the Water Carrier) to the southeast of the Milky Way, early May AD 96, during the early hours before sunrise.

These four angels are followed by a vast mounted army – the stars of the Milky Way. The horses of this army breathe red, blue, and

147

yellow flames, that is, fire, smoke, and sulfur, the fireworks from the open orifice into Hades towards the south.

I can't forget how I saw the Roman cavalry units during the Jewish War. I remember these animals with their riders as terrifying beasts since the Roman horsemen were often clothed in armor and flowing cloaks. Anybody who knows horses will agree that horses that have been ridden hard on a cold day breathe heavily with water vapor coming from their nostrils. Horses have big teeth and they often bite in self-defense, which make them terrifying beasts.

A battle between Roman and Germanic armies, depicted as a relief on a marble sarcophagus, *ca.* AD 180–90. The horse in the center, especially, has a head typical of an Arabian horse.

Some of the smoke and ash have been blown over Patmos and neighboring islands by a hot wind from the south, causing dis-comfort, disease, and the deaths of many people. These deaths must be the punishment for the perversions and pagan practices of these people and that was brought about by the four angels from the east.

While I s watch the sky, I reflect on the meaning of what I have seen the past few days.

Where the first four trumpets unleashed horrors onto the world at large, the fifth and sixth trumpets targeted human beings – especially those who were guilty of the following six sins: the worship of demons, the worship of inanimate idols made of gold, silver, stone and wood, murders, sorceries, sexual promiscuity, and theft. The number of six sins is another number that is connected to mankind. After all, man was created on the sixth day of creation. Sinful man tries to reach the sacred number of seven, but gets stuck at six. In other words, every conceivable human sin was meant by this list.

Some of the plagues connected to the first six trumpets coincided with six of the ten Egyptian plagues (Ex 7–11):

- First Egyptian plague – the water of the Nile turned red as blood (as also happened with the sea in Rev 8: 8);
- Fifth plague – an epidemic targeting livestock (in Rev 8: 9 a third of the marine creatures died);
- Sixth plague – painful boils on the Egyptians (a third of the people were stung by the tails of the poisonous locusts and endured great pain – Rev 9: 5 & 10);
- Eighth plague – locusts (the same happened in Rev 9: 3);
- Ninth plague – darkness (the sun and moon were also obscured, according to Rev 9: 2); and
- Tenth plague – all firstborns died (according to Rev 9: 18 a third of mankind was killed).

I am sure that the reason for all these plagues and calamities was to warn people to turn away from their idolatry and other sins. Six types of idolatry are involved, as far as I can make out: the worship of demons and idols of gold, silver, bronze, stone, and wood. Six is the number of evil and rebellious mankind, consisting of sinners and pagans.

Sexual immorality is especially applicable to Emperor Domitian, the present ruler of Rome, who lives quite openly in an incestuous relationship with his niece, the daughter of his late brother and predecessor, Titus.

My little congregation gathers shortly after dawn. Prochorus has made friends with two local men, Ajax and Argus, two brothers. They attend our little service here under the open skies because they want to learn more about the God of Abraham, Isaac, and Jacob, the God I serve as a prophet. I explain to them the sights we have seen during the recent past.

Ajax grabs my hands: "Dear Teacher, my brother and me are called after old Greek heroes. Just as them, we aren't afraid of anything. We are strong farmers who like to work with our hands. We will protect you against all those who are angry at you."

Argus: "I am supposed to see better than other people. I can clearly see that you are a man of God. And you opened our eyes to find the real and only God. Thank you!"

After the end of our service and after the other people have left, I and Prochorus talk to Andrew, the shepherd.

I ask him: "My friend, will you be able to become the leader, the overseer, the shepherd of this little flock when we are no longer around? After all, you were our first convert."

Andrew: "I wish I could do it. But I can't read and write and I don't know the Scriptures and the stories about Jesus as you do."

"Are you willing to learn to read and write?"

"Of course. I would love that."

"All right, then I and Prochorus will start to give you lessons, every evening after you have brought your sheep back to the cave.

150

And we will see to it that you receive copies of the Scriptures, as they are translated into Greek, so that you will be able to become God's messenger here on Patmos, after we have left."

Andrew grabs my hand and the tears are running over his cheeks.

Afterwards, Prochorus fetches a new sheet of papyrus, a pen, and ink. I dictate to him:

Revelation 9: 13–22
The Sixth Trumpet

13. The sixth angel sounded. I heard a voice from the horns of the golden altar which is before God,

14. saying to the sixth angel who had one trumpet, "Free the four angels who are bound at the great river Euphrates."

15. The four angels were freed who had been prepared for that hour and day and month and year, so that they would kill one third of mankind.

16. The number of the armies of the horsemen was two hundred million. I heard the number of them.

17. Thus I saw the horses in the vision, and those who sat on them, having breastplates of fiery red, hyacinth blue, and sulphur yellow; and the heads of lions. Out of their mouths proceed fire, smoke, and sulphur.

18. By these three plagues were one third of mankind killed: by the fire, the smoke, and the sulphur, which proceeded out of their mouths.

19. For the power of the horses is in their mouths, and in their tails. For their tails are like serpents, and have heads, and with them they harm.

20. The rest of mankind, who were not killed with these plagues, didn`t repent of the works of their hands, that they wouldn`t worship demons, and the idols of gold, and of silver, and of brass, and of stone, and of wood; which can neither see, nor hear, nor walk.

21. They didn`t repent of their murders, nor of their sorceries, nor of their sexual immorality, nor of their thefts

Musicians playing a Roman tuba, a water organ (hydraulis), and a pair of cornua, detail from the Zliten mosaic, 2nd century AD

Tuesday, 10 May AD 96

It is a pleasant Spring day and Prochorus and I are sitting outside the cave, watching the sea, the sky, and the scenery around us.

Prochorus asks: "Teacher, have you noticed? That must be a gigantic angel, there over the sea, over there, to our south. Look, there is a rainbow around his head, which is the sun. His body consists of all those clouds."

"Yes, you may be right. Well, I never, he even has legs of fire! Those thunder bolts jutting out of those clouds. One of them struck the sea and the other one touched that island over there."

"Yes, I also see it that way. And now we can hear his voice."

"And what a voice! Do you think that we can compare his voice with the roar of a lion? I have never seen a lion in my life, but I've heard that they have a terrible roar. Everybody shakes with fear when that beast roars. I wonder whether the voice of that angel can also be compared with a lion's voice."

"Teacher, you may be correct. And there he roars again!"

We sit and watch the spectacle. It thundered seven times before the storm to our south blew over. But the rainbow around the angel's head, the sun, stayed visible for some time.

After an hour, I remark: "My old friend, Mark, who wrote a book about Jesus and his disciples, recorded that two of Jesus' disciples, the sons of Zebedee, James and John, were called 'Sons of Thunder'.[118] That was because they had these hot tempers. They could become angry very easily, according to Mark. I knew this John before his death in Ephesus. I can't think why Jesus called him a 'Son of Thunder' because I experienced him as a soft, a saintly, a serene old man. He never raised his voice."

Prochorus: "Well, I remember that that nickname stuck and got transferred onto the seven most prominent of this John's pupils."

"Quite right. I wonder how they are doing right now. I haven't seen them since I was banished to this rocky island."

"I also wonder. It struck me that we heard the thunder seven times during that storm. And there are the Seven Thunders in Ephesus, the students of the apostle."

"You certainly have a point. Anyway, I got stuck in this place for the last four months. But God gave me a task. I must write down everything He tells me with his signs in the heavens so that we can send that off to the seven churches when the time is ripe."

"Do you want me to write down what we saw about this gigantic angel with the rainbow around his head and legs of fire?"

"No, not now. Perhaps later."

---

[118] Mark 3: 17 – " James the son of Zebedee; John, the brother of James, and them he surnamed Boanerges, which is, Sons of Thunder." The Greek word Βοανηργές (*Boanerges*) is derived from the Aramaic בְּנֵי רְגַז (*beney regaz* – sons of rage).

Wednesday, 11 May AD 96

My old friend from Ephesus, Gaius,[119] turns up unexpectedly at our cave. We grab each other and we laugh and cry because we are so glad to see each other again.

Gaius: "I happened to sail with one of our church members who owns a boat. He had to fetch some barrels of wine here from Patmos and I hitched a voyage. He is only leaving tomorrow and that gave me time to seek you."

"How did you find me?"

"A shop-keeper with the name of Jason told me that he belongs to your group and that he worships every Sunday with a few other Christians here at your cave."

"May the good Lord bless the soul of my dear Jason!"

"Anyway, here is a letter from the seven elders in Ephesus."

"Do you mean the Seven Thunders, of which you are one?"

"Yes. That's them. Hoe did you guess??"

"We watched a thunder storm yesterday when it thundered seven times. That reminded us of the Seven Sons of Thunder in Ephesus."

"Well, yes, read this letter. Take it. And then I advise you to swallow that letter because it may not fall into the hands of the wrong people. I saw the governor of Ephesus, Macinus Olivetius, over there in Skala where we landed. He is accompanied by a squad of guards and we must be very careful while he is around. It will be a disaster if he finds this letter."

I start to read the letter. It contains good news about the Christians in Ephesus, but it also mentions that our friend Antipas of Pergamum lost his life for being a faithful witness of Christ.

---

[119] See Rom 16: 23 where he is mentioned as a friend of the Apostle Paul in Ephesus.

Pergamum is described as the place where Satan lives. The letter also mentions a bag of golden coins that Gaius has to deliver.

Me: "Gaius, this letter tells me of a bag of golden coins that you are supposed to have brought along."

"Yes. Here it is. We held a collection and we exchanged all the small coins for a few golden ones. That made it easier to conceal so that it wouldn't get confiscated by a nasty soldier or a vicious official or stolen by a crafty thief. It is for your upkeep here on Patmos. But, please, forgive me, I have spent one coin on buying some fish for your supper tonight."

After I have chewed the letter, I get tears in my eyes because I feel sad and rather miserable. I know that the poor Christians in Ephesus must have sacrificed a lot to send me this money and this letter. I also mourn the loss of Antipas in Pergamum.

Me: "We must invite our friend and benefactor Andrew and his family to feast with us tonight when we roast this fish."

During supper and afterwards I tell Gaius of all the signs and messages that I have received from God. I also tell him that I am waiting for the seventh trumpet to be blown. That will, most likely, lead to some more signs and messages.

Zeus, the father of the Greek gods, hurling a thunderbolt; bronze statuette from Dodona, Greece, early 5th century BC, in the Staatliche Museen zu Berlin, Germany

Gaius: "You told me about the way you watched the thunderbolts yesterday. You must certainly know that the Greeks regard their chief god, Zeus, as the god of thunder? The people of this island must have thought that he was speaking to them yesterday."

Andrew: "But this holy old man, John, has taught us that the God of the Scriptures also spoke to the people of Israel with thunder when they camped out next to his holy mountain. I am glad that I know better than to believe in Zeus."

Thursday, 12 May AD 96

The three of us – Gaius, Prochorus, and I – walk to Skala to say good-bye to Gaius who must return to Ephesus. He slept with us in the cave last night.

Prochorus asks while we are walking: "Gaius, what are you? An angel or only a messenger?"

Gaius laughs: "Both, my brother, both. The same word describes both."[120]

After we have greeted each other with tears in our eyes, Gaius starts to step into the water to reach his boat. With one foot on dry land and the other foot in the water, he gives me a last message, while lifting his right hand up and pointing it to the sky: "I want to swear by the God who created the whole world and the heaven – and also the sea on which I will sail back – that the seventh trumpet will be heard very soon. God appointed you as a prophet, just as He has appointed many other prophets whose books we read in the Holy Scriptures. Therefore: you must prophesy again over many peoples, nations, languages, and kings – those four categories of people. Your message is meant for everybody on this earth. Carry on writing down God's messages."

Later during the afternoon, while the sun is still shining, I tell Prochorus: "It was very bad and sad to say good-bye to our old friend, Gaius. It almost makes me sick. Anyway, go and fetch your writing instruments."

Prochorus: "I think you must be careful about what you want me to write. You heard that Macinus Olivetius is here on Patmos. You must hide your words about Gaius as a messenger or an angel by linking him to that gigantic angel in the clouds two days ago."

---

[120] The Greek word ἄγγελος (*aggelos*) means "messenger, envoy, one who is sent, an angel".

"Yes, you're right. We don't want Gaius to run into trouble, do we? Let's disguise his visit in such a manner that the churches in Asia will get the message that we are grateful for his visit and his message to us – that letter with the sad news that he made me chew and swallow and which gave me indigestion and heartburn.

Revelation 10: 1–11
The angel and the little book

1.	I saw another mighty angel coming down out of the sky, clothed with a cloud. A rainbow was on his head. His face was like the sun, and his feet like pillars of fire.
2.	He had in his hand a little book open. He set his right foot on the sea, and his left on the land.
3.	He cried with a loud voice, as a lion roars. When he cried, the seven thunders uttered their voices.
4.	When the seven thunders sounded, I was about to write; but I heard a voice from the sky saying, "Seal up the things which the seven thunders said, and don't write them."
5.	The angel who I saw standing on the sea and on the land lifted up his right hand to the sky,
6.	and swore by him who lives forever and ever, who created heaven and the things that are in it, the earth and the things that are in it, and the sea and the things that are in it, that there will no longer be delay,
7.	but in the days of the voice of the seventh angel, when he is about to sound, then the mystery of God is finished, as he declared to his servants, the prophets.
8.	The voice which I heard from heaven, again speaking with me, said, "Go, take the book which is open in the hand of the angel who stands on the sea and on the land."

9. I went to the angel, saying, "Give me the little book." He said to me, "Take it, and eat it up. It will make your belly bitter, but in your mouth it will be as sweet as honey."

10. I took the little book out of the angel's hand, and ate it up. It was as sweet as honey in my mouth. When I had eaten it, my belly was made bitter.

11. They told me, "You must prophesy again over many peoples, nations, languages, and kings."

As Prochorus stores the sheet of papyrus and his pen and ink, he quips: "I don't think anybody outside our circle of friends in Ephesus and elsewhere in Asia will understand this jumbled message."

Thursday, 12 May AD 96

Tonight, I am sitting again on my habitual rocky seat outside the cave and I admire the open skies. There are no clouds and the smoke from the abyss of Hades has subsided. There is so much that the stars are telling me that I decide to drag Prochorus out of his bed and explain to him what the stars are telling me.

Prochorus isn't very friendly when I shake him awake, but he, nevertheless, gets into a cloak to join me outside. He asks: "Where is your sense of charity and generosity? Why must I come and sit here on a cold stone seat and suffer from the chilly wind?"

"I want you to see what I am seeing so that you can understand what I will dictate to you later. Understood?"

"Perhaps." He gives a long yawn.

"Look there, my friend, just beyond the throne of God, you will see the heavenly temple. It has the outlines of a Greek temple with a pitched roof."

"Do you mean that figure of Cepheus, the King of Aethiopia?"

"Yes. That's what the Greeks call it. But is has been revealed to me that it also represents the heavenly temple, not the destroyed temple of Jerusalem. It is there just beyond God's throne – there at the Chariot of Elijah – and the altar, which is represented by those seven stars in a semi-circle below the throne of God."

"Ah, yes. I see it. What's so special about it?"

"Two ancient prophets of Israel were instructed to measure the heavenly temple of God when it was showed to them – Ezekiel and Zachariah.[121] And that is also the instruction that the Lamb, who is sitting with God on the throne, gave me. I was told that I must

---

[121] Ezek 40–44 (especially Ezek 40: 3) and Zech 2.

measure only the temple itself – not the outer courts, because those belong to the gentiles, the pagan nations of the world."

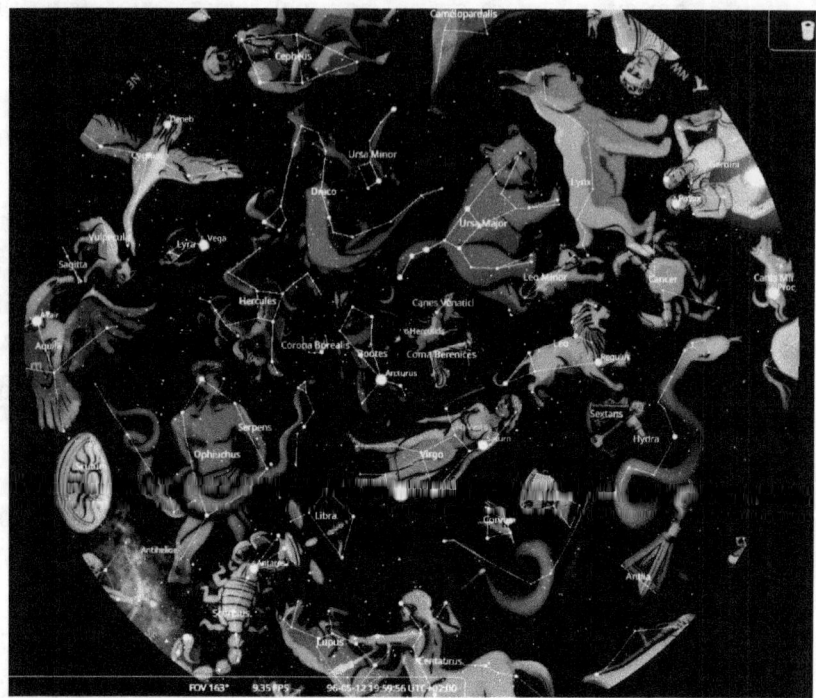

The temple of God is to be sought in the northern sky where the stars of the constellation of Cepheus are situated, forming the outlines of a building with a sloping roof. The "gentiles" are represented by the constellations of Auriga (the Charioteer), Gemini (the Twin Warriors), and Cancer (the Crab) on the north-western horizon. The constellation of Virgo (the Virgin – Jerusalem) on 12 May AD 96, had the planets Jupiter and Saturn (the two witnesses) within its borders. Scorpius (the Scorpion – Satan), with its bright red star, Antares, is rising in the south-east from the direction of the volcano just behind the horizon (the abyss).

"Do you still miss the temple of Jerusalem?"

"Yes, I do. I grew up in the shadow of that temple where my father was a priest. And that's where I also served as a priest. But that temple is gone. The idea is that I must become familiar with God's heavenly temple and count those who already dwell in there

– the souls of the deceased faithful. There is a sharp distinction between them and the pagan nations, the godless unbelievers."

"Where do you see these pagans?"

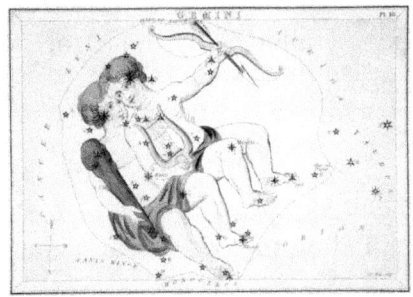

Gemini, the twin warriors, Castor and Pollux, as depicted in *Urania's Mirror*, a set of constellation cards published in London, c1825

"There on the horizon to the north-east. There you will see the Chariot Driver and the Twins, the two warrior brothers. Also, the Crab. They are ready to trample upon the holy city, the heavenly Jerusalem, the woman of God. There she is, allied with the Lion of Judah. Do you see them?"

"I do."

"Well, that woman of God is, of course, Jerusalem, the place where our Lord was crucified. These pagans will trample her for forty-two months or three-and-a half years – the same time the war of the Romans against the Jews lasted, from the time the Roman legions entered Palestine until Jerusalem went up in flames and sparks and smoke. One can also say that it was something like 1 260 days."

Although the Jewish War against the Romans started in AD 66 with some skirmishes and minor battles, the real fighting only commenced during March AD 67 when the Roman general and future emperor Vespasian attacked Judea with an army of 60 000 troops. Hostilities ended on 30 August AD 70 when Jerusalem with her temple

163

was destroyed by the Roman legions under the command of Vespasian's son, Titus – except for a few dozen die-hards who held out for three more years in the fortress of Masada and elsewhere.[122] The period between March AD 67 and the end of August AD 70 is exactly 42 months – the same period allotted by John for the trampling of the "holy city" by the gentiles.

Prochorus: "I seem to remember that the prophet Daniel also mentioned a period of three-and-a half years."

Yes, he did. Thanks for reminding me. He wrote about a certain king:

'He shall speak words against the Most High, and shall wear out the saints of the Most High; and he shall think to change the times and the law; and they shall be given into his hand until a time and times and half a time.'"[123]

"It's good that you remember that. I have been taught something about the meaning of numbers at our desert school. Three-and-a-half years amounts to 42 months. That is seven times six. Seven is the number that tells us something about God's work. He created heaven and earth in seven days. There are seven planets circling the earth. There are seven notes in a musical scale. On the other hand, six is the number that tells us something about mankind. Adam was created on the sixth day. Sinful man tries his best to emulate God's number of seven, but gets stuck at a six.

"So, you see, the time the Romans took to destroy Jerusalem has a great significance. That is also the time these pagans will use to attack that holy city up there in heaven."

"Remarkable."

---

[122] Mathis, "First Jewish-Roman War".
[123] Dan 7: 25.

164

"And now you must watch. Do you see those two bright stars within the woman of God, the city of God? They are prophets, the witnesses of God. Their task is to warn the pagans and all other unbelievers and godless people and to pronounce God's judgment on their sins, their crimes, their iniquities. During the time when they are doing their work there will fall no rain. One can compare these witnesses to lampstands that provide light in a dark world. One can also connect them to olive trees – very useful trees that bring us many blessings with their fruit and their oil."

"Yes, I see them."

"That's right. The pagans and sinners will see to it that these witnesses are killed. Their bodies will lie in the city of God for three-and-a-half days – only a short and limited period. In that time, the sinners will rejoice and celebrate. But God will justify these witnesses by taking them up into heaven. And God will pour fire over their enemies. The bright moon represents that fire."

"Do these witnesses, these martyrs, have names? Who are they?"

"Oh, yes! They do have names. Those bright stars depict really more than one prophet each. One can regard them as representing the two most prominent prophets in the history of Israel. Can you guess who they were?"

"Would that perhaps be Moses and Elijah?"

"Spot on! When both of them were doing their work, it did not rain. Moses led the Israelites through the dry desert and in Elijah's time there was a severe drought. Both were able to pour fire over their enemies. When Elijah prayed, God sent fire from heaven onto his altar. When Moses led the Israelites through the desert, God accompanied them in the form of a huge flame. That fire is portrayed by that shining moon, next to those two stars.

165

"They received the authority to turn the springs into blood and cause other disasters to strike the earth – just as our water supplies were struck with all that poisonous ash and dust blown out of Hades. Both were never buried in a grave but were taken up into heaven, very directly. They never died. But I think these two bright stars also tell us something about two other witnesses, men who lived quite recently."

"Yes?"

"Yes. John the Baptist and James the Just. Both were connected to Jesus. John – after whom I was named because I was born shortly after his head was chopped off – prepared the way for Jesus. James was Jesus' brother and he became the leader of the followers of Jesus in Jerusalem. He was killed by the priests shortly before the war started. Many people regarded the lost war as God's wrath against those priests who killed James. Both John and James are in heaven with Jesus, right at this moment, just like those two bright stars in the sky."

"I can remember that Jesus said that John was a second Elijah."

"That is so. And James was a second Moses. Both prayed for their people."

"It is wonderful what God is able to tell you about the war between good and evil by looking at the stars."

"But that's not all. Look in the direction of the abyss, where the fire and smoke used to pour out of that ugly entrance to Hades. There you can see the Scorpion. That is the Beast that comes from the abyss and he was ultimately responsible for the deaths of these witnesses."

"So, that must then be Satan, the prince of the evil spirits?"

"Dead right. All those sinners and pagans and murderers and killers are also his allies and that is why they trampled upon the holy

166

city. It was this Beast's influence that caused the two witnesses to be killed. That is the message I read when I look at the sky."

"You said that that woman represents God's woman, the city where our Lord was killed. Do you see this city as a good place?"

"Yes, and no. The killers of Jesus lived there and the real people of God were treated very badly there. I am almost tempted to compare this city with Sodom because of all her sins. Or even Egypt, where the Israelites were kept as slaves."

"I'm chilled to the bone. Thanks for the lecture, but I'm going back to my bed now."

Sunday, 15 May AD 96

My little congregation of about two dozen souls gathered again early this morning and I told them about the temple in Jerusalem where I served as a young priest and teacher of the Law before the war against the Romans of thirty years ago. This temple was destroyed at the end of the war. That was God's way of telling the world that the Jews are no longer his only people. All people who believe in Jesus are now God's children. I recite the words of some prophets to demonstrate that they promised the arrival of the Messiah.

Not long after my audience has left again, a gigantic earthquake overcomes us – even worse than any one from the recent past. We see the dust rise from some homes down in Skala, as well as the villages at Sapsila Bay and Groikos Bay, just below us to the east and south-east respectively.

Prochorus: "We must go to see what is going on there. Perhaps some of our friends had some damage and need help."

We reach the village of Sapsila a little while later and we find our friends safe and sound. However, a few homes have fallen in and that caused the dust to fly in all directions as we have seen. Our friends inform us that almost all the people in those buildings have died. We help to dig out survivors.

Our friends, who have survived the destruction of a part of the village, ask me to hold a short service to say thanks to God for their survival. A few other villagers join us to praise God.

Back at our cave, I instruct Prochorus: "It's time to write."

Revelation 11: 1–19

The two witnesses

1.	A reed like a rod was given to me. One said, "Rise, and measure God's temple, and the altar, and those who worship

in it.

2. Leave out the court which is outside of the temple, and don't measure it, for it has been given to the gentiles. They will tread the holy city under foot for forty-two months.

3. I will give power to my two witnesses, and they will prophesy one thousand two hundred sixty days, clothed in sackcloth.

4. These are the two olive trees and the two lampstands, standing before the Lord of the earth.

5. If anyone desires to harm them, fire proceeds out of their mouth and devours their enemies. If anyone desires to harm them, he must be killed in this way.

6. These have the power to shut up the sky, that it may not rain during the days of their prophecy. They have power over the waters, to turn them into blood, and to strike the earth with every plague, as often as they desire.

7. When they have finished their testimony, the beast that comes up out of the abyss will make war with them, and overcome them, and kill them.

8. Their dead bodies will be in the street of the great city, which spiritually is called Sodom and Egypt, where also their Lord was crucified.

9. From among the peoples, tribes, languages, and nations will people look at their dead bodies for three and a half days, and will not allow their dead bodies to be laid in a tomb.

10. Those who dwell on the earth will rejoice over them, and make merry. They will send gifts to one another, because these two prophets tormented those who dwell on the earth.

11. After the three and a half days, the breath of life from God entered into them, and they stood on their feet. Great fear fell

> on those who saw them.
>
> 12. I heard a loud voice from heaven saying to them, "Come up here!" They went up into heaven in the cloud, and their enemies saw them.
>
> 13. In that hour there was a great earthquake, and a tenth of the city fell. Seven thousand people were killed in the earthquake, and the rest were terrified, and gave glory to the God of heaven.
>
> 14. The second woe is past. Behold, the third woe comes quickly.

Prochorus: "Is this all for today?"

"Yes. I hope you understood what you were writing after I have shown you the other night what was revealed to me."

"But I don't understand how you could say that seven thousand people perished in the earthquake. There are not even so many people down there in the whole of Sapsila Village."

"All my numbers mean something. Seven is the number that tells us that God brought this earthquake about as a warning. The number of a thousand merely tells us that there were many victims."

"You also made me write that 'the peoples, tribes, languages, and nations' were watching the bodies of the two prophets. How could the people in Greece or Italy or Egypt see the bodies of these prophets lying in Jerusalem?"

"You will notice that I mentioned four groups. Four is the number that describes the earth. I meant that all the sinners, godless people, worshippers of idols, and pagans from all over the world are the enemies of God and his people.

"You must also have noticed that I mentioned that the second woe was over. We can expect the third woe together with the seventh trumpet at any time now."

Friday, 20 May AD 96

It is late at night and I and Prochorus are walking home from Skala where we attended a wedding feast yesterday. Penelope, the eldest daughter of Jason, the shopkeeper, got married to Perseus, the son of Xenophon, a neighbor. It was my task to bless the marriage and to baptize Perseus who decided to join my little congregation of Christians.

There was much singing and dancing during the service and I and Prochorus entertained the guests with a Hebrew Psalm:

> "Why do the nations rage, and the peoples plot a vain thing? The kings of the earth take a stand, and the rulers take counsel together, against the Lord, and against his anointed, saying, 'Let us break their bonds apart, and cast away their cords from us.' He who sits in the heavens will laugh. The Lord will have them in derision."[124]

It was a pleasant day and we celebrated till long after darkness set in. There was much singing and dancing and joking and toasts on all conceivable and inconceivable people and things and events. I had to teach the people some Hebrew songs from my youth.

Jason offered to accommodate me and Prochorus for the night, but we decided that a bright moon would illuminate the road back to our cave and we started to walk. Unfortunately, the amounts of wine we had swallowed slowed our progress considerably.

During our march to the south, we hummed the Psalm we had sung during the wedding ceremony. I declare: "Those millions of stars high above us... must be singing along with us... I'm certain."

---

[124] Ps 2: 1–4.

171

Prochorus: "I hear them. There is a ringing sound in my ears, which won't go away."

A few minutes later we hear a loud bang and I explain: "That must be the seventh angel. He just blew his trumpet."

Prochorus: "I think that bang was the roof a house that fell in because of all the rocks that accumulated upon it."

"That must still be that seventh angel. And he is joined by the twenty-four elders."

The moon later disappears behind the western horizon and it becomes very dark. We are tired and we sit down on some rocks next to the path. I look up to the northern sky to see whether I can see the seventh angel with his trumpet.

I grip Prochorus' shoulder: "Now watch carefully, my friend. Do you see the temple of God, up there?"

"The constellation that looks like a house with a sloping roof?"

Cassiopeia, the queen of Aethiopia, as depicted in Urania's Mirror

"That's it."

"The one the Greeks call the king of Aethiopia?

"That's it."

"Well, what about him?

"The temple that Solomon had built housed the Ark of the Covenant. That Ark disappeared when the Babylonians sacked Jerusalem many centuries ago, but I think it must still be hidden somewhere, perhaps in a cave below the temple mount, or somewhere else in a cave or something."

172

"I think I can see the heavenly Ark of the Covenant up there."

"Where, my dear friend?

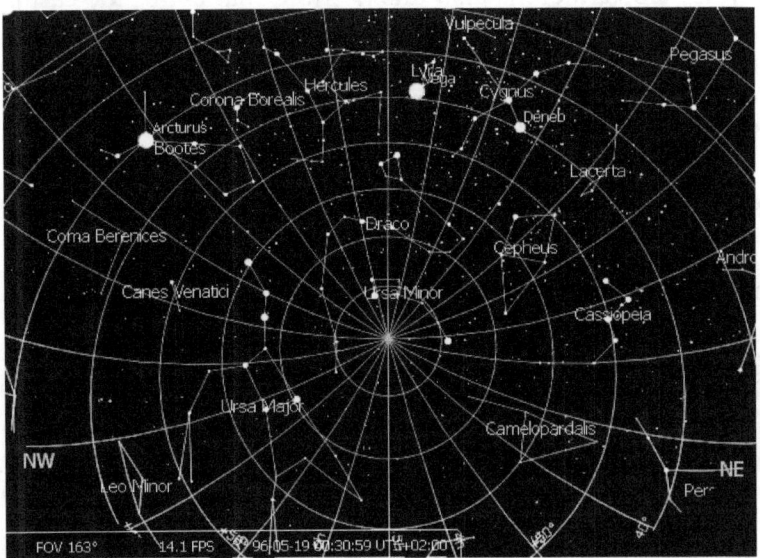

The sky above Patmos towards the end of May AD 96 at more or less midnight local time, looking towards the northern astronomical pole. The throne of God is situated at the northern celestial pole, the point around which everything revolves, and his temple is to be found where the constellation of Cepheus is just to the right of it. The constellation of Cassiopeia represents the Ark of the Covenant.

"Right next to Cepheus, as the Greeks call him. The King of Aethiopia. It's his wife, who is sitting on her chair. Her Greek name is Cassiopeia."

"At our school in the desert we called her Bathsheba, the mother of King Solomon."

"And the wife of King David. If you look carefully, you will notice that it also looks like a big box with an angel or two sitting on top of it."

"Yes! Yes! You've got it. The heavenly temple of God simply must have the Ark of the Covenant with it. Thanks for that insight!"

173

"I think it's that wine that made me dizzy and that opened my eyes."

"My good friend, we can't sleep here. I see a thunder storm brewing. Oops, there is also this horrible shaking of the earth. Was that a real earthquake, or was it the after-effects of the wine?"

"Both. Let's get going. You can tell me later what to write after we have had a good rest."

"Remind me to include that Psalm we sang during the service in the part I'm going to dictate to you."

Revelation 11: 15–19

The seventh trumpet

15. The seventh angel sounded, and there followed great voices in heaven, saying, "The kingdom of the world has become the kingdom of our Lord, and of his Christ. He will reign forever and ever!"

16. The twenty-four elders, who sit before God on their thrones, fell on their faces and worshipped God,

17. saying: "We give you thanks, Lord God, the Almighty, the one who is and who was; because you have taken your great power, and reigned.

18. The nations were angry, and your wrath came, as did the time for the dead to be judged, and to give your servants, the prophets, their reward, as well as the saints, and those who fear your name, the small and the great; and to destroy those who destroy the earth."

19. God's temple that is in heaven was opened, and the ark of the Lord's covenant was seen in his temple. There followed lightnings, sounds, thunders, an earthquake, and great hail.

Friday, 17 June AD 96

Our supply of money was getting low and, therefore, I and Prochorus decided to approach two farmers for work, namely our friends Argus and his brother Ajax. Although both of us are scholars, we don't regard ourselves too good or too important to perform manual work. We helped to plow some fields, to sow some wheat and to gather grapes for the wine presses – even if I'm not so young.

We were so tired at night that I didn't have time to watch the heavens for messages from God. However, our employers decided to declare today a day of rest and festivities because all the fields were plowed and all the seeds were sown. We need this rest because much hard work with the vineyards is still waiting.

This gives me time with the heavens again tonight after our supper. Prochorus announces that he will sacrifice his sleep to watch what I am watching and hear what I can tell him. I sit again on my usual seat on a rock from where I can observe the whole sky.

Prochorus remarks: "That rock belongs to you because you always use it. Have you written your name on it?"

"Not yet. But it's a good idea. Thanks. Then later generations can identify the spot where God gave me his messages."

"Don't use ink because that will get washed away when it rains. Use the hammer and chisel of George."

We sit in silence while we watch the heavens. The very last few rays of the sun are still faintly visible on the western horizon. After about half-an-hour I get a big smile on my face because the stars suddenly tell me a story.

I ask Prochorus: "My friend, what do you see in the heavens? Anything remarkable?"

"Well, yes, there is a rather bright moon. It is a little more than half full. Just to the west of it – or her – I see three rather bright

175

stars. Do they have any significance?"

"Oh, certainly."

"What do you mean, old Master?"

"What is the name of the star furthest away from the moon?"

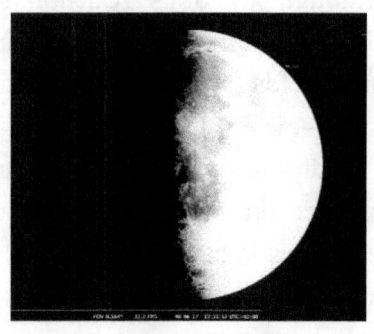

The moon with 64% of her surface illuminated as she appeared at the feet of Virgo on 17 June AD 96.

"Why, it is Shabtay. The star connected to the Jewish holy day, the Sabbath." [125]

"Correct. The pagans call it Saturn. That star, or rather planet, is Israel's special planet because it got its name from the Sabbath. It's the seventh planet, the slowest of the lot, and also the furthest away. I believe it isn't a coincidence that we watch these stars on the Jewish Sabbath tonight. And do you know the brightest planet just next to the moon?"

"That is the king star. The Greeks call him Zeus or Dios and the Romans call him Jupiter. We Jews call him Tzedeq,[126] the Just One or the Righteous One."

"Do you agree that we can see that as a good description of Jesus Christ?"

"Yes, you must be right."

"And that less bright star between the two planets, do you

---

[125] Hebrew: שַׁבְּתָאִי (*Shabray*); שַׁבָּת (*Shabbath*).
[126] Hebrew: צֶדֶק (*Tzedeq*).

know what it is called?"

"No. You tell me."

"It is Shibbolet.[127] You know enough Hebrew to know that is the word for a sheaf of wheat. The Greeks call it Spica."

"Thanks."

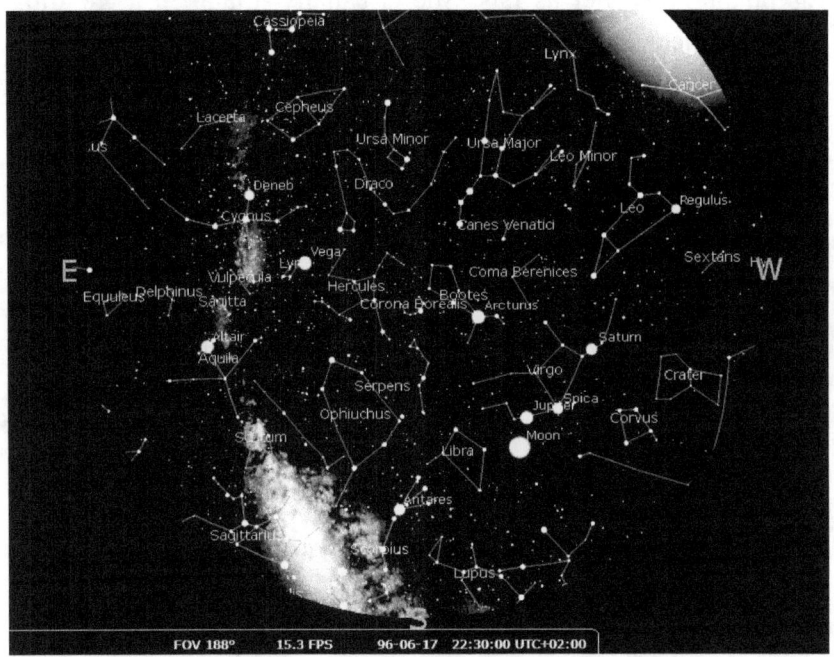

FOV 188°   15.3 FPS   96-06-17   22:30:00 UTC+02:00

The moon, Jupiter, and Saturn in Virgo (the Virgin), with the last rays of the sun in the north-west, together with Scorpius (the Scorpion) and Ophiuchus (the Serpent Catcher) to the south – 17 June AD 96, as seen from Patmos. Also visible are Coma Berenices (the hair of Berenice), Serpens (the Serpent), Aquila (the eagle) and Hydra (the Water Snake – partly behind the western horizon).

"Can you tell me what is that sheaf of wheat doing there? Is there anybody holding it?"

"That must be somebody who is connected to the harvest. A few weeks ago, you explained that that constellation represents

---

[127] Hebrew: שִׁבֹּלֶת (*Shibboleth*).

Israel. Directly, next to this woman, I can see the Lion, the sign of the tribe of Judah, the tribe of King David, as well as the tribe of Jesus."

"You have it. It's a woman. The Greeks call her the goddess of the harvest, Demeter. The Romans call her Ceres and the Egyptians know her as Isis. She is usually imagined as holding a sheaf of wheat and often also a horn full of fruit. The Jews know her as Bethulah,[128] the young woman. You correctly stated that we are dealing with the people of Israel, the woman of God."

Detail of the antique zodiac mosaic floor at Hamat Tiberias Synagogue National Park, Tiberias, Galilee, Israel (4th century) showing Virgo (the Virgin), called בְּתוּלָה, (Bethulah – young woman). She holds a sheaf of wheat.

"That's what you explained a few weeks ago."

"Indeed. That woman does represent the people of Israel. She is connected to Saturn, the special planet of Israel, as well as with the Lion of Judah. Israel is often called the wife or bride of God in the Scriptures. She has brought a son into the world, that bright planet at her feet. He must, therefore, be the Son of God. You already agreed that the planet Jupiter is a representation of Jesus Christ."

"That's remarkable."

"Now you must watch carefully. Do you notice that cluster of twelve faint stars next to this young woman? The pagan name for that group is Coma Berenices – the Hair of Berenice. For me, it is a

---

[128] Hebrew: בְּתוּלָה (Bethulah). This constellation is nowadays known as Virgo, the Virgin.

crown with twelve stars given to this young woman, God's wife."

"Let me guess: those twelve stars must indicate the twelve tribes of Israel. An I right?"

"Dead right. That bright moon would be the archangel Gabriel from God who announced the birth of Jesus to his mother and the archangel that guarded the baby Jesus and led the shepherds to the place where his mother nursed him."

"Remarkable. Fantastic!"

The Egyptian goddess Isis with the sun disc on her head and Horus, her son, at her breast (bronze figurine in the Egyptian Museum, Berlin).

The Greek goddess Demeter (Roman Ceres) holding a sheaf of wheat in one hand and a cornucopia (horn of plenty) brimming with fruit in the other. She is crowned with a wreath of fruit (Hermitage Museum, Saint Petersburg).

"Now you must watch the southern horizon. What do you see there?"

"Ah, that's easy. The Jews call that constellation the Serpent or the Dragon, as you pointed out a few weeks ago. But it is also known as the Scorpion. You have already explained that that group of stars is a depiction of Satan."

"Do you know the name of that red star in the body of that monster?"

"No."

"The Greeks call him Antares. He is just as red as the planet Ares or Mars, the god of war. This tells me that this red dragon is ready to make war on the woman and her child. He is ready to pounce upon her."

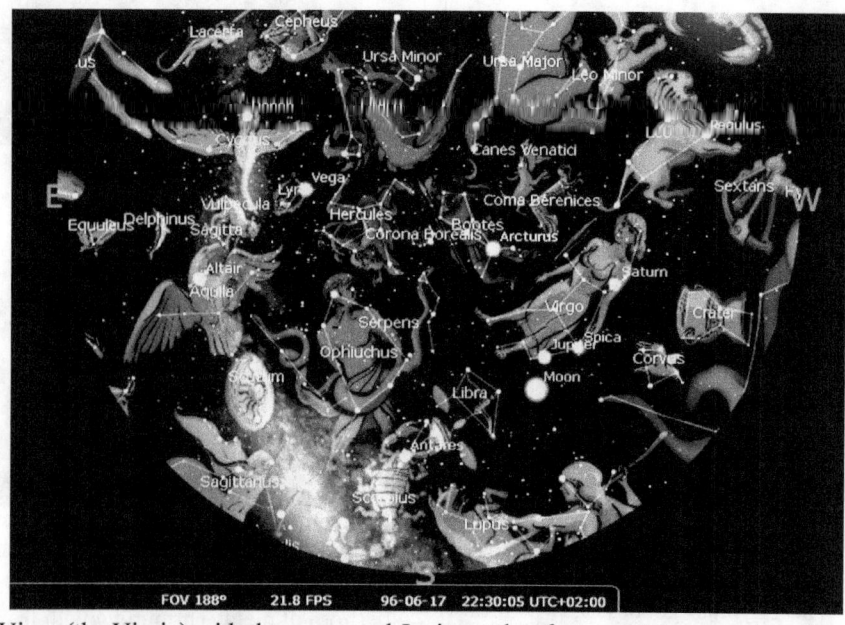

Virgo (the Virgin) with the moon and Jupiter at her feet on 17 June AD 96, after sunset – as seen from Patmos. To her north, the constellation of Coma Berenices (the Hair of Berenice) can be seen. To the south, Scorpius (the Scorpion), as well as Ophiuchus (the Serpent Catcher), together with Serpens (the Serpent), lie next to the Milky Way. Aquila (the Eagle) is to be found next to Ophiuchus, and Hydra (the Water Snake) is lying directly on the south-western horizon.

"That's perfectly clear."

"Certainly. He is just the opposite of Jesus Christ, the Righteous One. The prophets Isaiah and Zecheriah both promised that the Messiah would be a man of justice. Satan is the most evil enemy of God and he did his best to get rid of Jesus. Can you tell me how he did it?"

"Yes. That was when that cruel king Herod tried to kill all small boys in and around Bethlehem when he heard that a new king was born there. Satan also inspired Judas to betray Jesus so that he could be crucified. Fortunately, he didn't succeed because Jesus was resurrected and taken up into heaven."

"Do you see anything significant in the position of the red dragon between all the other stars?"

"Maybe. He lies next to the horizon. That must be where he was banished to the abyss when he was thrown out of heaven. That's in the direction from where the flames of hell shot out the other day. It's also directly opposite God's throne in the north."

"Can you remember what the prophet Enoch told us? Who was ordered by God to catch Satan and lock him up in the abyss?"

"That was, of course, the archangel Michael."

"Well done! I can see Micheal here in this scene. There is the constellation of Serpentarius, the Snake Catcher, trampling with his feet on the Scorpion or the Dragon. That was how Satan was kicked out of heaven. Let me quote to you from Enoch[129]:

> "And the Lord said unto Michael: 'Go, bind Semjâzâ and his associates who have united themselves with women so as to have defiled themselves with them in all their uncleanness."

"Yes! I can also see it."

---

[129] Enoch 10: 11.

"Have you noticed that dark regions next to the tail of the Dragon? It is as if he has swept a bunch of stars from the heaven. Those are the demons that followed him when he became the enemy of God. The prophet Daniel said something similar."[130]

"Would I be wrong if I see seven heads on that dragon?"

"No, you won't be wrong. I also see those seven prominent stars in this monster. One can also imagine that he has ten horns – those stars of the Balance in front of him. The Romans calls that constellation Libra."

A photo of the constellation of Scorpius with its outlines marked, against the background of the Milky Way. Dark areas in the Milky Way, due to dense dust clouds, obscure the stars behind them. The impression can be created that the Scorpion/Dragon swept some stars away with its tail.

We sit in silence for a long time to see what will happen next.

Prochorus: "Look, the woman is on the point of disappearing behind the horizon. And the Dragon has also disappeared into the earth."

---

[130] Dan 8: 9–10.

"I'm glad you notice that. Of course, the Dragon never had any success in his war against the son born from this woman. We know that Jeus was resurrected after his crucifixion and He was eventually taken up into heaven, where he shares God's throne. You can still see a little bit of the constellation of Hydra, the water snake. It looks like a stream of water flowing from the dragon. That must have been an effort of Satan to send a flood to wash the woman away or to drown her, but the earth swallowed that stream. It is almost gone now."

"An what happens with this woman?"

"This woman, who indicates the faithful of Israel, was taken to the wilderness, to the desert."

"Yes. If you mention the desert, that makes me think of the Israelites who travelled through the desert after escaping from Egypt. God looked after them in the desert."

"Yes, I agree. Look there, in the middle of the sky, you will see the constellation of the Eagle – one of the living beings that I saw in the beginning. That eagle with its strong and big wings helps the woman to reach safety in the desert."

"This story reminds me of the fate of the faithful followers of Jesus nowadays. Satan is still waging war against us."

"But we can rely on God to preserve us, just as that woman reached a safe place, although it is in the harsh desert."

"How long, do you think, did she have to hide in the desert?"

"Let's make it a period of three-and-a-half years or forty-two months, or even 1260 days. Let me remind you of how I explained it some time ago. This period of 42 months is the product of 7 and 6. The sacred number of seven symbolizes God's work; there were seven days of Creation, for instance. Six symbolizes sinful and godless man's unsuccessful endeavor to deify himself and also to reach seven. Mankind was also created on the sixth day of creation.

183

This period is therefore the time in which God is busy with mankind until the final Judgment arrives – a limited time that is sure to end but which is characterized by man's rebellion against God."

"That's a great mouth full of wise words."

"Thanks. But we must always remember that, although Michael has thrown Satan down into the abyss, he is not totally defeated or destroyed yet. We must continue to be wary of him. He tries his best to lure the woman's seed – that is, all the faithful – to give in to temptations."

A wooden statue of Mary, the mother of Jesus, and her child, with a crown with 12 stars on her head and a crescent moon at her feet, by the medieval sculptor Tilman Riemenschneider (*ca* 1490). This statue is meant to depict the woman featured in Rev 12 and she is shown as the queen of heaven. The woman seen by John cannot be identified with Mary, although she was the biological mother of Jesus Christ. For John, the woman in the sky symbolized the people of Israel, the people who brought the Messiah forth.

"Thank you for all your wisdom. You must be a real prophet who is able to read God's message from the stars and other events. But it's already late and I'm ready to go to bed."

"Not so hasty. I want you to stoke our fire so that we can

have some light in the cave and then I will tell you what to write."

"I have a surprise for you. With some of the money that we earned with our work, I was able to buy a little lamp and some oil. That will also provide some illumination."

Revelation 12
The pregnant woman and the dragon

1.	A great sign was seen in heaven: a woman clothed with the sun, and the moon under her feet, and on her head a crown of twelve stars.
2.	She was with child. She cried out, laboring and in pain, giving birth.
3.	Another sign was seen in heaven. Behold, a great red dragon, having seven heads and ten horns, and on his heads seven crowns.
4.	His tail drew one third of the stars of the sky, and threw them to the earth. The dragon stood before the woman who was about to give birth, so that when she gave birth he might devour her child.
5.	She gave birth to a son, a male child, who is to rule all the nations with a rod of iron. Her child was caught up to God, and to his throne.
6.	The woman fled into the wilderness, where she has a place prepared by God, that there they may nourish her one thousand two hundred sixty days.
7.	There was war in the sky. Michael and his angels made war on the dragon. The dragon and his angels made war.
8.	They didn't prevail, neither was a place found for him any more in heaven.

9.   The great dragon was thrown down, the old serpent, he who is called the Devil and Satan, the deceiver of the whole world. He was thrown down to the earth, and his angels were thrown down with him.

10.   I heard a loud voice in heaven, saying, "Now is come the salvation, the power, and the kingdom of our God, and the authority of his Christ; for the accuser of our brothers has been thrown down, who accuses them before our God day and night.

11.   They overcame him because of the Lamb's blood, and because of the word of their testimony. They didn't love their life, even to death.

12.   Therefore rejoice, heavens, and you who dwell in them. Woe for the earth and for the sea, because the devil has gone down to you, having great wrath, knowing that he has but a short time."

13.   When the dragon saw that he was thrown down to the earth, he persecuted the woman who gave birth to the male child.

14.   Two wings of the great eagle were given to the woman, that she might fly into the wilderness to her place, where she was nourished for a time, and times, and half a time, from the face of the serpent.

15.   The serpent spewed water out of his mouth after the woman like a river, that he might cause her to be carried away by the stream.

16.   The earth helped the woman, and the earth opened its mouth and swallowed up the river which the dragon spewed out of his mouth.

17. The dragon grew angry with the woman, and went away to make war with the rest of her seed, who keep God`s commandments and hold Jesus` testimony.

Saturday, 25 June AD 96

Something in the stew that Prochorus prepared last night did not agree with me and I got indigestion from it. My stomach cramped and I felt nauseous. The result was that I fled from my bed after midnight and sat down on my comfortable rock outside. The world is illuminated by a full moon and the night is quite warm.

I feel in the pocket of my robe and find one of the gold coins that Gaius has brought from Ephesus for us. In the moonlight, I have a good look at it again. It shows the head of Emperor Domitian on the one side and on the back side he is depicted as a great victor. I decide that God will understand if I loathe this despicable and detestable and diabolic dictator. I am a victim of his campaign to declare himself a living god because I refused to venerate him and accept his claim.

A golden sestertius minted by Emperor Domitian, showing him with a victor's crown. The reverse side shows him being crowned as a victor by the goddess Minerva, while he holds a thunder bolt, the sign of the god Jupiter. The inscription on the obverse reads: IMP(ERATOR) CAES(AR) DOMIT(IANUS) AUG(USTUS) GERM(ANICUS) CO(N)S(UL) XV CENS(OR) PER V(IR) M(AGNIFICUS) [EMPEROR CAESAR DOMITIAN AUGUSTUS, CONQUEROR OF GERMANY, CONSUL FOR THE FIFTEENTH YEAR, CENSOR, BY BEING A MAGNIFICENT MAN]. The abbreviation SC of the reverse stands for SENATUS CONSULTUM [BY AUTHORITY OF THE SENATE].

I feel somewhat better after some time and I want to stretch my legs.

In the light of the moon, I saunter down to the beach at Sapsila Bay, to the east of our cave. I hope that the fresh sea air will make me feel better.

The beach at Sapsila Bay on Patmos, the spot where John probably stood while viewing the monsters from the sea and from the earth.

While standing on the sandy beach, I couldn't help but to watch the heavens again. I expect a message from God and I'm not disappointed. Directly in front of me, on the eastern horizon, I see the constellation of Cetus, which the Jews call the Leviathan or Rahab, a monster from the sea, rising out of the water. This monster is mentioned in various spots in the Scriptures – in the Psalms, the book of Job, and the prophets Isaiah and Daniel.[131] According to Daniel, this monster has ten horns, and that is what I also see. The Psalms describes this beast as having several heads and I also count seven of them.

The Scriptures describe this beast as very dangerous creature and an enemy of God and his people. The beast I watch has spots

---

[131] Allen, *Star Names,* 162; Job 26: 13; Job 41: 1–34; Ps 74: 14; Ps 104: 26; Is 27: 1; Dan 7: 3–8.

like a leopard, a man-eating cat – the stars on its body. It has a cruel mouth with which it speaks blasphemous words. The red planet Mars lies directly next to one of the monster's head.

I decide that this monster must depict the epitome of anti-Christian forces, the emperor in Rome, Domitian himself, the man whose image I saw on that golden coin a little while ago and whose statue was unveiled in Ephesus a few months ago.

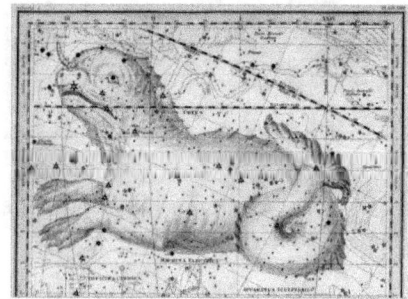

Cetus (the Sea Monster) from the Celestial Atlas by Andrew Jamieson, 1822.

I watch this beast carefully. I decide that he, as an emperor and a self-declared god, must have a throne and ten crowns on each of his ten horns, given to him by the Dragon. He rules over the biggest empire the world has ever seen. It was told to me that this empire includes the whole of Gaul, parts of Germania, the Islands of Britannia, most of North Africa, the whole of Asia, Syria, parts of Persia – and also Palestine.

He is certainly the most powerful man on earth. It is no wonder that regards himself as a god, somebody on the same level as Jupiter, Minerva, Venus, Mars, and other Roman disgusting and detestable deities. He reportedly insists on being addressed as *DOMINUS ET DEUS* (Master and God).

I decide that it is not a coincidence that the red and bloody planet Mars lies next this monster in the sky. That reminds me that it is well-known that he survived an assassination plot and that the governor of Germania started an unsuccessful rebellion against him.

190

The fact that this beast received an almost deadly wound, reminds me of Jesus Christ who also recovered from his wounds after he had been crucified. This means that this beast considers himself to be some sort of messianic figure, although he is exactly the opposite of Christ and his direct adversary.

While still standing on the beach, I also see another beast rising from the earth – the Goat, situated in the south over the land mass of Patmos. It has two horns, consisting of two prominent stars on its head, just like the Lamb I have seen in the past. That means that he is imitating the Lamb, who also has two horns, although he must be the exact opposite of the Lamb, of Jesus Christ.

This brute is clearly the Leviathan's servant. It dawns upon me that this Goat represents all the false pagan religions in the Roman Empire – the types of religion that would accept Emperor Domitian as a divine figure and whose adherents would gladly honor him as such. This beast represents all false prophets, including pagan priests, soothsayers, and magicians.

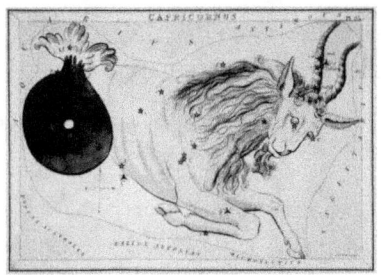

Capricornus (the Goat) from an old star atlas – the beast from the earth.

This second beast seems to have the ability to bring fire from the heaven onto earth – consisting of the full moon that is situated directly next to it. That means that he claims magical powers – much in the same way as many pagan priests and priestesses. He must also try to emulate a genuine prophet of Israel, Elijah, who prayed and fire fell from the heaven on his sacrifice in King Ahab's time.

I have had some experience with goats. They are different from sheep, although they are more or less of the same size. Goats are destructive and belligerent animals. That must also be the case with this monster from the earth, from Hades in the netherworld, which lies to the south where I saw the fires and flames from hell some time ago.

I also remember that Jesus compared Judgment Day with a shepherd who separates his sheep and goats into two herds. The sheep represented the true believers, while Jesus regarded the goats as his enemies, those who rejected him.

My memory goes back to the suffering of many Christians in Ephesus and Asia. They often live in poverty because they are excluded from trade guilds or prohibited to be shopkeepers or merchants due to their refusal to display the official stamp of the Empire to certify that they worship the traditional gods and the Roman emperor as a living god. This beast from the earth is, ultimately, responsible for this sad and sorry state of affairs.

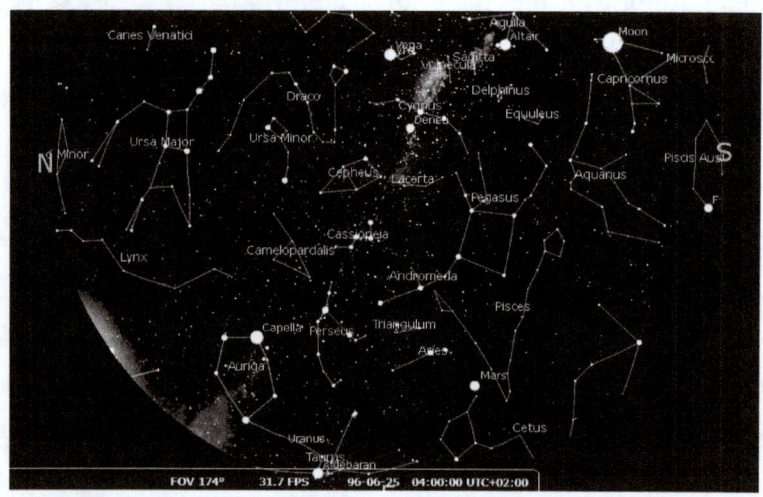

The positions of Cetus (the Sea Monster) and Capricornus (the fish-tailed Goat) shortly before daybreak, 25 June AD 96, as seen from Patmos and looking towards the east, with only the outlines of the constellations shown. There are seven stars in the head of Cetus – just as John described. Mars, the red planet, was situated just above the head of Cetus. The full moon is situated in Capricornus.

While I contemplate the destructive characters of these two contemptible creatures, I get the feeling that their days are numbered. They will not be able to survive Judgment Day and it is possible that especially the emperor will die a cruel and dishonorable death. God will certainly manage that.

When dawn arrives, I start walking back to our cave and I wonder how I must present my insights about the identities of these two brutes that I saw in the sky. I must use some or other code to let my flock on the mainland know who the Leviathan really is, but without using his name or his title because that could be dangerous if my documents fell into the wrong hands after I have delivered them to the seven assemblies in Asia.

Suddenly, I remember a trick that our Teacher at our school in the desert showed us. We were taught about the meaning of numbers and he demonstrated to us how we could conjure with the number of six hundred, sixty-six. This number is the sum of all the numbers between one and thirty-six. One may even arrange them in rows, like this:

$$
\begin{array}{l}
1+ \\
2+\ 3+ \\
4+\ 5+\ 6+ \\
7+\ 8+\ 9+\ 10+ \\
11+\ 12+\ 13+\ 14+\ 15+ \\
16+\ 17+\ 18+\ 19+\ 20+\ 21+ \\
22+\ 23+\ 24+\ 25+\ 26+\ 27+\ 28+ \\
29+\ 30+\ 31+\ 32+\ 33+\ 34+\ 35+\ 36 =
\end{array}
$$

666

This pattern forms a beautiful triangle – the Greek letter of delta (Δ).[132] And that is the first letter of the name of the beast from the sea, namely *Caesar Domitianus Augustus*. His name in Greek is

---

[132] Malina, *Revelation,* 185–87.

Δομετιανὸς (*Dometianos*) – a name that starts with the Δ. I am sure that some of my readers will be able to decipher my code.

The Qumran astrological calendar from the first century BC called Capricornus a kid goat (Hebrew: גדיא – *Gadya*), instead of the hybrid monster from the Babylonian and Greek mythologies. This was, no doubt, in accordance with the Jewish belief that such hybrids were blasphemous creatures, according to Lev 19: 19.[133] It is probable that John also saw an ordinary goat or a goat kid.

The monster from the sea is traditionally interpreted as the Antichrist (1 John 2: 18–22 and 4: 31; 2 John 1: 7; 2 Thess 2: 3-4) and the monster from the earth as the False Prophet (see Rev 19: 20).

I reach the cave just as Andrew arrives to take his sheep out.

He tells me: "I'm looking forward to our service tomorrow morning early. What are you going to tell us?"

"Wait and see. Perhaps I will tell you something about our emperor and his cult."

During the day, I discuss my visions of earlier this morning with Prochorus.

He remarks: "It seems as if there is a diabolic trinity – Satan or the Dragon, the Leviathan from the sea, and the Goat from the earth. It's almost a parody on the divine Trinity of God, the Father, God, the Son, and the Holy Spirit."

"My friend, that's a remarkable insight you have. Thank you. I am convinced that God will vanquish this unholy trinity. Their days are numbered. We can safely say that the beast from the sea will only have a limited time left."

"How long do you think?"

---

[133] Jacobus, "The Zodiac Sign Names", 323.

"A period of 42 months or three-and-a half years."

"When does this period start?"

"About three years ago."

"Why do you say that?"

"You know Marinus Vulvius, a Roman centurion and also a secret elder in our church in Ephesus. He told me three years ago that it was rumored that Domitian's days were numbered. He committed an unforgivable crime by executing some prominent senators and a popular general because he suspected them of plotting against him. These men called for a curse on his head. That was three years ag. If we count forty-two months from that time, the period God grants a sinner before He crushes him, it means that Domitian won't survive the end of this year."

"Remarkable. I have great respect for your powers and insights as a prophet of God."

"Thanks. And now you must fetch your writing apparatus. I must put on record what I have seen earlier this morning while it was still dark."

Revelation 13
The beast from the sea and the beast from the earth

1.	Then I stood on the sand of the sea. I saw a beast coming up out of the sea, having ten horns and seven heads. On his horns were ten crowns, and on his heads, blasphemous names.
2.	The beast which I saw was like a leopard, and his feet were like those of a bear, and his mouth like the mouth of a lion. The dragon gave him his power, his throne, and great authority.
3.	One of his heads looked like it had been wounded fatally. His fatal wound was healed, and the whole earth marvelled at the beast.

4. They worshipped the dragon, because he gave his authority to the beast, and they worshipped the beast, saying, "Who is like the beast? Who is able to make war with him?"

5. A mouth speaking great things and blasphemy was given to him. Authority to continue for forty-two months was given to him.

6. He opened his mouth for blasphemy against God, to blaspheme his name, and his tent, those who dwell in heaven.

7. It was given to him to make war with the saints, and to overcome them. Authority over every tribe, people, language, and nation was given to him.

8. All who dwell on the earth will worship him, everyone whose name has not been written from the foundation of the world in the book of life of the Lamb who has been killed.

9. If anyone has an ear, let him hear.

10. If anyone gathers into captivity, into captivity he goes. If anyone will kill with the sword, with the sword he must be killed. Here is the patience and the faith of the saints.

11. I saw another beast coming up out of the earth. He had two horns like a lamb, and he spoke like a dragon.

12. He exercises all the authority of the first beast in his presence. He makes the earth and those who dwell in it to worship the first beast, whose fatal wound was healed.

13. He performs great signs, even making fire come down out of the sky on the earth in the sight of men.

14. He deceives my own people who dwell on the earth because of the signs which it was given him to do in front of the beast; saying to those who dwell on the earth, that they should make an image to the beast who had the sword wound and lived.

15. It was given to him to give breath to it, to the image of the beast, that the image of the beast should both speak, and cause as many as wouldn't worship the image of the beast to be killed.

16. He causes all, the small and the great, the rich and the poor, and the free and the slave, to be given a mark on their right hand, or on their forehead;

17. and that no one would be able to buy or to sell, unless he has that mark, the name of the beast or the number of his name.

18. Here is wisdom. He who has understanding, let him calculate the number of the beast, for it is the number of a man. His number is six hundred sixty-six.

Tuesday, 5 July AD 96

It is necessary that I and Prochorus clean the cave daily. During the night, when the sheep of Andrew are housed inside the cave, they mess the place with their droppings, and these must be removed. We carry these droppings to a nearby vineyard to fertilize the soil.

The result of all this is that the cave doesn't smell very pleasant each day and night. That is the reason why we hold the meetings with our little flock on Sundays outside when the weather permits. That is also how Jesus addressed his audiences.

There was a thunder storm yesterday. The wet sheep slept again in the cave with us, but their wet woolly fleeces stank horribly and I fled from the cave during the early morning hours. It was somewhat of a struggle to find my way in the dark between all the sleeping smelly sheep to reach the mouth of the cave.

When I reached my favorite rock, I could start breathing the sweet fresh air again. It dawns upon me that God must have woken me so early so that I can watch for another message in the stars. I gaze upwards. All the clouds of the thunder storm of yesterday have cleared and there is a faint crescent moon in the west. The bright Mily Way stretches across the sky. I also notice the constellation of Aries, the Ram. We Jews used to call it the Lamb and that is what I perceive at this moment.

Aries, the Ram, from the Hamas Tiberias Synagogue Zodiac (4th Century AD). It is named a "lamb" (טָלֶה – *taleh*) (Isa 65: 25) instead of טְלָא (*tale*), which means a "spotted sheep" (Gen 30: 32) as called elsewhere.

198

Of course, that Lamb is none other than Jesus Christ, the Lamb of God.

The Milky way with its countless numbers of stars is, yet again, contains the crowd of faithful. When they were baptized, they received God's mark on their heads and hands. A few weeks ago, I decided to assign the symbolic number of 144 000 to this crowd.

I also see three of the four living beings that surround God's throne: the Eagle, the Bull, and the Man.

The Milky Way stretches from the southwest to the northeast across the sky during the early morning in July AD 96. Aries (the Ram) is rising on the eastern horizon The constellations of Aquila (the Eagle), Boötes (the Ploughman) and Taurus (the Bull) – three of the four living beings – are also to be seen. A crescent Moon is hanging in the east.

A slight wind starts blowing and it whistles over the cave's entrance. That must be the voices of all those faithful in heaven while they sing God's praise. Their hymn is accompanied by somebody playing the harp – the instrument that King David played. They all wear white clothes, the sign that all their sins have been forgiven and that their criminal records have been wiped clean because they trust Jesus. That means that they are ready to enter God's heaven where nothing bad or sinful can be allowed or tolerated.

Another thunder storm breaks over our heads during the afternoon. Where we sit inside the cave, we can hear the rain water splashing over the rocks. The sea is also restless and we can hear the waves crashing against the rocky shore. We are grateful for this rain, as well as previous showers, because that helped the pastures to become green again after the locusts and the wildfires.

After the storm has passed, I summon Prochorus with his papyrus sheet, pen, and ink. "My friend, please write down what I'm going to tell you. As you can see, there is a big smile on my face because last night I have witnessed the glorious future of all those who refused to worship the beast from the sea."

The Qumran astrological calendar of the first century BC substituted the constellation of the Ram with the Lamb.[134] Josephus noted that the Jews regarded this constellation as a representation of the sacrificial lamb that the Israelites had to slaughter when they were freed from slavery in Egypt.[135] It is certainly not too farfetched to conclude that John had the same idea.

Revelation 14: 1–5
The crowd singing God's praise

1. I saw, and behold, the Lamb standing on Mount Zion, and with him one hundred forty-four thousand, having his name, and the name of his Father, written on their foreheads.

[134] Jacobus, "The Zodiac Sign Names", 319.
[135] Allen, *Star Names,* 70.

2. I heard a sound from heaven, like the sound of many waters, and like the sound of a great thunder. The sound which I heard was like that of harpers playing on their harps.

3. They sing something like a new song before the throne, and before the four living creatures and the elders. None could learn the song except the one hundred forty-four thousand, those who had been redeemed out of the earth.

4. These are those who were not defiled with women, for they are virgins. These are those who follow the Lamb wherever he goes. These were redeemed by Jesus from among men, the first fruits to God and to the Lamb.

5. In their mouth was found no lie. They are without fault.

Monday and Tuesday, 11–12 July AD 96

Prochorus tells me when we reach our cave: "My old friend, go and get some rest. You must be very tired after working the whole day over there in the vineyards of Ajax and Argus. Go and sit on your favorite rock while Andrew's sheep get settled inside the cave. I want to go and buy some fish and bread at Groikos."

Groikos Bay on Patmos

Before I can respond, Prochorus disappears. He reappears just when the last bit of sunshine disappears.

He announces: "My old Master, let's go and watch how the stars come out while we sit on top of the hill behind us. I will grill the fish over a small fire and then we can sit and enjoy our supper there. I will pour some wine from the amphora that I've bought"

I agree with his plan and we enjoy our meal, while feeling very grateful for God's blessings and the willingness of Argus and Ajax to employ us as temporary farm workers during the grape harvest.

Here, from the top of the hill, we can watch the western horizon easily. The stars appear and immediately I receive a message from God. I address my friend: "I can see three angels up there. Each one has an important message or a warning."

"Where?"

"Do you see the constellation of the Virgin? Next to her lies the planet of Shabtai, which the pagans call Saturn. He carries the good news about Jesus Christ and he warns the people that Judgment Day is imminent. And the second angel is that bright planet, Tzedeq, the righteous one. The pagans call him Zeus or Jupiter."

"I know him. What does he say?"

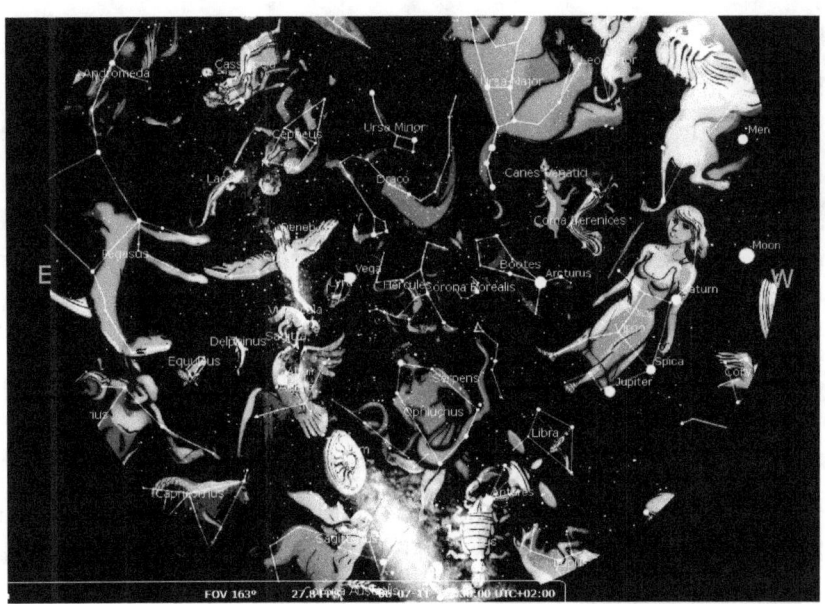

The constellation of Virgo (the Virgin – Babylon), is moving towards the western horizon, during the beginning of July AD 96. The crescent moon (13% illuminated) is to be seen near the south-western horizon and the planets Jupiter and Saturn are within Virgo's borders. Crater (the Chalice), is on the point of disappearing on the western horizon and Capricornus (the Goat – the monster from the earth) is on the south-eastern horizon.

"He warns that the fall of Babylon will happen very soon."

"But Babylon was destroyed by Alexander the Great more than three centuries ago, or am I wrong?"

"That was *four* centuries ago, not three. But it's not that Babylon. The angel gave that name to that woman, who's actually a prostitute. She symbolizes the people of God, the wife of God, the people of Israel, who drifted away from God by rejecting Jesus as their Messiah. The angel calls her Babylon because that was a horrible place where the people of God were held in captivity after Jerusalem was sacked."

"Oh."

"And that crescent moon, just above the horizon, looks like a third angel. He wants to warn all the people on this earth not to worship the two beasts and not to accept their marks on their foreheads and their hands."

"Can you see any of those monsters?"

"Yes. Look there, on the south-eastern horizon. There is the Goat, the beast coming up from the earth. There, just above that hill over there."

"Yes, I see it."

"And this third angel is warning the people, the pagans, and the unfaithful Jews, that they will be forced to drink from God's cup, which is filled with the wine of his anger, his righteous wrath. There, directly on the western horizon, you can see the constellation of Crater, the Chalice. That is the cup, filled with God's indignation, due to all the idolatry, wickedness, pagan idols, and immorality on earth."

I hold up my own cup of wine to emphasize my point.

Prochorus retorts: "I believe, God has the fullest right to be angry. He is, after all, the creator of heaven, earth, the oceans, and the waters of the underworld. He ought to be recognized as the ruler of the whole of creation."

"You are completely right. Let's douse this fire and go to bed. I will dictate to you tomorrow what to write."

Prochorus: "I seem to remember that the Scriptures mention somewhere something about the cup of God's anger."

"Yes, I also remember something like that. The prophet Isaiah wrote, if I remember correctly:

> 'Awake, awake, stand up, Jerusalem, that have drunk at the hand of the Lord the cup of his wrath; you have drunken the bowl of the cup of staggering, and drained it.'"[136]

After a while, I add: "There is also a Psalm that mentions something like this:

> 'For in the hand of the Lord there is a cup, full of foaming wine mixed with spices. He pours it out. Indeed, the wicked of the earth drink and drink it to its very dregs.'"[137]

We down the last drops of our wine and while we walk back to the cave in the dark, the wind starts blowing. I tell Prochorus: "This wind, this breath of God, tells me again that all those who believe in Jesus Christ will enter eternal life. There, they will rest of all their labors and hardships. They will be rewarded for all the cruelty and suffering they had to endure."

"I also feel this wind, God's breath of Spirit."

Revelation 14: 6–13

The three angels

6.	I saw another angel flying in mid heaven, having an eternal gospel to proclaim to those who dwell on the earth, and to every nation, tribe, language, and people.

---

[136] Isa 51: 17.
[137] Ps 75: 8.

7. He said with a loud voice, "Fear God, and give him glory; for the hour of his judgment has come. Worship him who made the heaven, the earth, the sea, and the springs of waters!"

8. Another, a second angel, followed, saying, "Babylon the great has fallen, which has made all the nations to drink of the wine of the wrath of her sexual immorality."

9. Another angel, a third, followed them, saying with a great voice, "If anyone worships the beast and his image, and receives a mark on his forehead, or on his hand,

10. he also will drink of the wine of the wrath of God, which is prepared unmixed in the cup of his anger. He will be tormented with fire and sulphur in the presence of the holy angels, and in the presence of the Lamb.

11. The smoke of their torment goes up forever and ever. They have no rest day and night, those who worship the beast and his image, and whoever receives the mark of his name.

12. Here is the patience of the saints, those who keep the commandments of God, and the faith of Jesus."

13. I heard the voice from heaven saying, "Write, 'Blessed are the dead who die in the Lord from now on.' 'Yes,' says the Spirit, "that they may rest from their labours; for their works follow with them.'"

Saturday and Sunday, 23–24 July, AD 96

Ajax and Argus held a feast tonight at the end of the grape harvest for all the workers, although their wheat harvest is still ongoing. We were fed mutton, fish, bread, olives, and grapes. Our drinking cups were regularly filled with red wine as soon as they were empty.

Argus: "The two of you may sleep over at our place tonight. It's warm enough so that you can sleep inside our stable with the horses."

I replied: "My blessed brother in Christ! Thank you very, very, very much for your wonderful, wonderful hospitality. Rest assured that the good Lord in heaven will reward you copiously, richly, abundantly, and … abundantly. But both of us must go home so that we can be ready for tomorrow's service directly after daybreak. I must still think about what I will tell the lot of you while we are walking back."

And now I and Prochorus are on our way. Fortunately, there is a full moon to illuminate the world.

Prochorus: "My good Master, my shaky legs and my sore foot can't carry me anymore. Please, let us sit down for a moment and rest on these rocks. Please, my left foot is still hurting where that cart horse trod on my foot when I wasn't paying attention."

"Yes, you should have been more careful. You know, horses are rather heavy animals – and Argus and Ajax have three of them."

After a little while, Prochorus asks me: "Master, do you see anything of importance in the sky?"

A warm southerly wind is blowing over us and I interpret that as God's Spirit edging me along to find a message in the sky.

"Yes. Look straight up, just below the throne of God. There is the figure of King David, that famous king and warrior of whom we read in the Scriptures. He gave the Philistines hell and even killed

207

a lion. Anyway, there he is in the sky, sitting on a cloud of stars. The Greeks call him Herakles and the Romans know him as Hercules. This pagan half-god was supposed to have killed a lion and he is pictured with the skin of a lion over his shoulders."

"So, both killed a lion. What must I notice about David?"

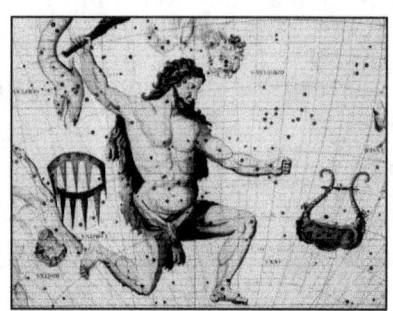

The constellation of Hercules with Corona Borealis (the Northern Crown) from 'Atlas Coelestis', by John Flamsteed, 1729.

"He is holding a sickle, one of those with which you were reaping wheat the whole week. I see in him 'a son of Man' – the title the prophet Daniel gave to the future figure of the Messiah and which Jesus used for himself, according to the stories I have gathered about him."

"So, you think David is actually representing Christ?"

"Spot-on. You have it. Good for you. Jesus was his descendant and he was also the king of the Jews. That's what Pontius Pilate called him, quite correctly, I must say. With his sickle, he is gathering the harvest of the souls of those who belong to God. That will happen on Judgment Day. Look carefully, there you can see his crown, next to him. The Greeks call it the 'Northern Crown'."[138]

"And that makes him a king?"

"Dead right. Perfect. I must agree. David was the greatest king of Israel. Everybody knows that. Jesus is the King of kings."

It is notable that there are superficial similarities between Jesus Christ and Hercules (Greek: Ἡρακλῆς– *Herakles*). Jesus was the

---

[138] The Hebrew name for Corona Borealis: עֲטָרוֹת *(Ataroth)*, which means "Crowns".

son of God, the Father, Creator of heaven and earth and the Virgin Mary. Hercules, the Greco-Roman hero and strongman, was the son of Zeus, the father of the Greek pantheon, and the virgin Alkmene, the granddaughter of Perseus.[139]

"Do you see that full moon, there on the eastern horizon?"

"Yes, I certainly do. I'm not blind or drunk or something. What about him? What is his task?"

"The moon is not a 'he', but a 'she'. You have had too much wine that messes with your mind. Anyway, that moon is an angel that calls upon the figure of Christ to carry on with the harvest with his sickle."

"I think my mind is clear enough. It's only my foot that is hurting. Anything else?"

A well-preserved ancient Roman sickle; its handle was probably covered by rope or leather straps for a better grip."

"Yes, of course. What do you think? Look at the west. There, hovering on the horizon and with the last rays of the sun behind her, you see the planet Mercury, also known as Hermes, the messenger of the Greek and Roman gods. He is calling on the Farmer or Ploughman with his sickle to tackle the grape harvest. I also think he's in charge of the fire on the altar – the very, very last rays of the sun behind the western horizon."

"And where is this Farmer, if I may ask?"

---

[139] Enc Brit, "Herakles".

"Just next to David. He also holds a sickle in his right hand. He is the representative of all the faithful who will help Christ to gather the harvest and assist him on Judgment Day."

"What is he harvesting? Also the wheat?"

"No. He cuts the bunches of grapes from the vineyard with his sharp sickle, as I was doing the whole week."

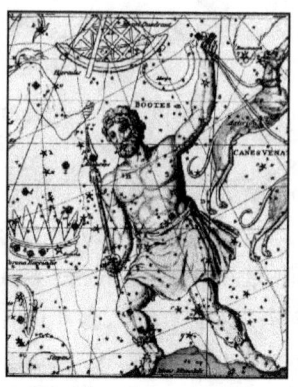

Boötes (the Ploughman) with a sickle in his hand, from the Celestial Atlas by Andrew Jamieson (1822).

"And you also helped with the wine press, where the grapes were crushed to collect the juice in a big bowl."

"Yes, you do remember correctly, even if you mind is foggy and your foot is hurting. That bowl is also there in the sky. The constellation of Crater, the Chalice. It is just disappearing in the west."

"And you were so over-eager that you splashed some of that grape juice onto one of the cart horses. You messed up his bridle."

"That's because this work is new to me and I didn't know how much force to use."

"That was why he trampled on this foot of mine. You can't blame him. Can you remember any parts of our Scriptures that tell us something of a wheat harvest and a grape harvest? And Judgment Day, as well?"

"Certainly. My mind is still clear enough that I can recollect something. The idea that Judgment Day can be compared to a harvest comes from Jeremiah. Let me recite to you two passages:

'For thus says the Lord of hosts, the God of Israel: The daughter of Babylon is like a threshing floor at the time when it is trodden; yet a little while, and the time of harvest shall come for her."[140] And –

"The stream of grape juice or blood that came from the wine press, comes from Isaiah. This is how he reported God's words: 'I have trodden the winepress alone; and of the peoples there was no man with me: yes, I trod them in my anger, and trampled them in my wrath; and their lifeblood is sprinkled on my garments, and I have stained all my clothing.'"[141]

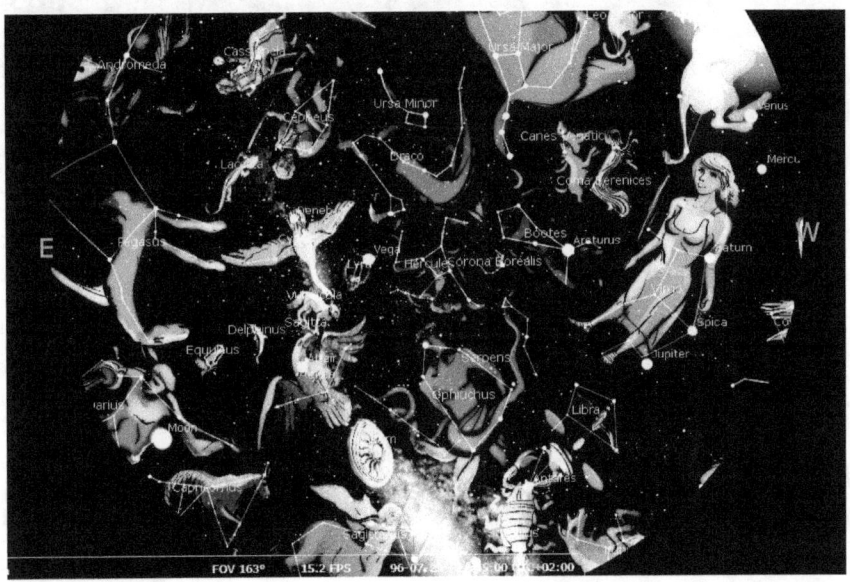

The constellations of Hercules, Coma Berenices (the Hair of Berenice) and Boötes (the Ploughman) with the sickle in his hand, appear in the middle of the sky. Hercules is situated next to the star clouds of the Milky Way. The full moon is rising in the south-east inside Aquarius and Mercury is in the west. The last rays of the sun are behind the horizon. Scutum (the Shield) lies in the south and on the western horizon, Crater (the Chalice) is disappearing on 23 July AD 96.

---

[140] Jer 51: 33.
[141] Isa 63: 3.

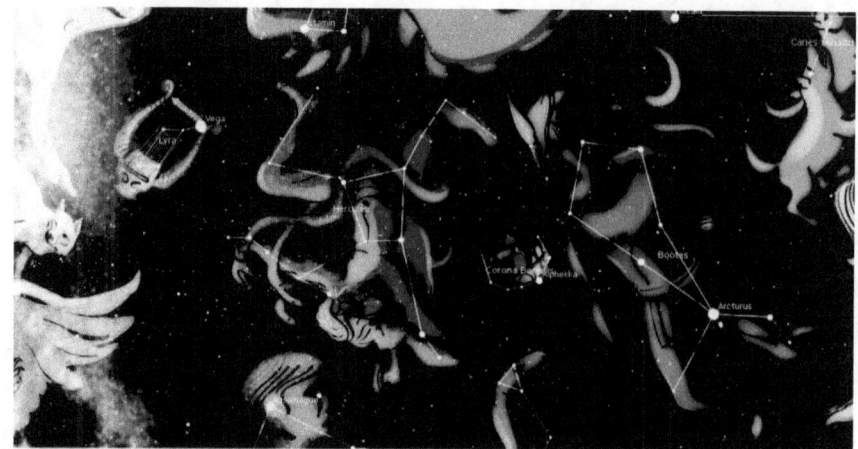

A close-up view of Hercules, Corona Borealis (the Northern Crown) and Boötes (the Ploughman) with a sickle in his hand. Hercules is not far from the star clouds of the Milky Way.

"You must have a wonderful memory. Remarkable. Did all that wine help you to remember better?"

"Ha-ha. That's not all. Listen to this prophecy in Joel:

'Put in the sickle; for the harvest is ripe. Come, tread, for the winepress is full, the vats overflow, for their wickedness is great'."[142]

"Really remarkable. Truly remarkable."

"I can also see the horses you mentioned. There, to the east, you can two horses: the Horse of Nimrod and its Foal. There, in the south, you can see another horseman, the Archer.[143] Which one trod on your foot, do you think?"

"I can't quite remember. It happened too fast. It was anyway the one whose bridle you messed up by splashing grape juice over him."

---

[142] Joel 3: 13.

[143] The constellations of Pegasus, Equuleus, and Sagittarius.

"Now, my friend, we must get going again. We must get some sleep and tomorrow, after I have spoken to our little flock and we have taught them a new song, I will then tell you what to write down."

This is what I will dictate to him:

Revelation 14: 14–20
The harvest of the earth

14.	I looked, and behold, a white cloud; and on the cloud one sitting like a son of man, having on his head a golden crown, and in his hand a sharp sickle.
15.	Another angel came out from the temple, crying with a loud voice to him who sat on the cloud, "Send forth your sickle, and reap; for the hour to reap has come; for the harvest of the earth is ripe!"
16.	He who sat on the cloud thrust his sickle on the earth, and the earth was reaped.
17.	Another angel came out from the temple which is in heaven. He also had a sharp sickle.
18.	Another angel came out from the altar, he who has power over fire, and he called with a great voice to him who had the sharp sickle, saying, "Send forth your sharp sickle, and gather the clusters of the vine of the earth, for her grapes are fully ripe!"
19.	The angel thrust his sickle into the earth, and gathered the vintage of the earth, and threw it into the great winepress of the wrath of God.
20.	The winepress was trodden outside of the city, and blood came out from the winepress, even to the bridles of the horses, as far as one thousand six hundred stadia.

An ancient winepress found in Israel. The grapes were gathered in the pit with a diameter of 5 meters where they were crushed by the feet of the harvesters. The juice flowed into the hole in the bottom and from there through pipes into receptacles. John would have encountered a similar winepress on Patmos.

Sunday and Monday, 24–25 July AS 96

Prochorus felt under the weather the whole day. His head was throbbing and his painful and swollen foot prevented him from walking. He stayed inside the cave while I held a service for my little congregation outside and I explained to them the passages from the prophets that I recited last night to my friend. The result was that I had to prepare supper. I made a delicious broth with enough leaves of the happy weed in the hope that it will make Prochorus feel better. It certainly lifted my spirits and I walk down to Groikos on the east coast after supper while the world is illuminated by the rising full moon.

And now, I am sitting on a rock above Groikos Bay and I watch the eastern horizon where the moon is rising. The moonlight is reflected upon the tranquil waters of the sea. The water is so smooth that it looks like glass. It almost seems as if there is some fire below the water's surface.

The rising moon reflected on the tranquil waters of Groikos (Γρικος) Bay, Patmos, looking eastwards. The Island at the entrance to the bay is Tragonisi Island (Τραγονήσι). The reflection of the moon on the water gives the impression of a "sea of glass mixed with fire".

My eyes fall on the seven stars directly next to God's throne. They represent the seven angels of the seven churches in Asia. I decide that they must have an important task tonight. It seems as if they came out of the temple or the tabernacle next to them (which is actually the figure of King Cepheus, but the outlines of the stars in this constellation look like a building or a tent with a sloping roof).

While I look at the temple in the heavens, I cannot help to think back at the time when I served as a priest in the Jerusalem temple. That temple is no more after it was consumed by flames and went up in smoke, twenty-six years ago. I am grateful that I was able to have had that experience. It was something special. But that also prepared me for my present role – that of a Christian prophet.

I remember that I saw two figures last night who were involved with God's harvest – Jesus Christ and a figure representing all the faithful souls. Tonight's scene must have a connection with that. Directly below God's throne I spot one of the four living beings – the man, the Farmer or Ploughman. The only other living being visible is the Eagle, but he is too far away to play any role.

This man points at the seven prominent stars in the tail and body of the Great Bear[144], just behind God's throne. A voice inside me tells me that those stars must be seven golden bowls, similar in shape to the bowls from which we drank wine yesterday. Those bowls must contain God's wrath, his anger, his condemnation of all the sins on this fallen, idol-infested, and crime-ridden world.

A hymn that we often sang in Ephesus suddenly pops into my mind. It is a translation of a part of the Torah, written by Moses.[145] The choir that sings this hymn consists of the thousands of stars in the Milky Way. Their song must be part of the "music of

---

[144] The constellation of Ursa Major, the Great Bear, was also known by the Jews with this name. In Hebrew it is עַיִשׁ ('Ayish) and it appears in Job 38: 32.
[145] The words of this hymn seem to come from Ex 15 and Deut 32.

the spheres", which was mentioned to me by a Greek philosopher in Ephesus, many years ago. Those who sing must be the faithful who withstood the two beasts and they are clothed in white.

The Milky Way reminds me of smoke clouds that Isaiah saw surrounding God's throne.[146] I hope that Prochorus will be ready to take down my description of this scene tomorrow. After that, I will have to keep my eyes open to discover the seven bowls.

The sky over Patmos on the evening of 24 July AD 96, after sunset. The Milky Way stretches across the whole sky. Draco (called The Quiver by the Jews) and Ursa Major (the Great Bear) are visible next to the north celestial pole – God's throne – which is marked by the converging lines. Boötes (the Ploughman with a sickle in his hand), lies next to the seven stars in the tail of Draco and Ursa Major. The full moon (inside Aquarius) rises over the Aegean Sea in the east.

---

[146] Isa 6: 4.

I composed in my mind the passage that Prochorus will have to write tomorrow when he feels better. I keep on singing the hymn that got stuck in my memory while I return to the cave and my bed.

Revelation 15: 1–8
Seven angels with seven plagues

1. I saw another great and marvellous sign in the sky: seven angels having the seven last plagues, for in them God's wrath is finished.

2. I saw something like a sea of glass mixed with fire. Those who overcame the beast, and his image, and the number of his name, standing on the sea of glass, having harps of God.

3. They sang the song of Moses, the servant of God, and the song of the Lamb, saying, "Great and marvelous are your works, Lord God, the Almighty; Righteous and true are your ways, you King of the nations.

4. Who wouldn't fear you, Lord, and glorify your name? For you only are holy. For all the nations will come and worship before you. For your righteous acts have been revealed."

5. After these things I looked, and the temple of the tent of the testimony in heaven was opened.

6. The seven angels who had the seven plagues came out from the temple, clothed with pure, bright linen, and wearing golden sashes around their breasts.

7. One of the four living creatures gave to the seven angels seven golden bowls full of the wrath of God, who lives forever and ever.

8. The temple was filled with smoke from the glory of God, and from his power. No one was able to enter into the temple,

until the seven plagues of the seven angels would be finished.

Monday, 8 August AD 96

Yesterday, Sunday, was a very eventful day and also not a pleasant day. We started off with our Sonday service just after dawn, before the activities of the day started.

When Ajax and Argus arrived, they asked me to say a special prayer of thanks that the wheat harvest and the grape harvest proceeded so well. They regard themselves as very blessed because the plague of locusts didn't reach their farm. These beasts only landed in the parts around our cave and the villages surrounding us, like Groikos village and Sapsila Village on the coast.

Directly after we have sung our last hymn, a loud bang was heard, like a thunder flash, only louder.

Argus: "That must be the voice of God, responding to our hymns and prayers."

I reply: "You may be right. But it may also be God expressing his anger about all the iniquity and insolence and insanity of the people in this world."

Andrew was still leading his sheep away when somebody from the village of Sapsila came to me. He asked: "Are you the healer, the medicine man?"

"Some people call me that."

"I would like you to look at me. I have these sores all over my neck and head. Can you do something about them, please?"

"Perhaps. Sit here and I will fetch something to try on you."

After about half-an-hour I returned with my sharp pointed knife, which George has given me. I heated it over the flames of the fire in our cave so that it glowed red. I also boiled some water in a bowl and dipped a cloth into the hot water. With the hot knife I punctured little holes in the boils. A yellow fluid seeped out. I wipe that off with the hot wet cloth. After I had treated all the boils in this

220

manner, I got another clean cloth, which I also immerse in the boiling water. I wrapped that, together with some leaves of the happy weed, around the neck and head of the suffering man.

"Keep that cloth around your neck and head till tonight and then you bring that cloth back to me tomorrow."

The man, whose name is Dimitrios, informed me: "There are many people down there at Sapsila and Groikos who suffer with sores like this."

"Do you think that I should go and help them?"

"I don't think that's a good idea. They won't allow you to touch them. They are angry at your God for causing all these troubles. They may even tear your clothes off your body and you will have to flee naked."

"What troubles?"

"Don't you smell all the rotting fish on the beach? I can smell them here where I sit. The sea water became red, almost like blood. That killed off all the fish. People who tried to gather the fish carcasses to dump them somewhere, got these boils."

To Prochorus I said: "That must be the first two bowls with God's anger and vengeance that were thrown upon the earth. Boils and bloody sea water. We can expect five more of them."

Prochorus: "Really remarkable. That must be due to all that smoke and ash still pouring from that gaping throat of Hades."

Andrew came back with his sheep and tells me: "My sheep won't drink the water in the pond over there. That water is poisonous."

Prochorus: "That also happened with the sea water. All the fish died and are rotting on the beach."

I added: "Stay away from the beach because that rotting fish made people sick. They got horrible boils from that mess."

221

Andrew: "That's because they refused to believe in Jesus. Now God is tormenting them. It's their punishment. We must empty our pools and reservoirs of this poisonous water. Let's pray to God to send u some rain with fresh water for ourselves and my animals."

Fortunately, the wind died down later during the day and the smoke and dust from Hades didn't fall down on us anymore. But then it became very, very hot and the sun scorched the earth. The coolest place was inside our cave. We were very grateful that the harvest was over and that we didn't need to work in this heat. Fortunately, we still had some fresh water with us and we decided not to use the water from the pools and reservoirs that got dirty from all the ash and dust from hell.

We decided that the dirty water and this hot sun must be the third and fourth bowls with God's fury and rage that the angels threw down onto the earth. This is also, as it were, a cloak repetition of Judgment Day. This must serve as a warning to the people to mend their ways, just as the prophet Jonah warned the wicked and worthless and wayward people of Nineveh to turn to God and get rid of their crimes and cruel habits.

When the sun settled in the west, I told my friend: "There are still three more bowls left. I wonder when they will be poured out."

"Perhaps tonight."

And now, today, both of us are sitting outside the cave on our usual rocks to watch the skies. The thirsty and restless sheep in the cave made sleep difficult and we fled the cave long before dawn arrived.

As usual, I look up into the heaven to see whether God is sending me any messages. I notice that the beast from the sea in the southern sky, which represents the emperor in Rome, is partly obscured by the smoke and vapors coming out of the throat of Hades.

I tell my companion: "Do you see how that sea monster is being obscured? I am convinced God is telling me that this is the fifth bowel of his anger and that He will make that monster vanish. His days are numbered. He will be gone, one of these days."

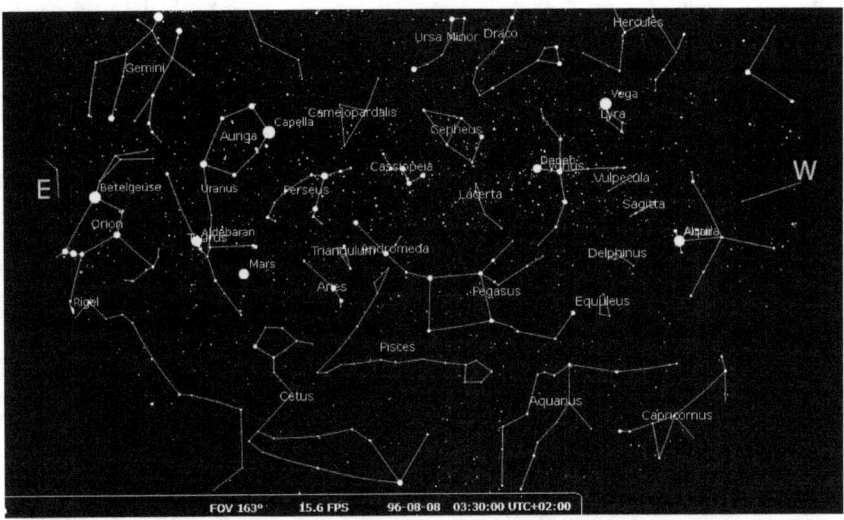

The sky over Patmos during August AD 96 with the constellations of Cetus (the Sea Monster), and Eridanus (the Celestial River) to its left, on the south-eastern horizon before sunrise. Capricornus (the Goat and monster from the earth) lies in the south-west. The three stars in the belt of Orion (the Hunter) are rising in the east; they are the kings who were preparing for war against the Lamb (Aries) at Armageddon – the red planet Mars, lying between Orion and Aries.

Prochorus: "He's not the only one who faces a bleak future. Andrew's wife told me that many people in Groikos and elsewhere are suffering terribly will all these painful boils and sores."

"That is also God's work."

"And they are very angry at God. They swear and blow blasphemies and proclaim profanities."

I continue watching the sky and I spot the long river, called Eridanus by the Greeks, but which the Jews call the Euphrates – the river that irrigated the Garden of Eden, but also the river in Babylonia where the Jews spent some decades in exile – just as I am also in exile at this moment. This river lies on the south-eastern horizon.

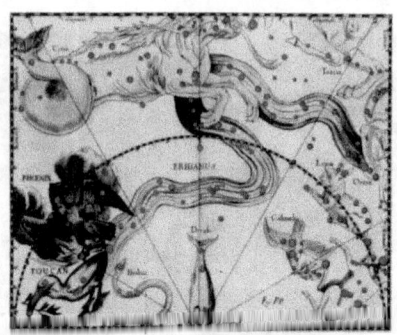

Eridanus, the celestial river, together with a part of Cetus, the sea monster, from an old star atlas by Hevelius.

The hot summer sun of yester-day, which dried up most of our fresh water supplies, gives me the idea that this river has also dried up. That enables the kings of the east to advance and attack the children of God. These kings must be the three promi-nent stars in the belt of Nimrod, the ancient Hunter or Warrior of whom we read in the books of Moses.[147]

The red planet, Mars, catches my eye. He is inside the constellation of the Bull, one of the four living creatures that surround God's throne. As the pagan god of war, he has the color of blood. I am convinced that these kings from the east are on their way to wage war against the saints, who are to be found in the Milky Way. It is also noticeable that the Lamb of God, in the guise of Aries, the Ram, lies directly next to the Bull and the planet Mars. He must be the ultimate target of these kings from the east. I wonder where this battle will take place.

I describe my observations to Prochorus. He tries to help me: "You told me you saw those Roman legions on their way to attack Jerusalem, many years ago. Where, exactly, did you see them?"

---

[147] The constellation of Orion.

"Ah, thank you! I saw them when I was overlooking the plain of Jezreel, at Megiddo, where King Salomon kept his war horses and chariots. I was standing on the mountain next to Megiddo in Galilee. That plain was the scene of many battles between the Israelites and their foes.[148] You must be right, that is where this fierce battle between the forces of evil and God's angels must take place – at the mountain of Megiddo, or Armageddon in Greek."[149]

The same scene as the previous illustration, only with the pictures of the various constellations added. Cetus (the Sea Monster) and part of Eridanus (the Celestial River) to its left lay on the south-eastern horizon during August AD 96, in the early morning. Capricornus (the Goat and the monster from the earth) is in the south-west. The three frog-like figures are the two fishes in the constellation of Pisces and the constellation of Delphinus (the Dolphin). The three stars on the belt of Orion are the kings from the east and they are preparing for a battle at Armageddon, the spot occupied by the red planet Mars, lying between Orion and Aries (the Ram or Lamb).

---

[148] Josh 12: 21; Judges 5: 19; 2' Kings 23: 29–30; Zechariah 12: 11.
[149] The name Armageddon is a transliteration of *Har-Magedon* (Greek: 'Αρμαγεδών; Hebrew: הַר מְגִדּוֹן) and it means mountain or hill of Megiddo.

"That will certainly be a bloody, brutal, and barbaric battle. You mentioned the beast from the sea. Is his friend, the beast from the earth, the False Prophet, also in attendance?"

"Yes, I see both of them. Both are spitting out damned demons. I would describe these demons as filthy frogs, although they are actually fishes in the sky. The constellations of the two Fishes and the Dolphin are clearly coming from the beaks of these monsters."

"What are these demons supposed to do?"

"They are the hidden allies of those kings from the east. Their task is to stab the Lamb in the back."

"But I suppose the Lamb will be ready for them?"

"Oh, certainly, of course. We know Jesus Christ will come like a thief during the night, very unexpectedly, and he will crush his enemies swiftly and securely. We must be ready for that day – not like a man who had to flee from his house without any clothes when floods or other disasters overtook him."

Andrew appears at dawn to look after his sheep: "Let's hope it will rain today and will provide some fresh water for these poor thirsty animals."

Prochorus reminds me during the day: "Master, I can clearly remember that you predicted that these woes and calamities and disasters would endure five months when they started. That was four months ago. Do you think that we must be ready for these things for another month?"

"That's quite possible. Even likely. Some of these signs from heaven are a repetition of the horrors that befell us when those seven angry angels sounded their thunderous trumpets at that stage."

"Master, who could ever foresee the horrible events we are experiencing during your stay here on this little Island?"

226

"You are correct. But I can see God's plan. He is righteous and fair. He sent me here at specifically this time, with all these horrors and hellish nightmares, so that I could receive some important messages that have to be passed on to the faithful in Ephesus and elsewhere. He also wants me to warn the pagans to destroy their idols and listen to the Gospel. Therefore, my friend, go fetch your papyrus, ink, and pen. I will tell you what to write about the first six bowls, filled with God's judgments."

Revelation 16: 1–16

The seven bowls of God's anger

1.	I heard a loud voice out of the temple, saying to the seven angels, "Go and pour out the seven bowls of the wrath of God on the earth!"
2.	The first went, and poured out his bowl into the earth, and it became a harmful and evil sore on the men that had the mark of the beast, and that worshipped his image.
3.	The second angel poured out his bowl into the sea, and it became blood as of a dead man. Every living thing in the sea died.
4.	The third poured out his bowl into the rivers and springs of water, and it became blood.
5.	I heard the angel of the waters saying, "You are righteous, who are and who were, you Holy One, because you judged this way.
6.	For they poured out the blood of the saints and the prophets, and you have given them blood to drink. They deserve this."

7. I heard the altar saying, "Yes, Lord God, the Almighty, true and righteous are your judgments."

8. The fourth poured out his bowl on the sun, and it was given to him to scorch men with fire.

9. Men were scorched with great heat, and they blasphemed the name of God who has the power over these plagues. They didn't repent and give him glory.

10. The fifth poured out his bowl on the throne of the beast, and his kingdom was darkened. They gnawed their tongues because of the pain,

11. and they blasphemed the God of heaven because of their pains and their sores. They didn't repent of their works.

12. The sixth poured out his bowl on the great river, the Euphrates. Its water was dried up, that the way might be made ready for the kings that come from the sunrise.

13. I saw coming out of the mouth of the beast, and out of the mouth of the false prophet, three unclean spirits, something like frogs;

14. for they are spirits of demons, performing signs; which go forth to the kings of the whole world, to gather them together for the war of the great day of God, the Almighty.

15. "Behold, I come like a thief. Blessed is he who watches, and keeps his clothes, so that he doesn't walk naked, and they see his shame."

16. He gathered them together into the place which is called in Hebrew, "Har-magedon."

Wednesday and Thursday, 10–11 August AD 96

Around midday, a huge thunder storm starts and torrents of rain pour down onto the earth out of God's heaven. We are relieved that God has sent some relief and we sing a hymn in praise of God. I am sure that the angels in heaven are singing along with us.

The rain is so heavy that we can't see very far. The small islands outside Groikos Bay and all the hills around the bay become invisible. But while we are still singing, a gigantic earthquake is felt. It causes rocks to loosen from the hills, especially where the earth is soft and soggy from the rain. These boulders roll down onto the villages below and we can hear how some houses are destroyed and demolished. The earthquake must also have collapsed and crushed some of them. We can even hear how people howl and cry.

To top everything, huge hail stones rain down upon us and we decide that they must have been thrown from those gaping jaws of Hades. The devil must be vomiting these lumps to show his bad temper and his defiance against God who sent us the rain.

This thunderstorm, together with the earthquake, must be the seventh and final bowl of God's anger.

My companion asks me: "Master, do you agree with me that these calamities, cataclysms, and catastrophes are a replay of the ten Egyptian plagues?"

"My good friend, you make a very valid point. Yes, let me quote to you a passage from the Scriptures:

"Moses stretched forth his rod toward the heavens, and the Lord sent thunder, hail, and lightning flashed down to the earth. The Lord rained hail on the land of Egypt. So there was very severe hail, and lightning mixed with the hail, such as had not been in all the land of Egypt since it became a nation. The hail struck throughout all the land of Egypt all

229

that was in the field, both man and animal; and the hail struck every herb of the field, and broke every tree of the field."[150]

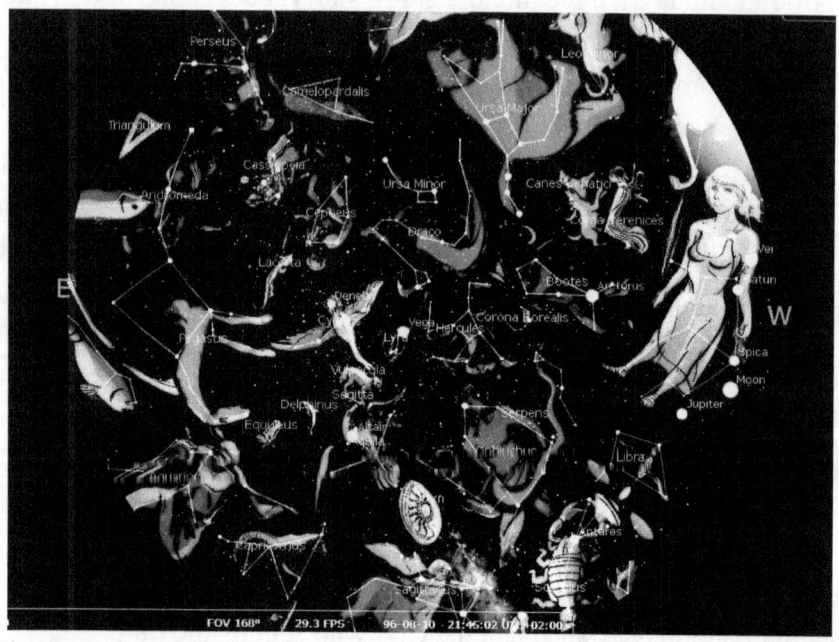

The starry sky over Patmos, on 10 August AD 96, after sunset. Virgo, the Virgin (Babylon), is seen towards the west. The moon, with 15% of its surface illuminated, lies next to Virgo, together with Venus, Saturn, and Jupiter. Ursa Minor represents the throne of God in the temple.

I continue: "These afflictions and adversities were sent to warn the pagans of our time to get rid of their idolatry and to accept Christ. God sent all those plagues on the ancient Egyptians to warn them."

After supper, the two of us sit outside the cave to give the sheep some time to get settled and fall asleep. I watch the sky for a message and my eyes fall again on the Virgin, whom I saw in the past as the woman or bride of God and who delivered the Messiah, Jesus Christ.

---

[150] Ex 9: 23–25.

But then it dawns upon me that this woman, who symbolized the city of God, actually became untrue to God. I notice that the planet called Venus by the Romans is closely associated with this woman. The Jews know this planet as the "she star", while the Greeks call her Aphrodite. The Canaanites called her Astarte and the Egyptians know her as Isis. This pagan goddess is the personification of lust, sexual desire, procreation, and sensual love.

The people of Israel, and especially Jerusalem, rejected Jesus as their Messiah and called for his crucifixion. With that, this woman must have transformed herself into something akin to the most evil city in the whole world, namely Babylon.

This thought makes me sad, because the real Jerusalem was indeed destroyed. God's wrath has descended upon this place. I see the cup filled with God's verdict and vengeance – one of the stars next to God's throne.

We return to the cave. I tell my companion: "Light your lamp. I have a few sentences for you to write down. This storm was so bad that I must describe it in the strongest terms possible. It reminded me of Judgment Day that is still to come.

Revelation 16: 17–21

The seventh bowl

17.	The seventh angel poured out his bowl into the air. A loud voice came forth out of the temple, from the throne, saying, "It is done!"
18.	There were lightnings, sounds, and thunders; and there was a great earthquake, such as was not since there were men on the earth, so great an earthquake, so mighty.
19.	The great city was divided into three parts, and the cities of the nations fell. Babylon the great was remembered in the sight of God, to give to her the cup of the wine of the fierceness of his wrath.

> 20.   Every island fled away, and the mountains were not found.
>
> 21.   Great hailstones, about the weight of a talent, came down out of the sky on men. Men blasphemed God because of the plague of the hail, for the plague of it is exceeding great.

It proved impossible to sleep after I had dictated this passage to Prochorus and silently I creep out of the cave again. I want to watch that adulterous woman once more. Her immorality is something I struggle to understand and I wait for guidance from heaven to fully understand the scene.

The seventh angel in front of God's throne, who threw out the seventh bowl of God's wrath, tells me that I must have another good look at the constellation of the Virgin, which is a representation of the people of Israel and to keep in mind how the city of Jerusalem was a few decades ago, before the war with Rome.

I do as I am told and watch the sky with interest. I notice again how the planet of Venus or Aphrodite is associated with this woman and I find this association mind-boggling. After all, a few weeks ago it was revealed to me that this woman symbolized the people of Israel, the people from whom the Messiah was born. The Messiah, Jesus Christ, was represented by the planet Jupiter at her feet. This woman also stood on the moon.

A red dragon, Satan, the constellation of the Scorpion, wanted to devour the child born from this woman. She was given the wings of an eagle and she fled to the wilderness. The Archangel Michael, in the form of Serpentarius, the Serpent Catcher, trampled upon the Scorpion and kicked him out of heaven. That was when Satan was banished to the abyss, as Enoch reported.

But now, the scene has changed. This woman does no longer represent the faithful people or the city of God, but became the exact opposite. Instead of being God's bride, she changed herself into a

232

prostitute. The association with Venus or Aphrodite demonstrates that switch. Jerusalem was, after all, the scene of the execution of Jesus, the Messiah, the Lamb of God.

The fact that the planet Saturn is inside Virgo is a confirmation that this constellation must be identified with Israel and Jerusalem. Saturn was always associated with Israel since the Jews celebrate Saturday, the day connected to Saturn (the seventh planet), as their Sabbath or holy day. The Hebrew name for Saturn is Shabtay and it is related to the word for Saturday or the Sabbath.[151]

This woman is near the western horizon, just above the waters of the Aegean Sea. Those waters represent the unruly, unholy, and ungodly pagan peoples of the earth, where this whore will feel at home.

She is dressed as a harlot with lots of jewels – the planets of Jupiter, Saturn, and Venus on her body. Her crown, with twelve stars, consists of the nearby Hair of Berenice. She wears a scarlet cloak – the last rays of the sun after it had disappeared behind the horizon.

And now this prostitute has made friends with the red or scarlet Dragon, Satan himself. This Dragon has seven heads and ten horns – a terrifying and appalling apparition. I imagine him as having blasphemous and scandalous names written all over him. It is hard for me to comprehend how this came about. In the Scriptures, the people of Israel were often accused of prostitution when they served pagan gods and forgot their special relationship with their God.[152]

The woman is holding a golden cup full of abominations, the crescent moon next to her. The name Babylon must be given to this woman. This name occurs more than once in the Scriptures. Moses

---

[151] Stieglitz, "The Hebrew Names", 135–37; Zucker, "Hebrew Names"304.
[152] Is 57: 3; Nah 3: 4-5

wrote about the Tower of Babel (Babylon) as a sign of man's rebellion against God.[153] Babylon was also the place where the Judeans were taken into exile after Jerusalem had been destroyed by the Babylonians.

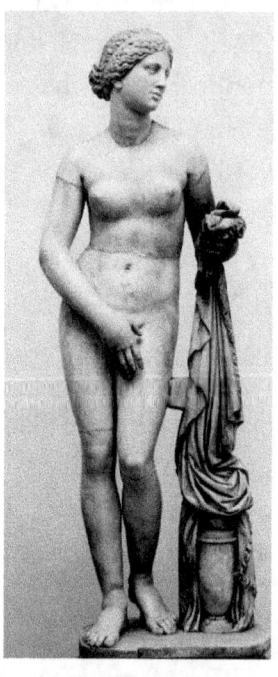

'Αφροδίτη (*Aphrodite*) – the goddess of love, lust, passion, pleasure, beauty, and sexuality. The Ludovisi Cnidian Aphrodite, Roman marble copy (torso and thighs) with restored head, arms, legs, and drapery support

The insight is given to me that the seven heads of the scarlet animal, on which the woman sits, must be seen as seven mountains. It is well-known that the city of Rome is built on seven hills and that means that the red dragon must also be regarded as the city of Rome, the capital of Satan's empire and the seat of the emperor.

In addition, the seven heads of the beast are also seven kings

who rule in the city of Rome – in other words, the Roman emperors. Of these seven kings, five had fallen, while one was still ruling and

---

[153] Genesis 11.

234

another one still had to come as seen from the time before the fall of Jerusalem. The whore is in league with these kings. I believe that an eighth king will appear later tonight, the beast from the sea that I have seen in the past – one who ruled after the fall of Jerusalem.

John saw that seven kings (or emperors; Greek used the same word for "king" and "emperor", namely βασιλεύς – *basileus*).), while the beast from the sea was an eighth king, yet he was also one of the seven. That meant that the eighth emperor had family ties with some of the previous emperors The list of Roman emperors until the time of John is as follows:

1. Augustus (reigned: 27 BC – AD 14)
2. Tiberius (AD 14–37)
3. Caligula (AD 37–41)
4. Claudius (AD 41–54)
5. Nero (AD 54–68)
6. Vespasian (AD 69–79) – he commanded the Roman army at the start of the Jewish War, but became emperor after the death of Nero;
7. Titus (AD 79–81) – he succeeded his father, Vespasian, as commander of the Roman army during the Jewish War and became emperor after Vespasian's death;
8. Domitian (AD 81–96) – another son of Vespasian.[154]

The close association between the woman and the scarlet beast suggests a close relationship or alliance between the ruling class in Jerusalem and the emperors who resided in Rome. The Sadducees, whom we often encounter in the Gospels, were the Jewish elite during the first century AD, consisting mostly of the priestly families

---

[154] Enc Britt, "Roman Empire".

and rich merchants. They were disliked by the common folk due to their haughty and superior attitude, but they managed to entertain cordial relationship with the Roman authorities.[155]

The angel tells me, in addition, that the ten horns of the scarlet beast are also ten kings who committed sexual immorality with the harlot – and they are the ten kings from the House of Herod. They were not real kings and they only ruled with the permission of the Romans. Most of them only ruled for a short time and none of them have survived to the present time.

The angel reminds me that the beast with ten horns is also mentioned in the book of Daniel[156] –

"As for the ten horns, out of this kingdom shall ten kings arise: and another shall arise after them; and he shall be diverse from the former, and he shall put down three kings."

These ten horns or kings are to be found in the constellation of Libra, the Scales or Balance, directly to the west of Scorpius.

The members of the house of Herod who ruled various parts of Palestine during the time of the New Testament on behalf of the Roman Empire were as follows:

1. Antipater the Idumaean (procurator of Judaea) 47–44 BC
2. Herod the Great (governor of Galilee 47–44 BC; tetrarch of Galilee 44–40 BC; appointed as king of all Judaea by the Roman Senate 40 BC, reigned 37–4 BC) – son of Antipater and mentioned in Matt 2

---

[155] Encyclopaedia Britannica, "Sadducee".
[156] Dan 7: 24

3. Pheroras (governor of Perea) 20–5 BC – brother of Herod the Great

4. Phasael (governor of Jerusalem) 47–40 BC – brother of Herod the Great

5. Herod Archelaus (ethnarch of Judaea) 4 BC–AD 6 – son of Herod the Great and mentioned in Matt 2: 22

6. Herod Antipas (tetrarch of Galilee) 4 BC–AD 39 – son of Herod the Great and mentioned in Mark 6: 7–28, Luke 13: 2, and Luke 23: 7–11

7. Herod Philip (tetrarch of Batanaea and Iturea) 4 BC–AD 34 – son of Herod the Great and mentioned in Mark 6: 17

8. Herod Agrippa I (king of Batanaea AD 37–41; king of Galilee AD 40–41; king of all Judaea AD 41–44) – grandson of Herod the Great and son of Antipater, son of Herod the Great who was executed by his father, and mentioned in Acts 4: 27 and 12: 1

9. Herod of Chalcis (king of Chalcis and Judea) AD 41–48 – grandson of Herod the Great

10. Herod Agrippa II (tetrarch of Chalcis AD 48–53; king of Chalcis and Trachonitis AD 53-93) – son of Herod Agrippa I and mentioned in Acts 25: 13

No member of the house of Herod was ever popular with the Jews and they were all seen as allies of the Roman oppressors. The Jews never accepted them as fellow Jews, due to their Idumean (Arab) descent and their support of the Roman army during the war of AD 66–70. The last member of the house of Herod to occupy a throne,

Herod Agrippa II, died a few years before John was banished to Patmos. Since they were not acknowledged by the Jews as kings, yet enjoyed royal status, it can be said that they "have received no kingdom as yet, but they receive authority as kings, with the beast, for one hour.

> Their collaboration with the priestly class in Jerusalem, their exploitation of the Jews and their friendship with Rome amounted in the eyes of John to "sexual immorality" with the prostitute.

It is clear to me that, in the end, these ten kings and the beast would wage war against the prostitute and they will hate her, and burn her utterly with fire. This is exactly what happened when Judea was conquered and Jerusalem was destroyed by fire by the Roman army during the Jewish war of twenty-six years ago, a war in which the remaining members of the House of Herod were allied with Rome.

There is no doubt in me that the red dragon, together with the seven Roman emperors, and the ten kings from the House of Herod, also waged war against Christ, the Lamb. Christ is represented in the sky by the figure of King David, known to the Greeks and the Romans as Herakles or Hercules. He is the King of Kings with the Northern Crown[157] next to him. I can see this royal figure just below the throne of God with the arc of seven angels in front of the throne.

All these insights disturb me to such an extent that I stay sitting on my rock till after midnight. I see again the beast from the sea, rising in the south-east, the monster which I previously identified as the Antichrist and as the present Roman emperor. This wretch is coming out of the abyss, the direction from which the flames and glowing stars were shot out into the sky a few weeks ago. He must be characterized as one who wasn't yet on the throne in Rome at the time when Jerusalem was destroyed, although he was alive at that time and only became emperor after the death of his

---

[157] The ancient Hebrew name for this constellation was עֲטָרוֹת (Ataroth – Crowns).

brother, Titus, who died without a son. [158]

The conviction takes hold of me that God will cause the downfall and death of this evil emperor who persecutes the followers of Jesus and whose image I refused to worship, which led to my banishment to this island.

It becomes very chilly and a cold wind starts blowing. That forces me to return to the cave and creep into my bed. It is impossible to switch my thoughts off and I start to compose in my mind the vision I will dictate to Prochorus tomorrow when the sun is shining again.

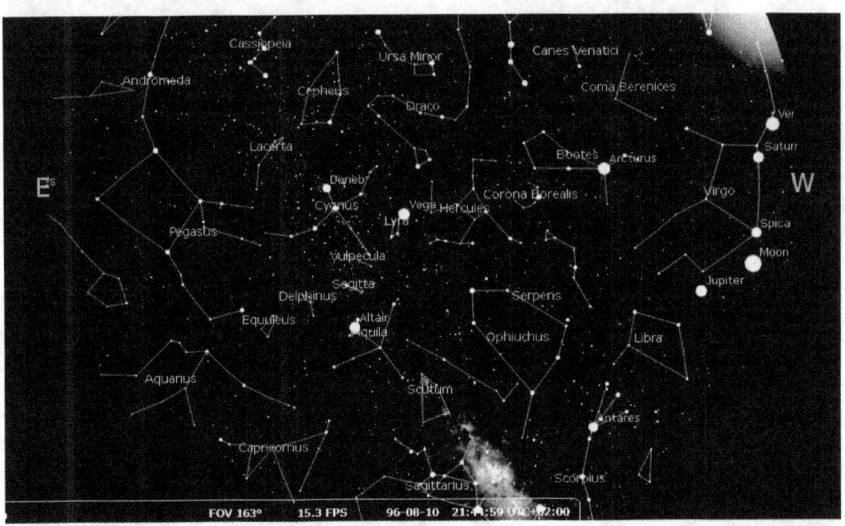

Virgo (the Virgin, but actually the whore) was setting in the west with the planets Venus, Jupiter, and Saturn and a crescent moon (15% of its surface illuminated) inside its borders. Coma Berenices (the Crown or Hair of Berenice) lies next to Virgo. Scorpius (the red beast) lies on the south-western horizon. Hercules and Corona Borealis lie just below God's throne.

While I lie and wait for dawn to arrive, I recite some passages from the Scriptures to myself, while I stay angry at the Jews who urged

---

[158] Enc Brit, "Titus".

the Roman authorities to crucify Jesus. I see that as adultery and prostitution since Israel was supposed to be God's beloved wife on earth. Isaiah declared:

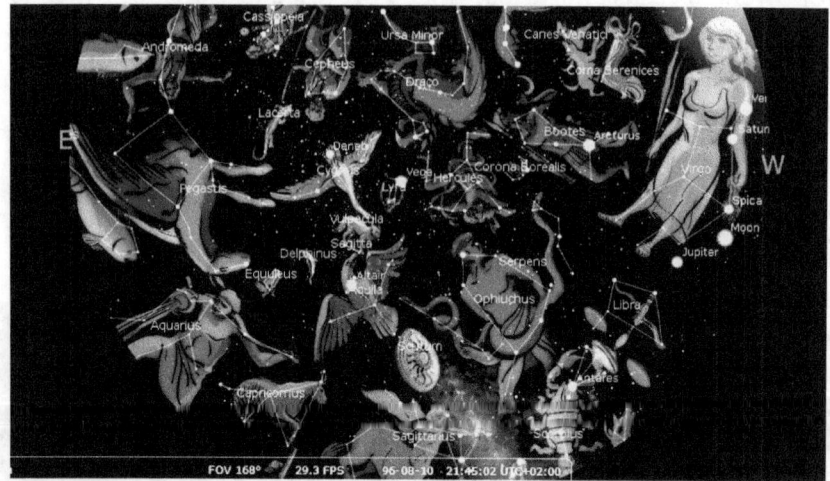

The same scene as the previous illustration, but with pictures of the personages, animals, and objects of the constellations added.

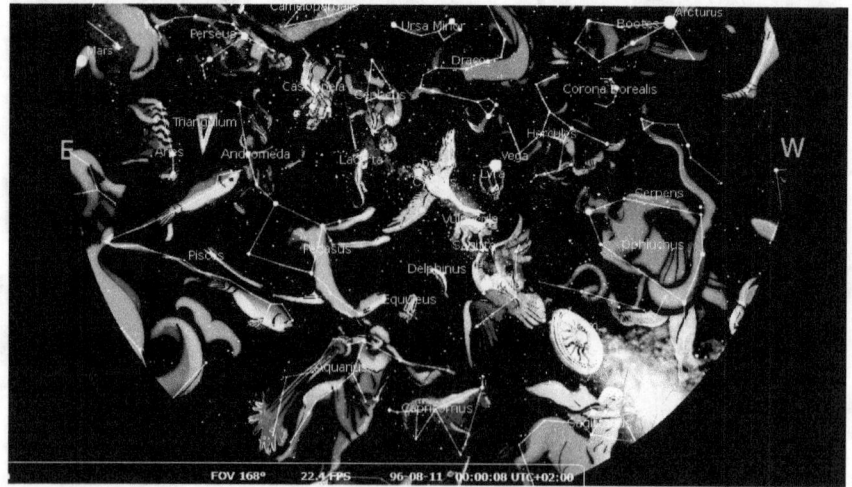

Cetus, the monster from the sea with seven stars in its head – the Antichrist – is rising in the south-east, the direction of the abyss (the volcano on Nisyros).

"For your Maker is your husband; the Lord of Hosts is his name: and the Holy One of Israel is your Redeemer; the God of the whole earth shall he be called. For the Lord has called you as a wife forsaken and grieved in spirit, even a wife of youth, when she is cast off, says your God."[159]

Israel was accused of prostitution more than once in the Scriptures when the people forgot their relationship with their God. Nahum also wrote:

"But draw near here, you sons of the sorceress, the seed of the adulterer and the prostitute."[160] The prophet Nahum called Israel "the alluring prostitute, the mistress of witchcraft, who sells nations through her prostitution, and families through her witchcraft."[161]

It is my recollection that Jerusalem or Babylon in the sky held a cup in her hand. That meant that she was getting drunk, together with the other enemies of God. The prophet Jeremiah said something similar about the real ancient Babylon:

"Babylon has been a golden cup in the Lord`s hand, who made all the earth drunken: the nations have drunk of her wine; therefore the nations are mad."[162]

After the sun has appeared and Andrew has led his flock out of the cave, I tell Prochorus: "Please get a clean piece of papyrus and write down my words. I will help you to prepare our breakfast after that.

---

[159] Isa 54: 5–6.
[160] Isa 57: 3.
[161] Nah 3: 4.
[162] Jer 71: 7.

Revelation 17
The Prostitute

1. One of the seven angels who had the seven bowls came and spoke with me, saying, "Come here. I will show you the judgment of the great prostitute who sits on many waters,

2. with whom the kings of the earth committed sexual immorality, and those who dwell in the earth were made drunken with the wine of her sexual immorality."

3. He carried me away in the Spirit into a wilderness. I saw a woman sitting on a scarlet-colored animal, full of blasphemous names, having seven heads and ten horns.

4. The woman was dressed in purple and scarlet, and decked with gold and precious stones and pearls, having in her hand a golden cup full of abominations, even the unclean things of her sexual immorality,

5. and on her forehead a name written, "MYSTERY, BABYLON THE GREAT, THE MOTHER OF THE PROSTITUTES AND OF THE ABOMINATIONS OF THE EARTH."

6. I saw the woman drunken with the blood of the saints, and with the blood of the martyrs of Jesus. When I saw her, I wondered with great amazement.

7. The angel said to me, "Why do you wonder? I will tell you the mystery of the woman, and of the beast that carries her, which has the seven heads and the ten horns.

8. The beast that you saw [previously] was, and is not; and is about to come up out of the abyss, and to go into destruction. Those who dwell on the earth will wonder, whose name has not been written in the book of life from the foundation of the world, when they see the beast, how that he was, and is not, and will come.

9.   Here is the mind that has wisdom. The seven heads are seven mountains, on which the woman sits.

10.   They are seven kings. Five have fallen, the one is, the other is not yet come. When he comes, he must continue a little while.

11.   The [other] beast that was, and is not, is himself also an eighth, and is of the seven; and he goes to destruction.

12.   The ten horns that you saw are ten kings, who have received no kingdom as yet, but they receive authority as kings, with the beast, for one hour.

13.   These have one mind, and they give their power and authority to the beast.

14.   These will war against the Lamb, and the Lamb will overcome them, for he is Lord of lords, and King of kings. They also will overcome who are with him, called and chosen and faithful."

15.   He said to me, "The waters which you saw, where the prostitute sits, are peoples, multitudes, nations, and languages.

16.   The ten horns which you saw, and the beast, these will hate the prostitute, and will make her desolate and naked, and will eat her flesh, and will burn her utterly with fire.

17.   For God has put in their hearts to do what he has in mind, and to come to unity of mind, and to give their kingdom to the beast, until the words of God should be accomplished.

18.   The woman whom you saw is the great city, which reigns over the kings of the earth."

Thursday, 11 August AD 96

During breakfast, Prochorus says: "We are now eating the last pieces of bread we have. We must go to Skala to buy some provisions with the money that Argus and Ajax gave us for all our hard work. It's market day today in Skala and it will be a good opportunity to buy whatever we need."

Me: "Will you be able to walk there with that sore foot of yours?"

"We have no choice. We can't sit here and starve to death."

"All right. Then we must get moving before the sun gets too hot. I am tired because I haven't slept last night, but I will manage."

It takes us quite some time to reach Skala because Prochorus struggles to walk and I feel weak and dizzy. We reach the house of Jason, the shopkeeper. George, his neighbor, is with him and we all greet each other with warm embraces.

George: "You found us just in time. We plan to visit the market square and the harbor today. But first, have some lunch."

There is much activity at the harbor where ships are being loaded and offloaded. The merchants of Patmos export amphoras with wine, wool, and marble blocks. The dock workers offload metal objects, foodstuffs, fish, wheat, carpets, and clothes.

Roman mosaic, depicting a ship with crew at work, from the domus in Diotallevi Palace at Rimini, Italy

We see many ship wrecks where they are stranded on the beaches after the gigantic wave that caused havoc on the fishing fleet of the island.

We purchase some fish imported from the mainland because the fish stocks around Patmos were decimated by the poisonous dust and ash blown out of Hades in the south.

The market is very busy with merchants and clients discussing and haggling over prices. We buy a bag of wheat for our bread, some cheese, olives, oil, and dried fruit.

In one corner, some slaves are being sold to the highest bidders. I don't like this practice, since I grew up in an Essene home and we never kept any slaves.

A group of musicians perform on a platform while a young boy walks around with a basket into which he collects money from the onlookers. The singer in the group sings naughty and uncouth songs and the crowd loves the group's performance. The money basket seems to get filled easily.

Roman Mosaic of Musicians, Pompeii, Italy (Naples Museum, Italy).

Jason warns us: "Don't look too much in the direction of these half-clothed harlots. If you seem to be only mildly interested in them, they will force themselves upon you and demand that you take them to bed – of course, at a preposterous price."

245

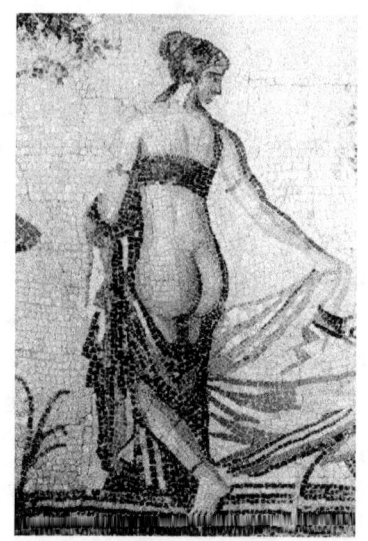

Leda and the Swan – Mosaic, circa 3rd century AD, Roman Imperial period, the Cyprus Museum

George: "They are a pest, especially on market days."

Me: "There are enough of them in Ephesus, as well. God isn't blind and He will certainly condemn and punish these ladies of pleasure and their eager admirers and customers."

I and Prochorus agree to ignore these women, as we did in Ephesus. They do remind us, though, of the prostitute we saw in the sky last night.

After Jason and George have done their purchases, they invite us to an early supper at Jason's home.

After I have recited a passage from the Psalms of David and did a prayer in which I begged God to bless this house, I tell Prochorus: "Get your things. We must go home before it becomes dark."

Prochorus: "Old Master, I can't. I just can't. We have been walking around the whole day, over there at the harbor, as well as through the market. My swollen foot can't take it anymore. It will just be too painful to walk another few steps."

"What can we do, my friend? I can't go home on my own and leave you here as a beggar on the streets of this turbulent town."

George: "I insist that both of you sleep in my home tonight. There is enough space. We can store your purchases in a safe place."

Jadon: "And then I can take you back tomorrow on my cart. We can't allow poor Prochorus to become a cripple by forcing him to walk with that painful foot."

This is the first opportunity I have of sleeping in a proper house since my arrival on Patmos and I accept the offer gratefully – especially because I am also very tired.

After we have dumped our purchases at a cool spot in George's home, we join him and his family on the flat roof of their house on stools and benches. Jason and his wife join us with a jug of wine and some bowls.

When it becomes dark and we all feel in a festive mood after a good supper and some wine, I start to explain to my hosts what I am seeing in the heaven right now.

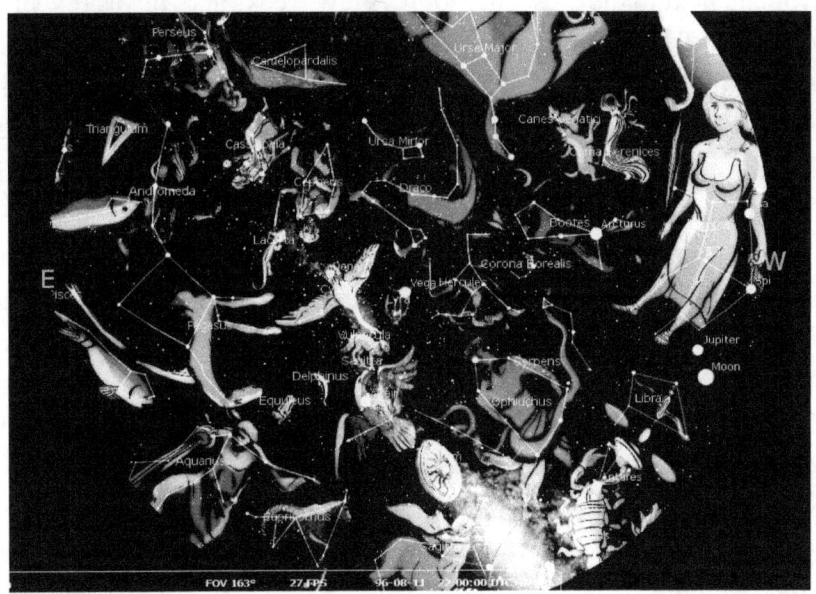

The crescent moon (23% illuminated) is situated in the western sky while the constellation of Virgo is disappearing behind the horizon in the west, following the sun that had set a short while earlier on 11 August AD 96. The constellations of Perseus, Sagittarius, Cepheus, Aquarius, and other mythological personages are distributed throughout the sky.

"My friends, as I've explained to you more than once, God has called me to be his prophet. This calling has often been confirmed by signs in the heavens. It is my task to interpret God's message on account of what I see in the sky, in God's heaven. I have, on occasion, explained to you what God revealed to me through the stars and other occurrences and events, such as a locust plague and all that glowing and burning lumps thrown out of Hades with its flames and fires.

"What I see in the sky tonight is simply a continuation of what God showed me last night. Look at that constellation near the western horizon. There you will see the constellation of the Young Woman, next to the crescent moon. A few weeks ago, it was revealed to me that that group of stars depict the people of Israel, the people who brought Jesus Christ forth. She and her new-born child were attacked by Satan, the Dragon, just below her. But God helped her to flee to the wilderness, while the Archangel Michel kicked this Dragon out of heaven.

"But then this woman changed sides and befriended the Dragon. The evening star, the planet of Aphrodite, who has disappeared a few minutes ago, became associated with this woman. And that demonstrated to me that she became a prostitute, worse than all those women of loose morals, the ladies of the night, we saw today."

Jason's wife: "There is a temple of Aphrodite, here on Patmos. That's why we have so many bad women on our streets. They worship at that temple and that's where they entertain their clients. It's too horrible for words."

Jason: "You said earlier today that you are sure that God will punish these immoral women and their clients. Is that also the fate of that bad woman in the sky?"

"Oh, certainly. You can see the red sky behind her, the last

248

rays of the sun behind the horizon. It is remarkable that the sunsets are much redder since all that dust and smoke was blown into the air when Hades started spitting fumes and flames. That bad woman, as you call her, is already being consumed by flames."

Prochorus: "Are you referring to the destruction of Jerusalem by flames at the end of the war against the Romans?"

"Yes, that's what happened. Jerusalem with her temple was completely and totally destroyed. That was God's punishment because the Jewish leaders sought the crucifixion of Jesus. The priests serving in the temple were also guilty of the murder of James, the brother of Jesus and leader of Jesus' followers. The Jews also stoned Stephen, one of the leaders of the group of Jesus people.

"If you look at the Milky Way, called the River of Fire by the Jews, you will see all the saints killed in Jerusalem, before and during the war. There they are in heaven and all are clothed in white because their sins have been wiped clean by the blood of the Lamb."

Procession of saints, clothed in white, each holding a crown (mosaic in S. Apollinare Nuovo, Ravenna, Italy – 6th century)

George: "So, Jerusalem is gone?"

249

"Totally, yes. That's because this city transformed herself into something ugly and unholy and I was informed by that angel next to the throne of God, that a more fitting name for her would be Babylon. That's the city where the godless people tried to erect a high tower to reach God's heaven on their own. That's also the place where the Jews were taken into exile a few centuries ago."

Prochorus: "Did this angel tell you anything more about Babylon?"

"Certainly. He actually quoted the prophet Isaiah:

'Fallen, fallen is Babylon; and all the engraved images of her gods are broken to the ground.'[163]

"The angel also told me that Babylon became the dwelling place of demons and unclean birds. He quoted Isaiah once again:

'But wild animals of the desert shall lie there; and their houses shall be full of doleful creatures; and ostriches shall dwell there, and wild goats shall dance there.'"

Prochorus: "Remarkable."

"That angel also reminds us of what the Jeremiah said:

'Then the heavens and the earth, and all that is therein, shall sing for joy over Babylon; for the destroyers shall come to her from the north, says the Lord.'"[164]

George's wife: "I suppose many people must have been sorry and disappointed that this city has disappeared."

"You are right. Jerusalem was a rich city and many merchants and ship masters made lots of money there. The kings

---

[163] Isa 21: 9.
[164] Jer 51: 48.

from the house of Herod, who sided with the Romans during the war, were also sorry that this city was razed because that prevented them from regaining the throne of the whole of Palestine in Jerusalem, the throne that belonged to their father and grandfather, Herod the Great. The last member of the house of Herod, Herod Agrippa II, king of Chalcis and Trachonitis, died a few years ago and with him this dynasty disappeared. These kings are represented by the constellation of Libra, the Scales, which may also be regarded as the horns of the Dragon.

"It can be said that these kings committed sexual immorality with this prostitute, Jerusalem, which may also be called Babylon. They frequently visited the temple while it still stood and made friends with the Sadducees, the ruling priestly class who were fierce opponents of Jesus and of John the Baptist, who was killed by one of these kings."

Jason, the shopkeeper: "You said that Jerusalem was a rich city and that the merchants made much money there. These merchants must have been sorry when Jerusalem was destroyed, if I'm not mistaken? They must have lost fortunes."

"I must agree with you. Four groups of men were sorry: kings, merchants, mariners, and shipmasters. Here I have a golden coin that was minted by Caesar Vespasian to commemorate the destruction of Jerusalem. It shows Judea as a captured woman who is guarded by a Roman soldier. This coin was meant to show people all over the Roman Empire that it won't do to start a rebellion."

Jason's wife: "I have heard that some tribes in Germania also started a rebellion against Rome at the same time when the Jews tried to get rid of the Romans. That rebellion was inspired by a pagan prophetess with the name of Veleda. That rebellion started well when a whole Roman legion was destroyed, but it also failed in the end and Veleda was captured by the Romans. She foretold the deaths

251

of Emperor Vespasian and his two sons."

"Thanks for that. I never knew of it."

George: "You told us that you fled from Jerusalem when the Roman army started its attack on the city."

"Thank you for reminding me of that. That angel over there (and I point to the Quiver) also called upon all the faithful in Babylon to get out, to leave this sinful city to her fate when God allowed the foreigners to destroy her. Most followers of Jesus did exactly that.[165] This call is an echo of the prophet Jeremiah, who wrote:

> "Flee out of the midst of Babylon, and save every man his life; don't be cut off in her iniquity: for it is the time of Yahweh's vengeance; he will render to her a recompense."[166]

After some silence, I continue: "I can hear that prostitute boasting about herself: 'I sit a queen, and am no widow, and will in no way see mourning.' That is the exact opposite of what was said of Jerusalem after the city was sacked by the Babylonians a few centuries ago:

> 'How does the city sit solitary, that was full of people! She has become as a widow, who was great among the nations!'[167]

"In other words: Jerusalem, this harlot who had rejected Jesus as Messiah, was very satisfied with herself – but that attitude did not save her."

Prochorus: "Truly remarkable!"

"Thanks. While I was strolling along the waterfront and

---

[165] Eusebius, *Hist Eccl,* Liber III/V/3.
[166] Jer 51: 6.
[167] Lam 1: 1.

through the market place today, my eyes fell on a wide variety of goods that were being bought and sold. That was also the case with Jerusalem. If you look up to all the stars in the sky, you can see some of these kings, merchants, mariners, and shipmasters – the constellations of the Water Carrier, the Snake Catcher, Perseus, the Charioteer, and others.

"I made a mental list of all the merchandise that went into and out of Jerusalem. Allow me to give you a list of these:

> *Jewelry*: objects of gold, silver, precious stones, and pearls;
> *Materials for clothing*: fine linen, purple, silk, and scarlet;
> *Vessels*: vessels made of ivory, vessels made of most precious wood, vessels made of durable materials, namely brass and iron, and vessels made of marble;
> *Spices*: pure cinnamon, incense, ointment, and frankincense;
> *Agricultural produce*: wine, oil, fine flour, and wheat;
> *Living beings*: cattle, sheep, horses with chariots, and the bodies and souls of men."

Prochorus: "I couldn't help but to notice that you mentioned four examples of each category of merchandize. I know you are fond of the number of four and you explained that it is the number to describe the world with its four elements and four winds."

"You have it, my friend. I also listed six categories of merchandize. Six is the number of man who was created on the sixth day after the beginning of the world. When you multiply six by four you get the number of twenty-four, which is a biblical number. There are twelve tribes of Israel and twelve apostles of Jesus."

Just as we get ready to go to bed, Jason cries out: "Look there, there to the south!" We all watch as a big glowing stone comes flying in our direction. It splashes into the sea outside Skala.

Jason's wife: "We have had enough of these demons from hell flying around. When will this stop?"

I console her: "That glowing stone, much heavier than a millstone, must remind us of God's judgment when Jerusalem, with the nickname of Babylon, was devastated. That was on account of this city's adultery and whoring. The people of Patmos must also repent."

Friday, 12 August AD 96

Last night, I slept badly in George's home. The bed was unfamiliar and there were constantly noises from the streets. I could hear George snoring and I missed the restless sheep in our cave. After breakfast and after I recited a part of one of the prophets and did a prayer, Jason took us back in his cart. We are relieved that we don't have to carry our purchases of the previous day.

After Jason has left again, I tell Prochorus: "It's time to write down what we saw and heard last night. Although the scene in the sky told us about what had happened many years ago, I will tell it as if it is a prophecy about the future."

"But why?"

"It must serve as a warning for any Christian assemblies in future not to follow the example of Israel and Jerusalem by embracing the big powers of the world."

Prochorus fetches a sheet of papyrus, a pen, and ink and I dictate:

Revelation 18: 1–24
The fall of Babylon

1.	After these things, I saw another angel coming down out of the sky, having great authority. The earth was illuminated with his glory.
2.	He cried with a mighty voice, saying, "Fallen, fallen is Babylon the great, and has become a habitation of demons, and a prison of every unclean spirit, and a prison of every unclean and hateful bird!
3.	For all the nations have drunk of the wine of the wrath of her sexual immorality, the kings of the earth committed sexual

immorality with her, and the merchants of the earth grew rich from the abundance of her luxury."

4.   I heard another voice from heaven, saying, "Come forth, my people, out of her, that you have no participation her sins, and that you don`t receive of her plagues,

5.   for her sins have reached to the sky, and God has remembered her iniquities.

6.   Return to her just as she returned, and double to her the double according to her works. In the cup which she mixed, mix to her double.

7.   However much she glorified herself, and grew wanton, so much give her of torment and mourning. For she says in her heart, 'I sit a queen, and am no widow, and will in no way see mourning.'

8.   Therefore, in one day her plagues will come: death, mourning, and famine; and she will be utterly burned with fire; for the Lord God who has judged her is strong.

9.   The kings of the earth, who committed sexual immorality and lived wantonly with her, will weep and wail over her, when they look at the smoke of her burning,

10.   standing far away for the fear of her torment, saying, 'Woe, woe, the great city, Babylon, the strong city! For your judgment has come in one hour.'

11.   The merchants of the earth weep and mourn over her, for no one buys their merchandise anymore;

12.   merchandise of gold, silver, precious stones, pearls, fine linen, purple, silk, scarlet, all expensive wood, every vessel of ivory, every vessel made of most precious wood, and of brass, and iron, and marble;

13. and cinnamon, spices, incense, ointment, frankincense, wine, oil, fine flour, wheat, cattle, and sheep; and merchandise of horses and chariots and slaves; and souls of men.

14. The fruits which your soul lusted after have been lost to you, and all things that were dainty and sumptuous have perished from you, and you will find them no more at all.

15. The merchants of these things, who were made rich by her, will stand far away for the fear of her torment, weeping and mourning;

16. saying, 'Woe, woe, the great city, she who was dressed in fine linen, purple, and scarlet, and decked with gold and precious stones and pearls!

17. For in an hour such great riches are made desolate.' Every shipmaster, and everyone who sails anywhere, and mariners, and as many as gain their living by sea, stood far away,

18. and cried out as they looked at the smoke of her burning, saying, 'What is like the great city?'

19. They cast dust on their heads, and cried, weeping and mourning, saying, 'Woe, woe, the great city, in which all who had their ships in the sea were made rich by reason of her great wealth!' For in one hour is she made desolate.

20. Rejoice over her, O heaven, you saints, you apostles, and you prophets; for God has judged your judgment on her."

21. A mighty angel took up a stone like a great millstone and cast it into the sea, saying, "Thus with violence will Babylon, the great city, be thrown down, and will be found no more at all.

22. The voice of harpers and minstrels and flute players and trumpeters will be heard no more at all in you. No craftsman,

> of whatever craft, will be found any more at all in you. The sound of a mill will be heard no more at all in you.
>
> 23. The light of a lamp will shine no more at all in you. The voice of the bridegroom and of the bride will be heard no more at all in you; for your merchants were the princes of the earth; for with your sorcery all the nations were deceived.
>
> 24. In her was found the blood of prophets and of saints, and of all who have been slain on the earth."

During the day, I take a nap to catch up on my lost sleep of the last two nights. While I am dreaming, the four living creatures and the twenty-four elders of previous scenes appear to me. They tell me that there was joy in heaven when that prostitute, Babylon, was destroyed.

After I have woken up, I call upon my companion to fetch another piece of papyrus and write the following words – and I adapt some of the hymns we used to sing in Ephesus to fit the occasion:

Revelation 19: 1–4
The song of the multitude

> 1. After these things I heard something like a loud voice of a great multitude in heaven, saying, "Hallelujah! Salvation, glory, and power belong to our God:
>
> 2. for true and righteous are his judgments. For he has judged the great prostitute, her who corrupted the earth with her sexual immorality, and he has avenged the blood of his servants at her hand."
>
> 3. A second time they said, "Hallelujah! Her smoke goes up forever and ever."

258

> 4. The twenty-four elders and the four living creatures fell down and worshipped God who sits on the throne, saying, "Amen! Hallelujah!"

When Prochorus puts down his pen, he announces: "This was our last piece of papyrus."

Me: "Really! Really! This is a very nice time to tell me this! We were in Skala just yesterday. We could have bought some sheets there."

"We must ask Jason when he turns up this Sunday to bring us some the week after that."

"Please, don't forget to ask him that, otherwise I may become frustrated, irritated, and extremely disappointed. Let's hope that I don't receive any messages before our stocks of papyrus are replenished."

Thursday, 25 August AD 96

During the past fortnight, we helped to bring in the grape harvest at the farm of Argus and Ajax. We returned to our cave this afternoon when work became impossible when a violent thunder storm started. Where we sat in the entrance of the cave, we could hear and see the thunder bolts crashing down onto the earth. Rain fell in a deluge and we heard streams of water running off the hill outside the cave.

Prochorus: "The Scriptures tell us that those thunders are God's voice. What is He telling us?"

"He tells us that He is the ruler of the world. He is the Almighty and we must honor him."

After Andrew has brought back his wet sheep to the cave and we had a late supper, we sit outside to admire the sky that has cleared after the storm of this afternoon. It was rather unpleasant inside the cave with all the stinking wet sheep and, therefore, we stayed outside as long as possible before going to bed. We feel relaxed and happy after having eaten a delicious broth with lots of leaves of the happy weed.

The full moon rising over the Aegean Sea, as seen from Patmos

One of the angels in front of God's throne warns me that I must watch a preview of how the marriage of the Lamb is to take place when the time is ripe. Directly next to the Lamb, an almost full moon is rising out of the waters of the Aegean Sea to the east.

I look around to find the Lamb. He is, of course, to be found

260

in the group of stars known to the pagan as Aries, the Ram, but known to the Jews as the Sheep or the Lamb.

The light of the moon is reflected on the waters of Sapsila Bay and I explain that to Prochorus as the beautiful wedding gown of the bride. I remember that Solomon said of his beloved that she is "fair as the moon".[168]

The stars in the Milky Way are producing appropriate music for the occasion. They remind me of the thunderstorm and streams of water of earlier today.

> The Jewish astrological calendar from Qumran of the first century BC substituted the constellation of the Ram with the Lamb[169] and it is certainly not too farfetched to conclude that John had the same idea. Although he wrote in Greek, it is clear that he was steeped in the Hebrew Scriptures and shared many ideas about the starry skies with his contemporaries.

The Zodiac mosaic on the floor of the Beth Alpha Synagogue (5th century AD) shows the constellation of Aries as a sheep. It is named a טָלֶא (tale), which means a "spotted sheep" (Gen 30: 32). This word sounds rather like the Hebrew word for "lamb" (טָלֶה – taleh) (Isa 65: 25).

I tell Prochorus: "This marriage of the Lamb is something that will only happen after Judgment Day. That is when all the faithful – typified by the moon – will be united with Christ in heaven. We are now looking into the future.

---

[168] Song 6: 10.
[169] Jacobus, "The Zodiac Sign Names", 319

This scene is so overwhelming that I can't help it – I want to honor the angel who showed me this wonderful scene of the new bride of the Lamb after the prostitute, Israel, has been vanquished by the pagans.

Prochorus: "I will light our lamp and then I can take down your words while your memory of this scene is still fresh."

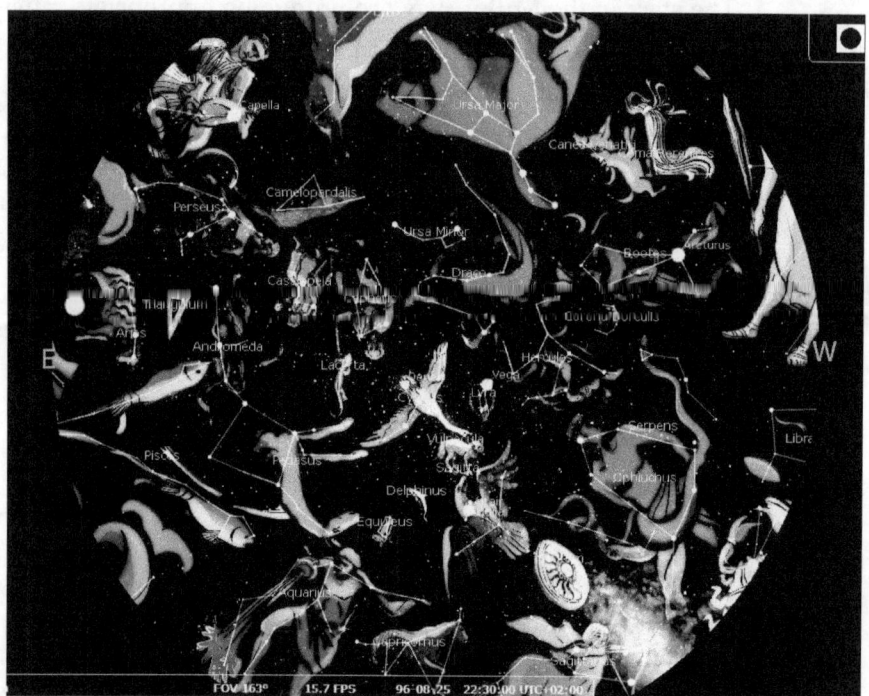

The rising moon (84% illuminated) inside Aries, the Ram, above the eastern horizon on 25 August AD 96. The Milky Way stretches along the middle of the sky.

Revelation 19: 5–10

The marriage of the Lamb

5. A voice came forth from the throne, saying, "Give praise to our God, all you his servants, you who fear him, the small and the great!"

262

6. I heard something like the voice of a great multitude, and like the voice of many waters, and like the voice of mighty thunders, saying, "Hallelujah! For the Lord our God, the Almighty, reigns!

7. Let us rejoice and be exceedingly glad, and let us give the glory to him. For the marriage of the Lamb has come, and his wife has made herself ready."

8. It was given to her that she would array herself in bright, pure, fine linen: for the fine linen is the righteous acts of the saints.

9. He said to me, "Write, 'Blessed are those who are invited to the marriage supper of the Lamb.'" He said to me, "These are true words of God."

10. I fell down before his feet to worship him. He said to me, "Look! Don't do it! I am a fellow bondservant with you and with your brothers who hold the testimony of Jesus. Worship God, for the testimony of Jesus is the Spirit of Prophecy."

Friday and Saturday, 26–27 August AD 96

More than six months have passed since my arrival on Patmos. I felt very miserable at that time, but my circumstances have changed remarkably since then and I can see that God is using me in this forlorn spot. I have gathered a small congregation of followers of Christ and God has revealed to me on various occasions what his intentions with this evil world is and how Satan and his assistants, including Emperor Domitian, will come to their end.

After God has shown me how that woman with loose morals, Jerusalem, and the Jews who rejected Jesus Christ, have been crushed – to serve as a warning to all Christians who wish to get allied to the godless powers of this world – I expect that God will demonstrate to me how everything will end. It is, therefore, with great expectations that I sit again on my habitual rock outside the cave to investigate the heavens for a message from God. Something tells me that I must remain here all night.

Last night, I viewed the coming marriage of the Lamb. I won't be surprised if God demonstrates to me tonight how this wedding was made possible. One of the angels surrounding God's throne in the north calls upon me to watch the southern horizon. There I notice the horse rider whom I have seen in the past – the knight on a white steed, the constellation of Sagittarius or the Archer, as the Jews know him.

I've seen the Roman cavalrymen on their way to lay siege to Jerusalem thirty years ago and I can't erase that memory from my mind. This horseman wields a very sharp sword with which he will cut down all his foes. He is a conquering hero with a crown to demonstrate his royal status – the constellation of the Southern Crown or Corona Australis, next to him. He has a name, "the Word of God", and a title, "KING OF KINGS, AND LORD OF LORDS" – the same title that the Lamb had in another context. This knight is, of course, none other than Jesus Christ, the faithful and trustworthy judge and ruler of the world. His robe has blood on it – the blood of his enemies, but also the blood that He lost when he was crucified. With fire in his eyes, he can see everything.

Roman cavalry from a mosaic of the Villa Romana del Casale, Sicily, 4th century AD

The horseman's role as a judge can be compared with the work of a wine farmer who crushes all the juice out of his grapes – just as we were doing the past few days. All the juice is squeezed out thoroughly and that will also be the fate of those who are being judged by this knight.

An ancient wine press. The grapes were crushed with the stone on top and the grape juice flowed into the receptacle on the right (Rev 14: 20)

265

This winepress illustrating the wrath of God must be sought in the constellation of Scutum, the Shield, directly next to Sagittarius. A shield and a winepress, after all, both have a round shape.

The bright evening star, called the "She-Star" by the Jews, is on the western horizon with the last rays of the sun behind her. She is the brightest object in the sky at this time. With the voice of an angel, she calls upon all the birds in the heavens, the Eagle, the Crow, and the Swan, to come and feast on the enemies of God, those enemies slain by the hero on the white horse.

The knight is followed by a big crowd, clothed in white – the stars of the Milky Way. This is the army to which all the happy souls in heaven belong – the deceased saints and the angels of God. They share in the victory of the hero on the white horse.

This hero wields a rod of iron, which is a sign of his invincibility. I recite a passage from the Psalms of David to myself:

> "Make your request to me, and I will give you the nations for your heritage, and the farthest limits of the earth will be under your hand. They will be ruled by you with a rod of iron; they will be broken like a potter's vessel."[170]

The Scriptures tell us of more than one occasion when God or the angels assisted the Israelites in their battles against their enemies – for instance, with the fall of Jericho or when Gideon and his band of 300 men vanquished the hordes of the Amalekites.[171]

One of the enemies of God and an ally of the Dragon, namely the monster from the earth, the Goat or the False Prophet, lies next to the Archer. Although he plans to pounce upon the knight, his fate is decided and sealed. I want to await the appearance of the beast from the sea, who is due to become visible later during the night.

---

[170] Ps 2: 8–9/
[171] Jos 6 and Judg 7.

Early the next morning, I see both the Antichrist, the beast from the sea and the beast from the earth, the False Prophet. Their allies and helpers must be six classes of people – the kings of the earth, captains, other mighty men, horses, those who sit on horses and the rest of sinful mankind, whether free or slave, whether old or young. They all prepared for war against the rider on the white horse and they are to be found all over the sky in other constellations.

These two beasts are then thrown into the lake of fire that burns with sulphur by the conquering hero. That happens when they disappear behind the western horizon as dawn approaches. I really smell some sulphur, which must have blown over from Hades in the south. The first rays of the sun are a sign of this big fire. The Antichrist, Caesar Domitian, cannot escape his destiny.

I remember that a similar outcome for the sea monster is to be found in Isaiah:

> "In that day the Lord with his hard and great and strong sword will punish leviathan the swift serpent, and leviathan the crooked serpent; and he will kill the monster that is in the sea. (…) It shall happen in that day, that the Lord will punish the host of the high ones on high, and the kings of the earth on the earth. They shall be gathered together, as prisoners are gathered in the pit, and shall be shut up in the prison; and after many days shall they be visited."[172]

I am quite sure that the same danger and doom awaits the Dragon, some or other time. He won't be able to escape because his downfall and destruction was already announced by the ancient prophet, Enoch.

---

[172] Isa 27: 1 and Isa 24: 21–22.

Only the outlines of Sagittarius (the Archer), Corona Australis (the Southern Crown), Capricornus (the Goat) and Scutum (the Shield), are shown in this computer-generated image of the night sky towards the end of August AD. Venus, the brightest object in the sky, lies on the western horizon while the last rays of the sun are still visible. Aquila (the Eagle) and Cygnus (the Swan), are gliding high in the middle of the sky.

A close-up view of Sagittarius (the Archer) on the southern horizon, together with Corona Australis (the Southern Crown), towards the end of August AD 96. Part of the Milky Way is to be seen in front of Sagittarius. Scutum (the Shield) is situated above the head of Sagittarius and may be regarded as a winepress.

268

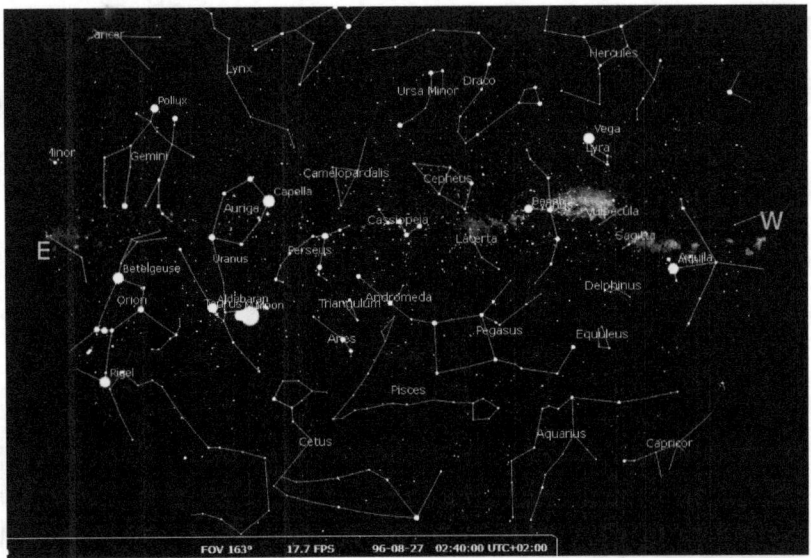

Cetus (the Sea Monster) and Capricornus (the Goat), visible during the early morning hours towards the end of August AD 96. Capricornus is on the point of disappearing behind the south-western horizon and Cetus followed a few hours later. Aquila (the Eagle) and Cygnus (the Swan) lie on the western part of the Milky Way. There is a near conjunction of the moon (72% illuminated) and the planet Mars next to the constellation of Aries (the Ram).

As dawn is approaching, I slide into my bed and I succeed in sleeping a few hours. When I wake up, the cave is empty. I find Prochorus sitting outside, waiting for me to wake up. After breakfast, I ask him to start writing:

Revelation 19: 11–21

The rider on the white horse

> 11. I saw the heaven opened, and behold, a white horse, and he who sat on it is called Faithful and True. In righteousness he judges and makes war.

12. His eyes are a flame of fire, and on his head are many crowns. He has names written and a name written which no one knows but he himself.

13. He is clothed in a garment sprinkled with blood. His name is called "The Word of God."

14. The armies which are in heaven followed him on white horses, clothed in white, pure, fine linen.

15. Out of his mouth proceeds a sharp, two-edged sword, that with it he should strike the nations. He will rule them with a rod of iron. He treads the winepress of the fierceness of the wrath of God, the Almighty.

16. He has on his garment and on his thigh a name written, "KING OF KINGS, AND LORD OF LORDS."

17. I saw an angel standing in the sun. He cried with a loud voice, saying to all the birds that fly in the sky, "Come! Be gathered together to the great supper of God,

18. that you may eat the flesh of kings, the flesh of captains, the flesh of mighty men, and the flesh of horses and of those who sit on them, and the flesh of all men, both free and slave, and small and great."

19. I saw the beast, and the kings of the earth, and their armies, gathered together to make war against him who sat on the horse, and against his army.

20. The beast was taken, and with him the false prophet who worked the signs in his sight, with which he deceived those who had received the mark of the beast and those who worshipped his image. They two were thrown alive into the lake of fire that burns with sulphur.

21. The rest were killed with the sword of him who sat on the horse, the sword which came forth out of his mouth. All the birds were filled with their flesh.

The best-known chorus in Händel's oratorio, the Messiah, the Hallelujah chorus, is a musical setting of words from Rev 19 and Rev 11. These words, taken from the Authorized Version, are as follows:

"Hallelujah: for the Lord God Omnipotent reigneth" (Rev 19: 6). "The kingdom of this world is become the kingdom of our Lord, and of His Christ; and He shall reign for ever and ever" (Rev 11: 15). "King of Kings, and Lord of Lords" (Rev 19: 16).

"Hallelujah!"

Sunday, 4 September AD 96

Introductory notes

Many Christian fundamentalists explain Revelation 20: 1–10 in such a way that they see there a prediction of a literal earthly kingdom of Christ of exactly one thousand years, somewhere in the future – a position known as millennialism or chiliasm (from the Greek word for thousand: χίλιοι – *chilioi*).

The church father, St Irenaeus (ca AD 180), may be regarded as the first theologian to have espoused chiliasm in chapters 30–35 of Book V of his work Against Heresies. He argued that just as God created the world in six days and rested on the seventh day, the history of mankind will endure for 6 000 years and that a period of rest of 1 000 years is to follow during which the saints would inherit the earth after the second coming of Christ – those who "have part in the first resurrection".

It will become clear that these millennialists misread and distort the biblical text. The main difficulty with the millennialist point of view is that it requires Christ to return twice – at the start of the millennium and when Satan must be overpowered and again on Judgment Day. The Bible nowhere teaches that Christ will return again and again. There will only be a single second coming.

The text of Revelation makes it clear that this book only deals with the time during which John and his reader lived, as well as the immediate future.

- Rev 1: 1 states explicitly – "This is the Revelation of Jesus Christ, which God gave him to show to his servants the things which must happen soon…"
- Rev 1: 3 adds – "Blessed is he who reads and those who hear the words of the prophecy, and keep the things that are written in it, for the time is at hand."

- According to Rev 1: 19, John received the following instruction: "Write therefore the things which you have seen, and the things which are, and the things which will happen hereafter."
- Rev 22: 10 contains the warning: "Don`t seal up the words of the prophecy of this book, for the time is at hand."
- It is clear from Rev 3: 11; 22: 7 and 12 that John expected the second coming of Christ and Judgment Day to happen very soon.

That millennialism is an artificial construct, which has little bearing on what John has really written can be demonstrated by following John's train of thought.

My little congregation visited me again this morning. I gave them the good news that the Antichrist – in fact, Emperor Domitian – and the False Prophet, a symbol for all false religions and cults, stand no chance against the Word of God, which is Jesus Christ. I expect and proclaim the final downfall of Satan on Judgment Day, which will occur very soon.

And tonight, I wish to see how God will see to it that Satan will not survive. I have often read in the book of Enoch how that prophet described Satan's banishment to the underworld to await his final annihilation on Judgment Day. I expect that God will reveal something similar to me.

One of the angels in front of God's throne addresses me and asks me to notice what is happening with the constellation of the Scorpion, which the Jews regard as a snake or a dragon.[173] In the past, I had no doubt that this figure represented Satan, the serpent of whom we read in Moses' report of how Eve was lured by this devil to eat from the forbidden fruit.

---

[173] Allen, *Star Names,* 362.

The Dragon is lying on the horizon, in the south-west, directly over the spot where the smoldering stars, sparks, and smoke from Hades or die abyss poured out a few weeks ago. It is certain that that is where Satan belongs – just as happened to the other two evil beasts.

Next to the Dragon, I see the Snake Catcher, called Ophiuchus by the Greeks.[174] He tramples upon the Dragon with his feet and he holds a long chain in his hands. The angel informs me that this figure also has the key to the Abyss. During the first vision I had after arriving on Patmos, Jesus as the Lamb of God told me that he holds the key to Death and Hades. That means that this figure must have received the key from Jesus. He is none other than the Archangel Michael. According to Enoch, God ordered Michael to arrest Satan and his delinquent demons and throw them out of heaven.

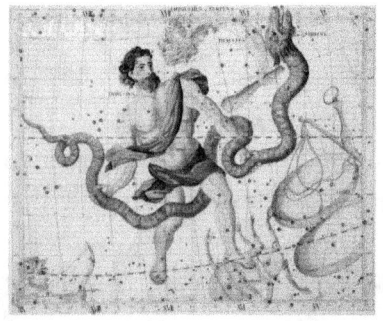

Ophiuchus, the Snake Catcher (also called Serpentarius), with Serpens, the Serpent, from an old star atlas. Scorpius, the Scorpion, is faintly visible under his feet. John saw the snake in his hands as a chain.

According to Enoch, Satan was initially an angel with the name of Semjâzâ, but he and his friends lusted after earthly women and made them pregnant. Their offspring were ghastly giants. That awakened the anger of God and Satan was expelled from heaven – and this

---

[174] The Greek name, *Ophiuchus*, is derived from the Hebrew and Arabic name *Afeichus*, which means "the serpent held" (Bullinger, "The Witnesss"). This name is also derived from the Greek word for a snake namely *ophis* (Greek: ὄφις).

scene I am witnessing is a reminder of what has happened many ages ago.[175]

I decide to calculate the time between Satan's apprehension and his eventual demise as a period of a thousand years. The number of a thousand isn't just a number. It conveys a meaning, a message, as all other numbers that I've used. A thousand is ten times ten times ten or ten multiplied twice with itself. Ten symbolizes God's work – such as the Ten Commandments, the ten Egyptian plagues, and the ten fingers on both hands with which we do our work. Three is the number that tells us that God is involved – God on the throne, the Lamb, and the Sevenfold Spirit of God. This period of a thousand years is, therefore, the whole long time between Satan's expulsion from heaven shortly after the creation of heaven and earth and Judgment Day.

To give Satan a fair chance in the final battle with the knight on the white horse, he will be released for a short time before the final battle and his exile into the pool of fire and sulphur. I can even smell some sulphureous odors and fumes, blown out from Hades in the south.

An important question is: what is meant by the "Abyss"? The Greek word is ἀβύσσος (abyssos), from which the English word abyss is derived. This word is also used in Rom 10: 7; Rev 9: 1, 2 & 11; Rev 11: 7 and Rev 17: 8. It is clear from these verses that the present abode or prison of Satan and his helpers is meant – and not hell. According to Rev 20: 10, Satan, together with the beast from the sea and the False Prophet, were only to be thrown into "the lake of fire and sulphur" on Judgment Day, somewhere in the future.

John had in mind the ancient Greek idea of a place where the gods incarcerated their enemies. This place was called the "nether-

---

[175] Enoch 5–10 (especially 10: 11).

"world" or *Tartarus* (Greek: Τάρταρος). In those days, people thought of this abyss as being somewhere below the surface of the earth. Tartarus was sometimes called *Hades* (Greek: ᾅδης) – the abode of the dead. The word "Hades" was used in the Greek translation of the Old Testament for the Hebrew word "*Sheol*" (שְׁאוֹל) the place of the dead – and it is also used in this sense in the New Testament (Matt 16: 18).

The only place where the name Tartarus is being used in the New Testament is 2 Pet 2: 4 – "For if God didn't spare angels when they sinned, but cast them down to Tartarus, and committed them to pits of darkness, to be reserved to judgment". In this text, Tartarus is the name of the place into which the rebellious angels – devils and demons – were imprisoned, while awaiting Judgment Day. The name Tartarus is, therefore, a synonym for the "Abyss".

I take another look at God's throne in the north. It is surrounded by many other thrones and those who are seated upon these thrones are the departed saints. They are to assist God and the Lamb to judge Satan and all his godless assistants and associates. This scene reminds me of a passage in the prophet Daniel:

"I saw until thrones were placed, and one who was ancient of days sat: his clothing was white as snow, and the hair of his head like pure wool; his throne was fiery flames, [and] the wheels of it burning fire. A fiery stream issued and came forth from before him: thousands of thousands ministered to him, and ten thousand times ten thousand stood before him: the judgment was set, and the books were opened."[176]

---

[176] Dan 7: 9–10.

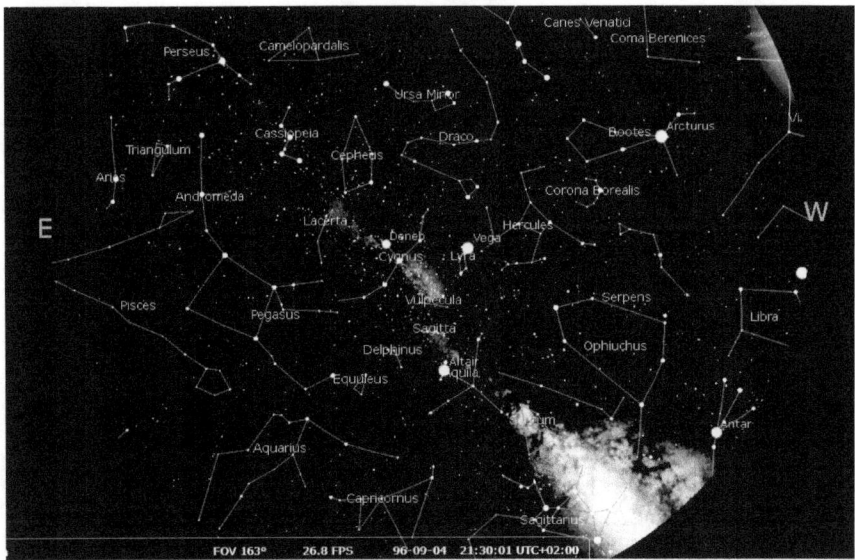

The outlines of Ophiuchus (the Serpent Catcher) and Scorpius (the Scorpion or Dragon) with its brightest star, Antares, on the south-western horizon towards the beginning of September AD 96. The last rays of the sun are visible in the west.

The same scene as in the previous illustration, but with the celestial figures of the various constellations added.

The "fiery stream" in front of God's throne in this vision of Daniel must have been the Milky Way with its "thousands of thousands" of stars. Likewise, the saints that I am watching must also be sought amongst the clouds of the Milky Way across the middle of the sky.

I feel somewhat confused because the scene that I am seeing contains events from the past and the future at the same time. The banishment of Satan to the Abyss happened a long time ago. The throne of God, with the thrones of the departed saints, show me something about Judgment Day, which lies in the future, although this judgment is also to take place during the whole time of a thousand years. The souls of these departed saints must have reached heaven directly after their cruel deaths, whenever they died or were killed. The only explanation is that time disappeared for them when they died and that they reached Judgment Day and God's eternity directly after that. After all, a thousand years and a single day are the same for God.[177]

The idea of the millennialists that these deceased saints will rule together with Christ *on earth* during the period of 1 000 years cannot be deduced from Rev 20. We also cannot say that those who die are waiting somewhere until Judgment Day and that they are then to be admitted into heaven. There are various biblical pronouncements that teach that the souls of those who die are immediately taken up into their eternal destinies (Luk 16: 22, 23; Luk 23: 34; 2 Cor 5: 1; 2 Tim 4: 18 & Heb 9: 27) – although we, who are still alive on earth and bound to the passage of time, have to await Judgment Day and the resurrection sometime in the unknown future (Matt 25: 31–46; 1 Cor 15: 23–24 & 1 Pet 1: 5).

The deceased martyrs of Rev 20: 4 are, therefore, in heaven – not on earth. From a terrestrial perspective, this is still in the un-

[177] Ps 90: 4 and 2 Pet 3: 8.

known future. Those who have died and have left the restraints of time, however, arrive in heaven immediately after they have departed from this life. These martyrs do not sit on thrones on earth during the period of 1 000 years; they are already experiencing heavenly bliss, together with Christ, while those who are still living on earth are experiencing the symbolic millennium, the period between Satan's expulsion from heaven and Judgment Day.

Thrones on which the saints are to be seated are mentioned elsewhere in Revelation (Rev 3: 21; 4: 1–6; 4: 10–11; 5: 8–9). In all these cases, these thrones are in heaven and that must also be the case with the thrones mentioned in Rev 20.

Where Rev 20: 5 says that the rest of the dead were not resurrected until the end of the 1000 years, one has to realize that this is being said from a terrestrial point of view. When viewed from the dimension of time, Judgment Day and the resurrection are still somewhere in the unknown future. The rest of the dead are, therefore, the people who were still alive in John's day and awaiting Judgment Day. This paradoxical situation may be illustrated by the following diagram:

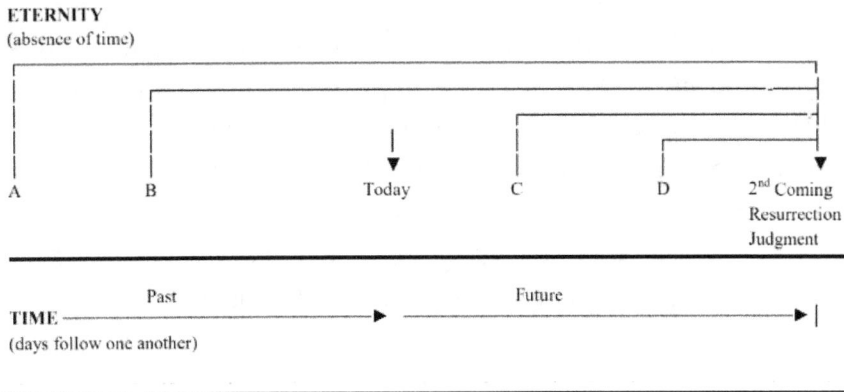

The state of affairs from the perspective of eternity is given above the thick line. Below the thick line, time rolls on as we experience it on earth where one day is followed by another, while we are powerless to stop this flow. Points A, B, C, and D are the dates of death of four imaginary people – two of them in the past and two in the future. Seen from the dimension of time, their dates of death are far apart, even centuries. Viewed from the perspective of eternity, it transpires that each one's date of death coincides with the resurrection and the final judgment. Time, to which we on earth are bound, simply disappeared for those who have died because they have left the time-bound existence on earth and entered God's timeless eternity. The person who dies, appears instantly before God's judicial throne and receives either life everlasting or eternal damnation.

For people who are still living on earth that is something still awaiting them in the unknown future.

While I watch the souls of those martyrs who refused to worship the beast and stayed true to their testimony, and who are helping Christ with the judgment, I conclude that they must have been resurrected and opened their eyes in God's eternity directly when they had died. This resurrection is much more preferable that the eternal death of those who are condemned by God. I prefer to contrast the two alternatives by calling them the first resurrection and the second death, to emphasize the glory of the resurrection and the horror of eternal damnation.

The last rays of the sun are visible in the west and that must be the lake of fire and sulphur, the place to which Satan is to be extradited and exiled. A wind is blowing and it carries the smell of sulphureous fumes to my nose – and this sulphur must come from this lake of fire and sulphur in the south-west.[178]

Because God is fair, he will give Satan a sporting chance by releasing him at the end of the thousand years so that his defeat and final judgment must be seen to be righteous and justified. In this time, Satan will certainly do his best to recruit as many allies as possible and to attack God's people in their camp in the harsh and dry desert where they are living as outcasts from pagan society.

Those who are misled by Satan, the pagan and heathen nations of the world, I prefer to call the "Gog and Magog". That is to confuse those unbelievers and godless people who may happen to obtain copies of my notes, without knowing what I mean with these names. For me, the Roman military might and all false pagan religions are meant.

> The expression "God and Magog" needs an explanation. The name Magog appears in Gen 10: 2 as a son of Japheth, the son of Noah. A certain Gog is mentioned in 1 Chr 5: 4 as the son of Joel. Both these names are also encountered in Ezek 38 and 39 as enemies of Israel where Gog is the prince of the land of Magog. The names "Gog" and "Magog" also occur in the extrabiblical Book of Jubilees, which contains comments on the stories of Genesis.

I notice that there is fire coming down out of heaven, which devours the Gog and Magog, the followers of Satan. This fire is the bright dense cloud of the Milky Way, between the Snake Catcher and the knight on the white horse.

This fire that descended from heaven is a reference to the fire that God sent onto the sacrifice of the prophet Elijah, through which

---

[178] The dormant volcano on Nisyros is still emitting sulpherous fumes today (Sattin & Franquet, *Greek Islands,* 160).

he triumphed over the prophets of Baal.[179]

The expression "fire and sulphur" comes from a Psalm of David, which I recite to myself:

> "On the wicked He will rain blazing coals; fire, sulphur, and scorching wind shall be the portion of their cup."[180]

Satan, the Dragon or the Serpent, on the other hand, is dumped into the fiery lake, together with the two beasts. It is as Enoch prophesied in his book:

> "And on the day of the great judgment he [Azazel, the devil] shall be cast into the fire."[181]

---

[179] 1 Kgs 18.
[180] Ps 11: 6.
[181] Enoch 10: 5.

Monday, 5 September AD 96

During breakfast, Prochorus asks me: "Old Master, what did you observe last night when I was already asleep?"

"You will find out as soon as you fetch your writing instruments and I tell you what to write."

Revelation 20: 1–10
Satan bound

1. I saw an angel coming down out of heaven, having the key of the abyss and a great chain in his hand.

2. He seized the dragon, the old serpent, which is the Devil and Satan, and bound him for one thousand years,

3. and cast him into the abyss, and shut it, and sealed it over him, that he should deceive the nations no more, until the thousand years were finished. After this, he must be freed for a short time.

4. I saw thrones, and they sat on them, and judgment was given to them. I saw the souls of those who had been beheaded for the testimony of Jesus, and for the word of God, and such as didn't worship the beast nor his image, and didn't receive the mark on their forehead and on their hand. They lived, and reigned with Christ one thousand years.

5. The rest of the dead didn't live until the thousand years were finished. This is the first resurrection.

6. Blessed and holy is he who has part in the first resurrection. Over these, the second death has no power, but they will be priests of God and of Christ, and will reign with him one thousand years.

7. And after the thousand years, Satan will be freed out of his prison,

8. and will come forth to deceive the nations which are in the four corners of the earth, Gog and Magog, to gather them together to the war; the number of whom is as the sand of the sea.

9. They went up over the breadth of the earth, and surrounded the camp of the saints, and the beloved city. Fire came down out of heaven, and devoured them.

10. The devil who deceived them was thrown into the lake of fire and sulphur, where are also the beast and the false prophet. They will be tormented day and night forever and ever.

Friday, 9 September AD 96

A nightmare woke me up during the night and it frightened me so much that I couldn't fall asleep again. During this nightmare, I saw myself standing once more in a court room with a raving Roman judge questioning me and sentencing me to a permanent, life-long stay in prison. After rolling around on my bed for some time, I decided to go outside and watch the stars from my favorite rock.

It is still dark and I can see a very faint glimmer of the approaching daybreak. My dream of a Roman judge forces me to watch God's throne in the northern sky from where Christ will judge the world. I am certainly not the first prophet who gazed upon God's throne from where he rules his creation. For instance, Isaiah wrote:

> "In the year that king Uzziah died I saw the Lord sitting on a throne, high and lifted up; and his train filled the temple."[182]

King David also wrote in one of his Psalms about God as a judge:

> "But the Lord reigns forever. He has prepared his throne for judgment. He will judge the world in righteousness. He will administer judgment to the peoples in uprightness."[183]

Although God is not visible to human eyes, I am sure that his majesty must be so overwhelming that no creature can endure that sight. I can imagine that the whole of creation with all its evils, crimes, and iniquities must flee from God on his throne.

While I look northwards to God's throne, I also notice the tranquil waters of the Bay of Skala to the north. Many of the stars in

---

[182] Isa 6: 1.
[183] Ps 9: 7–8.

the sky are reflected upon this water. This gives me the idea that all the dead people, also those who have drowned in the sea, will be collected in front of God's throne on Judgment Day.

The books of Daniel and Enoch taught me that God will consult his books on Judgment Day. These books will contain the criminal records of all the sinners on earth.

An ancient scroll containing the book of Esther

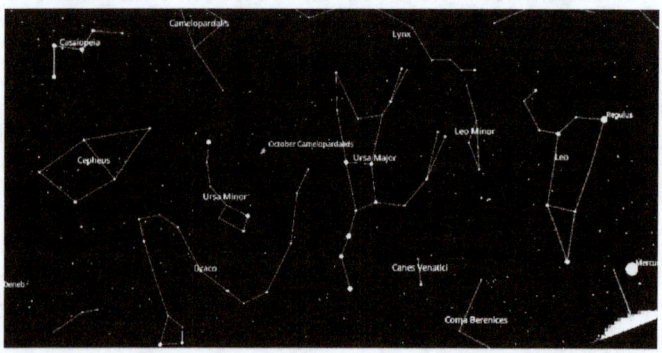

The constellations of Cepheus, Ursa Major, Ursa Minor, and Leo in the vicinity of the northern celestial pole (the throne of God at Ursa Minor), each containing a configuration with a square – the books consulted by God that John saw

286

I recite to myself again the following words from Daniel:

> "A fiery stream issued and came forth from before him: thousands of thousands ministered to him, and ten thousand times ten thousand stood before him: the judgment was set, and the books were opened."[184]

Enoch wrote in this regard:

> "And I saw till a throne was erected in the pleasant land, and the Lord of the sheep [lamb?] sat Himself thereon, and the other took the sealed books and opened those books before the Lord of the sheep."[185]

Mosaic of Christ in his glory as heavenly judge, holding the book of life (Rev 3: 5 and 20: 12), in the Hagia Sophia Cathedral in Istanbul (Constantinople) from the 13th century.

The most important book is also opened – the book of life. All those whose names are not written in this book were thrown into the lake of fire – the sun behind the eastern horizon whose first rays are becoming visible as dawn approaches. This book contains the names of those who are the property of God and their names were already entered into this book at the beginning of the world because God knew who would be the faithful.

---

[184] Dan 7: 10.
[185] Enoch 90: 20.

It is revealed to me that Death and Hades are thrown into the lake of fire and sulphur on this day, Judgment Day. In other words: death is abolished because God's children will receive eternal and everlasting life. They will be immortal. Hades is being destroyed and emptied of its inhabitants.

In a previous vision, when I saw the four horsemen, I mentioned "a pale horse. He who sat on him, his name was Death. Hades followed with him." This pale horse was identified as the constellation of Equuleus, the Foal of Pegasus with his wings, Nimrod's Horse. While I am watching, the Foal is situated on the western horizon, ready to disappear – together with Nimrod's Horse. In other words, Death and Hades are to be annihilated by the rays of the rising sun in the east.

The flames and fires from Hades in the south-east have died down and that also gives me the conviction that God will eliminate and eradicated Hades, the abyss. As the faintest stars disappears as daybreak is arriving, I feel much better after my ugly and disturbing nightmare. I lie down again and I drift off into a peaceful sleep because I know that God is the judge and ruler of the world.

The traditional Roman Catholic cycle of hymns known as the Requiem or Mass for the Dead (named for the beginning of the Latin words of the Introit "Requiem aeternam dona eis, Domine" – "Give them eternal rest, O Lord") contains a hymn known by its opening words in Latin "Dies Irae" ("Day of Wrath"). This hymn, ascribed to Thomas of Celano († c. 1256), deals with Judgment Day and was inspired by the words of Rev 20: 11–15 and Matt 25: 31–46. The dramatic and moving musical dramas composed by Wolfgang Amadeus Mozart and Giuseppi Verdi to accompany this cycle of hymns are often performed.[186]

---

[186] Enc Brit, "Dies Irae".

Christ as cosmic judge and clothed as a Roman senator, with the book of life in his left hand and the crown of life in his right hand, flanked by two archangels, Saint Vitalis, and Bishop Ecclesius (mosaic in the apse of the basilica of San Vitale, Ravenna, Italy, 6th century).

After a hearty breakfast consisting of bread, cheese, and sheep's milk, I instruct Prochorus to start writing as follows:

Revelation 20: 11 –15
The last judgment

11.	I saw a great white throne, and him who sat on it, from whose face the earth and the heaven fled away. There was found no place for them.
12.	I saw the dead, the great and the small, standing before the throne. Books were opened. Another book was opened, which is the book of life. The dead were judged out of the things which were written in the books, according to their works.
13.	The sea gave up the dead who were in it. Death and Hades gave up the dead who were in them. They were judged, each one according to his works.

14. Death and Hades were thrown into the lake of fire. This is the second death, the lake of fire.

15. If anyone was not found written in the book of life, he was cast into the lake of fire.

Tuesday, 20 December AD 96

A few days after I have given a description of Judgment Day for Prochorus to write down, the Beast from the Sea with the secret number of 666, Caesar Domitian, appeared before God's judicial throne directly after he had been assassinated. I often felt confident that this godless, cruel, and immoral emperor's days were numbered. I was only informed on a Saturday of this development by my friend Jason a whole fortnight after the emperor's inglorious end because the news took some time to reach Patmos.

A thanksgiving service was held the next morning and my whole little flock attended. I know it's not polite to be glad about the death of any person, but we all agreed that an exception had to be made in this case, although I told my flock not to tell everybody about our gratitude and relief that this godless and blasphemous emperor, the Antichrist, has met his end.

Prochorus declared: "My friends, brothers, and sisters in Christ, I don't have the same prophetic gift as this master of ours, but I think that I can predict with confidence that our master's exile on this island will soon come to an end. He will be pardoned, somehow or other, sooner or later."

I agreed with my companion.

It took more than two months, though, before I was allowed

to sail back to Ephesus after the Senate in Rome had decided to grant a pardon to all religious and political prisoners and exiles.

Because we had to pay for our own passage back to Ephesus, my little congregation provided most of the money to be paid to a shipmaster who took us to the mainland last week.

The congregation on Patmos unanimously voted Andrew as my successor because he was my first convert and he had learnt much from me and Prochorus – including the art or reading and writing. I promised to send him copies of the Scriptures and the books describing the life of Jesus, so that he could instruct the little flock and win new converts. His hut, on a spot overlooking the sea, below my cave, would become the new meeting place.

It is tempting to think of the little ancient chapel below the cave in which John lived according to tradition, as the spot where John's little flock assembled after his departure from the island. This chapel, dedicated to Saint Andrew (Greek: Ἅγιος Ἀνδρέας – *Hagios Andreas*), is about 300 meters from the cave.

We arrived in Ephesus three days ago, on a Saturday. Nobody expected us and we proceeded on our own to our old home. The place was empty and dirty, but we tried to make ourselves at home. Somebody must have broken in and stole everything, including my books. The next morning, we attended the meeting of the Christian congregation and everybody was very glad to see us back. A special collection was held to help us to buy some food. We also received some donations of furniture to make our home habitable.

One of my colleagues brought me a stack of books: "My brother, I am becoming blind. I can't read these books anymore. God persuaded me to donate them to you."

Since I knew the Scriptures by heart, I didn't need some of these books and I decided to send them to Andrew on Patmos.

Tonight, Tuesday night, an angel urged me to climb onto one of the hills outside Ephesus to watch the stars from this vantage point. I took Prochorus along and we wore thick robes and took some rugs along due to the winter cold.

Ancient Ephesus lies in a valley between hills. The amphitheater of the city – mentioned in Acts 19: 29 – lies at the foot of one of these hills.

In comparison with the low hills on Patmos, this hill feels like a high mountain to me. I am sure that I will see the stars clearer from here. I haven't been able to receive any messages from heaven during the last two months and I am confident that the Spirit of God will show me something important tonight.

It is indeed remarkable that the stars are brighter here than on Patmos – perhaps because I am higher above sea level and nearer to the sky than on Patmos.

While I am watching the sky, it dawns upon me that I am watching a new heaven and a new earth, here on the mainland. The sky and the environment are different from that on Patmos. The sea is invisible. I quote the following words from the Book of Jubilees to Prochorus to make my point:

> "The heavens and the earth shall be renewed and all their creation according to the powers of the heaven, and according to all the creation of the earth, until the sanctuary of the Lord shall be made in Jerusalem on Mount Zion, and all the luminaries be renewed for healing and for peace and for blessing for all the elect of Israel…"[187]

The prophet Isaiah wrote something in the same vein:

> "For, behold, I create new heavens and a new earth; and the former things shall not be remembered, nor come into mind. But be you glad and rejoice forever in that which I create; for, behold, I create Jerusalem a rejoicing, and her people a joy."[188]

---

[187] Jub 1: 28.
[188] Isa 65: 17–18.

Prochorus: "It is a relief to know that the hardship of living in a cave, filled with stinking and squealing sheep, is something of the past and that a new future awaits you, even if you're not so young anymore. The words of the prophets give us the expectation that God will show us his New Jerusalem, the replacement of the old Jerusalem that was destroyed almost thirty years ago. You were shown this New Jerusalem briefly a few weeks ago on Patmos, but I am sure that you will see her, the bride of the Lamb, much better here."

I agree and I remind him that Enoch also thought of God's heaven as a big city because he mentioned "the gates of heaven".[189]

I add: "There can be no doubt that this New Jerusalem will be a much better place than anything on the present earth with all its warfare, crime, pain, and suffering. In the New Jerusalem, people will live in peace and all their tears will dry up."

Prochorus: "In contrast, there are some people who will be condemned to the second death, the lake of fire and sulphur"

"That's right. It will be the corrupt cowards, the sacrilegious sinners, the merciless murderers, the shameless sexual offenders, the scheming sorcerers, all insincere idolaters, and all loathsome liars."

It is no coincidence that I mention six categories since six is the symbolic number of sinful man.

When I start to study the whole heaven when it becomes dark, I look it from east to west and from north to south.

Me: "My friend, I just discovered that the New Jerusalem has twelve gates, each of them a prominent star that glitters like a shiny pearl. Each gate is guarded by an angel. On each of these gates the name of one of the tribes of Israel is written and that demonstrates to me that only the true people of God will live in this city."

"Interesting, remarkable."

---

[189] Enoch 9: 9–10.

"Yes. There are three gates in each direction. The following constellations on the four corners of the sky each has three prominent stars in a row, forming the gates of this city. There, in the east, you will see Nimrod, the Hunter[190]. The stars forming his shoulder, his belt, and his knee lie in a neat row. The Sea Monster lies to the south and there are three prominent stars in a row on its body.[191] In the west, you will see the Eagle.[192] Both his wing tips and his head form a straight line. The Great Bear in the north has three bright stars in his tail. These twelve gates will never be closed because there will never be night in this fabulous and fantastic city."[193]

"Did any of the prophets have anything on this matter?"

"Certainly. The prophet Ezekiel had a similar vision of the New Jerusalem in the last part of his book.[194] He describes the gates of this city as follows:

'And the gates of the city shall be after the names of the tribes of Israel, three gates northward: the gate of Reuben, one; the gate of Judah, one; the gate of Levi, one. At the east side four thousand and five hundred [reeds], and three gates: even the gate of Joseph, one; the gate of Benjamin, one; the gate of Dan, one. At the south side four thousand and five hundred [reeds] by measure, and three gates: the gate of Simeon, one; the gate of Issachar, one; the gate of Zebulun, one. At the west side four thousand and five hundred [reeds], with their three gates: the gate of Gad, one; the gate of Asher,

---

[190] Orion.
[191] Cetus.
[192] Aquila.
[193] Ursa Major.
[194] Ezek 31–35, 40–48.

one; the gate of Naphtali, one. It shall be eighteen thousand [reeds] round about: and the name of the city from that day shall be, the Lord is there'."[195]

Prochorus: "Truly remarkable."

I continue: "My vision of the New Jerusalem also reminds me of the camps of the wandering Israelites during the exodus on their way to the Promised Land. The twelve tribes were required to camp in a large square with three tribes occupying each of the four main directions. The tribe of Levi with the Tabernacle was to be protected in the center."[196]

John's description of the heavenly Jerusalem fascinated Christians through the ages. A medieval depiction of this city shows how an angel demonstrates to John the heavenly Jerusalem, while standing on a mountain (Manuscript illumination from the Revelation to John, *c.* 1020; in the Staatsbibliothek in Bamberg, Germany)

I show my companion that there are also twelve foundation stones at each gate, each with a name of an apostle of the Lamb on it and made from a shiny jewel or precious stone. The main street of the city is made of pure gold, the Milky Way stretching from east to west. I find the sight so breath-taking that I conclude that this heavenly city must be immensely huge. I estimate that the four

---

[195] Ezek 48: 33–35.
[196] Num 2.

walls, enclosing the city, are each twelve thousand stadia or Roman miles long. Of course, the number of twelve thousand tells me something. I explain to Prochorus that twelve is the number that demonstrates completeness or perfection and that thousand tells me that it is immensely huge, filling the whole sky.

Prochorus: "You mentioned jewels as the foundation stones. Which jewels do you mean?"

"The first foundation is jasper; the second, sapphire; the third, chalcedony; the fourth, emerald; the fifth, sardonyx; the sixth, sardius; the seventh, chrysolite; the eighth, beryl; the ninth, topaz; the tenth, chrysoprasus; the eleventh, jacinth; and the twelfth, amethyst."

"Where did you get those names? Are they mentioned somewhere in the Scriptures?"

"Oh, yes. They are the twelve gems on the breastplate of the high priest, as described by Moses.[197] When I was serving as a priest in Jerusalem before the war, I saw that breast plate regularly. It was a replacement because the original one got lost when Jerusalem was sacked by the Babylonians a few centuries ago."

"Remarkable. Will all the needs of those in this celestial city be satisfied in any way?"

"Look there, to the south-west. Do you see the Water Carrier with his bucket?[198] That water is from the spring of life, which is to be given to those who are thirsty. You will also see the evening star, which is sometimes also the morning star, next to the Water Carrier. This star is sometimes called the planet that is 'bringing light, giving light' and we may see it as a symbol of Christ who gives light and

---

[197] Ex 28: 15–21; Pratt, 2005.
[198] Aquarius; Jacobus, 2012: 323.

the water of life.[199] It is certainly the brightest thing in the sky and it draws the attention to the Water Carrier. This spring of the water of life is a gift of Him who is called 'the Alpha and the Omega, the Beginning and the End' – in other words: Christ."

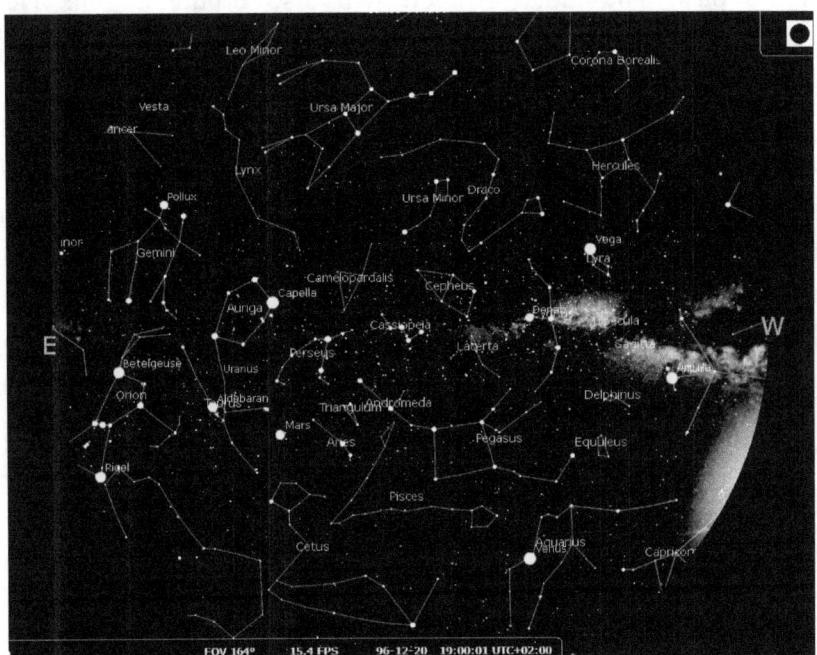

The sky over Ephesus, looking south, on the night of 20 December AD 96, shortly after sunset. The following constellations are visible: Orion (the Hunter ore Nimrod) in the east, Cetus (the Sea Monster or Leviathan) towards the south, Aquila (the Eagle) in the West and Ursa Major (the Great Bear) in the north – each containing three prominent stars in a row. Also visible is Aquarius (the Water Carrier) in the southwest. The bright Milky Way stretches from east to west. The only two planets visible are Venus as the evening star in the southwest in Aquarius and Mars in the southeast.

Prochorus: "I do agree that that planet is the brightest object in the

---

[199] The planet Venus is given the name of φωσφόρος *(fosferos* – bringer of light) in 2 Pet 1: 19.

sky because the sun and the moon are absent."

"I also think so. This heavenly Jerusalem doesn't need the sun and the moon because Christ is its lamp. God is sitting on his invisible throne, over there in the north, as I have pointed out to you in the past. The glory of God will also illuminate this New Jerusalem."

"Is there a temple in this city?"

"I can't see any temples, really. Because God resides directly with his people in this place, it is not necessary to have a temple where he can be worshipped. He will no longer be hidden in a far-away heaven but will be in direct contact with the blessed souls – just as He was in contact with his people during their travels through the desert and He resided in his tent."

"I suppose that if God is residing in this city, there will be no place for Satan, one of the other beasts, or Hades. Am I right?"

"Totally right, my friend. Satan, in the form of the Dragon, and the other two beasts, are absent here. We can't see the flames and sparks and smoke from Hades anymore and, therefore, I believe that death will also be something of the past when this city arrives."

"Do you agree that this New Jerusalem will be a perfect place?"

"Most definitely. Nothing that is sinful, evil, wrong, bad, malicious, or reminds one of any pagan gods can be tolerated in God's presence. May I remind you of what the prophet Enoch said? He promised:

'And in their days shall no sorrow or plague or torment or calamity touch them.'[200]

This New Jerusalem will be infinitely better than the horrible world

---

[200] Enoch 25: 6.

in which we are living at present. God's plans for his creation and his children will be realized completely when this heavenly city arrives after the defeat of Satan and his godless forces."

"So, the wedding of the Lamb has taken place, I believe?"

"This beautiful city is certainly the bride of the Lamb. All the angels and the souls of the martyrs will rejoice."

"You also said that this wonderful place will have no sea?"

"That's right. The sea is often seen in the Scriptures as constantly producing chaos. The sea is the dwelling of Rahab or the Leviathan, a frightening and dangerous sea monster.[201]

> Eusebius of Caesarea, the first church historian, wrote that John was freed after the death of Emperor Domitian, which occurred in September AD 96. After he had "returned from the isle of Patmos to Ephesus, he went away upon their invitation to the neighboring territories of the Gentiles, to appoint bishops in some places, in other places to set in order whole churches ...".[202]

---

[201] Job 9: 13; Ps 87: 4; Ps 89: 9–10.
[202] Eusebius, *Hist Eccl,* Liber III/ XVIII/1 and III/XX/10.

Wednesday, 21 December AD 96

Today is a special day: the shortest day of the year and the longest night of the year. The pagans sometimes do something special on this day but the followers of Jesus just take note of this date without celebrating it.

Last night, we struggled during the dark to descend from the hill outside Ephesus. We didn't want to stay up there in the cold the whole night. And this morning, we sit down so that I can dictate to Prochorus what he must write.

Revelation 21: 1–27

The new heaven and the new earth

1.	I saw a new heaven and a new earth: for the first heaven and the first earth have passed away, and the sea is no more.
2.	I saw the holy city, New Jerusalem, coming down out of heaven from God, made ready as a bride adorned for her husband.
3.	I heard a loud voice out of heaven saying, "Behold, God's tent is with men, and he will dwell with them, and they will be his people, and God himself will be with them as their God.
4.	He will wipe away every tear from their eyes. Death will be no more; neither will there be mourning, nor crying, nor pain, any more. The first things have passed away."
5.	He who sits on the throne said, "Behold, I make all things new." He said, "Write, for these words are faithful and true."
6.	He said to me, "It is done! I am the Alpha and the Omega, the Beginning and the End. I will give freely to him who is thirsty from the spring of the water of life.

7. He who overcomes, I will give him these things. I will be his God, and he will be my son.

8. But for the cowardly, unbelieving, sinners, abominable, murderers, sexually immoral, sorcerers, idolaters, and all liars, their part is in the lake that burns with fire and sulphur, which is the second death."

9. One of the seven angels who had the seven bowls, who were laden with the seven last plagues came, and he spoke with me, saying, "Come here. I will show you the wife, the Lamb's bride."

10. He carried me away in the Spirit to a great and high mountain, and showed me the holy city, Jerusalem, coming down out of heaven from God,

11. having the glory of God. Her light was like a most precious stone, as if it was a jasper stone, clear as crystal;

12. having a great and high wall; having twelve gates, and at the gates twelve angels; and names written on them, which are the names of the twelve tribes of the children of Israel.

13. On the east were three gates; and on the north three gates; and on the south three gates; and on the west three gates.

14. The wall of the city had twelve foundations, and on them twelve names of the twelve Apostles of the Lamb.

15. He who spoke with me had for a measure a golden reed to measure the city, its gates, and its walls.

16. The city lies foursquare, and its length is as great as its breadth. He measured the city with the reed, twelve thousand stadia. Its length, breadth, and height are equal.

17. He measured its wall, one hundred forty-four cubits, by the measure of a man, that is, of an angel.

18. The construction of its wall was jasper. The city was pure gold, like pure glass.

19. The foundations of the city's wall were adorned with all kinds of precious stones. The first foundation was jasper; the second, sapphire; the third, chalcedony; the fourth, emerald;

20. the fifth, sardonyx; the sixth, sardius; the seventh, chrysolite; the eighth, beryl; the ninth, topaz; the tenth, chrysoprasus; the eleventh, jacinth; and the twelfth, amethyst.

21. The twelve gates were twelve pearls. Each one of the gates was made of one pearl. The street of the city was pure gold, like transparent glass.

22. I saw no temple in it, for the Lord God, the Almighty, and the Lamb, are its temple.

23. The city has no need for the sun, neither of the moon, to shine, for the very glory of God illuminated it, and its lamp is the Lamb.

24. The nations will walk in its light. The kings of the earth bring their glory into it.

25. Its gates will in no way be shut by day (for there will be no night there),

26. and they will bring the glory and the honour of the nations into it.

27. There will in no way enter into it anything profane, or one who causes an abomination or a lie, but only those who are written in the Lamb's book of life.

The elders requested me to restart my lectures on the books of Daniel and Enoch to some students during the afternoon when the School of Tyrannus is not in use by the pagans.

While I and Prochorus walk back home after the lecture, I tell him: "I want you to add a few sentences to the part I dictated to you this morning. I have been thinking about our vision of the New Jerusalem last night and there are a few thoughts I wish to add."

"That scene was so overwhelming that I am sure that you can tell your eventual readers a lot more."

"Yes. We didn't only see the New Jerusalem, the city of God. He also revealed to us the restored garden of Eden, the garden from which Adam and Eve were banned after having eaten from the forbidden fruit."

"What did you see of this garden?"

"The bright Milky Way in the middle of the sky, stretching from east to west, is not only the main street of this fantastic city. It can also be regarded as the river that irrigates this garden, streaming along this main street. There are wonderful fruit trees on its banks, bearing fruit throughout the whole year. Those who reside there will never go hungry, just as they will never be thirsty with the water of life at their disposal."

"All right, as soon as we get home, we can start to write down what you just told me."

Rwevelation 22: 1–5
The heavenly garden

1.	He showed me a river of water of life, clear as crystal, proceeding out of the throne of God and of the Lamb,
2.	in the midst of its street. On this side of the river and on that was the tree of life, bearing twelve kinds of fruits, yielding its fruit every month. The leaves of the tree were for the healing of the nations.
3.	There will be no curse any more. The throne of God and of the Lamb will be in it, and his servants will serve him.

4. They will see his face, and his name will be on their foreheads.

5. There will be no more night, and they need no lamp light, neither sunlight; for the Lord God will give them light. They will reign forever and ever.

Sunday, 1 January AD 97

During the past few days, I was so busy visiting the elders and other members of the congregation to hear from them what had happened during my absence, that there was no time to work on the completion of my book about the visions that God had given me.

However, on this Sunday morning before daybreak, I am sitting outside the city and mediating about what I should tell the congregation today. Today is supposed to be a special day for the pagans because it is the beginning of the Roman year and the first day of the month consecrated to their god Janus – a two-faced awful abomination and a freakish fraud. With one face on its usual place, he is supposed to look forward to the rest of the year ahead and with his other face, at the back of his head, he purportedly looks back at the previous year. For us, as the followers of Christ, this day holds no special meaning and we will carry on as usual.

While I am awaiting daybreak, I watch the sky – the habit I acquired while I was on Patmos. My eye catches the brightest object in the sky – the planet Jupiter on the eastern horizon. This bright planet with the pagan name of Jupiter or Zeus, is called by the Jews the "Righteous One". It is almost as if I hear that Christ reminds me that He is the bright Morning Star, heralding a new day with hope and new prospects. He reminds me that his return is imminent.

According to me, this name of the "Righteous One" for Christ as the judge on Judgment Day is appropriate. The prophet Zechariah promised that the Messiah would be a man of justice:

> "Rejoice greatly, daughter of Zion; shout, daughter of Jerusalem: behold, your king comes to you; he is just, and having salvation ...."[203]

---

[203] Zech 9: 9.

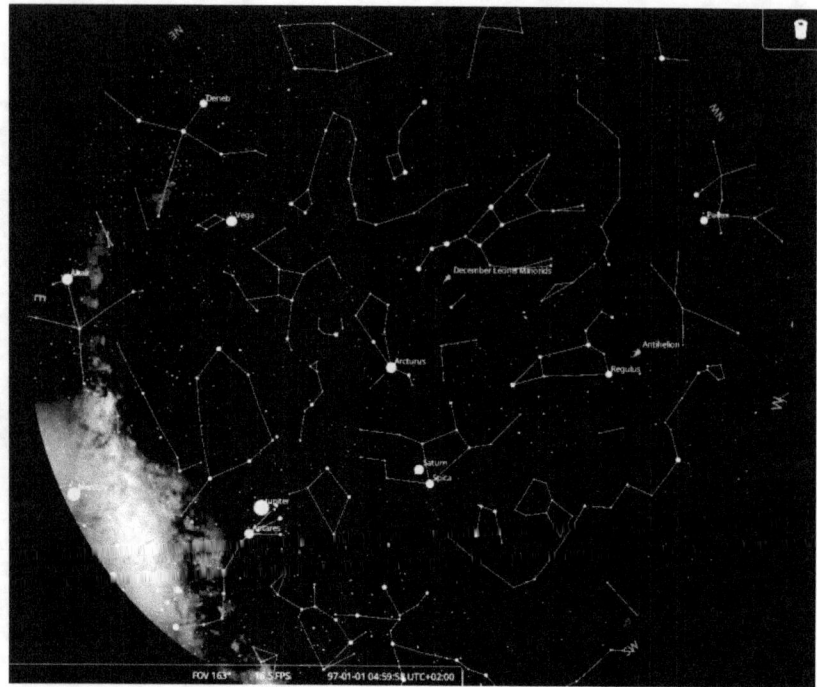

Jupiter rising as a morning star in the south-east on 1 January AD 97 in the sky over Ephesus, shortly before daybreak. Jupiter was the brightest object in the sky, with a magnitude of -1,89. Saturn, by comparison, had a magnitude of 0,45.

One of the angels next to God's throne gives me the assurance that the messages I have received are true and trustworthy and that I ought to complete my book with which I must instruct my fellow-Christians. This message gives me so much joy that I feel like worshipping this angel, but then I remember that I am supposed to worship only the one true God. After all, angels are only servants of God, just as I am.

As the Alpha and Omega, the beginning and the end, Christ is the equal of God, the Father, who is also the Alpha and the Omega. He is the firstborn of creation, as well as the one who will bring human history to a close on Judgment Day. Since the return of Christ must be expected at any moment, there would, as it were, not even be enough time before the arrival of Judgment Day for evil people to repent and turn to God and, therefore, the angel tells me that sinners could just as well carry on with their iniquities and vices. Those people who belonged to God, on the other hand, had to persist in their ways because the coming of Christ is due at any time now.

The contrast between those saints and martyrs who belong to Christ and the crude godless sinners is very apparent to me. The faithful deserve to enter the New Jerusalem, enjoy the fruit of the tree of life and drink from the fountain with the water of life. The evil sinners have as their destiny the second death, eternal punishment and perdition in hell.

I believe that those who will arrive in hell can be classified in six classes (the symbolic number of sinful mankind): the dirty dogs, the scandalous sorcerers, the filthy fornicators, the messy murderers, the ignorant idol worshippers, and all those who twist the truth.

During the day, after I have delivered a sermon to the congregation on what believers may expect after they have died, I ask Prochorus to get hold of a sheet of papyrus, a pen, and some ink. I dictate to him as follows:

Revelation 22: 6–17
The coming of Christ

6.	He said to me, "These words are faithful and true. The Lord, the God of the spirits of the prophets, sent his angels to show to his servants the things which must happen soon."
7.	"Behold, I come quickly. Blessed is he who keeps the words of the prophecy of this book."
8.	Now I, John, am the one who heard and saw these things. When I heard and saw, I fell down to worship before the feet of the angel who showed me these things.

9. He said to me, "See you don't do it! I am a fellow bondservant with you and with your brothers, the prophets, and with those who keep the words of this book. Worship God."

10. He said to me, "Don't seal up the words of the prophecy of this book, for the time is at hand.

11. He who acts unjustly, let him act unjustly still. He who is filthy, let him be filthy still. He who is righteous, let him do righteousness still. He who is holy, let him be holy still."

12. "Behold, I come quickly. My reward is with me, to repay to each man according to his work.

13. I am the Alpha and the Omega, the First and the Last, the Beginning and the End.

14. Blessed are those who do his commandments, that they may have the right to the tree of life, and may enter in by the gates into the city.

15. Outside are the dogs, the sorcerers, the sexually immoral, the murderers, the idolaters, and everyone who loves and practices falsehood.

16. I, Jesus, have sent my angel to testify these things to you for the assemblies. I am the root and the offspring of David; the Bright and Morning Star. "

17. The Spirit and the bride say, "Come!" He who hears, let him say, "Come!" He who is thirsty, let him come. He who desires, let him take the water of life freely.

Prochorus asks me afterwards: "Is this the very last part of your book?"

"I don't think so. I was ordered to deliver my book to the seven churches in Asia. The only way will be to deliver a copy to each one of those churches. I am convinced that God appointed me

310

as a prophet – just as he called Isaiah, Elijah, Ezekiel, Amos, or Daniel. My book was inspired by the Spirit of God and that means that it contains God's message to these churches. But we will have to go and visit these churches and deliver copies of this book there personally. I can't trust anybody else to do that."

"Will that mean that we will have to make six more copies of your book?"

"That will be necessary, yes. But before we start with that task, I think I must add a few thoughts in my own hand to complete the book. It is necessary that I add an introduction to greet my readers and tell them what this book is about. And then I must add an ending in which I will warn anybody who makes further copies to be careful not to change anything in this book. Nothing may be added or left out because that will mean that God's message will be distorted. It has happened far too many times that scribes who copied parts of the holy Scriptures made mistakes or added their own words to those of the prophets or the apostles.

"I must also remind the readers of this book, yet again, that the things described in this book are dealing with the present and the very near future. They must be ready for Christ's unexpected return at any moment, just as death may strike when nobody expects it."

Prochorus provides me with two sheets of papyrus and I start writing with my own hand:

Revelation 1: 4–8
Introduction

4.	John, to the seven assemblies that are in Asia: Grace to you and peace, from God, who is and who was and who is to come; and from the seven Spirits who are before his throne;

5.	and from Jesus Christ, the faithful witness, the firstborn of the dead, and the ruler of the kings of the earth. To him who loves us, and washed us from our sins by his blood;

6.	and he made us to be a kingdom, priests to his God and Father; to him be the glory and the dominion forever and ever. Amen.

7.	Behold, he is coming with the clouds, and every eye will see him, including those who pierced him. All the tribes of the earth will mourn over him. Even so, Amen.

8.	"I am the Alpha and the Omega, the Beginning and the End," says the Lord God, "who is and who was and who is to come, the Almighty."

Prochorus asks: "Why don't you introduce yourself better? You simply called yourself John on two occasions now, without informing your readers who and what you are."

"I don't think it's necessary, my good friend. All the Christians know me and I am the only church leader in these parts with the name of John after the death of the apostle with this name."

On the second sheet I add the following ending to my book:

Revelation 22: 18–21
Last words

18.	I testify to every man who hears the words of the prophecy of this book, if anyone adds to them, may God add to him the plagues which are written in this book.

19.	If anyone takes away from the words of the book of this prophecy, may God take away his part from the tree of life, and out of the holy city, which are written in this book.

> 20. He who testifies these things says, "Yes, I come quickly." Amen! Come, Lord Jesus.
>
> 21. The grace of the Lord Jesus be with all the saints. Amen.

Prochorus places my sheets at the beginning and end of the stack of sheets he keeps in a box.

Sunday, 8 January AD 97

My completed book with God's messages must be delivered to the seven churches in Asia. The first church is my home congregation, Ephesus, and during today's service I present a copy to my friend Gaius, the man who visited us on Patmos and who acted as leader during my exile.

  Prochorus helped me to make a neat copy of the book, which he has bound into a codex. On the outside cover, he provided a description of the contents of the book:

A codex is the Roman name for a book, made of pages, and usually bound on the left (illustrated: a page of the Codex Vaticanus, 4th Century)

Revelation 1: 1–3
Contents of the book

1.	This is the Revelation of Jesus Christ, which God gave him to show to his servants the things which must happen soon, which he sent and made known by his angel to his servant, John,
2.	who testified to God's word, and of the testimony of Jesus Christ, about everything that he saw.
3.	Blessed is he who reads and those who hear the words of the prophecy, and keep the things that are written in it, for the time is at hand.

It is my intention to start my visits and inspection tour to the other six churches tomorrow. I will spend a fortnight at each to hear about their problems and challenges and to help them to function better and to stay true to their calling. My first stop will be at Smyrna, north of Ephesus.

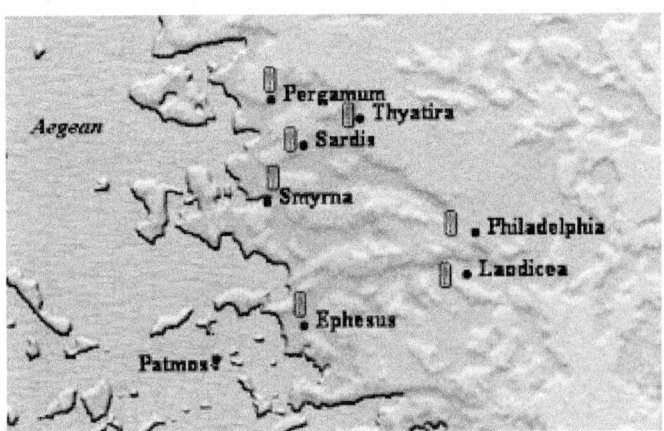

The seven churches of Asia that received letters from John, together with the island of Patmos.

Together with the book, I hand over a letter addressed to the leader of the congregation of Ephesus, the assembly where I spent the last thirty odd years after I had fled from Jerusalem during the war against Rome. It is impossible not to feel emotional about the Christians in this city because I have made many friends and I have received much love from so many people. It is an honor they have bestowed upon me to appoint me as their leader and overseer.

It will be necessary to present a letter to each of the other churches in which I will provide them with a report about their spiritual health.

Ephesus is an ancient Greek city that was founded centuries ago. After becoming part of the Persian Empire and revolting against foreign rule, it became part of the empire of Alexander the Great until it was taken over by the Roman Empire more than a century ago.

Although Ephesus is not the capital city of Asia – Pergamum holds that honor – she is, nevertheless, the most important and richest city of the region due to her harbor that handles almost all the traffic and commerce between Mesopotamia and the Mediterranean countries to the west, including Greece and Italy. Its main attraction is the ancient temple of Artemis.[204] This temple is regarded as one of the seven wonders of the world. Artemis is the Greek goddess of the hunt and of fertility.[205]

Site of the Temple of Artemis in Ephesus

The apostle Paul founded the church in this city and he visited the elders afterwards again[206]. One of Paul's letters was addressed to the church in Ephesus. Paul also instructed his pupil, Timothy – who was my predecessor as overseer here – to stay in Ephesus and engage Christians who taught a "different doctrine" and kept themselves busy with "myths and endless genealogies, which caused divisive disputes".[207] Paul also wrote his letter to the church

---

[204] See Acts 19: 27–34.

[205] Enc Brit, "Ephesus".

[206] Acts 19 & 20: 17.

[207] 1 Tim 1: 3–4.

in Rome from Ephesus.

I plan to address the leaders or bishops of the seven churches as "angels" (messengers) of Christ. It will be their tasks to read the letters to their congregations since many people are not be able to read the letters themselves. Each of these angels of the churches has a heavenly counterpart, the angels in the form of stars next to God's throne.

It seems fitting to me to introduce the real and primary, but hidden, author of the letter to Ephesus as "He who holds the seven stars in his right hand, he who walks in the midst of the seven golden lampstands." This is how I saw Christ during my first vision after having arrived on Patmos almost a year ago. The seven stars in his right hand were symbols of the angels or messengers of the seven churches and the golden lampstands symbolized the seven churches. The members of this church are to be reminded that their church is dependent upon Christ, but also that He protects the church.

A statue of Artemis in the Vatican Museum – probably a copy of the statue that stood in her temple in Ephesus. As goddess of fertility, she was depicted with many milk-filled breasts.

It is certainly prudent to point to the positive points in this church, which I noticed during my conversations with the elders and others.

317

I want to praise the steadfast Christians who suffered persecutions, due to their refusal to venerate Caesar Domitian as a living god.

They must be commended for the fact that discipline in this church was strict and that those who held heretical views were warned to change their convictions. There were wandering teachers, who called themselves apostles, whose false teachings had to be resisted and rejected.

One of these teachers is a certain Nikolaos. I praise the congregation for repudiating his ideas. He followed the example of Balaam[208] and taught that it was acceptable for Christians to participate in pagan feasts in the temple of Artemis with their sexual licentiousness. The Nicolaitans taught that Christ has fulfilled and abolished the Law and, therefore, they may do whatever they like. They confused Christian freedom with promiscuity.

Something that bothers, is my evaluation that the love for Christ of the members has waned. They do not try very hard to find new followers of Christ as in the past.

It is necessary to emphasize that those who persevere may rely on God's promise that they will have the privilege of eating the fruit from the tree of life in the restored paradise.

Revelation 2: 1–7
The Letter to Ephesus

1.	*To the angel of the assembly in Ephesus write:* He who holds the seven stars in his right hand, he who walks in the midst of the seven golden lampstands says these things:
2.	I know your works, and your toil and perseverance, and that you can't tolerate evil men, and have tested those who call themselves apostles, and they are not, and found them false.

---

[208] Num 24: 14; 1–3; 31: 8 &16.

318

3. You have perseverance and have endured for my name's sake, and have not grown weary.

4. But I have this against you, that you left your first love.

5. Remember therefore from where you have fallen, and repent and do the first works; or else I am coming to you, and will move your lampstand out of its place, unless you repent.

6. But this you have, that you hate the works of the Nicolaitans, which I also hate.'

7. He who has an ear, let him hear what the Spirit says to the assemblies. To him who overcomes I will give to eat of the tree of life, which is in the Paradise of my God.

Although John sent the seven letters on behalf of Christ it becomes clear that he composed them himself. He started each letter with a command from Christ to write to the angel of a particular church and the impression is created that the contents of the letters were dictated to him. But then he gave himself away by using the phrase "my God" repeatedly (Rev 2: 7; 3: 2; 3: 12 – four times in the last text) – an expression that would not have fitted in the mouth of Christ since Christ was identified with God Himself. Elsewhere in these letters, Christ refers to God as "my Father" (Rev 2: 27; 3: 5) – as in the Gospels.

Sunday, 22 January AD 97

A journey on horseback of three days took me and Prochorus to the city of Smyrna, a beautiful city and the second most important city in Asia after Ephesus. It is a very old city, which has been destroyed more than once by earthquakes and wars, but rebuilt every time.

A meeting of the elders was called for the day after our arrival and we heard from them about their problems. They complained that the emperor worship in this city is very strong and that some Jews even participate in these ceremonies. These Jews make life difficult for the Christians and I feel compelled to condemn these Jews as a synagogue of Satan.

The congregation suffered from a lack of strong leadership with more than one elder vying for the position of bishop or overseer. After two more meetings, I made an end to this strife and I appoint Polycarp, a former disciple of some of the apostles and certainly the most acceptable candidate for this position.[209]

The ancient agora (marketplace) in Smyrna (today: Izmir)

---

[209] Eusebius: *Hist Eccl*, Liber III/XXXVI/1.

During the past few days, I gave Polycarp some training in leadership. I also visited the homes of many Christians to hear from how they cope with their poverty and persecution.

Early this Sunday morning, I and Prochorus sit down to write the necessary letter to this congregation. I decide to address them in the name of Christ, who is the first and the last, the eternal Son of God, who is his Father's equal, and who called Himself the Alpha and the Omega during my visions of Him. With that, I want to assure these Christians that they have the eternal God on their side. Although they are poor, they are really rich with the promise of eternal life with the crown of life.

The Greek letters Alpha and Omega (A & ω appear on either side of this pain-ting of Jesus Christ from the catacomb of Commodilla in Rome. There are faint stars surrounding Him. The painting was created in the fourth century A.D.

In addition, they won't be subjected to the second death, the eternal death in the lake of fire and sulphur.

It is necessary that I warn this congregation that their troubles are not over and that they may expect prison sentences. Those will be of a limited duration and I express that idea with the announcement that imprisonment would only be for ten days – a sign that God is in command, just as He sent ten plagues to Egypt and gave Ten Commandments to Israel.

I find it necessary to condemn the Jews of this city because their meeting place is nothing but a synagogue of the devil. They cannot regard themselves anymore as the people of God after they have rejected Jesus as their Messiah.

During the Sunday service, which is being held after dark, I bless Polycarp as the new bishop. I also hand him a copy of my book and a copy of my letter to this church. I request him to read the latter to the believers who have assembled:

Revelation 2: 8–11
The Letter to Smyrna

8.	*To the angel of the assembly in Smyrna write:* "The first and the last, who was dead, and has come to life says these things:
9.	'I know your oppression, and your poverty (but you are rich), and the blasphemy of those who say they are Jews, and they are not, but are a synagogue of Satan.
10.	Don't be afraid of the things which you are about to suffer. Behold, the devil is about to throw some of you into prison, that you may be tested; and you will have oppression for ten days. Be faithful to death, and I will give you the crown of life.
11.	He who has an ear, let him hear what the' Spirit says to the assemblies. He who overcomes won't be hurt by the second death.

Sunday, 5 February AD 97

Our next stop is Pergamum, the ancient capital city of the Roman province of Asia and it took us two days of hard riding to travel from Smyrna.

Pergamum is situated on the river Caicus. It is famous for its temple of Aesculapius and the invention and manufacture of parchment as a writing material. In fact, the word "parchment" is derived from the city's name. It is the birthplace of the famous physician Galen, and has a great royal library and a school of medicine. It is a beautiful city with temples and other civic buildings; the best-known of these is the gigantic Altar of Zeus.

The Altar of Zeus from Pergamum (nowadays called Bergama in Turkey), as reconstructed in the Pergamon museum in Berlin. Was this "Satan's throne"?

Pergamum also has temples dedicated to the worship of the deified emperors Augustus and Tiberius and all inhabitants are required to worship there to prove their allegiance to the Roman Empire – although they are also allowed to worship any other deity of their choice. Most Christians in Pergamum, of course, refuse to partake in these pagan ceremonies because Christ was their only Lord, and that sparked persecutions against them.

These persecutions resulted in the execution of Antipas, the previous bishop who was consecrated by the Apostle John during the reign of Nero. He was killed to make an example of him of what could happen to people who refuse to honor the official state religion.

A meeting of elders was called the day after our arrival and we met the present bishop who was chosen by the congregation. We held talks with many Christians and, today, Sunday, I am ready to dictate to Prochorus my letter to this church. As was the case with my two previous letters, I write it on behalf of Christ who I saw in my first vision with a double-bladed sword protruding from his mouth.

The Spatha

John uses the Greek word ῥομφαίαν (*rhomphaia*) for a "sword". By the middle of the 1st century AD, the "gladius" [or short sword] of Roman soldiers had been replaced by the spatha *(spada* is the modern-day Italian word for sword). It had a much longer blade (60—80 *cm / 23.6*—*31.5* in) and a shorter point. The sword was Celtic in origin and it is probable that Gallic soldiers introduced the sword to the Roman Army during the time of Julius Caesar (100–44 BC) and Augustus (63 BC–AD 14). It was a slashing weapon and designed to be used by both the Roman cavalry and infantry."

Found in Spain, this is the only known actual example of a spatha with an eagle-headed hilt. It would have been used by a tribune in the early 4th century AD" .[210] This is probably the sword that John had in mind when he wrote about a "sharp two-edged sword" (Rev 2: 12).

---

[210] Weapons Universe, "Ancient Roman Weapons".

The two-edged sword signified that when Christ speaks, one must listen carefully. It is an indication that his words are incisive and decisive and nobody can contradict Him. I remember that the Roman Empire is being ruled by the might of the sword. The sword of Christ – his Word – will prove in the end to be mightier than any Roman military might.

I must give a positive diagnosis of the spiritual health of this church on behalf of Christ. The Christians clung steadfastly to their faith, even in this city with the Throne of Satan and where Antipas was executed.

I can't stay silent about the tendency of some Christians to make compromises with the pagans and partake in their ceremonies with their sexual perversities. That reminds one of the sins of Balaam who motivated the Israelites to become guilty of fornication.[211] That means that there are some church members who follow the teachings of the Nicolaitans.

Because of the failure to discipline the Nicolaitans, this church is advised to repent, otherwise Christ would smite them with his sword

The promise is given to this church that they will be fed with the hidden or secret manna. The faithful will also receive a white stone with a new name written on it.

The secret manna is something that the pagans would not understand – only those familiar with the history of the Israelites' exodus from Egypt when God fed them miraculously in the desert with manna. In other words: the faithful will receive everything to sustain them in the afterlife. The white stone with a new name is the admittance token to heavenly glory for those who remain faithful and overcome the temptations to submit to worldly standards and behavior.

Prochorus is ready to write:

---

[211] Num 24: 14; 1–3; 31: 8 & 16.

Revelation 2: 13–17
The Letter to Pergamum

12.	*To the angel of the assembly in Pergamum write:* "He who has the sharp two-edged sword says these things:
13.	I know your works and where you dwell, where Satan`s 'throne is. You hold firmly to my name, and didn`t deny my faith, even in the days of Antipas my witness, my faithful one, who was killed among you, where Satan dwells.
14.	But I have a few things against you, because you have there some who hold the teaching of Balaam, who taught Balak to throw a stumbling block before the children of Israel, to eat things sacrificed to idols, and to commit sexual immorality,
15.	So you also have some who hold to the teaching of the Nicolaitans in the same way.
16.	Repent therefore, or else I am coming to you quickly, and I will make war against them with the sword of my mouth.
17.	He who has an ear, let him hear what the Spirit says to the assemblies. To him who overcomes, to him will I give of the hidden manna, and I will give him a white stone, and on the stone a new name written, which no one knows but he who receives it.

Sunday, 19 February AD 97

We arrived at Thyatira three days after having left Pergamum. We easily found the home of the bishop after asking around and he provided us with lodging. He promised to convene a meeting of the elders for the next day's evening, after work.

Before this meeting, I and Prochorus sauntered through the city. The bishop informed us that this city was a colony of Macedonian Greeks, situated between Sardis and Pergamum on the river Lycus. It became part of the kingdom of Pergamum three centuries ago and was later incorporated into the Roman Empire.

The cotton industry is important and employs many people. The Apostle Paul met a woman from this place, a certain Lydia, when he came to Philippi.[212] She was a rich woman who dealt in expensive purple dye for garments made of cotton.

During the meeting with the elders, I was informed of a woman – whom I prefer to call Jezebel, after King Ahab's promiscuous pagan wife – who acts as a prophetess. The elders didn't know what to do with her because she is no better than a harlot and she seduced many men from the congregation into her bed. She tells other Christians that one should first know the "deep things of Satan" before one can experience and appreciate the grace of God.

The elders told me where I could find her and we went to her home the next morning, together with the bishop. I severely reprimanded her and called upon her to repent if she didn't want to kindle the anger of God. She only laughed in our faces.

After this episode, I had many meetings with elders and other people in their homes to hear all the news about recent events that had an impact upon the church.

During this Sunday, I and Prochorus prepare for the service tonight after dark and I discuss my planned letter to this church with Prochorus.

---

[212] Acts 16: 14.

"Since I am writing this letter in the name of Christ, I must introduce Him as the sender of the letter. I will take something from my first vision again and introduce Him as the Son of God who has flaming eyes with which he can see everything. He also has feet of brass with which can trample upon all his enemies and evil forces."

"Old Master, are you going to say anything about that bad brothel-keeper of a woman who laughed at us when you told her that she was risking the wrath of God?"

"Oh, certainly. I won't use her real name, but continue to call her Jezebel. It must be mentioned that she hasn't been disciplined yet by the elders, who have forsaken their duty. I am also disappointed that some Christians take part in pagan ceremonies and eat food that was sacrificed to idols, which are nothing but demons.

"But I will also praise the congregation for their love and their good works. It is clear that they are active with good works. As usual, I will remind them that Christ is fully aware of what they do, what they think, what they desire, and what they hate."

"What will happen to this Jezebel?"

"I foresee that her immoral lifestyle will ruin her health and that she will face a dishonorable end."

"What type of promises do you think will Christ make towards these people?"

"Those who stay loyal to Christ will certainly aid Him on Judgment Day to rule over the nations of the world. Are you ready to write what I tell you?"

"Almost. May I suggest that you remind them that Christ is the Morning Star, the herald of a new day?"

"Good idea. Thanks."

Revelation 2: 18–29
The Letter to Thyatira

18.	*To the angel of the assembly in Thyatira write:*

"The Son of God, who has his eyes like a flame of fire, and his feet are like burnished brass, says these things:

19. 'I know your works, your love, faith, service, patient endurance, and that your last works are more than the first.

20. But I have this against you, that you tolerate your woman, Jezebel, who calls herself a prophetess. She teaches and seduces my servants to commit sexual immorality, and to eat things sacrificed to idols.

21. I gave her time to repent, but she refuses to repent of her sexual immorality.

22. Behold, I will throw her into a bed, and those who commit adultery with her into great oppression, unless they repent of her works.

23. I will kill her children with Death, and all the assemblies will know that I am he who searches the minds and hearts. I will give to each one of you according to your deeds.

24. But to you I say, to the rest who are in Thyatira, as many as don't have this teaching, who don't know what some call 'the deep things of Satan,' to you I say, I don't lay on you any other burden.

25. Nevertheless that which you have, hold firmly until I come.

26. He who overcomes, and he who keeps my works to the end, to him will I give authority over the nations.

27. He will rule them with a rod of iron, shattering them like clay pots; as I also have received of my Father:

28. and I will give him the morning star.

29. He who has an ear, let him hear what the Spirit says to the assemblies.'"

Sunday, 5 March AD 97

Sardis, our next destination, used to be the capital city of the kingdom of Lydia from eight centuries ago, according to the bishop whose home we found after asking a few citizens where we could find him. The city's most famous king was the ridiculously rich Croesus. This place is famed for the fact that the first gold and silver coins in the world were minted here.

The inhabitants thought that nobody would be able to conquer their city because it is situated upon a hill top and is protected on three sides by steep cliffs and this attitude undermined their vigilance. However, the armies of both the Persian King Cyrus in and Antiochus the Great succeeded in captured Sardis by scaling the undefended cliffs. It became part of the Roman Empire more than two centuries ago.

The most imposing building of Roman Sardis is the (much reconstructed) courtyard of the Bath-Gymnasium Complex.

Emperor Tiberius helped to fund the rebuilding of the city eighty years ago when it was destroyed by a violent earthquake – the sort of catastrophe we also encountered on Patmos. The place slipped into a quiet and sleepy way of life and that is what I also found when we met the bishop and his elders the day after our arrival. This lazy and careless attitude and tradition must be a left-over of previous centuries when the city neglected her defenses.

Bishop Melito, a Jew by birth, received us in his home and promised to convene a meeting of the church council the next day.

While I and Prochorus were walking though the market square, a young man didn't look where he was running and he bumped into Prochorus. Both fell and the young man hit his head against a wall. Blood poured from his head where he suffered a gash. We helped him onto his feet and took him to Melito's home to nurse his injury.

He gave his name as Ignatius – which describes his fiery character. While I fixed his wound, I told him about Jesus Christ and he listened with attention.

After I have cleaned the wound with wine and oil and fastened a strip of clean cloth around his head to protect the wound, he asked: "Master, may I stay some time with you? I want to learn more about this Jesus."

"You must ask bishop Melito, whose house this is."

Melito immediately granted permission and asked: "But Ignatius, don't you have a home of your own?"

"No. I am visiting Sardis, looking for work. I hail from Thessalonica."

Between a meeting with the church council and visits to the homes of elders and other Christians to get an idea of what is going on in this church, I and Melito instructed Ignatius about our faith.

I discuss with Prochorus and Melito the letter I want to write. I explain that I write this letter on behalf of Christ. I will introduce Him as author by mentioning that He appeared to me while sitting on God's throne with seven stars in his hand and seven stars in front of him. The stars in his hand represented the angels or bishops of the seven churches in Asia, while the seven stars in front of him depict lamp stands, as well as the seven-fold Spirit of God.

Melito: "Interesting."

Prochorus: "It's really remarkable."

I continue: "I will provide an appraisal of the spiritual health of this church. There are good things that I've noticed, but also some things that worry me."

Melito: "What good things?"

"The members of this church are extremely busy and have the reputation of being a lively body of people with all the activities they undertook. Their faith and their love for Christ, however, has waned and Christ will pronounce this church to be almost dead. However, a small number of Christians remained steadfast and led exemplary lives and I may assure them on the authority that Christ gave me that they are worthy to receive white spiritual clothes, the proper clothing for heaven. Their names will never be removed from the Book of Life, the book containing the names of all those who belong to God."

Melito: "I agree that we are a sleepy lot. We must certainly wake up if we don't want to displease Christ."

Me: "Christ has warned me on many occasions that his return is imminent. We must be ready for that at all times."

Today is Sunday and I deliver a sermon to the congregation. Melito baptizes Ignatius, a very handsome young man, who joins the congregation.

I tell Melito: "Please look after this young man. Treat him as your own son. I also regard him as my spiritual son because I have led him to Christ."

Thereafter, Melito reads the letter to the congregation:

Revelation 3: 1–6
The Letter to Sardis

1.	*And to the angel of the assembly in Sardis write:*

He who has the seven Spirits of God, and the seven stars says these things: "I know your works, that you have a reputation of being alive, but you are dead.

2. Wake up, and establish the things that remain, which were ready to die, for I have found no works of yours perfected before my God.

3. Remember therefore how you have received and heard. Keep it, and repent. If therefore you won`t watch, I will come as a thief, and you won`t know what hour I will come on you.

4. Nevertheless you have a few names in Sardis that did not defile their garments. They will walk with me in white, for they are worthy.

5. He who overcomes will be arrayed like this in white garments, and I will in no way blot his name out of the book of life, and I will confess his name before my Father, and before his angels.

6. He who has an ear, let him hear what the Spirit says to the assemblies.

Sunday, 19 March AD 97

It was a long journey to Philadelphia, south-east of Sardis. This city, whose name means "brotherly love", was founded two centuries ago by King Attalus II Philadelphus of Pergamum and was given this name out of love for his brother, Eumenes. It became part of the Roman Empire afterwards. The city was devastated by an earthquake eighty years ago – which happened frequently in these parts of Asia – and the rebuilding was partly funded by Emperor Tiberius. At the present time, Philadelphia is a thriving city with many temples and schools.

It is not known when and by whom this Church was established, but most probably some of Paul's converts in Ephesus spread the Gospel in this city. The present bishop is the very elderly Epaphras who is mentioned in two of Paul's letters.

As usual, our first stop was at the bishop's home and he invited us in. He promised to convene a meeting of all the elders and the deacons in two days' time.

In between visits to the homes of most of the elders and other church members, we roamed the streets and talked to strangers to hear how they experienced the Christians. It seems that the church in Philadelphia has a very good reputation and enjoys the respect of all.

Prochorus helps me to write the letter that Epaphras must read to his congregation later today.

I ask him: "Do you agree that it will be a good thing if I call Christ, as the real author of this letter, holy and the keeper of the key of David with which he opens heaven for the believers and locks heaven for the unbelievers?"

"That sounds appropriate. Perhaps you can add that He is sincere and truthful – apart from being holy."

"Yes, that's acceptable."

Basel Lion

An ancient Roman key with a
Lion's head

"I seem to remember that the prophet Isaiah mentioned the 'key of David' somewhere in his book."

"That's right. I can also remember that he wrote about David's key to his house":

"The key of the house of David will I lay on his shoulder; and he shall open, and none shall shut; and he shall shut, and none shall open."[213]

"The person who was to receive this key was Eliakim, the son of Hilkiah, master of King Hezekiah's household. In other words: Christ received the authority as the descendant of King David, to be in control of God's kingdom and household."

"I get the impression that this church doesn't deserve to be criticized."

"You may be right. One can only say positive things about these people. They were not afraid to tell their fellow-citizens about Jesus and they lived exemplary lives, while preserving their faith. The Word of God was preached in all its purity.

"The poor Christians here have problems with the jealous Jews, just as other churches. It may be foreseen that these Jews will have to admit that the Christians worshipped God more steadfastly than they did. I can call them in the name of Christ a 'synagogue of Satan'. He also promised that these false Jews will come to the realization that they were wrong and that they will prostrate themselves before the Christians of Philadelphia."

"Those are harsh words. What type of promise will Christ give to these people?"

---

[213] Isa 22: 22.

"They will receive the promise that Christ will preserve them on Judgment Day, when all the ungodly, unbelieving, and unholy people will be judged. They may expect to become pillars in God's heavenly temple and to receive crowns as God's children."

"Here is my writing apparatus. I'm ready to write."

Revelation 3: 7 –13
The Letter to Philadelphia

7.	*To the angel of the assembly in Philadelphia write:* "He who is holy, he who is true, he who has the key of David, he who opens and no one can shut, and that shuts and no one opens, says these things:
8.	'I know your works (behold, I have set before you an open door, which no one can shut), that you have a little power, and kept my word, and didn't deny my name.
9.	Behold, I give of the synagogue of Satan, of those who say they are Jews, and they are not, but lie. Behold, I will make them to come and worship before your feet, and to know that I have loved you.
10.	Because you kept the word of my patience, I also will keep you from the hour of testing, that which is to come on the whole world, to test those who dwell on the earth.
11.	I come quickly. Hold firmly that which you have, so that no one takes your crown.
12.	He who overcomes, I will make him a pillar in the temple of my God, and he will go out from there no more. I will write on him the name of my God, and the name of the city of my God, the new Jerusalem, which comes down out of heaven from my God, and my own new name.
13.	He who has an ear, let him hear what the Spirit says to the assemblies.'"

Sunday, 2 April AD 97

When we reached the last stop of our inspection tour, the city of Laodicea, we enquired where we could find the home of the bishop. Nobody seemed to know, until we found a Christian who told us that the previous bishop was deposed by the elders after having been caught with money from the church he stole. The elders are fighting amongst themselves who should succeed him. This Christian can't tell us where any of the elders live, but he invites us to the service next Sunday in the home of a rich Christian.

Ruins along the main road of the ancient city of Laodicea

We find lodgings in a guest house and explore the city and its environment. Outside the city, there are some hot springs where people with all sorts of ailments bathe in the hope of receiving some relief of their pains and aches. We do the same to rest our weary legs after having travelled many stadia on horseback.

337

We talk to some bathers and they tell us that this city was founded four centuries ago by King Antiochus II and named after his wife Laodice. It is a rich city where woolen garments are manufactured and where various apothecaries prepare medicines for several ailments, including a salve for sore eyes.

The city was destroyed by an earthquake forty years ago and rebuilt by the inhabitants from their own resources. Nobody can tell us when and how a Christian church was established in Laodicea. I remember that Paul knew some Christians in this city and he sent greetings to them via his letter to the Colossians.[214]

We found the home of the Christian where the Sunday service was to be held after dark. The home has big peristylum where the members of the church congregate.

Reconstruction of a Roman peristyle surrounding a courtyard in Pompeii, Italy.

When I introduced myself as John of Ephesus, the overseer of the

---

[214] Col 4: 15–16.

churches in Asia, we were heartily welcomed. Most of the elders knew of me and they declare that they are honored to receive us here. I asked them to hold an impromptu meeting of the church council after the service.

The elder who was supposed to lead the service, was only too glad to allow me to conduct the service with a sermon because he declared that some members of the congregation don't like his sermons.

During the meeting afterwards, the elders invited me to their homes. I accept the invitations. The Christian, in whose home the service was held, who is one of the elders, declared that we are welcome to stay with him until we leave again.

After a week of visits and conversations with elders and deacons, I and Prochorus compose the letter to this church.

Me: "It is important that I introduce Christ properly to impress upon the minds of these Christians that He must be taken seriously. I intend calling Him 'the Amen, the faithful and true witness, the head of God's creation". This is a summary of all the other descriptions of Christ in the letters to the other six churches."

Prochorus: "That ought to impress them."

"May I remind you that the Hebrew word 'Amen' signifies reliability, truthfulness, and trust. The description of Christ as the 'faithful and true witness' says essentially the same. As the head of God's creation, his majesty is emphasized."

"This city has a whole industry to heal people with diseases and disorders. Their physicians diagnose their clients. How will you diagnose the health of this church?"

"I can't really say anything positive about them. Everything is in chaos and it's a miracle that the congregation does still function. There is very little order. They feel very satisfied with themselves and regard themselves as being rich, although they are spiritual paupers. Their attitude reminds me of the water of the hot springs outside the city. That water is undrinkable and if you get a mouth full of it, you immediately spit it out. Christ cannot accept their luke-warm attitude. They are not enthusiastic about their faith, although they haven't abandoned their faith totally. Christ will spit them from his mouth."

"That's a very harsh appraisal."

"I know. But they will have to hear it. If things go on as at present, they won't stand a chance when Christ returns and Judgment Day arrives. They are spiritually blind and they need some spiritual ointment for their eyes to see themselves better. They are, in fact, spiritually poor and even naked. It is necessary for them to repent and turn away from their tolerant attitude towards pagan rituals and feasts."

"Has Christ given up on them?"

"Not totally. It is as if He is standing outside the door of this church and knocks so that He can be admitted. He wants to be invited inside, just as we were invited into this house. He is ready to grant them a royal status by allowing them to sit on thrones next to Him when he judges the world."

"You gave an accurate summary, I'm sure."

"Fetch your pen and some papyrus."

Revelation 3: 14–22
The Letter to Laodicea

14.	To the angel of the assembly in Laodicea write: ""The Amen, the Faithful and True Witness, the Head of God's creation, says these things:
15.	'I know your works, that you are neither cold nor hot. I wish you were cold or hot.
16.	So, because you are lukewarm, and neither hot nor cold, I will vomit you out of my mouth.

17.	Because you say, 'I am rich, and have gotten riches, and have need of nothing;' and don't know that you are the wretched one, miserable, poor, blind, and naked;
18.	I counsel you to buy from me gold refined by fire, that you may become rich; and white garments, that you may clothe yourself, and that the shame of your nakedness may not be revealed; and eye salve to anoint your eyes, that you may see.
19.	As many as I love, I reprove and chasten. Be zealous therefore, and repent.
20.	Behold, I stand at the door and knock. If anyone hears my voice and opens the door, I will come in to him, and will dine with him, and he with me.
21.	He who overcomes, I will give to him to sit down with me on my throne, as I also overcame, and sat down with my Father on his throne.
22.	He who has an ear, let him hear what the Spirit says to the assemblies.'"

At the start of the service on this Sunday night, I take the word and tell the congregation: "There has been too much infighting and discord in this church. We must appoint a bishop right now. Which one of your elders will be the most suitable person?"

Some names are mentioned and then I let the members vote. They choose Sagaris[215] and I bless him in his new position directly afterwards. After my sermon, I request Sagaris to receive a copy of my book and to read my letter to those who are gathered.

---

[215] Eusebius, *Hist Eccl,* Liber V/XXIV/5.

EPILOGUE

Sunday, 1 December AD 99

My inspection tour to the churches of Asia ended more than a year ago. Prochorus made a few more copies of my book and inserted the seven letters to the seven churches directly after the first scene. Many members of the various churches assure me that they regard my book as just as valuable as the books of the prophets of the Hebrew Scriptures.

I often receive positive reports from the bishops who write letters or who travel personally to Ephesus to seek my advice. All this gives me the assurance that my work was not in vain.

The conviction grows in me that my work as a prophet is drawing to a close. I have produced a book, containing God's message to the churches and I don't know whether God has any other plans for me. Perhaps the time has come to retire and appoint Gaius as my successor. My exile on Patmos with all its hardships took its toll on me and I can see that I am not the man that I was ten years ago.

There was, though, one thing that perturbed me and to which I had to pay urgent attention. I received a letter from bishop Melito of Sardis and he bade me to visit him and his church as soon as possible to help him with a serious problem. I immediately took my horse and travelled to Sardis, accompanied by Prochorus.

Today, I lead the service in Sardis and the parishioners are glad to see me again.

Afterwards, Melito takes me to his home for a dinner. He looks worried: "John, do you remember that handsome young man you entrusted to my care two years ago?"

"Do you perhaps mean Ignatius?"

"That's him."

"What about him?"

"He is the biggest disappointment of my life. Both of us instructed him in the Christian faith and he was baptized as a

345

member of this church. He led an exemplary life for some time, but then he returned to his old type of life."

"How? Why?"

"He told us in the beginning that he came to Sardis to look for work and that he hailed from Thessalonica. That was a lie. He was really a fugitive from justice and he came from Antioch where he was sought for robbery and murder. He joined our church with the sole goal of finding a place where he could hide."

"How did you learn about his past?"

"The magistrate of Sardis visited me after the disappearance of Ignatius to hear whether I knew where he was to be found. He had received a request from the authorities in Antioch to arrest him and to deliver him to be tried there."

"You say, he disappeared?"

"Yes. He got involved with a bad and criminal lot. He became the leader of a band of highway robbers and they are hiding somewhere in the mountains. He became a bold bandit-chief, the most violent, most blood-thirsty, the most cruel of them all. He returned to his old type of life and forgot about Christ."

"Have you tried to find him and lead him back to Christ?"

"It's too damned dangerous. His gang of cutthroats and assassins and slayers have a terrible reputation. People avoid those parts like the plague. These robbers appear every so often on the highways and byways to rob the travelers and kill anybody who resists them. It's a huge problem. It gives me sleepless nights. I blame myself for not caring more and better for this young man with so many talents and gifts. He could have become an elder or presbyter in the church if he had persevered."

I stay silent for a while and then I say: "Let me sleep tonight here and tomorrow I may perhaps do something."

Monday, 2 December AD 99

Just after daybreak I saddle my horse and ride in the direction of the mountains where Ignatius and his gangsters are hiding. The sun is already high in the sky when the outpost of the cabal of criminals stops me. Since I am unarmed, they don't seem to regard me as a threat. I also show them that I have no money or other valuable items with me, save for my horse.

I cry out: "Take me to your captain! I have a message for him. From Jesus Christ."

The bandits take me deeper into a valley where the gang has its hide-out.

When Ignatius sees me, he turns pale and runs away. I break free from the guards and pursue him on my horse while I shout at the top of my voice:

"Why, my son, do you flee from me, your own father? I am unarmed. I am an old man with gray hair! Pity me, my son; fear not; you have still hope of life. I will give account to Christ for you. If need be, I will willingly endure your death as the Lord suffered death for us. For you will I give up my life. Stand, believe; Christ has sent me!"

Something in my urgent voice must have had an effect upon him. He stops, drops his sword and knife, and looks down to the earth. He is, apparently, too ashamed to look me in my eyes.

And then Igantius starts to sob. The tears stream from his face and it is as if he is baptizing himself again with his own tears. He sinks down onto his knees and allows me to embrace him. He kisses my right hand.

I hold him a long time while his body trembles. I can't help it, but I follow his example by shedding some tears myself. I dry my own tears and my running nose with the sleeve of my cloak. And then he confesses all his crimes. I give him the assurance that God will forgive him if his repentance is genuine.

I kneel next to him and start to pray for his soul with a loud voice so that the other robbers and gangsters can hear.

After about an hour, we both stand up and Ignatius calls his men together: "Men, I am leaving you. This man of God took a great risk to come here, but God guided him to me. And God touched my heart and I decided to leave this type of life. Farewell, my men!"

Ignatius gathers all his possessions, save his armaments, and gets onto his horse.

"Father, take me back to the church. I will confess all my sins and beg everybody whom I wronged for forgiveness. Here, in this bag, is all the money that we have stolen. I promise to give it back to those from whom I took it."

While we ride away, back to Sardis, I look over my shoulder at the rest of the squad of killers and marauders. They are too surprised and caught off-guard to do anything while we disappear with all their treasures.[216]

When Sardis comes into sight, I say a silent prayer of thanks that I was able, even at my age, to find a dangerous lost soul and lead him back to God – just like the Prodigal Son in the story of Jesus who went back to his father after a sinful and wasteful life. Miracles certainly do happen when people change their ways. I am confident that Ignatius, whose name means "ignited" or "set on fire" or "full of passion and enthusiasm" will become a saint.[217]

---

[216] This story was recorded by the Christian historian, Eusebius of Caesarea: *Hist Eccl*, Liber III/XXIII.

[217] A certain St Ignatius was bishop of Antioch and he was martyred around AD 140 while travelling to Rome. Nothing else of his life is known.

I would not have been able to undertake this task if I wasn't prepared by my exile on Patmos to shake off all fears and learnt to trust on God in all situations, even in highly dangerous circumstances.

BIBLIOGRAPHY

Editions of the Bible and Apocrypha
Passages from the Bible are quoted from the *World English Bible* as found on a CD with the title *The Bible Collection, Deluxe Edition*, and published by ValuSoft, a division of THQ Inc, Waconia MN, 2002. This CD also contains several English translations, translations of the Bible in various other languages, the Hebrew text of the Old Testament and the Greek text of the New Testament, as well as *Strong's Complete Greek & Hebrew Lexicon*.

The following editions of the biblical text in the original languages were consulted:

Elliger, K. and W. Rudolph, eds. *Biblia Hebraica Stuttgartensia*. Stuttgart: Deutsche Bibelgesellschaft, 1997.

Nestle, E. and E. Nestle, eds. *Novum Testamentum Graece*. Stuttgart: Deutsche Bibelstiftung, 1981.

The Book of Enoch. From: *The Apocrypha and Pseudepigrapha of the Old Testament*. Tr. R.H. Charles Oxford: The Clarendon Press. Section I: Chapters I–XXXVI.
https://www.ccel.org/c/charles/otpseudepig/enoch/ENOCH_1.HTM

Other Publications
Allen, Richard Hinckley. *Star Names: Their Lore and Meaning*. New York: Dover, 1963.

Anaema, "Nisyros: A Volcanic Island in the Aegean Sea". Http://Www.Anaema.Gr/Nisyros/

Bottenberg, C. *et al.* "The Mediterranean Climate". http://www.meteor.iastate.edu/~kuballc/portfolio/406%20Version%202.pdf

Bullinger, E.W. "The Witness of the Stars". http://philologos.org/__eb-tws/chap13.htm

Clarke, J.C.C. "Jacobs Zodiac". *The Hebrew Student*.

https://books.google.co.za/books/about/Old_and_New_Testamen t_Student.html?id=DSg4AQAAMAAJ&redir_esc=y

Cornelius, F.: *Geistesgeschichte der Frühzeit II/1.* Leiden, 1962.

Dann, Moshe. "The Essenes and the Origins of Christianity: How the Essenes played a part in history". Jerusalem Post: 13 July, 2018. https://www.jpost.com/jerusalem-report/the-essenes-and-the-origins-of-christianity-562442

Decker, R.W. & Decker, B.B. "Volcano". Chicago : Encyclopeadia Britannica, 2010.

Encyclopaedia Britannica. "Dies Irae." Chicago : Encyclopeadia Britannica, 2010.

———. "Ephesus." Chicago : Encyclopeadia Britannica, 2010.

———. "Herakles." Chicago : Encyclopeadia Britannica, 2010.

———. "Locust." Chicago : Encyclopeadia Britannica, 2010.

———. "Roman Empire." Chicago : Encyclopeadia Britannica, 2010.

———. "Sadducee." Chicago : Encyclopeadia Britannica, 2010.

———. "Spartacus." Chicago : Encyclopeadia Britannica, 2010.

———. "Vesuvius". Chicago : Encyclopeadia Britannica, 2010.

Epiphanios. *Panarion, Liber I.* Translated by Frank Williams. https://web.archive.org/web/20170916133936/http://www.masse iana.org/panarion_bk1.htm

Eusebius of Caesarea. *Historia Ecclesiastica,* Libri II, III et V. http://www.documentacatholicaomnia.eu/03d/0265-0339,_eusebius_caesariensis,_church_history,_en.pdf

———— . *Ευσεβιου Καισαρειας, Εκκλησιαστικη Ιστορια.* http://www.documentacatholicaomnia.eu/03d/0265-0339,_Eusebius_Caesariensis,_Historia_Ecclesiastica,_GR.pdf

Fox, Alex: "Archaeologists Identify Traces of Burnt Cannabis in Ancient Jewish Shrine."
Smithsonian Magazine, June 4, 2020.
https://www.smithsonianmag.com/smart-news/cannabis-found-altar-ancient-israeli-shrine-180975016/#:~:text=Roughly%2035%20miles%20south%20of,r eports%20Kristen%20Rogers%20of%20CNN.

Franz, G. "The king and I : The Apostle John and Emperor Domitian.

Bible and Spade, Spring 1999.
http://www.biblearchaeology.org/post/2010/02/11/The-King-
and-I-Opening-The-Third-Seal-Part-3.aspx

Hachlili, R. "The Zodiac in Ancient Jewish Synagogal Art: A Review."
Jewish Studies Quarterly, Volume 9, 2002, 219—258.

Hammond, M. "Trajan". Chicago: Encyclopædia Britannica, 2010.

Jacobus, H.R. "The Zodiac Sign Names in the Dead Sea Scrolls (4q318):
Features and Questions". *Aram*, 24 (2012) 311–31.
file:///c:/users/user/downloads/the_zodiac_sign_names_in_the_d
ead_sea_sc.pdf

Jong, P.C. *Kommt das Zeitalter des Antichristen, des Martyriums, der
Entrückung und des Tausendjährigen Königreiches?* (I & II).
Hephzibah Verlagshaus, New Life Mission. 2004.

Jordaan, T. *Openbaring vandag : die Boodskap Agter die Beelde.* Lux
Verbi : Wellington, 2006.

Kinvig, H.S. *et al.* "Analysis Of Volcanic Threat From Nisyros Island,
Greece, With Implications For Aviation And Population
Exposure." Nat. Hazards Earth Syst. Sci., 10, 1101–1113, 2010
[www.nat-hazards-earth-syst-sci.net/10/1101/2010/
doi:10.5194/nhess-10-1101-2010

Kinzig, Wolfram. "The Nazoreans". In Oskar Skarsaune and Reidar
Hvalvik, Eds., *Jewish Believers in Jesus,* Peabod, MS,
Hendrickson, 2007, 463–87.

Kovacs, J. & Rowland, C. *Revelation: The Apocalypse of Jesus Christ.*
Oxford: Blackwell, *2004.*

Malina, B.J. *On the Genre and Message of Revelation: Star Visions and
Sky Journeys,* Peabody, Ms, 1995.

Mason, J. "Rhodes Island Hit by Locusts". *Greek Island Travel,* May
2013.
http://www.greek-islands
travel.co.uk/dodecanese/rhodes/locusts-on-rhodes.html

Mathis, R.L. "First Jewish-Roman War." *Military History*, December
1995
http://www.historynet.com/first-jewish-roman-war.htm

NASA. "Eclipse Web Site: Catalog of Solar Eclipses, 0001 To 100 Ce –

0029 Nov 24".
https://eclipse.gsfc.nasa.gov/5mcsemap/0001-0100/29-11-24.gif

———. "Eclipse Web Site: Catalog of Lunar Eclipses, 0001 To 100 Ce – 0029 Dec 09."
https://eclipse.gsfc.nasa.gov/5mclemap/0001-0100/le0029-12-09p.gif

———. "Eclipse Predictions: Lunar Eclipses from 0001 to 0100, Jerusalem, Israel."
http://eclipse.gsfc.nasa.gov/jlex/jlex-as.html

Ngo, R. "Judaea Capta Coin Uncovered in Bethsaida Excavations." Biblical Archaeology, 09.07.2016
http://www.biblicalarchaeology.org/daily/ancient-cultures/ancient-israel/judaea-capta-coin-uncovered-in-bethsaida-excavations/

Sattin, A. & Franquet, S. *Explorer Greek Islands*. Basingstoke : AA Publishing, 2000.

Scholtz, Adelbert. *The Prophecies of Revelation*. Mauritius: Lambert Academic, 2017.

Stellarium Astronomy Software. https://stellarium-web.org/

Stieglitz, R. "The Hebrew Names of the Seven Planets". *Journal of Near Eastern Studies*, April 1981, 40 (2): 135.

UNESCO. The World's Heritage. Paris : Unesco Publishing, 2009.

Valdez, A. Number 666 and the Twelve Tribes of Israel. *Revista Bíblica* 68/3–4 (2006) 191–214.
https://www.academia.edu/12773260/Number_666_and_the_Twelve_Tribes_of_Israel

Visser, A.J.: *De Openbaring aan Johannes*. Nijkerk, 1962.

Volcano World, " Nisyros, Greece"
http://volcano.oregonstate.edu/vwdocs/volc_images/europe_west_asia/nisyros.html

Weapons Universe, "Ancient Roman Weapons".
http://www.weapons-universe.com/Swords/Ancient_Roman_Weapons.shtml

Zucker, S. "Hebrew Names of the Planets ". *Proceeding of the International Astronomical Union, 2011.*

LIST OF ILLUSTRATIONS

Star charts
The maps of the starry skies at various dates during AD 96–97 over Patmos and Ephesus were produced by an astronomical computer program called *Stellarium* that may be downloaded, free of charge, from http://www.stellarium.org/

Maps of Solar and Lunar Eclipses
These were downloaded from the following websites:

NASA. "Eclipse Web Site: Catalog of Solar Eclipses, 0001 To 100 Ce – 0029 Nov 24".
https://eclipse.gsfc.nasa.gov/5mcsemap/0001-0100/29-11-24.gif

———. "Eclipse Web Site: Catalog of Lunar Eclipses, 0001 To 100 Ce – 0029 Dec 09."
https://eclipse.gsfc.nasa.gov/5mclemap/0001-0100/le0029-12-09p.gif

———. "Eclipse Predictions: Lunar Eclipses from 0001 to 0100, Jerusalem, Israel."

Frontispiece
St. John, the author of Revelation
https://sterx.ru/en_a_cave.htm

Monday, 12 April AD 43
Drawing of Jewish High Priest
https://www.mediastorehouse.com.au/north-wind-picture-archives/ancient-history/jewish-high-priest-levite-ancient-israel-5878130.html

Saturday, 5 September AD 43
Lunar eclipse
https://pikbest.com/templates/lunar-eclipse-orange-red-clouds-texture-night-background_8916790.html

Saturday, 23 April AD 50

Lunar eclipse

https://www.thesouthafrican.com/lifestyle/can-you-see-lunar-eclipse-if-its-cloudy/

Friday, 8 January AD 96

Roman prison cell

https://gronology.wordpress.com/2011/08/17/when-in-rome/

The Beth Alpha mosaic with the Zodiac

https://en.wikipedia.org/wiki/Beth_Alpha

Ancient Hebrew world-view

https://www.stpeterslist.com/

Statue of Roman soldier

https://www.vroma.org/images/mcmanus_Images/legionary.jpg

Dead Sea caves

https://en.wikipedia.org/wiki/Qumran_Caves

Mosaic: Roman ship

https://www.researchgate.net/figure/The-common-spiny-lobster-P-elephas-in-a-third-century-CE-Roman-mosaic-known-as_fig4_275968722

The restored house in Ephesus in which the Virgin Mary purportedly lived

https://turkisharchaeonews.net/object/house-virgin-mary-ephesus

Ruins of the Library of Celsus in Ephesus

https://greekreporter.com/2023/07/20/ancient-greek-city-ephesus-unesco-world-heritage-site/

Mosaic of Roman legionaries

https://europe.factsanddetails.com/article/entry-429.html#group=429&photo=3

Sunday, 10 January AD 96

Ancient Roman prison

https://za.pinterest.com/pin/844776842605991434/

A golden coin minted by Emperor Vespasian after the destruction of Jerusalem https://en.wikipedia.org/wiki/Judaea_Capta_coinage

Sunday, 17 January AD 96
Roman shackles
>	https://www.caitlingreen.org/2015/02/some-roman-slave-shackles-and-figurines.html

Map of Patmos
>	http://www.angelfire.com/super2/greece/patmos-map.html

The cave in the southern part of Patmos in which John is said to have lived
>	http://www.patmos.gr/

Aerial photo of Patmos
>	http://www.patmos.gr/the-island-of-patmos/?lang=en

Sunday, 31 January AD 96
The menorah with seven lamps, looted from the Jerusalem temple in AD 70, as depicted on the Arch of Titus in Rome.
>	http://www.myjewishlearning.com/article/ancient-judaism-101/

Christ on his throne and dressed as a Roman judge, with four archangels
>	https://commons.wikimedia.org/wiki/File:Sant'Apollinare_Nuovo_(Christ).jpg

The deified son of Emperor Domitian who died at the age of nine, is depicted on this coin
>	https://biblearchaeology.org/research/new-testament-era/3080-the-king-and-i-the-apostle-john-and-emperor-domitian-part-1?highlight=WyJqb2huIiwiam9obidzIiwiJ2pvaG4iXQ==

Tuesday and Wednesday, 2–3 February, AD 96
A map of the northern sky (viewed from above) by the medieval German artist, Albrecht Dürer
>	https://www.metmuseum.org/art/collection/search/358366

The symbols of the Four Evangelists
>	https://www.2kdenmark.com/stories/the-book-of-kells

Sunday, 14 February AD 96

Flock of sheep on Patmos
    http://mygreecetravelblog.com/2011/05/10/greece-holiday-2010-
    patmos/
Mosaic on the ceiling of the Basilica of San Vitale, Ravenna
    http://beautifulnow.is/bnow/check-out-ravenna-a-city-
    beautifully-obsessed

Sunday, 13 March AD 96
Roman mosaic of a gladiator spearing a leopard
    Encyclopaedia Britannica, 2010: Gladiator

Monday, 14 March AD 96
Roman commemorative stone depicting a horseman wielding a spear and
with a sword strapped to his side
    http://www.weapons-
    universe.com/Swords/Ancient_Roman_Weapons.shtml
Sagittarius (the Archer) and Corona Australis (the Southern Crown)
    http://prints.rmg.co.uk/art/504960/constellation-card-uranias-
    mirror-sagittarius-and-corona

Tuesday and Wednesday, 15–16 March AD 96
Centaurus, the Centaur, together with the Southern Cross
    http://www.underthenightsky.com/constellations/centaurus/
A silver denarius coin minted during the reign of Emperor Domitian
    https://www.antiquesboutique.com/roman-coins/ancient-roman-
    silver-denarius-of-emperor-domitian-minerva/itm50051

Thursday, 17 March AD 96
Pegasus, the winged horse (the red horse), and Equuleus, the Foal (the
pale horse)
    https://en.wikipedia.org/wiki/Pegasus_%28constellation%29

Friday, 18 March AD 96

https://en.wikipedia.org/wiki/Roman_tuba

Sunday, 1 May AD 96
A locust photographed on Rhodos, May 2013.
http://www.greek-islands-
travel.co.uk/dodecanese/rhodes/locusts-on-rhodes.html

Sunday, 8 May AD 96
A battle between Roman and Germanic armies
http://www.weapons-
universe.com/Swords/Ancient_Roman_Weapons.shtml
Musicians playing a Roman tuba, a water organ (hydraulis), and a pair of
cornua
https://en.wikipedia.org/wiki/Roman_tuba

Tuesday, 10 May AD 96
Circular rainbow around the sun
https://www.fromtheangels.com/spirituality/rainbow-around-the-
sun-spiritual-meaning/

Wednesday, 11 May AD 96
Zeus hurling a thunderbolt
Encyclopaedia Britannica, 2010: Zeus

Saturday, 17 May AD 96
Gemini
https://en.wikipedia.org/wiki/Gemini_(constellation)

Tuesday, 20 May AD 96
Cassiopeia, the queen of Aethiopia
https://www.greeklegendsandmyths.com/cassiopeia.html

Friday, 17 June AD 96
Detail of the antique zodiac mosaic floor at Hamat Tiberias Synagogue
National Park

https://biblelandpictures.com/product/1264-1-tiberias-synagogue/

The Egyptian goddess Isis

https://global.britannica.com/topic/Isis-Egyptian-goddess

The Greek goddess Demeter

https://www.theoi.com/Gallery/S3.1.html

A photo of the constellation of Scorpius

http://www.abc.net.au/science/starhunt/tour/virtual/scorpius/

A wooden statue of Mary

https://www.pinterest.com/yangzhijian100/religion-statue/

Saturday, 25 June AD 96

A golden sestertius minted by Emperor Domitian

http://www.romancoins.info/VIC-Historical1.html

The beach at Sapsila Bay on Patmos

https://www.greeka.com/dodecanese/patmos/villages/sapsila/

Cetus from the Celestial Atlas by Alexander Jamieson, 1822

http://www.peoplesguidetothecosmos.com/constellations/cetus.htm

Capricornus, the Goat, from an old star atlas

http://www.philaprintshop.com/leigh.html

Tuesday, 5 July AD 96

Aries, the Ram, from the Hamas Tiberias Zodiac

https://smarthistory.org/mosaic-decoration-at-the-hammath-tiberias-synagogue/

Saturday and Sunday, 23–24 July, AD 96

The constellation of Hercules with Corona

http://fineartamerica.com/featured/constellation-of-hercules-with-corona-and-lyra-sir-james-thornhill.html

A well-preserved ancient Roman sickle

https://www.scran.ac.uk/packs/exhibitions/learning_materials/webs/56/Legion.htm

Boötes, the Plowman
  http://www.peoplesguidetothecosmos.com/constellations/bootes.htm
An ancient wine press
  http://winetastingguy.com/page/7/

Sunday and Monday, 24–25 July AS 96
The full moon reflected on the tranquil water of Groikos Bay
  http://www.hotel-golden-sun.com/hotel-and-environs.html

Monday, 8 August AD 96
Eridanus, the celestial river
  https://www.raremaps.com/gallery/detail/41354/Eridanus/Hevelius.html
Aphrodite, the goddess of love
  https://en.wikipedia.org/wiki/Aphrodite

Thursday, 11 August AD 96
Roman mosaic, depicting a ship with crew at work
  https://ar.pinterest.com/pin/104075441379137963/
Roman Mosaic of Musicians and Masked Actors in a Play, Pompeii, Italy
  https://za.pinterest.com/pin/239464905176218135/
Leda and the Swan
  https://za.pinterest.com/pin/105342078778086648/
Procession of saints
  https://corvinus.nl/2016/07/25/ravenna-santapollinare-nuovo/

Thursday, 25 August AD 96
The full moon rising over the Aegean
  https://za.pinterest.com/pin/359021401560883560/
The Zodiac mosaic on the floor of the Beth Alpha Synagogue
  https://en.wikipedia.org/wiki/Beth_Alpha

Friday and Saturday, 26–27 August AD 96

Roman cavalry

> https://en.wikipedia.org/wiki/Roman_cavalry#/media/File:Roma n_cavalry_-_Big_Game_Hunt_mosaic_- _Villa_Romana_del_Casale_-_Italy_2015.JPG

An ancient winepress

> http://www.ancient-origins.net/news-history- archaeology/innocent-boys-meticulously-excavated-1400-year- old-winepress-israel-003089

Sunday, 4 September AD 96

Ophiuchus, the Snake Catcher

> http://themindunleashed.com/2013/08/the-13th-zodiac-sign- ophiuchus.html

Friday, 9 September AD 96

Ancient scroll of the book of Esther

> https://en.wikipedia.org/wiki/History_of_scrolls

Mosaic of Christ in his glory, holding the book of life

> http://www.approachguides.com/blog/hidden-gem-in-istanbul- the-deesis-in-hagia-sophia/

Christ as cosmic judge

> https://orthodoxartsjournal.org/heaven-round-earth-square/

Tuesday, 20 December AD 96

Ancient Roman ship

> https://commons.wikimedia.org/wiki/File:Detail_of_Roman_mo saic_from_Veii_%28Isola_Farnese,_Italy%29_depicting_an_Afr ican_elephant_being_loaded_onto_a_ship,_3rd- 4th_century_AD,_Badisches_Landesmuseum_Karlsruhe,_Germ any_%2818622028386%29.jpg

Chapel dedicated to Saint Andrew

> Google Earth

Ancient Ephesus lies in a valley between hills.

http://www.cultureaddicthistorynerd.com/wordpress/wp-
content/uploads/2012/06/ephesus-theatre2.jpg
An angel showing John the heavenly Jerusalem
Encyclopaedia Brittanica, 2010: Heaven

Sunday, 8 January AD 97

A Roman codex
https://en.wikipedia.org/wiki/Codex_Vaticanus
The seven churches of Asia
http://www.truthinprophecy.com/post/sevenchurches/
Site of the Temple of Artemis in Ephesus
https://en.wikipedia.org/wiki/Artemis#/media/File:Ac_artemisep
hesus.jpg
Statue of Artemis in the Vatican
https://bleon1.wordpress.com/2014/08/23/goddess-artemis-at-
vatican-museum/

Sunday, 22 January AD 97

The ancient agora (marketplace) in Smyrna (Izmir)
http://www.206tours.com/tour165/
The Greek letters Alpha and Omega appear on either side of this painting
of Jesus
https://www.lds.org/manual/new-testament-student-
manual/revelation/chapter-53-revelation-1-3?lang=eng

Sunday, 5 February AD 97

The Altar of Zeus from Pergamum, as reconstructed in the
Pergamonmuseum in Berlin
http://www.biblicalarRevaeology.org/daily/biblical-sites-
places/biblical-arRevaeology-sites/pergamon-2/
The Spatha
http://www.weapons-
universe.com/Swords/Ancient_Roman_Weapons.shtml

Sunday, 5 March AD 97

The most imposing building of Roman Sardis is the (much reconstructed) courtyard of the Bath-Gymnasium complex.

https://www.worldhistory.org/image/3794/the-bath-gymnasium-complex-at-sardis/

Sunday, 19 March AD 97

A Roman key

https://www.forumancientcoins.com/numiswiki/view.asp?key=roman%20keys

Sunday, 2 April AD 97

Ruins along the main road of the ancient city of Laodicea

http://www.geo.de/reisen/community/bild/447384/Denizli-Tuerkei-die-roemisReve-Ruinenstadt-Laodikea-bei-Denizli

Reconstruction of a Roman peristyle surrounding a courtyard in Pompeii, Italy

https://en.wikipedia.org/wiki/Peristyle

Monday, 2 December AD 99

Roman mosaic of a horseman, British Museum

https://www.britishmuseum.org/collection/object/H_1967-0405-18

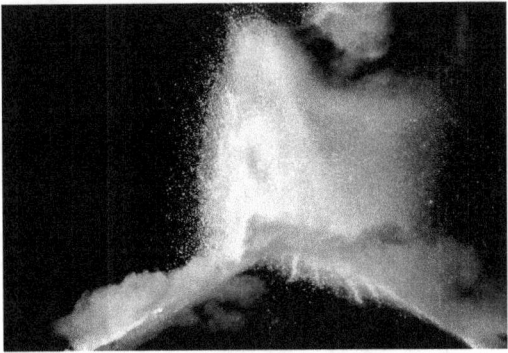

Mount Etna at night, 1 Dec 2023 (https://www.reuters.com/pictures/italys-mount-etna-lights-up-night-sky-stunning-eruption-2023-12-04/)

www.ingramcontent.com/pod-product-compliance
Lightning Source LLC
Chambersburg PA
CBHW060317100726
47907CB00002B/439